Mrs Sidhu's
DEAD
AND
Scone

Suk Pannu has written for some of Britain's best-loved Asian shows including *Goodness Gracious Me* and five series of the award-winning *The Kumars at No. 42*. He has also contributed to radio shows like *The News Quiz* and Armando Iannucci's *Charm Offensive*, and he has had several successful series and pilots of his own.

Suk grew up along the M4, the draughty corridor that connects London to Slough. The son of immigrants, his upbringing was filled with discipline, love and aunties. At an early age, he got his head stuck into books and escaped into other worlds. He has long believed that one of his aunties would be the perfect crime solver.

BBC Radio 4's production of *Mrs Sidhu Investigates* charmed audiences and won praise from across the national media. The show was pick of the week/day in every national daily and Sunday paper, and earned the top spot on Radio 4's *Pick of the Week*.

Mrs Sidhu's Dead and Scone is his first novel.

✕ @sukpannu

Mrs Sidhu's
DEAD
AND
Scone

SUK PANNU

HEMLOCK
PRESS

Hemlock Press
An imprint of HarperCollins*Publishers* Ltd
1 London Bridge Street,
London SE1 9GF

www.harpercollins.co.uk

HarperCollins*Publishers*
Macken House, 39/40 Mayor Street Upper,
Dublin 1, D01 C9W8, Ireland

This paperback edition 2024
1

First published in Great Britain in 2023 by HarperCollins*Publishers*

A catalogue record for this book is available from the British Library

ISBN: 978-0-00-856296-0

Typeset in Sabon LT Std by Palimpsest Book Production Ltd,
Falkirk, Stirlingshire

Printed and bound in the UK using 100% renewable electricity at
CPI Group (UK) Ltd

To Tess

PART I

Three mistakes to avoid when baking scones

1. Using warm ingredients
2. Overworking the dough
3. Getting yourself killed before you take them out of the oven

Life With a Knife, Mrs Sidhu's Memoirs

PROLOGUE

The great turning points in life are when two ideas smash into each other. Sometimes they come together too late. So it was for Wendy Calman on the evening she died. On that evening, Wendy was sitting in the half-light of her kitchen. A summer sunset boiled egg-yolk red through the window. She pored over the file open in front of her and tried to still her unease. She had read the words a thousand times but today she sensed she was missing something. It was like an itch, a grain of sand that had worked its way against her skin in a place she could not reach.

Justin and Sandra Pollock had died on Midsummer Day, 1997. They ate a simple meal, moved all their money into an offshore account in the Caribbean, put on white robes, and took overdoses together. While the drugs were taking effect, the cult leader doused their designer home in petrol and set it alight. Their bodies were found in the gutted remains of their own burned-out house. Wendy sighed. There was nothing new there. For a moment, before she closed the file, she looked at the photograph of a happy couple, smiling, at ease with each other.

Dr Wendy Calman was small and erect with a gently curved nose. She wore a pair of oversized glasses. Her clients thought these gave her the look of a startled owl. The same clients found her a good listener, and an insightful therapist, if a slightly distant presence. They could not know this, but she was often struck by the regret that her career was missing one piece in the jigsaw. She had never had her book published. She had read it so many times that there were deep creases in the brown folder. She had not known the Pollocks, she had never even met them, but she had the feeling that she knew them. Justin was a rising star in property development. Sandra was shy, and according to neighbours at the time, was slowly coming out of her shell.

The police had investigated. Wendy had investigated too, in her own way. Trying to understand how two people, deeply in love, with their lives ahead of them could come to the conclusion that they should take their own lives. The answer to that was in another file. That file had even more creases than the first one. This one was 'the bad guy' of the story. Maybe it was home to her unsatisfied sense of unease.

William Mackie disappeared on the same night Justin and Sandra Pollock died. A photograph showed dreaming eyes, a thousand-yard stare, a goatee beard, long hair. He was attractive, no mistake. It was no surprise to learn he had been diagnosed with a 'messiah complex' by his first psychiatric doctor. Somewhere he had slipped through the system and by 1997 he had arrived in the village of Benham as a penniless drifter. He did some odd jobs, gardening work around the village. Espousing ideas about interplanetary life forms, the end of the world and transcendence through death, he was considered a charming eccentric. Unknown to all, he was building a small cult following for his ideas – a following that included the Pollocks. Mackie was believed to have presided over and 'blessed' the Pollocks and set fire to their home. There was nothing new there either.

Frustration threatened to overwhelm her. Wendy put the file down next to the first. Wendy Calman understood people. She had the degrees, diplomas and certificates to prove it. Anyone could look at them on the walls of her office. William Mackie was supposed to be the final, culminating chapter in her book *Disorders of the Mind*, but in twenty years of researching she had not found one single person who would admit to being in William Mackie's cult. Not one interview; they had all slunk into the shadows. Perhaps some had followed him to South America. The police, moving too slowly, had not issued his description until well after he had landed at Santiago airport in Chile and disappeared completely. She reflected on this, calmly and with distance, just as her training had taught her. She wondered why today, of all days, she had picked up the files again. Was it just the thought of retirement and an unfulfilled dream? Or somewhere, from some direction, was the steam train of an idea racing along red-hot rails? She felt it, and she knew she could not force it to arrive any sooner than the timetable it was running to.

The itch was still there, all her attempts to scratch had made it worse, and now she needed to do something else. With a heavy heart she turned her attention to the kitchen.

* * *

3

It was the case of the Pollocks that had brought Wendy to Benham. A successful practice in London gave her the freedom to pick and choose her clients, and eventually as decisions about retirement beckoned, it was natural to move to the country. A draughty, Grade II listed, thatched cottage came up in Benham, and it seemed in keeping with the modern world that a primitive structure with a roof made from dried grass, when painted in pastel colours, could be worth a million pounds. She paid it, she had the money, and when a part-time job at a nearby retreat came up it seemed as if fate was smiling on her. She settled down to a reduced list of clients and to writing her career-defining book.

Five years on, full retirement was knocking on the door, Wendy's book was gathering dust, and the pressure to 'contribute to village life' was growing. Being a city girl, Wendy's vision of the move to the countryside had indeed involved cream teas on sun-kissed lawns, but she had not imagined she would be the one making them. More and more her simple life was cluttered with requests to help at the bring-and-buy, to sell raffle tickets, to collect litter from the verges. She complied; what else could one do?

Tonight, she approached the oven with the caution of someone warily entering a backyard with a BEWARE OF THE ROTTWEILER sign. When it came to cooking, Wendy had been bitten before. Perhaps if she snuck up on it, she thought, irritated at her own irrationality, perhaps if she snuck up on it, she could surprise it. In one movement she slammed the door open and hauled the baking tray out. Smoke and disappointment teared up her eyes. A dozen charred roundels of sugar and flour stared up at her, blackened and dead. For one moment she was reminded of the charred remains of the Pollocks' house, and of horrifying pictures of the blackened bodies, crying out silent, black-mouthed shrieks. Photographs which she had obtained through a police friend and wished she had not. It was an image so bleak and so at odds with her preceding thoughts about village fetes that she almost dropped the tray. She blinked the mental image away, but something had come alive in Wendy's mind and somewhere another train of an idea was skating on silver rails on a collision course with the first.

Her thoughts were interrupted by the phone, a matter-of-fact conversation about lost property from today's bring-and-buy sale followed. Yes, Wendy had the 'lost property'; yes, lost items could be collected from her house. Once the conversation had run its course, Wendy started again on another batch of scones and on a batch of jam. Futile though it may seem, she had made it her mission to learn to cook.

Following the recipe carefully, she set the berries on a low heat over the stove then, like a high board diver, looked up, raised her arms, took a short breath and plunged her hands into the flour. She watched distantly, as if someone else's fingers were chasing egg yolks into the powder, adding milk and sugar, pausing to add sugar to the berries. Sugar, it seemed, was the secret to winning friends and influencing people. Brain chemistry was predictable, measurable and repeatable, even if the products of her cooking were not.

The scones were in the oven and the antique grandfather clock in the hallway was chiming eight by the time the knock came at her door, but Wendy glanced at her watch anyway. Wendy tried to wipe her hands on the tea towel, spreading gooey flour on the cloth, checked on the fast-softening berries, made the necessary adjustments and made for the front door. Before she did, a glistening new thought came to her. It was important, and urgent. She unscrewed the cap of her pen and made a note on the final page of her manuscript. This was it. This was the breakthrough. She went to answer the door.

He stood there, or maybe it was a she, because it was hard to tell with the hood pulled down so low. 'Yes?' she said, then when there was no response, 'May I help you?'

Whoever it was stood absolutely still for a moment, and Wendy had time to take in the strangeness of the white robes and the curved iron implement in the right hand hanging down to one side as if held by a puppet. She had time to see this and time for fear to rise in her chest like a ball of burning bile, time enough to draw in a breath, time enough to start a scream, but not time enough to finish it. Time ran out for Wendy Calman as she was pushed back into her own kitchen. The only witnesses to her last moments were the photographs in her files. Suddenly the memory that had kept drifting away from her solidified in the bare face above her, and inside was the face she finally recognised.

Two trains of ideas ploughed into each other at the same instant, and in the twisted, metal-screaming shock-wave that followed as two truly disconnected ideas were forced together, Wendy knew exactly what had happened the night the Pollocks died, why it happened and why she had wasted the last five years of her life trying to under-stand a double suicide.

Too late.

The blade came up, crooked, rusty like a bent smile.

6

I

Mrs Sidhu's phone hummed rhythmically while she decided if she was going to wake up or not.

In her dream she was in a tumble dryer. It was hot and all the dead bodies were in there with her. As they jumbled around, a mass of steamy, flopping limbs, a face she half remembered came up close and stared through unseeing eyes. It was his face, she knew it, but no recognition stirred in her. With concern, turning to panic, she scrambled to assemble his features in her mind. Their wedding photo was on the mantel in the front room, for heaven's sake. She could get up, run downstairs, but sleep was not ready to let her go and nor was the dream. He came so close she could almost reach it. It may as well have been a stranger. The face was a repulsive, smooth orb, and with jerking hands she was pinning a nose, and eye and lips, but as quick as she put them up, they slipped off. Eventually, she almost had the semblance of his face. Just as she did, the tumble dryer's cylinder turned, a wheel of life, a wheel of death, a wheel of reincarnation. He was gone with not so much as a kiss goodbye. The memory of his face curled away like steam. She may as well open her eyes.

Two years of bereavement had not changed Mrs Sidhu's waking routine significantly. Her right hand woke first. Working on a primitive muscle memory, it wandered across the empty cold reaches of the bed to a place where it remembered there had once been a warm thing. After a few minutes fumbling around for what was not there, her other hand set off in the opposite direction. It walked and fumbled around, past the dagger glinting with blood dripping under a suitably brutal title. It pushed the splayed-open paperback to one side. It was looking for the other comforting warm thing that was not there. Her cup of tea. The two unwarm places were intimately related.

Every single day of their marriage, her husband had brought her a cup of tea in bed. She opened her eyes, confirming her worst fears. Her husband was still dead, and consequently she had no tea. As usual, the meringue swirl pattern on the ceiling wound into focus, reminding her of teacups. As usual, she smacked the tinny taste of sleep from her mouth which should have been rinsed away by tea. As usual she elbowed herself into a seated position, took a sip of water and wished it was tea. And, as usual she stared for a while at the crinkling wallpaper on the opposite wall of the room which for no good reason reminded her that she needed a cup of tea. Thus it was, and thus it had been for two years, and while as a series of waking thoughts it lacked profundity, it more than made up for it by its singular focus on tea. The final part of the ritual required Mrs Sidhu to clear her throat and airwaves before bellowing.

8

'Tez! Are you by any chance making a cup of tea?' As usual, the only reply was a distant and warthog-like snoring from another room. She shook her head and stared around vacantly. Slowly she recollected that she was alone in her own sagging bed, in her own bare bedroom.

The second time the phone rang she had a cup of tea in her hand. She was drifting around the kitchen, still in her dressing gown, taking an inventory of stock on a torn envelope with a blunt pencil. She examined the screen: *No Caller ID*. So, it was either someone intriguingly secretive or someone annoyingly secretive. Mrs Sidhu had had her fair share of both. She declined the call.

The third time the phone rang, she had finished the tea and had a shower. Dressed in neat slacks and practical cardigan, she was almost ready to meet the world. Of course, all three calls could be from different people, but then what three people call a caterer before nine in the morning on a Monday? Most likely it was one person with a pressing problem. Mrs Sidhu had instincts about such things, and very rarely was she wrong. She also had pressing problems of her own and so much work to do, and yet here was someone calling repeatedly, and each buzz of the phone fanned a tiny flame of curiosity deep in the seat of her brain.

'Hello?' The unknown caller was a woman, perhaps in her thirties. The word came out low, sultry, almost a whisper, as if the speaker was deliberately keeping her voice down. 'I've tried calling twice.' There was no hint of irritation, more a tint of desperation. This was confirmed by her next words. 'I'm afraid we have an emergency.'

Mrs Sidhu allowed herself a moment to preen herself on her deductions: she had called twice, so one caller with a problem, just as she had thought. Mrs Sidhu cleared her throat before answering. 'I am a caterer not an emergency service.' Everything was an emergency these days. Be it weddings, funerals or birthdays it was urgent business, and in business you could not kowtow to people's whims and fancies.

'Please.' Again, the hushed voice, with a hint of desperation in it. The woman broke off, the phone went silent as if she had placed her hand over it. Enough time passed for Mrs Sidhu to wonder if the call had been ended, or the connection lost. She was about to end the call herself when the woman spoke again. 'Dr Eardley could really use your help.' A sharp pang of intrigue plucked at Mrs Sidhu's chest. Dr Eardley? Could that be Stephen Eardley, the eminent psychiatrist and self-help guru; the man they called Dr Feelgood? She had a copy of *Don't Let Life Get You Down* on one of her bookshelves. A frisson of delight shivered through her bones. Alas there was nothing she could do. There was no point in even contemplating whether the Dr Eardley in question was the eminent one, or an unknown dentist from Stoke Poges. With the phone wedged under her ear and a determined set to her chin, she replied clearly: 'I do apologise but I cannot attend to anything today. I have several hundred aubergines to prepare.' Her heart sank as she said the words.

'If you change your mind—'

'There are other caterers.'

'It's just your website. You have such a kind face. It reminds me of my aunty Jean.'

Either from kindness or just to get the woman off the phone, Mrs Sidhu found herself scratching out the directions with her blunt pencil on an old envelope which was already covered in partly crossed-out shopping lists, doodles and some mysterious symbols.

She squinted and cursed her handwriting. Was that an 'A'? Were those numbers? Her best guess was 'Ali33'. She knew plenty of Alis. She counted on her fingers. Ali the butcher, Ali the bus driver, Ali the independent financial consultant and so on. She did not know as many as thirty-three Alis, and she had never taken to numbering her friends. Maybe it was a client, an Ali with a thirty-third birthday. A puzzle for another time.

She finished writing the address. So, it was *the* Dr Eardley. The Benham House Retreat was world renowned. Every week, the rich and famous were photographed entering the iron gates with pale faces and dark sunglasses, in need of Dr Feelgood's magic touch to piece their wrecked lives back together. Mrs Sidhu rang off, then wondered if she should have asked what the job was about, or even the name of the insistent young woman on the phone. Outside, on the driveway, the summer sun winked on the polished paintwork of her old Nissan Micra. When was the last time she had taken a drive out of Slough into the Berkshire countryside? On her way to the kitchen, she picked out her copy of *Don't Let Life Get You Down* from the book-shelf. She needed something to get her through the day.

Catering Siberia, that's what this was.

She hefted a clean pan from the rack and lit the gas ring. It hissed and flamed. The pot hit the cooker grate with a clang as loud and clear as a temple bell. The kitchen was completely modern. A full-height Lincat combination oven shone its glassy perfection onto a run of stainless-steel countertops leading up to a state-of-the-art Charvet range with maximum power extraction. For cookware, however, she prized the frugal aluminium pots she could buy from the Indian and Pakistani hardware stores in Slough town centre.

Mrs Sidhu had no purpose, and while she had no purpose, her spirit felt thin and drawn out, like a sheet of clingfilm pulled to the limit before it tore. She felt weak in herself, as if she had a mild head cold. Her taste buds were off, her palate uncertain, and her stomach was easily upset. This was how it was when Mrs Sidhu had no purpose. This? This was work, but it could not be considered purpose. The constant and mechanical production of aubergine bhaji would never do as a purpose in life. Can you imagine just doing that for the rest of your days? No, you could not. Purpose was a flavour that came together from different ingredients, like bitter or sour, or the elusive umami. You just knew when the taste was right. Mrs Sidhu considered with frustration that her life was flavourless. This was not work, it was punishment.

Mrs Sidhu seethed. Had she really done anything truly bad? The problem was, these days, if you did something even the slightest bit unusual, people jumped on you. You were banished, outcast. Sent to the gulag, or the catering equivalent. In Mrs Sidhu's case, the gulag was being made to work on your own.

She cast her mind back to the fateful wedding day. Mrs Sidhu had worked hard through autumn to win the contract, even calling in favours from a distant cousin who was a friend of the bride's father. She took on waiters, bussers and even a sous chef. People were going to remember Sukhi and Gurpreet's nuptials for two reasons. First: local girl Sukhi Sharma was wedding Gurpreet, a

12

very eligible software programmer from the USA. Second: the perfection of the light, balanced, locally sourced and deeply satisfying menu – an effortless blend of haute cuisine and Mother India's stomach-growler family favourites. Weeks of wrangling over the details followed. Sukhi was allergic to nearly everything, Gurpreet seemed only to like plain rice and chicken, but none of the dishes should touch. Each set of parents, too, had their own demands. But when the day came, Mrs Sidhu wiped her brow and took pause to wonder. Somehow she had worked out and prepared a five-course dinner that wound a careful, yet delicious path through all of these restrictions. She did not know it, but there would be a third reason why people remembered the wedding of Sukhi and Gurpreet. Mrs Sidhu's downfall.

The day came. It was January, a winter wedding, and a cold draught howled on the heels of everyone who entered the hotel lobby that fateful day. There was the bride, in a beautiful sari. There was the groom, in a very respectable new suit. There was Mrs Sidhu's nemesis and arch catering rival, Mrs Prakesh, standing with a fake smile smeared on her overly made-up face, fakely congratulating Mrs Sidhu on winning the contract for the Slough wedding of the year. And there was the groom's uncle, a real charmer to be sure. Mrs Sidhu spotted that straight away when she had gone round with a tray of her tofu fusion samosas. He had grey eyes the colour of a distant shoreline, and a baritone voice which said he lived in California most of the year and was a widowed doctor. He even had hair. Within about ten seconds he had a swarm of Slough's most eligible widows buzzing round him like flies on dung. They flung questions at him.

13

Which part of California? I hear they have orange trees there.

Is that real hair?

The last one was not spoken out loud, but Mrs Sidhu could see it in the misty eyes of the women. While they were watching the hair, the eyes, the dancer's hips, they weren't watching the hands. This guy was no magician, but he was no Californian doctor either.

It was left to Mrs Sidhu to point out to the hotel manager that she might want to do a tally-up on the silverware. The doorman grabbed the uncle by the wrist at the door. He had a dozen cruet sets in his bag and an ashtray in his pocket. You would think that was bad enough, but that wasn't the shocking thing.

In the pot, white butter was foaming on the base. Working with quick fingers, her knife sliced easily through a red onion, releasing tear-inducing tangs. The slices joined the butter with a salty roar. She added the aubergines (organic, unskinned), all new parts for the choir. Then she added water, and the choir became a football crowd, roaring their team into life.

The shocking thing, the outrageous, insulting and frankly barmy thing, was that everyone blamed Mrs Sidhu for spoiling the wedding. For having the brass to out a thief, they called her an oddball, a nosy nag, a weirdo. When a few kinder souls pointed out that Mrs Sidhu had, in the past, helped the police in their investigations, that too was twisted around. She had got above herself, let a few lucky guesses go to her head.

Never shred people's dreams, that was the message, because if you do, you are the one they will shoot. In the end it came down to the hotel management, and they did not have the stomach to prosecute a confused old man who claimed mental health issues. The 'uncle' was released and everyone agreed it was all a misunderstanding conjured up by an overzealous older woman. As everyone left the reception there was only one thing that was genuine, and that was Mrs Prakesh's poisonous smile. 'What a wonderful occasion,' she purred. 'No one will ever forget it.'

After that, Mrs Sidhu was outcast. The word got round. Orders dried up. Mrs Sidhu was being cold-shouldered by the great and the good of the Slough and district Asian catering scene. She could wail all she wanted that they had the wrong woman, she was not the criminal. It mattered not one jot to them. The last thing anyone wanted was someone outing their misdeeds at a public event. She was like that man who killed the albatross in the poem. She had an uncle round her neck. Which was how she had ended up in catering Siberia.

'This will be better for you, Mrs Sidhu. Better for everyone,' Varma had said. Mr Varma was one of those Asian men who always wore a suit, always carried a briefcase, and conducted almost all his business from the lounge bar at the Heathrow Hilton. He had summoned her there after the wedding debacle. What he really meant was it would be better for him.

'You see, Mrs Sidhu, your culinary skills are indubitable, but your people skills are a little, shall we say, rusty.' Rusty! Mrs Sidhu knew people, and people who knew people knew that. In fact, it was Mrs Sidhu's long standing as an aunty and confidante to all that had given her a unique insight into human nature. Unfortunately, that was the problem as far as Varma was concerned. 'You need insight into human nature like you need a hole in the head, Mrs Sidhu. Now, I have an idea that will allow you to focus completely on cooking while I deal with the customer side of things.'

Varma was the one who had fixed her up after her husband died. He loaned her money, found her clients. She had to be grateful to him. So, she agreed to stay at home and cook pre-packaged aubergine bhajis to be sold in Varma's outlets. That was three months ago. Three months of cooking aubergine bhajis destined for the frozen section of Varma's cash-and-carry.

She reached into her shopping bag and pulled out one of the offending vegetables. She looked deep into its shiny skin and caught her own reflection, distorted, fat and purple. Great, she was turning into one now. To exorcise the image, she cut another aubergine into rough square chunks and, with the skin still on, tossed the pieces into a pan with butter, onions and spices. Soon a second and then a third pot was steaming next to the first.

For the first time since starting that morning she allowed herself a moment. She stretched a hand to her back and rubbed where the spine arched, massaging at the muscle. As smoke and steam overwhelmed the efforts of the extractor fan, Mrs Sidhu opened the back door. She rattled the keys in the lock. The plastic door complained about being asked once again to open. Oh, stop complaining and get on with life, she told it. After all, she had to.

Mrs Sidhu took a mug of tea ('Keep Calm and Curry On') and the *Slough and District Chronicle* out onto the patio. The kitchen exhaled a mist of delicately spiced aromas into the back garden, where Mrs Sidhu noted her husband's beloved lawn was fast turning into a four-inch-high jungle of grass and wispy dandelion heads. The sun was climbing

16

already but it was cooler out here than the kitchen. The *Chronicle* carried all the local stories and Mrs Sidhu spent a contented quarter hour with her tea, flipping her licked finger over a cascade of planning matters, the tribulations of local sports teams, memoirs of local events, school openings, hospital closures, burglaries. She sighed, folded the newspaper. An interesting haul but nothing worth picking up the phone to her friend at the police. She thumped her tea mug down. Time was getting on. To make the point, a jet roared overhead on its final descent to Heathrow in the East, to be replaced almost seamlessly by another one from the West. It was as if the sky was some space-age portal, a gateway, a womb, even – albeit one that gave birth to shrieking metal children every ten minutes or so. Children that, at first, drowned out every thought in your head. Then, just as it looked as if they were leaving, making their way forward, another one appeared. Or, if conditions were not right, the same one circled back round, making yet more agonising noise. Mrs Sidhu sighed and wondered where she came up with these things. What Varma needed was a demonstration. A clear signal that Mrs Sidhu was ready to take on an outside catering job and stay out of trouble, that she had learned her lesson.

Inside the house, she opened her copy of *Don't Let Life Get You Down*. The dedication read 'To Emily, who taught me to follow my dreams and to believe in the impossible.' She mused over Emily: a wife, a parent, a daughter, a teacher? As a young girl, Mrs Sidhu had always been driven by curiosity, an itch in her soul that meant she needed to know. Just like fidgeting or picking her nose, it was an urge that was carefully suppressed by concerned and traditional parents. Mrs Sidhu's mother believed that

17

all human wrinkles could be ironed smooth, with persistence and lecturing. Her mother would spend many hours watching her daughter caught up in her own play, puzzled and sometimes fearful of the intensity of this girl's curiosity about the world around her. Mrs Sidhu grew within the confines of this puzzlement until she pressed up against its sides like some wild verdant plant quickly outgrowing its glass bowl. Curiosity killed the cat, we all know that. It may well be that curiosity was how the evil Dr Schrödinger lured his cat into his box, slamming the lid shut and condemning the poor moggy to an eternity of hovering between life and death. Perhaps he garnished the box with some juicy tidbit, some ham or a piece of pan-seared tuna. Trains, motorbikes, automobiles were also hazards that could do for a cat, as well as getting locked in boxes. Cats, Mrs Sidhu reflected, faced uncertain futures, only and simply because they had the instinct to follow their noses into places that others did not.

She read the back cover once more. 'Often, the problem we face in life isn't that we're down for the count, it's that we feel powerless on our feet. I'll show you how to take back control of your life.'

Mrs Sidhu picked up the directions to the Benham House Retreat and thought back to the phone call. There was something about the woman's voice, a pleading quality perhaps, that would not let go of her. It was the same sound as one of her nieces in trouble, and to Mrs Sidhu the voice of someone in trouble was nails on a blackboard. It unsettled her, and she would find it hard to concentrate on her work until she had put it right. She went back into the kitchen and checked her vats of aubergine bhaji. Most of her tasks were in hand; all she had to do was be back in time for Varma when he came to collect them. She picked up the directions to Benham House. If she left now, there was time to find out what the job was and get back. Aubergines be damned. What Mrs Sidhu needed was a nice side job with no complications. What she needed was a trip to Dr Feelgood.

Upstairs, in the back bedroom Tez Sidhu was woken by the front door slamming shut and a car engine starting. He launched himself into an ear-shattering yawn, baring a gaping mouth and greying tongue and a smell that had escaped from a zoo. He checked the time on his phone against the Post-it note on his bedside table. 'Air India 133, 10:15am, Terminal 2.' Plenty of time. Tez Sidhu rolled over and fell fast asleep.

2

Rage, joy, depression, grief, jealousy, shame, horror: these are all flavours in the standard palate of the human heart. They are the sweet, sour, bitter and salty of emotions and are familiar to us all, and each of us can taste the tang of one, the heaviness of the other. We can experience each one separately or in delicately folded combinations. In between these feelings, Mrs Sidhu had discovered another emotion: Happysad.

Happysad was the umami of emotions. It was the feeling you got when you were alone under the sulphurous glow of a streetlight and it started to rain. Happysad was the sensation of standing next to a cold pane of glass, looking out onto an empty street at midnight, feeling loneliness turning to Aloneness, and in that moment, goosebumps prickling your entire body. Aloneness was Happysad; it was better than loneliness, because in loneliness you were voided and powerless like a stone sinking into the depths. Aloneness, on the other hand, gave your mind wings. Aloneness was a state where your feet were on the ground and your head was in the clouds.

Mrs Sidhu had experimented with other compound emotions. Rage-shame, sympathy-terror, worry-joy and once even lust-indifference, but none had produced anything as zen or productive as Happysad and Aloneness.

When Mrs Sidhu was in a deep state of Aloneness she was oblivious to the outside world. She could remain frozen with a sandwich halfway to her lips until the thread of thought ended or was ended for her by an outside distraction. That distraction, though, usually needed to be moderately forceful. A tap on the shoulder or a cough from a concerned bystander might do it. Once, when she had had a particularly intense attack of Happysadness brought on by watching a cat sitting under a tree in a storm – perfectly protected by the thick boughs of the tree – Mrs Sidhu had entered such a deep and involving state of Aloneness that Tez had found her on the staircase, balanced on one leg, with her right foot hovering over the last step. Tez had to shake her arm until she came back to the living world. It was a wonder that she had not fallen and broken her neck, but for Mrs Sidhu it was always worth the risk. Aloneness was a state where frothy ideas would separate under the heat of concentration and congeal back together into sharply acid conclusions. Aloneness had helped her solve some of the more interesting crimes that had come her way. Without these moments there would currently be a good number of murderers walking merrily around the Berkshire countryside instead of mouldering in prison.

There were shallower states of this Aloneness, and these came when Mrs Sidhu was not completely alone. These came when she was alone in a crowd. When this happened, it was as if people were wind-driven rain, trickling past her, running together into streams, twisting and spinning into eddies as they disappeared into the storm gutters of their lives. This Aloneness happened when she arrived at the Benham House Retreat.

The house itself was a great sandy-coloured mound of mellowed stone. Its colossal size belied its effect, which was gentle and calm, like someone had made the beach into a building. By the time Mrs Sidhu entered the lobby area, tension she had not been aware of was easing from her shoulders. Healthy houseplants abounded, filling the softly lit space with green. And yet Mrs Sidhu could not help but sense that something was wrong.

White-uniformed orderlies eased across thick carpets speaking in urgent whispered voices to well-dressed clients. The reception desk was unoccupied, and Mrs Sidhu tried to flag down one of the orderlies, a gap-toothed man who was wheeling an elderly woman in a wheelchair towards the door. He paid her weak wave no heed at all. She allowed herself to be carried along by the movement of people, until, like a leaf carried by a stream, she found herself outside an office marked DR EARDLEY.

The same clear grey eyes that had stared at Mrs Sidhu from the book jacket now stared at her in person. Mrs Sidhu sat up square to their level gaze, pushing out her chin and resisting the instinct to squirm. It was worth the journey just to be face to face with the man who could make all your problems go away.

The room smelled like a library. Or at least the way libraries used to smell, before they had been filled with clapped-out computers and shiny tables. It smelled of books. Old books, which smelled musty and acidic, and new ones, which smelled as smooth and velvety as their untouched pages. She wanted to open one and stuff her nose into it, breathe in all that knowledge. It looked like a library too, a library from way back when, with wood panelling and creaky leather armchairs and a big mahogany desk, where Dr Eardley was sitting. The only odd note was a pair of muddy walking boots, which sat on a shoe rack in the corner. Newspaper had been put down and had collected lumps of clay.

He rose to greet her, talking in soothing tones. 'I want to assure you that this is not an asylum, nor a hospital. This is a place to heal.' Stephen 'Dr Feelgood' Eardley was just like his book jacket photo: lean, silver-haired, grey-eyed, with a graceful smile that told you that everything was going to be all right.

Dr Eardley's office overlooked the grounds of his house. More of a stately home than a house. 'There are no drugs here, just good mental health practice.' Outside, in seeming answer to his promise, clients daubed canvases in the art therapy session or sat cross-legged, meditating. He circled the room, glancing around, checking his mobile phone, his mind not entirely present, as if he had forgotten something, or as if he were distracted by another pressing matter.

Mrs Sidhu sat awkwardly on her chair, with her handbag perched on her lap and her hands folded neatly on top. She pulled her feet underneath her. Something about Dr Eardley made her want to sit up straighter. She thought of Mr Varma and what he would think if she went against his express wishes. She pushed the thought aside; she was going to get back in time, but she could not resist a glance at her watch.

23

'Should we get started?' she said.

Dr Eardley's eyebrows rose in surprise. A man of his stature would be used to initiating meetings, but Mrs Sidhu had no time to dilly-dally. He nodded his assent. 'I understand that you're the chief executive of your company. A leader of industry.'

Mrs Sidhu smiled. She supposed she was. One didn't often think of oneself that way, but it was good to take stock of these things from time to time. She liked the sound of it. 'I never call myself that.'

'In my experience, those who work at the top of the tree are usually quite humble people.'

Mrs Sidhu accepted this with the grace she imagined went hand in hand with humble leadership.

'Where would you like to start?'

'How about the kitchen?'

'Excellent.'

Mrs Sidhu half stood up, thinking that Dr Eardley was going to show her the way. She settled back down slowly when he took a seat behind his desk, carefully angling his own chair so that he looked not directly at Mrs Sidhu but at a point in the distance out of the window. He took up a notepad and waited, his gold pen poised. 'And what do you see yourself doing in this "kitchen"?'

For a moment, a seed of doubt was pressed into the soil of Mrs Sidhu's mind. Both Dr Eardley's question and tone were not entirely consistent with the usual to and fro of an employer-employee relationship. She looked around herself, at the dark wood-panelled walls, the unsettling piece of abstract artwork on the wall. To Mrs Sidhu it resembled a splash of blood on a cornfield. However, the soil of Mrs Sidhu's mind, when in the mood for business, was not fertile ground for doubt. Being a woman of energy and decisive enthusiasm for her profession, she decided to press on. 'Whatever you like. If the kitchen is equipped properly. Otherwise. I'll have to bring my own knives for the chopping, the dicing, the slicing, et cetera.' She added the et cetera as a flourish to take into account that she was dealing with a learned man.

'Own knives, I see.' He nodded with interest and made a note of this. 'And when did all this start?'

It was not unusual for clients to ask after her curriculum vitae, her experience, and these days everyone wanted a story. A 'narrative', one of her nieces who worked in marketing had said. 'It was shortly after my husband died. I had a lot of debts and a lot of dark thoughts. I have to admit that hacking things up with a big knife gave me an outlet.' Mrs Sidhu broke out a smile. She was sure that the good doctor would understand.

It looked like the good doctor was understanding quite a lot, from the speed and density at which he was taking notes. His pen was flying along at a clip. Mrs Sidhu thought that was a good sign.

'And then there were the murders.'

Eardley's eyes opened wide. 'Murders?' He indicated that she should proceed, and doubled his writing speed. Mrs Sidhu spent a good while talking about some of the cases she had been involved in and how she had helped the police to solve several very difficult crimes. By the time she finished, Eardley's face wore the concerned look of a man who had just discovered a case history that could take years to unravel.

'Maybe we should talk about you, now?' said Mrs Sidhu. She drew out her own notepad.

Still scribbling with furious frenzy, Dr Eardley did not look up. 'Me?'

'Yes, if I'm to cook your meals, it would be handy to know if you have any dietary preferences or allergies.'

Eardley's pen stopped moving, the scrabbling of nib on paper ceased. 'I'm sorry, are you not my ten o'clock? Stress, hypertension and burnout?'

'Oh dear, no,' said Mrs Sidhu. She leaned forward seriously. 'There seems to have been a misunderstanding. I am a caterer.' Dr Eardley looked puzzled, so Mrs Sidhu pressed on, hoping to jog his memory. 'I was told it was an emergency. A woman called.'

'A woman? First I've heard of it.' Eardley's benign smile did its best to recover its place on his cheeks. 'I'm afraid we are at sixes and sevens this morning. One of our therapists hasn't turned up for work and it's caused some organisational problems.'

Mrs Sidhu sympathised. 'Getting good staff is a problem in my field too.'

Dr Eardley hastened to correct the impression he had given. 'Oh, no, no. Wendy Calman is a fine therapist. She has never been late before in the five years we've employed her here. It's most unlike her.' Eardley looked guilty momentarily.

Mrs Sidhu's head tilted to one side, and as she stroked her earlobe a distant look appeared in her eyes. 'Which is why you are concerned.' She nodded gently, speaking to a corner of carpet. 'You are clearly distracted enough to mistake me for a client; you are professional, and understand human nature, and yet you betray signs of guilt, and you're also ambitious and like to do things your own way. I imagine other therapists are a challenge to you.' Mrs Sidhu banged the desk suddenly, making Dr Eardley jump. 'Thus you had some kind of argument!' she concluded, coming out of her daze and smiling broadly at him.

Dr Eardley stared at Mrs Sidhu for some time. Mrs Sidhu, who was prone to saying what she thought, unfiltered, when she descended into one of her meditations, realised she may have been a little insensitive in her assessment of the doctor. For Mrs Sidhu, thinking and speaking sometimes got muddled in the heat of making her conclusions. The smile faded from her face and she said in a small voice, 'Though I don't like to pry.'

Dr Eardley leaned back and nodded. It was obvious that Mrs Sidhu had hit the mark. 'We did have something of a disagreement on Friday. Having had the weekend to cool off, I hoped we might make up. It may be that Dr Calman is sulking.'

'It must have been a serious row for her to not turn up to work.'

'It was a professional matter involving the trust.'

'Trust?'

'The trust. The governing body which oversees the retreat.'

Now it was Mrs Sidhu's turn to look puzzled. Dr Eardley chuckled. 'My books made me a lot of money, but not enough to run a retreat of this size. We need investment, and in return for that I have to accept oversight from the board.'

Mrs Sidhu's mouth went dry. 'I suppose everyone has a boss,' she said. The image of Varma berating her leapt into her mind. It was a cold reminder of why she was here. She checked her watch and groaned inwardly. Half the morning had gone, and she was no closer to finding out what her job was.

A curious look came over Dr Eardley's face. He turned his gold pen over in his hands thoughtfully while he recovered his poise. Then he snapped the lid on his pen and turned back to Mrs Sidhu. 'So, all that business about helping the police, it was true?'

Mrs Sidhu paused. 'Why do you ask?'

Clouds were gathering in those grey eyes; a frown wrinkled his forehead and he looked pale. Dr Feelgood wasn't feeling so good. His phone rang, breaking his gaze. 'You'll have to excuse me. I have to take this.' With that, the meeting was over.

Mrs Sidhu made her way to the door as Dr Eardley answered the phone. 'Anthony? No, Wendy hasn't turned up. How am I supposed to know? Did you talk to her?' He lowered his voice, and Mrs Sidhu strained to hear. 'And more important, did she say anything to anyone else?' He looked up, apparently surprised to see Mrs Sidhu was still in the room. He covered the phone for a moment. 'Is there anything else?' Of course there wasn't. He smiled wryly. Mrs Sidhu apologised and closed the door behind her.

Mrs Sidhu lingered in the outer office. The meeting had ended so suddenly, she had no idea what her duties were or what the job was in the slightest. She cursed herself for not taking down the name of her mystery caller. Naturally, she had tried to call the number back. Each time it had gone straight to a generic answerphone message. Mrs Sidhu thought back to her own kitchen: the waiting aubergines, her empty bank account and what Varma was going to say when she was late with her order. Perhaps this was not the best idea. She could leave now;

no one seemed to be expecting her. Mrs Sidhu had a job that paid the bills, and not only that, Varma would be waiting for her to call in the order. Then she thought back to the mess of aubergines, and having to package them up and freeze them, and she simply could not face it. She was out, out in the open air, for the first time in months, with the offer of a job. She just had to find out what the job was.

Maybe she should go back in and sort things out with Dr Eardley. No, he had been very firm in his dismissal. To interrupt now would only irritate him further, especially after the misunderstanding about her status. Mrs Sidhu was acutely aware that her time was running out, that she should go home. She could wait until his phone call was over. But then how would she know it was over? Then there was that phone call he was taking. His voice had sounded odd, out of control, thick with emotion. Mrs Sidhu did not consider herself an eavesdropper. True, yes, she had often had cause to hear things that were said around her, but that was only natural, and it was hardly as if she could help it. Nor could she help it if she stood too close to a door when someone was talking on the other side.

She stood near the door.

Sometimes, though, standing too close to a door was not good enough. She gave up the pretence and pressed her ear to the wood panelling. She could hear him talking. 'It had to be done. This is simply not the time to start dredging up all that nonsense. She had no right to treat her, she's my client now, Anthony. Which is why I'm terminating her.' Dr Eardley's voice was rising with anger. However, she heard no more of the conversation.

Someone behind her cleared their throat. Mrs Sidhu stood very still.

'You must be Mrs Sidhu,' the young woman said. 'I've been looking everywhere for you.'

3

'Come on, Jonny,' said Tamzin. She could hear Jonny a couple of paces behind her. She took a quick look back. He was pale-faced, pouting and looking wretchedly sorry for himself. Nothing new about that. There was something else about him today. She knew he would be watching her lycra-clad bottom pumping along, and she didn't care. 'Come on!' she repeated.

Tamzin upped her pace and Jonny's skinny legs stumbled into a higher rhythm as they turned the corner into the High Street. Benham village's idea of a high street. Not exactly Oxford Circus or Fifth Avenue, but Tamzin had chosen the village for that exact reason. A quiet little village with good links to London and plenty of space, fresh air and a place for clients like Jonny to get themselves off the bottle or drugs long enough for them to make some money so she could make her 10 per cent plus VAT. The only downside was that villages had people living in them, and those people objected – quite unreasonably – to newcomers coming in and improving things.

They were halfway down the street when she heard only one set of footsteps. She felt a wave of irritation. Despite the lure of her bum, Jonny had stopped. He was outside Dr Calman's house. She jogged back to him. 'Why have you stopped?'

'You look like you could use a break,' he said, breathing in and out reedily. Then he groaned and quietly threw up in a rose bush. Tamzin closed her eyes and began counting to a hundred. She only got as far as ten. When Jonny had finished watering the rose, he spoke again. 'And then I saw that.'

She followed his look to the front door of Dr Calman's cottage. Maybe the village was getting to Jonny. Maybe it was turning him into a nosy neighbour, or worse, a concerned citizen. The front door was open, and Dr Calman was the type to have seven locks and a keychain.

Jonny made his way towards the front door. 'Where are you going?' Tamzin asked.

'Maybe she's taken a fall. Hey, who knows, maybe the old bag is dead.' Then they saw the smoke pouring out of the window. 'You wait here,' Tamzin said. 'I'll go in.'

She was efficient and trim and had a red notebook under her arm and, yes, she would be very happy to show Mrs Sidhu where the kitchen was. Most gratifyingly, she never mentioned the compromising position she had found Mrs Sidhu in. Mrs Sidhu knew well enough she had already made a bad impression, and she wanted to get to work as quickly as possible before Varma called at her house for his bhaji order. She checked her watch; there was time still. However, the kitchen did not seem to be close at hand.

The woman guided Mrs Sidhu through endless old corridors, hung with modern paintings like the one in Dr Eardley's office. She wore a light summer trouser suit, casual but efficient. 'I'm afraid Dr Eardley's in a bit of a bad mood this morning,' she said. Mrs Sidhu explained that she understood.

Her name was Sienna Sampson, and it was she who had phoned Mrs Sidhu that morning. She had small features and black button eyes that ate up light and reflected nothing back. Her name sounded made up. In a sense it was, because all names are made up, and, in a sense, it had logic. 'My parents met there, in the Italian city.' Like the house, Sienna was beautiful and symmetric. She could have been made from the same beige marble the house was adorned with. The building was seventeenth-century and had belonged to an elevated family who fell on hard times. The retreat was new. Dr Eardley had purchased the house and transformed it. Mrs Sidhu realised that Sienna was warming to her role as tour guide, and that theirs was not the shortest route to the kitchen.

They passed through a door, but instead of entering the kitchen, they exited out onto a lawn as wide as one of Slough's public parks. Mrs Sidhu, as all urban residents treading onto public parkland, watched her feet instinctively. There was no need. No hint of dog poo here. She doubted fly-tipping was a problem either. The high walls along the perimeter looked like they had been built to keep the Normans out. The yellow stones were topped with altogether more modern precautions. Hair-like spikes of toughened wire sprouted along the ridge. To keep people in or to keep people out? The walls and hedges softened, but could not entirely deaden, the sound of the motorway.

The M4 crashed through Berkshire's countryside, a distant dragon's roar of thundering steel on hot tarmac. Sienna, meanwhile, continued her tour.

'We've got gyms, spas, a waterfall, meditation, a pottery studio, lots of treatments, even colonic irrigation. We treat the whole body, inside and out.' She painted a picture, a conveyor belt of self-realisation. Troubled executives arrived with stiff-shouldered anxiety and left with their innards washed and wrung out both figuratively and literally. It was like a laundry service for the soul.

'She doesn't look like one of your busy middle managers.' Mrs Sidhu pointed towards the elderly lady in the wheelchair she had seen in reception earlier. She was being wheeled across the lawn by the same gap-toothed man. 'And he has a different uniform to the others.'

'That's Elliot, he's an HCA – a personal healthcare assistant – and that's who he works for. Edith, but we call her the Witch.' When Mrs Sidhu enquired further, Sienna smiled mysteriously and said, 'You'll learn.'

Mrs Sidhu hesitated, then asked the question that was on her mind. 'Is there an Anthony working here?'

Sienna tapped her chin. 'No, I don't think so. There's Tony Hammond, you know, the guy behind Hammond Homes.'

Hammond Homes was the country's biggest housebuilder, and everyone knew who Tony Hammond was. 'He's having treatment?'

Sienna laughed. 'Oh no! Though he should, he's one of those red-faced men who look like they're going to have a heart attack any minute. No, his wife comes in. They live in the village.' There were two cushions next to Edith's wheelchair on the lawn. One was taken by a twitchy-looking woman of about thirty.

'She's a lot younger than Tony Hammond,' said Mrs Sidhu. Sienna couldn't hide a smirk. 'So who's the other cushion for?'

Sienna pulled her notebook tight to her chest. 'I can't say, but if you read the papers you'll know already.' Mrs Sidhu hadn't read the right papers, so she let it go.

One thing was for sure, Sienna seemed prepared for Mrs Sidhu's arrival, even if Dr Feelgood was not. She carried a folder – patient notes, she confided, then quickly changed 'patient' to 'client'. She explained Mrs Sidhu's role. Preparing lunches and teas for the various therapy groups, outside or in the dining room if the weather was bad. Later, there would be contracts to sign, and of course non-disclosure agreements – Dr Eardley had to maintain client confidentiality, so anything that Mrs Sidhu overheard was subject to strict limits. Everyone was expected to sign them, even herself, she said with a discreet smile. 'A number of the clients are high profile.'

The distant motorway roar was laced now with the sound of sirens. They jarred with the bucolic garden, the fine architecture of the house and the flowering shrubs bordering. It was as if the noises were from a different, bruising world, and this world, inside the walls, was a shelter from it.

'Stress is the biggest problem in modern society. Stress, addiction, burnout, breakdown. The clients here have been through hell. Therapy is a journey for each and every one of them.' Sienna handed Mrs Sidhu a brochure from an antique side table. If they were in hell, they certainly had the money to buy their way out. The rooms were rated five stars. There was a swimming pool and clients (not patients) were encouraged to exercise. Membership of a local golf club was included in the price. The price was high enough to draw a wince from Mrs Sidhu and a mental note to revise her quotation for the job, when she finally found out what it was.

They entered the house again, further up the building into the east wing, Mrs Sidhu estimated.

'The kitchen is newly installed,' said Sienna. She walked around the large central island, pointing out features like a housewife in a fifties advert. She stroked the granite counters, paused to identify the tower fridge and finished up with one hand on hip, the other waving airily over the Victorian-style porcelain sink. 'Dr Eardley buys only the best.'

He could afford to, with what he was charging, Mrs Sidhu thought. Sienna continued: 'Now, your most important job will be preparing cream teas for the village fete on Saturday. We host it every year and it is very important to keep the local people onside.' Sienna paused and added proudly, 'This year it's my job to organise it.'

Mrs Sidhu sensed there was another problem. 'I have no problem preparing cream teas.'

Sienna grimaced. 'I'm afraid that's not it. The problem is that someone has already volunteered to do the job. Dr Calman. She's one of our staff, and she is the most awful chef you have ever seen.'

Mrs Sidhu recollected the phone conversation, the undercurrent of panic, and tried to match it up with the prospect of some overcooked scones. The implication that Sienna would lose her job. Something here did not add up. 'And that was the emergency that you were so worried about?' Mrs Sidhu could not keep the dubious edge out of her voice.

Sienna laughed it off lightly. 'You haven't seen her scones. I nearly broke a tooth last year.' The kitchen was in the basement and had high, narrow windows along the corner walls. If a person was close you would see only their feet. Further away, because of the raised position of the house, there was a good view across the back garden. Sienna's eyes searched the lawn, finding the figure of a well-muscled gardener tending the flower beds. Her eyes flickered away quickly, but not quickly enough to escape Mrs Sidhu's attention. 'And who's that?'

Sienna's voice softened. 'That's Patrick. He's the gardener.' She pulled herself together. 'The real emergency is that I want you to break it to Dr Calman that she's not doing the cream teas. She's trying so hard, and I don't want it to sound like it's official or from Dr Eardley.' Sienna checked her watch. 'She should be here by now.'

The sirens were getting closer, no longer on the motorway but winding their way through narrower arteries. Mrs Sidhu was getting that sensation again: the narrowing of her arteries, the increase in her heart rate, the retreat to her inner world. 'Perhaps she's running late. Traffic was terrible on the motorway,' she mumbled, but she knew that was not it. Wife, mother, caterer and sleuth, Mrs Sidhu knew when something was wrong. A faint smell of smoke tickled Mrs Sidhu's nose. The sirens were very close now. Multiple sirens, like an ambulance and a fire engine.

Sienna frowned. 'No, she lives just around the corner.' Then a curious look passed over her face, a remembering of something. She shook her head, trying to dismiss the thought.

'How close?' asked Mrs Sidhu.

* * *

37

The road was picture-postcard perfect: a twisting lane, a line of thatched cottages. The only discordant note was that one of the houses had smoke pouring out of the open front door. In the front garden, sitting on his haunches and vomiting into a bush, was a man. He wore a leather jacket and tracksuit bottoms. He pulled his head out and Mrs Sidhu recognised him from somewhere. As she walked past, his hand gripped her wrist. It was a hand from the grave, sinewed, tattooed. 'Don't go in there,' he warned. His voice was deep, his eyes dark and his skin was shrunken like beef jerky. His voice was ravaged with use and abuse. Mrs Sidhu recognised his face but did not place it for a moment.

The human memory is a curious thing; so often we search the corridors of our minds for a word we want, or the name of a long-time friend, pushing into the room where we kept the thought, only to find it is empty except for ghosts. In this room, Mrs Sidhu found lizard-skinned demons and screaming and crashing sounds. She almost jumped.

'Jonny Snakeskin.' His crooked smile said he knew that she would know who he was.

The half-placed face, the demons, the shrieking – it all made sense. 'Mr Snakeskin! The rock star?' she said. 'I would love to tell you what a huge fan I am.' It was true, she would love to be able to tell him that. 'Are you all right?' she asked.

Jonny Snakeskin nodded. 'I'm fine.' He plunged his head back into the bush. His stomach heaved again. That was why Mrs Sidhu recognised him. She was more used to seeing his heavily mascara-ed eyes staring out from an album cover than from his backside sticking out of a hebe plant.

Mrs Sidhu craned her head to the top of the road. The sirens, and more importantly the vehicles producing them, were still nowhere in sight. When he came back up for air, Mrs Sidhu gripped him by the shoulders.

'Did you call the fire brigade?'

He looked confused. 'No . . . yes, I guess I did,' he said.

Mrs Sidhu forced herself to slow down. 'Is she inside? Dr Calman, I mean. Is Dr Calman inside?'

Snakeskin nodded then started to speak. 'Yes, but—' He started choking again.

Mrs Sidhu shook Snakeskin's hand free and made for the door.

Inside, the smell of burning was stronger, and smoke lingered close to the ceiling like a rain cloud. If it hadn't been on fire, an estate agent would call it a quaint cottage, where the word 'quaint' adds an extra zero to the price tag. It was Farrow and Ball outside and in. Small, bent windows allowed meagre portions of light, which did little but throw sunbeams at the smoke haze. To be honest, most of the estate agents Mrs Sidhu knew would probably have added even more for the fire – insisting that it added to the cosy feel.

Mrs Sidhu hunted around for the source. Everything seemed normal. The house was on fire, but there were no flames. She called out for Dr Calman. There was no reply. Mrs Sidhu took a breath to steady herself. If there was smoke, there was a perfectly natural source for it, and any chef knew where that was.

In the kitchen, the smoke was thicker still. Mrs Sidhu wrapped her chiffon choonie around her face and rushed across to the pan on the stove. There were two pans and from the first, the scent of apples, summer fruits, berries and sugar told her it was jam but burned hard onto the base of the pan. She looked underneath; the gas ring was still on. The other pan also smelled of fruit, but apples, and they were only half cooked. She instinctively moved to take it off the heat before she realised it was not necessary. The ring under it was off, but the one next to it was on. Clearly, Dr Calman had already taken it off. Neither pan was the source of the smoke.

Mrs Sidhu turned her attention to the oven. She covered her mouth, trying not to cough. She opened the oven door. Black smoke tumbled out, smarting her eyes. Inside were a dozen charred lumps of what she guessed had once been scones. Sienna's assessment of Dr Calman's cooking skills seemed to be pretty on the nose. She turned the oven off and closed it. Smoke continued to gush from the oven vent. Mrs Sidhu opened the main oven. Two black ovals lay on a baking tray. Mrs Sidhu's guess, from the salty smell, was pork chops. Jam and scones, for the village fete. Two pork chops and apple sauce, someone was coming to dinner. She turned the main oven off and slammed the door shut.

Dr Calman took the apples off the stove but had left both ovens and the jam on. She must be nearby somewhere.

Mrs Sidhu cast her eyes around the kitchen. It was hard to see through the choking fog. She scooped her hands to part it, like a swimmer doing breaststroke. Shapes slowly came into focus: a kitchen table in the corner was scuffed; the back door, tiled floor and walls in the same muted pastel shades as the paintwork, and glimmers of gold in every corner. She squinted and the glints formed into tiny discs. There were pound coins scattered around the room, leading a trail to the back door.

Mrs Sidhu's eyes swung back to the table. There was a fountain pen, uncapped. Mrs Sidhu looked around and under the things on the table. There was no sign of any paper. Then there were more coins scattered on the top and underneath—

Her train of thought stopped. Mrs Sidhu suddenly understood what Jonny Snakeskin had been trying to tell her, what had made him sick and why he warned her not to go in. From under the table, a pair of feet stuck out, clad in dark, sensible shoes. A thick, congealing slick of red lapped around them. It wasn't jam. Mrs Sidhu knew from past experience that she was standing in the middle of a crime scene. Her heart sank like a stone plunging into the depths. Mr Varma was not going to like this.

4

Mrs Sidhu had a bad habit. At moments of crisis, she talked to herself, or rather, her 'better self' talked to her. Right now, her better self was screaming at her. *You need to get out of here. Now!*

Heat flushed her face, and it wasn't from the cooker. She let out a low groan. She knew what this feeling was. This was Trouble. Pure, boiled down, single origin, concentrated, straight from source nectar of Trouble. She should turn round and leave right now, because if she stayed a minute longer the Trouble would stick to her like the burned fruit in Dr Calman's sad little pans, like the curdled blood pooling around Dr Calman's sad little body.

She stifled a cough. In the stillness, smoke swirled around her, and the choonie over her mouth was only doing so much to keep it from her burning lungs. She ignored it, like she was ignoring her better self. What was wrong here? Other than a dead woman with her throat cut open?

Go now! Or explain all this to Varma. Do you want that?

Was it possible to envy Wendy Calman? Because she was no longer part of the living world, the world that would have to explain to Mr Varma why his delivery of aubergine bhaji had been delayed? That would also have to explain to the same Mr Varma that it had been delayed because she left the house, went in search of alternative employment – against his express wishes – and then had somehow contrived to stumble on a corpse? It did not bear thinking about. The body itself though, now that was another story.

Her better self already knew she was screaming at a brick wall. *All right then, look at the corpse, be a weirdo, I don't care.*

The sight of a dead body had presented no difficulties to Mrs Sidhu. She knew at a young age that for all living things, life parted company with the body in a mysterious moment called 'death'. If it was someone you knew, or a pet, or something like that, you were devastated by it; looking on the lifeless remains, it was a shock to learn that this living thing would never speak or bark or lick your hand ever again. Like the time when she was eleven and had found Sherlock at the back of the hutch. He wouldn't come out, however much she waved the carrot. When she touched him, he was cold and as stiff as cardboard, watching her with whited-out eyes. Dad lifted him out of the hutch by the back legs and slid him into a black bin bag. At the time she had been devastated. Now, years on, so much life and death behind her, she wondered what he would have tasted like with a cranberry and peppercorn sauce.

If it was not someone you knew, or your rabbit, the effect of death was muted, shocking still to sense the end of a life, but nonetheless inevitable. All that lived, died.

This body, Dr Calman's body, had stopped being alive some time ago. From the abandoned and burned cooking, the preparations for a meal, Mrs Sidhu would have guessed she died sometime last night before dinner time. The money was a confusing factor. Was she going to pay someone, or had someone robbed her, killed her and run away in a panic? The sound of sirens outside jolted her from her thoughts.

What did you think was going to happen? Her better self was actually being smug.

Another groan escaped her throat. More trouble on the way. She pictured a fire engine approaching from the village end of the street, and Mrs Sidhu knew a police car would soon be behind it. If they interviewed her now, she would be here for hours. It was not that she was going to lie, exactly, but a complication with the police right now was not what she needed. The police, she reasoned, would ask questions, questions that they could answer for themselves.

Wendy Calman's body was actually the least interesting thing in the room. It was other things in the kitchen that struck Mrs Sidhu as strange; small things. The most curious of these was the arrangement of the jam and apple sauce and the presence of the overcooked scones. Those were very interesting. Then there were the pork chops, plural, but no vegetables or salad. Then there was the money. In Mrs Sidhu's fertile and ever-moving mind, these were seeds that could be left to sit and grow, and grow they would. That was enough for now.

All right, she said to her better self, *I'm going*. She really needed to get a grip of herself.

*　*　*

Mrs Sidhu made short, fast strides out the front door. Outside, Jonny Snakeskin was gone. She skipped across the road before the fire engine screeched to a stop, and she mingled with a fast-growing crowd of onlookers. She finally allowed fresh air into her lungs, and the cough that had been tickling up under her ribs for the last few moments came on like an earthquake. She hacked and gurgled until someone offered her a tissue. She recognised the face, the beaming gap-toothed smile, the orderly's white uniform. 'You all right, luv?' he said. Mrs Sidhu grabbed the tissue, spat into it as decorously as she could and smiled as if this was normal, then handed it back to him. For an instant his gaze hardened and the smile flickered. 'Thanks,' he said. Mrs Sidhu said he was welcome in a distracted way, because her mind was elsewhere.

Mrs Sidhu pulled out her phone to check the time and found a list of missed calls from Varma. He would be on his way over. Mrs Sidhu would have to rely on Tez. Thank the stars he answered his phone.

'Tez? You awake?'

There was a delay and a rustling that could only be bedsheets. 'Course I'm up.' He yawned. Mrs Sidhu wondered if there was much difference between 'up' and 'out cold'. She imagined him, getting out of bed and scratching himself. Scratching in areas that Mrs Sidhu did not want to contemplate. Mrs Sidhu was an enthusiastic observer of human nature. She had noticed that men were scratchers in a way that the fairer sex were not. Her departed husband had been a vigorous scratcher and Tez was, if anything, an even more avid fan. So much so, Mrs Sidhu had wondered on more than one occasion if he had fleas. Impossible of course, though

45

she had discreetly dusted his bed with anti-flea powder just to be sure.

'Tez, I need you to get downstairs to the kitchen. You'll find three vats of aubergine bhaji. I want you to pot them up into the Tupperware because Mr Varma is coming to collect at midday. Have you got that straight? Tez?' She heard snoring. 'Tez!' The snoring stopped abruptly.

'What?'

'Please can you pot up the aubergine bhaji for Varma to collect?'

Silence for a while, accompanied by the sound of more scratching. 'Yeah, yeah, I'm on it, Mum. But what about the pickup?'

Mrs Sidhu clasped her head, which right now felt like it was full of angry bees. For the third time, Mrs Sidhu explained what she wanted Tez to do. This time she used short words with long pauses between them. 'Yeah, I heard, but I mean the other pickup—' he started to say.

She looked back up to the cottage. While Tez had been testing her sanity, time had passed. The fire engine had left, the smoke was dispersing and a police constable was patiently wrapping blue plastic POLICE, DO NOT CROSS tape across the front gate. 'I have to go, they're wheeling the body out.' Mrs Sidhu watched as the formless mass on the trolley jumped and juddered over each bump. Wendy Calman made her way for the last time out of her cottage, covered in a blanket. It was not the sort of blanket that offered any kind of warmth, Mrs Sidhu noted, but then it did not need to. Wendy's sensibly shod feet stuck out from underneath, turned out at the ankles, making a V sign, a parting gesture perhaps.

There was a pause on the phone while the gears of Tez's mind revolved. 'They're wheeling the what out?'

'I'll be home before Varma gets there. I'll see you soon.' She ended the call. Hai, hai, she just prayed he would wash his hands after all the scratching. The catering manuals were very clear about hand hygiene standards.

The police were very keen on hygiene too. Men and women in gloves and puffy white suits attended to the body of Dr Wendy Calman. They looked like clouds, as formless, unreal and shapeless as the poor woman herself. Mrs Sidhu wondered if a strong wind could blow them all away, or if, in the way of clouds, they might slowly change shape and come to resemble cushions or lighthouses or (gulp) even aubergines.

Mrs Sidhu adjusted the strap on her bag and turned to leave. If Tez got the food ready to go, she still had time to get home to meet Varma. She was confronted by a white shirt and a black tactical vest. She looked up and found the policeman's eyes. She sighed, her shoulders slumping. 'Hello, officer. How can I help?'

'I understand that you entered the building and found the body. We need to take a statement, if you don't mind.' She was about to ask how the officer knew, when the gap-toothed orderly gave her a cheery wave and dropped the tissue in a bin.

It was lunchtime when Mrs Sidhu finished giving her statement to the constable. More missed call alerts from Mr Varma bounced up on her screen when she checked her phone, accompanied by one from Tez. She should phone Varma. Her thumb hovered over the call button and wavered. There was a lot to explain, and some begging of forgiveness. Such things were better done in person. She must get back; her catering business had to be her priority here. She put the phone away.

47

Back at the Benham House Retreat, the sun was high and a light sweat prickled her forehead. Mrs Sidhu allowed herself to open one button on her cardigan. Any thoughts of hurrying back to Slough were quickly scotched. Her bottle-green Nissan Micra was parked where she had left it on the gravel forecourt. She unlocked the door, hot air flushing across her arms from the miniature greenhouse inside. It reminded her again of the oven in Dr Calman's house. The picture was clear in her mind: jam (on the stove), apple sauce (off the stove), two pork chops (in the upper oven), scones (in the lower oven). Inside the car, the oven theme persisted. Mrs Sidhu's fingers leapt from the plastic steering wheel. The fabric of the seat burned her back. She wound the windows down and hopped out of the car. While waiting for it to cool she watched. Waiting is watching, and to watch is to observe.

Dr Calman's passing seemed to have had no lasting impact. Was that disturbing? She crossed her arms. It was downright annoying. A woman was dead, yet the mass of sandstone that made up Benham House's frontage was unchanged and the atmosphere around the place was as reflective and soothing as it had been earlier in the day. On the lawn a circle of intense-looking men and women sat cross-legged, arms on knees, fingers splayed as they tried to expel their all too obvious tensions. Another group made tight pencil sketches of the fine mature trees that dotted the garden, and in depositing lead on paper exorcised the pressure of running stock-market-listed companies or making their fortunes on social media.

These people thought they knew pressure. They never worked in a kitchen during a wedding with the bride changing her mind twenty times about what she wanted

48

to accompany the main course. They had never worked with Varma on their shoulders. The man was relentless; blood from a stone was an everyday miracle for him. On cue, a message from Varma popped up on her phone. Where are you?????. Mrs Sidhu felt her blood pressure rising and silently envied the meditators and sketchers on their perfect lawn. What would she give for an hour with a half-decent therapist!

Inside, the car creaked and clicked as it cooled like an old man settling into a favourite chair. The seat was no longer hot to the touch, and the steering wheel would soon be bearable on the ends of Mrs Sidhu's fingers. The people who designed car interiors were obviously sadists.

Mrs Sidhu remembered the sensible black shoes on the hospital stretcher, and some faint tendril of sympathy for a woman whom she had never met played and tickled against her conscience. Perhaps, she wondered, for a moment giving everyone the benefit of the doubt, the news had not yet reached them. The high walls, the electric gates, these might insulate this island of calm from the outside world. That was the advertised promise of the Benham House Retreat. The skin on Mrs Sidhu's neck tingled. She knew there was a sweet zone, a time between the happening of bad things and the arrival of bad news, and in that sweet zone, answers could be found to questions. Not that it mattered. She had invested far too much in building up her catering business to let that distract her.

A man locked up his bicycle outside the retreat. He wore the white tunic of an orderly and red cycling gloves. The contrast, and the goatee beard, made him look oddly theatrical, like a magician. He was young and serious, brows hitched together in a frown. He was also in a hurry.

He cursed as he fumbled and dropped his bike lock. Bad news was on the way. Inside the car, the steering wheel was cool to the touch. Her back would accept the hot plastic of the seat without too much complaint. There was no good reason why Mrs Sidhu should stay a moment longer at the Benham House Retreat.

So it was a mystery even unto herself that moments later, Mrs Sidhu slammed the door shut on her little car, locked it, and made her way inside the doors of the retreat. On the way she accidentally kicked the serious young man's bike lock into a drain. 'Oh my, I'm so sorry. And there are so many bike thieves.' The man glowered at Mrs Sidhu's departing back and rolled up his sleeve. Mrs Sidhu had questions about Dr Calman's dinner arrangements. Surely that was catering business.

'Did you talk to Wendy?' Sienna asked.

So news had not reached Sienna yet. They were in Dr Eardley's outer office. Mrs Sidhu had brought cups of chai from the kitchen for both of them. They absorbed them-selves in pleasant conversation for a while, Sienna looking out of the window, swaying and sipping her tea. Mrs Sidhu mumbled a reply: 'She wasn't very talkative, as it happens.'

Sienna turned away from the window and eyed Mrs Sidhu curiously, picking up on the catch that Mrs Sidhu couldn't keep out of her voice. Mrs Sidhu's cheeks burned. She should tell Sienna that Wendy Calman was lying dead in a police morgue, but she hesitated. It was wrong, of course, to keep such things back, but there was so much Mrs Sidhu wanted to know, and the news of death would destroy any opportunity to ask questions. Perhaps, she told herself, it was a mercy to delay spreading such terrible news. 'I was going to ask you about Dr Calman's routine in the evenings.'

Sienna looked puzzled and asked why Mrs Sidhu wanted to know. This was a good question, and Mrs Sidhu scratched her head for a moment before coming up with an answer. 'Some of my clients want me to cook their evening meals too.' It was weak, but Mrs Sidhu pushed on. 'Especially if they have dinner guests.' Keeping her voice as light as she could, she asked, 'Did . . .' She changed that quickly to the present tense: '. . . Does! Does Dr Calman have dinner guests over in the evenings?'

Sienna played with a strand of hair, pulling it down over her eyes and staring at it. 'I don't know. I can't imagine anyone would put themselves through her cooking. She is really, really bad. Did I not say?'

Mrs Sidhu scratched her head again. 'You know, I think you did. Yes, now I mention it, you did. Silly of me to forget. I just thought that maybe Dr Calman would have her clients over to dinner so she could talk to them informally.'

With a grave look, Sienna confirmed that such a thing would never happen, that it would be unprofessional, and Dr Calman was very professional and a stickler for rules. As if reminded of this, Sienna stopped playing with her hair and started moving around the office, tidying up, putting away files.

Mrs Sidhu's shoulders relaxed and she let out the air that seemed to have built up in her chest. It looked like she was being silly after all. There was nothing in her suspicions. She felt disappointed. She should feel relieved, shouldn't she? Now she felt guilty that she felt disappointed instead of relieved. She took a breath and some time to untangle herself from this knot of emotions. The simple fact of the matter was that she could go home with a clear conscience, apologise to Mr Varma for being late on her order, try to explain where she had been all morning, and return to her normal everyday life. Yes, that was exactly what she should do. She forced a smile to her lips but it didn't manage to go all the way up to her eyes. She was about to leave the room and go back to her car when Sienna spoke again.

'Actually, it'd be a mercy to Patrick if you did cook dinner instead of Wendy.' Sienna laughed, showing bright white teeth, small under her luminous eyes and her pert nose, like one of those animals that people trapped for fur. A mink, that was it.

'I beg your pardon?' said Mrs Sidhu.

'Patrick, the gardener. He has to put up with her cooking. I tell him not to, but what can he do? He's a captive audience. I think half the time he sneaks a veggie burger in, to be honest.'

Mrs Sidhu was about ask what Sienna could possibly mean when the inner door opened and Dr Eardley's head appeared around it. 'Errr . . . Sienna?' he said as if he struggled to remember names. 'What are you doing in here?' His jaw clenched. He strode across the outer office, ignoring Mrs Sidhu completely, and took Sienna by the elbow. It must have been a little rough because he quickly withdrew his hand and regained his composure. 'You should be with Dr Calman.'

'Mrs Sidhu says Wendy's taken a sick day. I thought I'd be more use out here, tidying up and waiting for you.' A tiny frown wrinkled Sienna's smooth forehead, her mink eyes glazed cloudy. 'Have I done something wrong?'

Eardley melted in the gaze of those little black eyes. He wiped the concern from his face and smiled beatifically. 'You've done nothing wrong at all. I was just surprised to see you here.' He seemed to notice Mrs Sidhu for the first time, his spectacled eyes zoning in on her like glow lamps. 'What's up with Dr Calman?' Mrs Sidhu swallowed and tried to think what she was going to say. Fortunately, she was saved by the serious young orderly she had seen outside earlier, the one with the dark hair and the red cycling gloves. He arrived at the office door out of breath. 'I came as quick as I could, Dr Eardley, but I was delayed.' He threw a malevolent glance at Mrs Sidhu.

Eardley eyed the orderly sympathetically. 'No need for agitation, Arif. Give yourself a hug.' He waited while Arif, reluctantly, complied. 'Now, tell me what is going on. Is it Jonny Snakeskin again?'

Arif shook his head and recovered his breath. 'Dr Eardley, you have to come. I was in the village. The police are at Dr Calman's house. People are saying something has happened to her.' Shame burned Mrs Sidhu's brow but she carefully watched the reactions as the news sank in. Sienna's eyes turned to Mrs Sidhu in horrified confusion. The sun caught Eardley's glasses at that moment and Mrs Sidhu could not read his eyes. He stood very still for a while. 'I see. Let's go. You can fill me in.' As they all left the room, Mrs Sidhu made sure she was last out and peeled off in the opposite direction. She had a sudden hankering to be out in the garden.

5

The late-morning sun shone through the kitchen window onto the floor and spilled out into the hallway. What it was illuminating was not very illuminating.

Detective Chief Inspector Burton was in Dr Calman's kitchen. The coroner had already done her work. The crime techs had taken the body away. He had snatched a look before they did. It had been no mystery what killed her. Her throat was cut open in an untidy gash. The skin on his own neck prickled and he rubbed the sensation away. He never liked looking at bodies; it interfered with the detachment he had to preserve. That's what he told himself, anyway.

Now, her shape was marked out in blood, like a photographic negative. Burton glanced around and wondered if there was anyone here who was old enough to remember photographic negatives. Perhaps not. Elsewhere, there were pots on the stove; otherwise the kitchen was clean and tidy. So was the hall and living room. Not a thing out of place. Burton put on examination gloves and opened the oven.

Inside were some blackened lumps. He went to the back door and tried the handle, which turned easily. The door swung open. Burton left it that way; maybe it would clear the smell. He swivelled around, examining the scene, and drew a line with his arm from the front door to the impression of Wendy's prone body and to the back door.

'Attacker came in the front, she was trying to get to the back door to get away,' Burton said to the room. Around him, crime scene technicians continued their work, minutely sweeping for fingerprints and DNA. 'She never made it,' he concluded.

A crime technician popped his head in through the back door and held up a plaster cast.

'Got some good shoe prints,' he said. Outside, the new sergeant was interviewing the neighbour. Burton thrust his hands into his pockets and wondered why he could no longer keep the names of his fellow officers in his head. They came and they went. He seemed to be the only one who stayed.

Still in a thoughtful mood, he drifted towards the front door. Burton was disturbed by the smell of charred pork. He had missed breakfast and his mouth was salivating. The fact that he knew from personal experience that it smelled like burned human flesh did nothing to dull the growling in his stomach. That was even more disturbing. Burton wondered idly if he was becoming desensitised to the horrors of the world. He had worked crime scenes after fires, where the bodies had to be identified by dental records.

He stepped outside into the front garden. Very nice, winding path, flowers at the edges, the archetypal rose-covered cottage. Burton knew this village. He had dim memories of the summer fete, strawberry jam, scones and clotted cream, the coconut shy and winning a big teddy bear for his wife. Then wife; she was his ex-wife now. He remembered her hugging the teddy, her dark eyes on him, shining as if he was Buck Rogers or something. That was long ago. His face soured. She was hugging someone else's teddy bear now.

'Sir?' The sergeant broke his chain of thought.

'What?' he growled back. The sergeant waited patiently on the front path, young and keen and nervous. Burton massaged the back of his own neck. He softened his tone. And he finally remembered his colleague's name. 'What is it, Sergeant Dove?'

'It's just the neighbour, sir.' Dove checked his notes, to get the name right. 'Ms Tamzin Grey. She lives behind, their gardens are back to back. She works in entertainment, an agent.' The sergeant looked up at him.

The chief inspector was a tall man. His size, however, put him at a disadvantage among what he liked to call the cultural elite. He felt awkward, a proverbial bull in a china shop. In fact, one of his greatest fears was moving too fast and knocking over one of their precious vases or objets d'art. 'Did she see anything last night?' he said.

'No, but she says that the victim was selling raffle tickets and the like at the bring-and-buy sale earlier.' Dove snapped his notebook shut.

'Fascinating,' Burton said, not bothering to keep the sarcasm from his voice. This prompted more from Dove. 'She says Jonny Snakeskin found the body. You remember him, sir. Rock star at one time. His fans were into a load of satanic worship and stuff.'

Burton mused unhappily around the flower beds. 'I remember.' Burton did. He had all his albums at home and not a shred of satanism in him. He doubted Jonny Snakeskin did either. 'So is he the one who threw up in these bushes?' Dove supposed that he was and, crestfallen, started organising a sample and a DNA test to confirm it while Burton eyed the Farrow and Ball walls, the thatched roof, in pristine condition. 'These places must be a fortune in upkeep. What sort of doctor was she? A consultant?'

'She was a psychiatrist, a therapist,' Dove said. 'She worked round the corner at the Benham House Retreat.'

The afternoon sun was shining brightly and the well-watered lawn felt springy and welcoming under Mrs Sidhu's feet. The air was sweetened by the aromas of scented flowers, and gentle tinkles emanated from a wind chime. Somewhere in the distance a senior manager at a retail company sublimated her stress next to a water feature. All in all a perfect day in a perfect English garden, and everything that Mrs Sidhu had hoped for when she had ventured out. It must be stated, however, that a relaxing walk in the garden was not the limit of Mrs Sidhu's ambitions on setting out from the kitchen shortly before lunchtime. It was not long before she found the object of her search: a shed.

Mrs Sidhu did not share her late husband's fascination – no, obsession – with temporary outhouse structures. Two years after his death, she was still throwing out the catalogues. This shed was the possible hiding place of one handsome, if hairy, gardener. From what Sienna had said, Patrick must have been Dr Calman's dinner guest. What had she meant by 'captive audience'? Mrs Sidhu approached the shed with trepidation. The news of Dr Calman's death was still a ripple on a pond, unrevealed. Such knowledge, when released, quickly became a tidal wave.

'Hello?' she said, pulling the door open.

After the bright afternoon light, Mrs Sidhu blinked. The shed was dark, with little light falling through the one window because it was obscured by an overgrown bush. Patrick, she guessed, did not like to be overlooked. He was shy. Then she saw the drawings. 'Oh my, look at these,' she said when her eyes adjusted and fell on the papers spread across the workbench. There were dozens of them, darkly lined sketches. Some of the pencil strokes were so deep they had torn through the thick paper.

Mrs Sidhu picked one up. She turned it around in her hands, trying to find an angle to view it that would make it clear. There were strange apparitions with heads of beasts, what looked like altars and twisted pillars, and in the centre a single, all-seeing staring eye looked out. Not the sort of thing Mrs Sidhu would hang in the vestibule at home. She was unsure what that eye was seeing.

'You shouldn't be looking at that.' Mrs Sidhu jumped. The stuttering voice had come from the door.

Mrs Sidhu dropped her hand from her heart. 'You must be Patrick.' She kept her voice calm. Patrick was broad-chested; Mrs Sidhu could tell because he wore no shirt. She could smell the work on him, from his skin, from his dreadlocked hair. He glared at her and snatched the picture from her hand. He gathered up the other ones and stuffed them under the bench, out of view. 'They're private,' he said. He hurried to make a pile out of the other pictures, but not before Mrs Sidhu pulled one out. It again featured the all-seeing eye. 'This one is good. Nice eyeball. Did you use a model, or is it something from your imagination?'

Patrick grunted. He had his back to her, preferring to

58

face the rough plank wall rather than Mrs Sidhu. He stood oddly statue-like and awkward.

'Do you exhibit?' Mrs Sidhu asked. Again Patrick grunted, possibly meaning (with an optimistic reading) that would be a nice thing to do one day. 'Did you have dinner with Dr Calman?' He stiffened and turned to face her; there was suspicion in his eyes and Mrs Sidhu chose her next words carefully. 'It's just that she hasn't come to work and people are worried.'

'I didn't sleep at home last night. I have another place I go to sometimes.' He crossed his arms. The muscles across his chest writhed, fighting over which one was going to be on top.

Suddenly it all made sense. Sienna had said that Patrick was a captive audience for Dr Calman's cooking. 'Home, Patrick? So you live with Dr Calman?'

He nodded stiffly. 'She's always been kind to me.'

Mrs Sidhu tried pacing around along the length of the shed. As she did, Patrick edged his huge body to one side. That was why he seemed so stiff. There was something on the workbench behind him and he was hiding it from her view. Mrs Sidhu kept up her questioning and moved back towards the door. 'She was expecting you for dinner. She was cooking pork chops, am I right? So why didn't you go home?'

Patrick's chin dipped to his chest, he looked confused. Mrs Sidhu pressed on. 'Was it her cooking? Her cooking was bad?' When Patrick grunted, Mrs Sidhu took it as agreement. That was one mystery solved. How many stolid chop dinners cooked by his landlady had Patrick run away from? 'I'll leave you to grunt along,' Mrs Sidhu said. 'Er, get along,' she corrected herself quickly. She turned to leave.

Patrick dropped his guard, moved a pace forward from the workbench. Mrs Sidhu moved fast. She executed a sharp 180-degree turn. She was small and had always been nimble on her toes and was behind Patrick in the second that it took him to reverse his significant momentum. 'What have we here?' she said.

Benham House. The thought of strawberries and happy memories came flooding back to Burton like sunshine warming his back on a winter day. 'Is that where they have the summer fete? The big old house, falling to bits?'

'Was a big old house, now it's some kind of rehab retreat,' said Dove. Burton's mental image of shivering junkies with needle marks in their arms was dispelled quickly by Dove's next words. 'For execs and celebs. You know, stress, booze, the pressures of the boardroom, the pressures of the stage. Holistic healing. Couple of Shiatzu sessions and a bit of aromatherapy and they're all set to make another million, sir,' Dove chuckled and petered out.

Under the afternoon sun, the front garden was a furnace. Burton fished a tissue out of his pocket and wiped it around his forehead and neck. So Benham House had changed ownership; it was the Benham House Retreat now. Nothing was the same. Burton had heard of it, of course, but had never made the connection with the Benham House of his memory. 'It's that self-help bloke, isn't it? Eardley?'

Dove nodded. 'Dr Feelgood, he calls himself. Naturopathy, making a mint off it.' Dove was overdoing it with the chummy banter, Burton thought, but such were the bonding rituals between men. He let it go and went back inside the house, where it was cooler and he could think alone.

There was a flyer on the hall table. Village fete, the date was for the coming Saturday. So Benham Hall had changed hands, but they still hosted the fete.

He turned his attention to the loose change scattered around the kitchen. It marked a trail in the back garden. It had all been counted, twenty-seven pounds in all. His eyes scanned the shelves for a missing jar or a broken piggy bank. Nothing seemed out of place. Burton raised his eyebrow and computed the possibilities. It took him a few moments to make up his mind. Burton was not a man who acted before he thought. He prided himself on deliberation. 'Raffle tickets, village fete,' he mumbled, then raised his voice, interrupting the work of half a dozen police constables and crime scene techs. 'OK, we're looking for something that would hold cash. The sort of thing people use on a market stall, or at a bring-and-buy sale. Most likely a lockable cash box.'

'It's a cash box.' The box was one of those metal ones which stallholders use for cash takings, or people used at jumble sales to keep change in. Oblong, flattened, about a foot and a half long and a foot wide. Across the lid, neatly printed, were the words *Village fete raffle*. Mrs Sidhu turned it over in her hand and hefted the weight. Inside, coins shifted and rumbled. Mrs Sidhu flipped the lid open. A raffle book with pink tickets bulged under a fat wad of notes and a pile of coins. Mrs Sidhu exhaled. 'Looks like the village raffle is doing well,' she said.

The effect on Patrick was immediate. All the breath seemed to leave his body. He buckled at the knees; his lips quivered. He reached out a weak arm towards the box. 'Sacred,' he whispered.

61

'What, this?' Mrs Sidhu's eyebrows shot up. She looked at the cash box carefully again, reappraising with squinted eyes. 'I've heard village raffles described in lots of ways, but never that,' she concluded. 'What's so special about this one?' She put a hand on it and pulled it away sharply as Patrick let out a tortured breath. 'Patrick, are you listening to me?'

Something strange was happening to Patrick. He was on his knees and his eyes were pressed tightly shut. He panted as beads of sweat pricked his forehead and slicked his face. Pulling his arms out wide, he started to talk, fast. 'There was a bad smell. The chops were overcooked. The apples were fine. I checked the apples, they were fine. She always said to be careful with the apples. Apples are the first fruit, the sin.' Tears glistened at the edges of his eyelids and tracked down his cheeks. 'I tried to talk to her, but she wouldn't listen.'

Mrs Sidhu shook her head; confusion and pity fought for control of her facial muscles. Pity won out. 'What happened, Patrick? What happened to Dr Calman?'

He was babbling. 'She was a good person. All she did was help people. She helped me. But she wouldn't listen. She was always asking about him.' Patrick nodded his head, setting his greasy yellow dreadlocks bouncing sadly. But with a new firmness he added, 'She wouldn't listen and now she's dead. There's nothing to be done about that.' He went quiet. His stream of consciousness seemed to have stopped just at that point. Mrs Sidhu took the cash box to him and tried shaking it. 'And this? What about this? Did you take it, Patrick?'

Patrick's eyes blasted wide open, shining with a holy light.

* * *

Time, in DCI Burton's experience, was an important factor. If this was a robbery with violence, and that was looking more and more likely, then getting a clear picture of what happened and a description of the suspect was going to be important. Catching him or her with the evidence was liable to be a deciding factor in getting a conviction. Burton knew there was no point in pushing his officers. The uniformed police were efficient in their search methods. Much of what they had found had already been bagged, tagged and labelled. So Burton did what good bosses did. He stayed out of the way under the shade of a cherry tree in Dr Calman's back garden until they finished up. His wait was not a long one. Within twenty minutes Dove came and found him.

'It's not inside nor in the front or back gardens, sir.' Sergeant Dove was out of breath, he held up a hand to guard against interruptions. 'There's more.' He took a few sharp breaths while Burton tapped his finger on his forearm. 'The pathologist thinks the throat wound might have some dirt in it. Maybe she was dragged in from outside.'

'Or dirt was on the weapon that killed her,' said Burton.

'There's something else, sir. It looks like someone else was living in the spare room.'

'She had a lodger?' Burton's neck prickled with sweat.

Dove thumbed through his trusty notepad. 'He apparently stayed somewhere else last night. Bed wasn't slept in. He works as a gardener, at the Benham House Retreat, sir.'

Patrick stared through pin-prick irises at the cash box. Something was awake inside him, something growing and ominous. Patrick climbed to his feet and advanced with a new determination. 'It's mine.' His voice was choked and deep, and all doubt had left it.

Mrs Sidhu gulped and edged backward. 'Patrick, I don't know what happened, but I can help you. I promise. There's nothing to be frightened of.' It was an effort, but she kept her voice steady. She asked herself if Patrick really believed that he would be the frightened one in this scenario.

Patrick closed in; he grabbed at the cash box, catching Mrs Sidhu unaware. As with any lady of a certain age and disposition, Mrs Sidhu's instincts in a cash box wrestling competition were entirely predictable. The edges of her mouth moved into a determined snarl and she wrapped her arms around the smooth metal box in a vice-like hold. 'You're not having it!' she said.

Patrick became wild, rage filled his eyes. He snorted air in through his nose. His expanding lungs made him seem twice as big, like some mythical beast. 'Give it to me.' In the grip of his giant hands the cash box looked more like a matchbox.

Mrs Sidhu's knees weakened. She tried not to imagine Patrick ripping her arms out of their sockets like a raging child with a doll. It might be the last thing she did, but an Indian aunty did not give in to an overgrown man-child having a tantrum. She thrust out her chin, fought back the urge to drop to her knees and then shook her head. 'Nuh-uh. Not until you tell me what happened.' Amazingly, she said this with a steady voice.

For a moment they were face to face like dancers frozen in time. She could feel his breath on her, smell his unique bouquet, 'Eau de Patrick' – sweat, soil, and sweetpeas. In his eyes she read only indecision and turmoil. Then it came. The dance began, and it was not going to be a waltz. Like thunder after lightning, Patrick's eyes blackened to storm darkness. He bared his teeth and he thrashed. His long, braided hair swung like a thousand serpents, and in a snap and crack Mrs Sidhu flew away, bouncing her head off a bench vice on her way.

Mrs Sidhu fell to the ground; the world swirling around her. She fought to keep her concentration as darkness seeped in from the edges of her vision, narrowing to a small circle at the centre. Patrick leaned into it, his face filling her head. 'Warn them,' he said, 'for I am returned, Death, destroyer of worlds.' Then all was blackness. Mrs Sidhu fell into a dark hole with no bottom, her body forever twisting and jerking through the void.

6

If dreams were going to be like real life they should make more sense. Or perhaps it was the other way round, life should make less sense. There should be less a to b to c, less reason for this to connect to that. Death, after all, made senselessness out of life, and Wendy Calman's death made no sense.

When Mrs Sidhu opened her eyes she was staring at soft-edged clouds. The clouds, oddly, were brown, square and very dark. Her eyes came into focus and after a few moments she realised she was lying down, that the shapes above her were mouldings in an antique wood panelled ceiling. She was lying on firm leather, and a pair of concerned grey eyes stared at her through round eyeglasses. In a moment of free-floating non-thought, the kind that occupies the territory between sleeping and waking, Mrs Sidhu felt the urge to confess, to let loose all the pain she kept tightly bound up in her chest. It would be so much easier.

'Might be some mild concussion.' The grey eyes turned to talk to someone out of Mrs Sidhu's sight. 'Probably best to get that checked with a medical doctor. My qualifications are in healing the mind, not the body,' he finished.

She was lying on the couch in Dr Eardley's consulting room, looking up at the wood-panelled ceiling. Well, she said she wanted time with Dr Feelgood. She just wished she'd been conscious for more of it.

'What exactly are your qualifications, sir?' another voice asked. This was a slow voice, a familiar voice. She lay still and listened for now, still trying to pin down the second voice.

Meanwhile, Eardley rose and cast a hand across his bookshelves where his name featured prominently on the spines of an entire row. 'My qualifications are that I've helped millions of people across the world come to terms with everything from losing their jobs to losing their loved ones.' He plucked a book from a shelf and handed it to Burton. 'Please, this may help you.'

Burton read the cover: '*You Are More than Your Last Relationship.*'

When he looked up, Eardley smiled. 'I have a sixth sense for these things. Please.' He pushed it into Burton's hands, who thanked him. 'It's four ninety-nine. Tell you what, just make a donation to the retreat.'

Burton ripped a fiver from his wallet and thanked him again, with less sincerity, before returning to his question. 'I meant your academic qualifications. I mean stress, addiction? You're stretching yourself a bit, aren't you?'

'My doctorate is an honorary one, I admit. But they don't just hand those out. It was in recognition of the work I've done. The medical establishment aren't always ready for new ideas. But I am not against scientific methods.

That's why I hire people like Wendy Calman. Her psychiatric credentials were impeccable.'

'You weren't forced to hire her, then, by the board of trustees you mentioned this morning?' Mrs Sidhu spoke from the couch. She identified the second voice with a small flutter of joy.

'Take it easy, Mrs Sidhu, you've had a nasty knock. Take your time,' DCI Burton said.

'No need, I'm fine,' she said. She sat up and tried to push herself off the couch, but all too quickly. Everything went blank for a moment. When she came to, strong arms supported her and a face frowned at her. 'My goodness, are they calling out chief inspectors for minor accidents now?' she said. She waved away any further help and took a few wobbly steps for herself, concluding, entirely differently from the two men in the room, that she was as right as rain. 'There.'

'In answer to your question, Mrs Sidhu,' Eardley said, 'it was the board's suggestion that I take on a medically qualified professional, but it's one I welcomed with open arms. At Benham House, we are here for the whole person: body, mind and spirit. I agree with you, Chief Inspector, these are serious conditions, and no one wants a lawsuit, do they?'

Dr Feelgood's compassion was bottomless, thought Mrs Sidhu.

'Mrs Sidhu, I think you should sit down for a bit,' Burton said. They knew each other, of course. They were old adversaries and old companions. The DCI was a good man, and he had helped her in her previous cases. Though, in his opinion, he was certain that she had helped him.

Their paths had last crossed six months previously in 'The case of the cycle thief of Newton'. That was what

68

Mrs Sidhu called it in her mind (and much later in her memoirs). It started off as a case that no one was interested in. To Mrs Sidhu's outrage, cycle theft was not a crime the police devoted much attention to, other than issuing crime numbers for insurance claims. So it was Mrs Sidhu, with her usual dogged determination, who had connected the random-seeming thefts to the murder of a hedge fund manager in Windsor. Donald Peake was now serving twenty years for murder and three months for stealing bicycles. Mrs Sidhu was secretly more pleased about the latter. All this was before Mrs Sidhu's exile to her kitchen in Slough and the back-breaking toil of the *brinjal bhajis*.

Now, once again, here was Burton waiting for answers. It was like old times, like a fruit she had not savoured for a long time that was now back in season. Old times, except that now there was a gigantic headache in her left temple and the room was moving around like a ship in a storm – but, otherwise, like old times. 'Do you remember what happened to you in that shed?' Burton asked.

Mrs Sidhu rubbed the lump on the side of her head. She remembered Patrick, his wildness, the animal fear in his eyes, the struggle with the cash box. 'I slipped, must have bumped my head, but I'm completely fine. Now, I have to get back home before lunchtime. Mr Varma will be very annoyed.'

DCI Burton and Dr Eardley exchanged a look. Outside the sky was darkening, Mrs Sidhu now realised. 'My goodness, how long have I been asleep? What happened to Patrick? Is he all right? The poor boy is half scared out of his wits.'

'Maybe we'd best have a chat,' Burton said, finally convincing Mrs Sidhu to take her seat again. 'That boy murdered Dr Calman. I've no doubt about that,' said Burton. He handed over to Eardley and she listened with growing dismay.

Patrick was not just a simple gardener; he was a man with deep-rooted mental health issues. Dr Calman got him a job and took him in as a lodger. 'It was typical of Wendy, she always wanted to help,' Eardley said. 'It's what make us therapists in the first place. Patrick was a bit of a project for her. He was once a brilliant young man and she was determined he would return to his profession.'

'You mean as an artist?' Mrs Sidhu said.

'A few years ago Patrick became obsessed with certain numbers and eventually had a breakdown. He had some very strange ideas. Wendy was helping him put his life together. I suggested gardening – growing things is a healing experience. I say as much in my book *The Green-Fingered Executive*.' Eardley modestly pressed a hand to his chest. 'Yes, guilty as charged, I was the man who introduced the Busy Lizzie to the boardroom.'

'That's very impressive, sir.' Before Eardley could wind up the momentum to sell him another book, Burton took up the story, helped her join the dots. Patrick had a relapse, killed Wendy with some kind of garden implement, and then ran off with the cash box, for reasons relating to his number obsession. He probably suppressed all memory of the crime until Mrs Sidhu reminded him of the cash box. It was hard to come to any other conclusion, for the two men, anyway. Mrs Sidhu was less inclined to see things the same way. The police arrived only to find Mrs Sidhu unconscious on the floor of the shed; Patrick had fled and was still at large. 'We don't know where he is, but we need to find him quickly,' Burton finished.

It was when DCI Burton took his notebook out that she realised the tone of their conversation was a police interview. That Burton had only told her the details of the case to impress on her the seriousness of the situation. 'Now, I've already heard that you found Wendy Calman's body,' he snapped, 'I've also heard you failed to raise the alarm here at Benham House. So can we finally have the truth, the whole truth and nothing but the truth.' He raised his pen, and for the second time in one day Mrs Sidhu had her statement taken.

Outside, the night air was cool when Mrs Sidhu left the retreat, and Burton was already almost at his car. She hurried to catch up with him. 'Chief Inspector, fancy running into you here,' she said.

Burton agreed with dead eyes that it was always a pleasure. 'Well, you know, where there's a body, there's a policeman,' he said. So much time had passed since they last met, there was a distance in the way he talked. He was polite, professional like a stranger. 'Anyway, it's nice to see you again.' If he thought that was enough to give Mrs Sidhu the brush-off, he was wrong.

Mrs Sidhu scuttled around, getting between him and his car, smiling pleasantly and bringing Burton up short. Mrs Sidhu remembered Wendy's body, laid out with her throat open. 'Do you really believe Patrick killed Dr Calman?' Mrs Sidhu thought back to Patrick, his gentleness. Gentle until she found the cash box, that was. Then he turned altogether more aggressive. She shook her head clear, refusing to accept Burton's line on the subject. 'Just because someone is unusual doesn't mean there's something wrong with them.'

71

Burton pursed his lips and rubbed the back of his neck. Eventually he said, 'It doesn't mean there isn't either.' He took a long look at the bandage around Mrs Sidhu's head. 'What was it that Patrick Kirby said before he clobbered you?'

Mrs Sidhu's heart sank. '"I am returned, Death, destroyer of worlds."'

Burton's jaw hardened. 'Sounds like a completely sane thing to say. Maybe leave this one to us, eh? And be careful.' He looked directly at Mrs Sidhu with those placid eyes, and there was warning in them. 'Because this man is dangerous. You got between him and what he wanted, and what he said sounds like a threat to me.'

She shrugged it off, sure that she was in no danger, but she still had an uneasy feeling. As her car spluttered and rolled on the bumpy road out of Benham village, she remembered something she had forgotten in her statement to Burton. Patrick had started his sentence with 'Warn them.' Mrs Sidhu could not help but wonder who Patrick wanted to warn and about what. She had the feeling that this was not the end of the matter. Wendy Calman's death still made no sense to her.

Eardley found Arif in the dispensary, tidying up.

'It's been a very upsetting day. We need to take extra precautions tonight. Make sure the front gates are locked and the security system is on.' He threw Arif a sharp look. 'Things have been getting lax around here.'

Arif shifted from foot to foot apologetically. 'They are saying it was Patrick?'

Eardley watched the darkening skies. 'He's out there somewhere and I don't know what he's feeling. I just wish

I could be there to talk to him, even if I could get one of my books to him.' But it was an impossible dream. 'He might come back.'

'If he comes back, I call the police?' Arif asked.

Eardley put up a cautioning hand, like a traffic cop slowing down traffic. 'Let's work that through. I feel I'm responsible for his welfare. I should talk to him first, see what triggered this, what I can do to help, what he might recollect about the night Dr Calman died.'

Arif's face was implacable, stoic, but it was obvious he understood. He unlocked the drugs cabinet and scooped up a vial of clear liquid and a syringe. 'If he comes here, you leave him to me.'

By the time Mrs Sidhu jiggled the key in her front door it was late. After a few tries she persuaded the lock to cooperate, and with a barge of the shoulder she stumbled onto her welcome mat. She closed the door behind her. Mrs Sidhu exhaled and leaned against it for a moment. It had been a long day.

Why was her life like this? A nice side job with no complications, that's all she had wanted when she left the house. Now she was standing here with a bruise and a head-shattering headache, worrying about a dead woman she had never met.

The house was in darkness but for the streetlight coming through the front door. Her own shadow was cast in broken angles, like a cubist painting of a spreadeagled spider.

Mrs Sidhu knew about cubism, the art movement that had formed the idea that you could look at something from all sides at once. She liked it, even if sometimes it was confusing. Her own attention fell on what she heard from different corners of her house, building a picture from all angles. The sound of snoring drifted down the stairs, a hushed roar from the water boiler, the faint smell of cardamom, distant traffic, a cat in a neighbour's back garden. Was there something else? She listened for a while. She heard only conversation from the television from next door seeping through the cardboard walls.

She made for the sitting room, keeping her steps quiet so as not to rouse Tez. She reached for the light switch but changed her mind. Her head was throbbing, and her eyes were feeling sensitive. She lowered herself wearily into her favourite chair, the contours mating perfectly with her backside through the effort of time and repeated application. Here she rubbed the sore spot on her left temple, making circles with the tips of her fingers. Things were still a bit jumbled in her mind. She made a conscious effort to pull the shattered parts into one picture. She had been attacked by, for want of a better word, a maniac. The same maniac who had murdered a woman, his land-lady, for nothing more than the contents of a charity collection. The story seemed to scan, and yet the parts did not seem to add up to the whole. There was something she had forgotten, something important.

The main point was that she could not afford any involvement in anything right now. With all those auber-gines to cook and with everything else in her life, it was impossible. Yet Mrs Sidhu could not deny that all her old instincts were tingling again. This lad, Patrick, a cold-blooded killer? For the contents of a cash box? What had he said about Dr Calman? 'She always helped people.' Mrs Sidhu snorted; she knew what that was like. The reward for those who helped people was not meant to be finding themselves dead on the kitchen floor, she remarked to herself, even if the martyred mother in her imagined ruefully that was where she would end up herself. Pain was a lesson you did not forget. Mrs Sidhu had her fair share; her thoughts wandered briefly back to her departed husband. She wondered what pain poor Patrick had endured. If 'poor' was the right word for a murderer. One was not supposed to feel sympathy.

Suddenly a wave of tiredness washed over her. Such a long day. These were questions for the police, she surely had no time for them. Mrs Sidhu leaned back in the chair and used a foot to steer a wayward pouffe into position so she could get her feet up. Her eyelids were becoming heavy and she had no real hope of making it up to bed. That was when she saw in the half-light that there was someone else in the room. The figure was sitting ramrod straight on the sofa.

'I've been waiting,' the voice said.

7

A torchlight flicked around the velvety edges of the darkness. Soon hands appeared on the rough, charred edges of the wooden panels. With a groan the wooden boards parted and he was inside. Quickly the boards were pushed back into place. The torch went out. After a hiss, a flash, and then a match was held to a wick. Light grew out from the pale yellow flickerings of a candle.

The night was warm but Patrick shivered. He let out a shuddering breath and the candle flame spluttered and threatened to go out. He rushed to protect it in the crook of his hand. When the flame was steady he trusted it enough to place the candle on an upturned box. Next to it he put the cash box.

The space was big enough to walk around, and old furniture was stacked in one corner. Patrick's hands trembled as he opened the drawer of a rotting desk. Inside, still sealed, were his provisions and the book. Some of the tension that clenched his back eased. He turned his eyes upward to thank his protector that he had the foresight to see this day coming.

He ate. He broke off chunks of bread and swallowed them, barely chewing. He drank soup from the can, cold, and washed it down with bottled water. When he was sated, he turned his attention to the cash box. He pulled out the contents, making small reverent piles of coins and notes, then placing the raffle book in front of them in the manner of an offering at a shrine. Then he took the three tickets torn roughly from the counterfoils and placed them on top. Three numbers, three sacred numbers.

If the police caught him before he succeeded, he would not be able to do his work, the work that Wendy had given him, the work that he now realised was the reason for his being on earth. She had trusted him. He could see now that her death was necessary. He must save them; he was the only one who could save them. But if he showed them the raffle tickets he would suffer the same fate as Wendy. The same demon would be on his back. There must be a way.

In the corner was some derelict furniture. Patrick's strong hands reached under an old table. Good, the box was still there. The hands dragged it out and pulled out the papers, holding them up in the light in a moment of reverence and wonder. His quaking fingers turned the pages. Finding the right page, his index finger traced out the shape of an ancient, angular symbol. His eyes lit with devotion, Patrick grabbed the paint spray, then with a shuddering, halting breath, turned to the wall, drawing the mark out.

Mrs Sidhu sat absolutely still and held her breath. *I am returned, Death, destroyer of worlds.* The voice was grating and formal like nails on a metal colander. This jarred with the smell in the room, a smell that only now was creeping into Mrs Sidhu's consciousness. The scent of cinnamon and cardamoms wafted across, warm and welcoming. Mrs Sidhu realised it came from the cup that the other figure was sipping from, and with it came a pang of remembrance of younger days. Mrs Sidhu stifled a moan and pulled her scrawled-on envelope out of her pocket. It wasn't Ali33, it was AI133, Air India flight one three three, Delhi to Heathrow. Meanwhile the owner of the voice waited.

Respected Sister-in-Law Daljeet, her departed husband's sister, sat forward in her chair, the glow from the streetlight catching her iron-grey hair, bound in a tight bun at the back of her head. 'You keep long hours, sister,' she said. Then she nodded quietly, her mouth dragged down at the edges by gravity and grim reality.

How could Mrs Sidhu have forgotten that Daljeet was arriving? A gut-sickening wave of embarrassment threatened to drown Mrs Sidhu. She snatched her feet from the pouffe and sat up straight. Daljeet had that effect on people. It was like a sergeant major walking into the unkempt barracks of Mrs Sidhu's mind. Her thoughts flitted around covering up her untidy excuses: her work, the excitement of the day, her head injury.

Not that there was disapproval or rebuke in Respected Sister-in-Law Daljeet's comment. Quite the opposite, for the admission of the hardness of life, and the inevitability of back-breaking toil was offered as a shared platform, a brokering service in the diminished penny-stock market of Daljeet's emotions. Mrs Sidhu hesitated to trade. It would only lead downward.

'Luckily, I enjoy my job,' she said. Then, to assuage her guilt, 'Though naturally I was sad not to greet you personally. Did Tez—' Of course he hadn't. Mrs Sidhu had told

78

him not to, because she had confused the food pick up with the airport pick up. So her guest had waited some time and then took the bus. On a positive note, Tez had let her in, but on a negative he had also given her the TV remote control, some left-over fried chicken in a bucket and gone straight out. Daljeet's eyebrows curved upward. 'He came back at midnight with more fried chicken and went straight to bed.'

'I am so sorry, I can't believe I forgot to pick you up,' Mrs Sidhu said.

However, Respected Sister-in-Law Daljeet made allowances, she understood that work was more important than luxuries like being picked up from the airport. Daljeet would have happily walked from Heathrow to Slough, Mrs Sidhu thought. She could imagine her now, trudging out the miles with her grim countenance set against the wind, motorway traffic whirling her chiffon choonie around her. 'I hope you'll have time to enjoy your trip,' Mrs Sidhu said. 'Are you staying long?' she added, hoping she kept the concern out of her voice.

Daljeet stiffly glanced around the room. 'This is undecided. For now, it is enough to experience the joy of speaking once more with relatives,' she said, somehow failing to convey any sense of joy about the situation. 'I see you've hurt your head.'

Mrs Sidhu put a hand to the bandage on her forehead, stroking at the sore lump beneath. 'It's nothing,' she said.

Daljeet stood and put her arm around Mrs Sidhu's shoulder and led her up the stairs, though Mrs Sidhu would rather have slept on her chair for a while. 'It's time you went to bed,' she commanded, 'tomorrow we have so much catching up to do.'

PART II

Finding out what the client wants is the key to a successful catering contract, just as finding out what the murderer wants is the key to a successful investigation.

Life With a Knife, Mrs Sidhu's memoirs

MIDSUMMER DAY, 1997

He knew he was going to have to get out of the house before midnight. That gave him twenty minutes.

Moonlight picked out the house as it nestled easily into a piece of ancient English woodland. Yellow light crept out of the windows, shining splayed rectangles onto the gravel courtyard below. Inside, he could see the Happy Couple were sitting on a plush leather sofa. They were holding hands and watching television with sightless eyes. It looked like some distorted children's playhouse and they the children. The house was built into a hill and stood on stilts on one side, with a gaping, crooked mouth underneath, big enough to swallow two large cars. He moved past the cars. Behind them was a door. He strained with the weight of the jerrycans weighing down each arm. Even with the lids fastened, the stink of petrol found its way into his nostrils, causing his eyes to stream. He forced back a choke and climbed the stairs quickly. The cans gurgled and wobbled.

Inside, the house was perfect down to the last beam, the last nail, the last fitting. Blond Scandinavian pine,

German engineered wooden beams. Once on the top level he put the jerrycans down on the soft pile carpet next to the other two. It would be a shame to see the house go, but it was necessary. He appreciated things of beauty and things that people had worked hard for. On the other hand, it would burn beautifully. People would see it for miles around. That was important, that it be seen. He checked his watch. Eighteen minutes.

Everything had to be perfect. He pressed the eject button on the sound system. The tray eased open. He dropped the CD into it. Why not a little music while he worked? He turned the volume up to maximum. There was no one to hear it.

He decided to start on the top floor. He heaved one of the jerrycans up the final set of stairs into the bedroom and began to splash the fuming liquid around. By the time he got back to the main level, he was sweating with the effort.

He moved around the airy, Nordic-inspired spaces of the house, dousing petrol. He hummed along as Frank Sinatra's 'Fly Me to the Moon' belted out of the perfectly balanced Wharfedale speakers. The stodgy remains of a vegetarian lasagne and a bottle of Montepulciano stood on the table next to two wine flutes stained red. Next to them, the jarring presence of a bottle of Coca-Cola. It was laced with phenobarbital: a quick painless death and to his mind the masterstroke of the plan. Their last meal. He chuckled mirthlessly about that. Last meal, it turned out, was exactly what it was. Did people have a way of predicting their own futures? As he passed through the living room, he turned the music up. Sinatra's voice soared and invited him to play among any number of heavenly bodies. He chuckled. 'The skies await you,' he said to the corpses, and moved with his jerrycan through the house. The thick carpet on the stairs soaked up so much that he worried he wouldn't have enough. He had to have enough for a really big, really hot fire.

Back in the living room the television was showing Patrick Moore explaining again the trajectory of the comet Hale Bopp. How a lifeless lump of ice and rock tumbling through space had made the light show of a lifetime. That was two months ago. The couple watched on. They looked so beautiful together he almost smiled. Their eyes stared back at him, empty of all thoughts, of all pain.

Was everything in place? He had a moment of panic. Had he forgotten something? No, he need not have worried; everything was laid out as it should be, he reassured himself.

'Well, this is it. Goodbye,' he said, 'I commend you to the stars. Have a happy new life.'

The remark was addressed to the house as a whole, as well as to the Happy Couple.

He lit the match, dropped it. The blue flame spread out quickly. It coated the floor and climbed the walls. It was so beautiful he stopped to watch it. Flames always had a hypnotising effect on him, ever since he had been a boy.

Fire.

The heat hit him like a red brick wall. His eyes widened. He had to run.

By the time he got to the stairs, he could feel the air leaving the room. His chest heaved, his legs felt weak. He pounded on, wheezing for air, but the only air he could get was hotter than a desert wind. He made a final burst, jumping the steps two at a time to keep ahead of the flames.

He landed hard on the last one and tripped, twisting his ankle. He cried out, clawing at the door. His hands slipped on the brass handle twice before he got purchase on it. He slid the rest of the way out on his belly, landing in a quivering heap in the garage.

Outside, cool night air finally reached his lungs. He sobbed it down gratefully. Somehow he got into the car and with shaking hands turned the ignition. The engine gunned, the wheels spat gravel and he was gone. He checked again that the passport and plane ticket were on the seat beside him. In the rear-view mirror he could see that the fire had reached the roof. The windows gave with a splintering groan and the fire tumbled out. He feared for one moment that somehow it would reach out and grab him back. But he steadied himself.

He was the master of the fire. He gave it life, and he controlled it.

He accelerated up the long drive and was at the main road by the time the pile of jerrycans exploded, sending a thunderbolt of flame into the starry sky. He reached the motorway junction before he saw the first emergency vehicle, a police car. He pulled the hood of his robes over his head. On the motorway, he hit ninety. But no one was interested in a speeding motorist. No human being anyway. Only the silently watching eye of the speed camera flickered, then strobed and flashed. Two hours later he was sitting in first class sipping a cool glass of Sancerre. Never had he felt so alive. He had so much more to do with his life. There was nothing left here to bring him back. He had burned his bridges. He would never return to the village of Benham. He swallowed the wine, acid on his lying tongue. He would have to come back one day. All he could do was hope that it would not be for a long time, long enough for people to forget – and for him to alter his appearance significantly.

8

Tony Hammond had two big secrets in his life, and he was forced to share both with Stephen 'Dr Feelgood' Eardley.

'Where the bloody hell were you?'

Stephen Eardley seemed to ignore the interruption as he made a couple of annotations to the case notes open on his desk. After a moment or two, when it became apparent that he was not going to respond, a curled, plump red fist smashed down on the notes. The owner left it there. Eardley turned his calm grey eyes up to meet the smouldering bloodshot gaze of Tony Hammond. Hammond's jowls wobbled. 'I said, where the bloody hell were you?'

Dr Eardley pressed the tips of his fingers together. He offered Hammond a chair. Hammond shook his head, jowls wobbling, fried egg eyes steady. 'You look very pale, Anthony.' Tony hated being called Anthony. Only his father had ever called him Anthony, and that was usually before he expressed his disappointment in him. Of course, Dr Eardley knew all that. They knew everything, didn't they, bloody shrinks. Tony growled. 'Don't start with me.'

Eardley stood up from his desk. 'Physical contact is known to release a host of endorphins and chemicals that enhance mood and lower stress.' Wearing a beaming smile, he stepped around his desk with arms outstretched. 'Nothing feels better than the common or garden hug.'

Tony Hammond was a big man, he played rugby as a boy before injury ended his career. He raised a warning hand. 'I swear if you come one step closer to me you'll be feeling my mood very clearly.'

Eardley sighed, waved his hands in surrender and retreated. 'Fine. I was there, at the agreed time, agreed place. So if I may rephrase your own question, my dear Anthony, where on earth were *you*?'

Tony's chin dropped, his mouth hanging slack and open. 'I was there.' He shook his head as if to clear any doubt. 'I was there,' he repeated. A crease of concern appeared on his brow. 'My train was delayed. I couldn't have been more than ten minutes late.' He pointed a stubby finger at Dr Eardley, finding his anger again. 'You should have waited!'

Stephen Eardley smirked. 'Come now, Tony, if you were up to your late-night activities you need have no shame in front of me. I understand.'

Hammond disguised his embarrassment with contempt. 'You don't understand anything, not in this world anyway. In your la-la fairyland maybe. But on this earth I make things work, which is why you need me. Never forget it.' Hammond smiled with satisfaction.

Stephen Eardley's faint smile remained where it was. He took his glasses off and stared out of the window. Midsummer was nearly here and the sun had been up some hours already. Under its glare, rough-cut oblong silhouettes could be made out in the distance. 'You know that thing up there is a calendar. That was what the ancient Druids were doing out there, making sense of the repeating patterns of the year, making sense of time, space and the human spirit.'

Tony grunted. 'Are we in for another one of your mystical talks?'

Eardley pursed his lips before continuing with a snip in his voice. 'I'll be brief, then. Am I right in thinking that you don't have someone to vouch for your whereabouts night before last?' asked Eardley.

Hammond spluttered that he didn't need someone to vouch for him. He was Tony Hammond, for God's sake. 'What were we doing wandering about in the night like a pair of halfwits anyway?' He was about to smash his fist down on the table again when he stopped. 'Hey, hang on a minute, nor do you! And it's bloody convenient for you that Dr Calman is dead.'

'Just convenient for me, Anthony? Or do you benefit too?' Tony fell into silence. Eardley stroked the spine of a book on the bookshelf. It was his first bestseller, *You Don't Have to Be Unhappy, You Just Need to Be Understood*. The public had been generous, but the book reviewers had been unkind: 'therapy lite' they called it. They missed the point. People wanted to be listened to and comforted, and Stephen Eardley's genius was that he heard and he soothed. He had tried to help Anthony, tried to listen to him, tried to help him reach the light of a new understanding of himself. Hammond, he reflected with sadness, seemed immune to happiness. 'People come here to get better, Anthony. My belief is that they're the ones standing in their own way. I merely help them get themselves out of the way of their own recovery. You're in your own way Anthony.'

Tony looked at Eardley, nonplussed. 'Save your holistic babble for the middle management crowd and the Hollywood has-beens. I don't need it.'

Eardley explained patiently: 'It's obvious what happened, isn't it? It was dark and we simply missed each other.' Hammond nodded curtly and Eardley continued, 'But the business with Wendy Calman. It's a complication.'

This left Hammond blank-faced. He stroked his chin before rubbing his tired, bloodshot eyes. 'So what do we do about it?' he asked.

Dr Eardley nodded thoughtfully. 'Do our jobs, Anthony. Do our jobs.' He put his glasses back on. 'We must proceed with our plans. The Sanctuary must become a reality.'

'I'll get to work. As long as you have your end in hand. You do, don't you? Good, leave it with me. I can get started.'

'Won't we have to wait for the results of the public consultation? The local people will surely have a say in our plans,' Eardley asked, his face earnest.

For a moment, Tony seemed to have a fly in his throat. He choked, spluttered and a slow rumble gurgled up from his lungs and exploded from his mouth. Eardley realised he had never heard Tony laugh before. A deep bass throb filled the room; tears filled his eyes and wet his pink cheeks. He left Eardley with a bemused look on his face.

Tony was still laughing when he got back to his folding bike. Tony liked his folding bike. Once upon a time he had taken his Bentley everywhere, but when they had moved out to the country he had become a train commuter, joining the army of bleary-eyed espresso suppers who chugged their way from the counties into the capital. But the ten-minute ride between house and station and then between station and office afforded him a sense of freedom. Long ago he had left the Bentley to Kate. Which is what he found her climbing out of as he put his bicycle clips on, still chuckling at Eardley's naivety.

'What's so funny?' Kate asked. The Bentley suited her better anyway. The stretched leather, the ivory white and smoothness matched Kate's young skin closer than Tony's puckered pink features.

Tony thought of himself as a lucky man. All his life, the wind had been at his back. Born with a bit of money, he had applied himself, and with a bit of luck a bit of money turned into a fortune. That fortune was built on mud, concrete and brick, and forged in a house-building boom that started in the eighties and did not look like letting up anytime soon. Because he was lucky, Tony was forever young, he told himself.

'Nothing, my dear.' Eardley wiped his eyes. 'Just a joke I heard about local democracy.' He unlocked his bike, seeming to realise something. 'What are you doing here?'

'Therapy, Tony. I'm having therapy. You don't take anything I do seriously. Not my blog, not my Instagram account, not my home farm idea.' Kate unclipped her seatbelt and allowed it to snap back into its sheath, then slid her feet out of the Bentley and onto the gravel.

Tony had no daughters, only sons, but in marrying a woman a fraction of his age (a fraction too small for the British public to be really comfortable with) he felt like he was getting the experience anyway. 'There's nowt wrong with you that I can see. You look absolutely lovely, my dear.'

The compliment, old-fashioned though it was, did the job. She pouted but with humour. 'Flatterer. And do I have to guess what you're doing here? Should you be doing that silly project? People in the village won't like it.'

Tony retracted his jowly expression, his face reddening again. He loved her, but it was still possible for him to be angry with her. 'You haven't told anyone, have you?' When Kate didn't reply he looked exasperated. 'I did happen to mention it's a secret, didn't I?'

Kate's perfectly plucked brows formed a wavy line over haunted eyes. 'I thought you'd be more worried for me than your silly project. There's a madman running around, haven't you heard?'

Irritation rumbled in Tony's stomach. 'We moved out here for you, so you could feel safe. I was fine in London. But if you don't feel safe here, maybe we should move back. It would save me a commute.' He softened and shuffled closer to her. He loved her and he couldn't be angry with her for long. 'The police will catch up with that lunatic soon enough.' He patted her hand in a fatherly way. 'It doesn't affect you at all. You are perfectly safe.'

'It's just he's so strong and big. I mean, what if he comes after me or you?'

Tony's brow wrinkled. 'Is there any reason he would come after us? Has he ever said anything to you? Do you two talk or something?' He really had to calm down. He was frightening her. She was easily frightened these days. He wondered if he had done that to her, but he dismissed it quickly. Someone had to be in charge.

'Not really, I barely know him.' It was all Tony could do to hide his relief. 'But I hear stuff. He's a bit weird.

And he's into nature and the countryside, and your job is tearing those things up and covering them in concrete.'

'My job is making homes for people. I've made a home for us.' She nodded.

Conventional thinking was that their age difference was a gulf that, even these days, was too much. Conventional thinking was for dummies. Their age difference was the exact reason they were a perfect match. His experience gave her stability. Her energy revitalised him. He took a moment before he advanced another thought as casually as he could. 'I thought with Dr Calman dead, you'd pack this all in. I mean, it's her you come to see, isn't it?'

Kate shook her head slowly. 'Poor Dr Calman. Why do you think that gardener killed her?'

Tony blew through his cheeks. 'No one knows. Money they think, he nicked some cash. Whatever the reason, she's gone.' Tony's eyes darkened. 'Unless there's someone else you come here to see.'

'Honey, there is only one man in my life, but I have certain . . .' she struggled for the word, '. . . issues. And I want to be whole again, for you.' She put a hand on his chest and smiled. 'Dr Eardley says he's taking over Dr Calman's group. So, you see, I'm in good hands, the best of hands.'

Was she indeed? Tony pretended to check the brakes on his bike, while talking casually. 'Are you staying here tonight, or will you be home?' Then he watched her from the corners of his eyes.

There was a troubled look in Kate's eyes. She scratched at her forearms. 'If you're coming home, I'll stay at home.'

Tony gripped her hands. 'Good, I'll see you at home.'

'Please don't be late. You're always late back these days.'

A knot twisted in Tony's stomach. Did she know? How could she know? He was always so careful, covered his traces. Unless that weed Eardley had told her something. If he had, he'd crush him. Tony reflected again that he had two secrets in his life, and he was forced to share both with that man.

'You look so worried.' She stroked his pink face, closing down the desperation in her own. 'Don't be worried. I'll be better, I promise I'll be better soon, and everything will be the same again. Please get home before dark, you know how much I worry.'

He hugged her, more with relief than anything else. She didn't know, and while she didn't know, he could carry on. He wanted to stop what he was doing, but he knew he had to carry on. Suddenly Tony didn't feel revitalised. He felt tired and old, his eyes redder than his cheeks. The day was just beginning and he was already worn out. He put his feet to the pedals of his bike and tried to enjoy the ride to the station. Suddenly, annoyingly, the wind was at Tony's front. He was forced to pedal harder.

9

If Tony Hammond was already worn out, Mrs Sidhu took on the new day with customary vigour. Today the skies of Slough were bright and a fresh breeze blew. It revitalised the laundry on the carousel in the garden and blew away any thoughts of Dr Calman's murder from Mrs Sidhu's mind. Her head felt better; she had removed the dressing. There was certainly plenty to do.

She turned instead to the simple realities of life: clean clothes and cooking. Hers were the busy elbows, the scurrying feet, the nimble fingers. She tidied, washed, and sliced and diced. Everywhere you looked there was something to be done, and on top of that there was a house guest to entertain. Mrs Sidhu rapped the wooden spoon on the side of the pan, releasing chunks of aubergine, onion and ginger. The kitchen was hot and full of steam. The counters were crowded with half-finished dishes and Tupperware pots ready to be filled.

She exhaled. She was snowed. She soon came to the inevitable conclusion that something had to give. With her blunt pencil, Mrs Sidhu had scrawled three things on to her to-do list for the day. Daljeet, Varma and the Benham House Retreat, starting with Daljeet.

There she was, sitting at the table, stiff as a stick, with a frown on her face. Mrs Sidhu hadn't done a stock-take of the fruit yet, but if there was a banana missing you'd put money that it was currently up Daljeet's rear end.

'Good morning, respected sister. Any plans today?' Mrs Sidhu said. Daljeet's frown could cause a solar eclipse. As long as Mrs Sidhu had known her, Daljeet was like the dark. Darkness, the scientists tell us, is an absence of light. Daljeet was an absence of fun. Fun was the sun, and Daljeet was the moon blocking it out.

Mrs Sidhu shook her head. She could hardly abandon Daljeet. She already felt bad about forgetting her at the airport. Family duty was family duty. Daljeet was non-negotiable. She had to look after her, starting right now.

'What better start to the day than a fresh breakfast?' Mrs Sidhu placed a thali of pickles, butter, dohi and fresh soft parathas on the dining table. Then she returned to her stove, concentrating on getting her mise en place ready for her job at the retreat while scraping browning onions and aubergines from the bottom her aluminium patila. The thava smoked while she rolled another flat patty of dough for the next breakfast paratha.

Daljeet tore off a *boorkhi* of the flatbread the size of her palm. 'I see now in daylight that your injury is worse than I thought. Perhaps you should take the day off, sister,' she said. 'Your head must be sore.' Her voice had a commanding, metallic note, and (not for the first time) Mrs Sidhu was reminded of a dalek. Daljeet the Dalek, that's what they used to call her. She exterminated the thought, quickly, her cheeks flushing with shame. Daljeet was her husband's sister, after all. But there was the problem. For all these years they had played tug-o'-war over the same man. Mrs Sidhu knew two things. First, that Daljeet had tried to persuade her brother out of the marriage match. The second was worse, far worse: that once they were married, Mrs Sidhu had done her best to keep his sister at arm's length. Daljeet the Dalek. It was Mrs Sidhu who had coined the nickname. She suppressed the flush of guilt threatening to burst out onto her face. 'How I would love a day off,' Mrs Sidhu said. A day off with the dalek? It would certainly make up for the airport fiasco.

'Then take one, we can have some time together. My brother wrote to me often about a place called Bekonscot Model Village. I would very much like to see it.' Daljeet scooped up pickles and yoghurt onto the hot bread and chewed it down with hot tea.

Mrs Sidhu stifled a groan. Oh dear God, had Mrs Sidhu not spent enough time wandering around the knee-high dolls houses and miniature railway sidings of that place while her husband was alive? But she had to do something with Daljeet. 'Nothing would give me more pleasure,' Mrs Sidhu said, her heart sinking at the thought. 'But regrettably, respected sister, this is my live-lihood and I will have to ask for the day off.' If she still had a livelihood.

Which brought us to item number two: Varma. Of course she could turn down Mr Varma's work, but Varma was her bread and butter. Turning down work was not in Mrs Sidhu's nature. She would have to explain to him why she had turned him down. There was already enough explaining to do on the Varma front. The screen of her phone was blank, empty of missed call alerts and messages. The quiet before the storm; Varma was brooding. Mrs Sidhu had not talked to him at all since her unscheduled departure from her kitchen. It could not be put off for ever. Had he sacked her? Was he about to sack her? Just a blank screen shone her own reflection back at her.

Which brought her finally to item number three: the Benham House Retreat. Working there was a lot more fun than working for Varma, and a fairground ride compared to spending the day with Daljeet. With a sinking heart she had to admit that duty came first. It was the Benham House Retreat that would have to go. That was a decision. If she did that, and she worked extra hard and got some prep done for tomorrow, she might just be able to persuade Varma to give her some time off.

She looked again, still no messages from Varma. He was toying with her. The wind swung round; the laundry carousel creaked like a weathervane. A pair of Tez's pants pointed west. Now, that could easily be a sign, and not of something good. Mrs Sidhu moved the aubergines off the ring. They simmered down.

She took her phone into the living room. Begging forgiveness needed a modicum of privacy. She would rip the band aid off in one go, wipe the slate clean and tell Varma straight that she had made a mistake.

As anyone who's been on the internet will tell you, lies are faster than truth.

Mrs Sidhu had every intention of coming clean with Varma. She would beg his forgiveness, drop her prices, resign the job at the retreat and suggest alternative caterers for both the day-to-day work and the summer fete.

'Well, well, well look who's calling. I'm not talking to you. There's no point saying anything, I won't change my mind.' Silence. After a while Varma realised his mistake. He hurriedly said, 'I am talking to you again. I hope you've learned your lesson.' He coughed. 'You may speak now.'

She braced herself then, in her best voice, the one she usually kept for well-heeled clients, she started her pleading. 'Mr Varma, how lovely to hear from you. Now, you must let me explain.'

Varma interrupted sharply before Mrs Sidhu could say any more. 'Mrs Sidhu, I came by to collect the brinjal bhaji order yesterday. To my surprise you weren't there, and Tez mentioned something about a body. What could he have meant by that?'

Mrs Sidhu silently cursed herself for ever saying anything to Tez. All the truthful responses that Mrs Sidhu had practised came rushing forward to the front of her mind. Truth is slow and lies are faster. One got there first. 'Tez, as you know, is a good boy but doesn't always have the concentration levels that I need from him. He misheard. When he said body, he meant buddy. You may not know this, but my sister-in-law is visiting, and we are bosom buddies.'

Varma gasped. 'Daljeet the Dalek's in town? No wonder the birds have stopped singing.' Mrs Sidhu once again regretted coining the nickname.

'She is, and in fact, she was wondering if I could have the day off.'

There followed a fit of choking at the other end of the line and a garbled response that roughly translated as 'no chance'. The last time Varma had given someone the day off the British flag had flown over India. Well, she had tried.

'I have to go. I bumped my head quite badly yesterday and I'm getting a headache.' It was true, her lump was throbbing. 'Perhaps I should have gone to the doctor, but you know how it is in A and E.'

There was a cold pause. When Varma spoke again his voice was dry. 'You bumped your head?' Another pause followed. 'In the course of your duties?' Now a small, strangled squeak. 'While you were working for me?'

This was another moment where one of those truthful responses should have elbowed their way to the front of the queue. She simply had to admit to Varma that she had gone out on another job. 'Yes,' she found herself saying. 'That's right.'

Now Varma was using his own best voice, the one he used for business meetings and irate customers who were demanding refunds. His voice was as smooth as silk, or at least an inexpensive silk substitute. Was there such a thing as 'smooth as rayon'? 'Mrs Sidhu, when a valued colleague, nay friend, is injured in the line of duty, I simply have to make sure she is all right.' Mrs Sidhu could swear that she could hear the sound of a liability disclaimer sliding around Varma's desk.

'Mr Varma, I'm fine, honestly. And if you're worried about today's brinjal order, I can assure you I am running on time,' she said.

Varma oozed and smoothed that nothing could be further from his mind, in a voice sweeter than honey (produce of many countries, may contain nuts). His tone went up an octave. 'I'm just checking that you haven't been bothered by anyone.'

Mrs Sidhu's nose wrinkled up. What sort of people would be bothering her, she asked. Varma gulped, and in a voice fighting to remain light, he suggested, 'You know what those ambulance chasers are like. No win no fee! I mean, it sounds like an irresistible offer when you say it out loud,' he said. He then realised that he had ended on the wrong selling point. 'But it's not. It's not irresistible. So please resist.'

Mrs Sidhu did not know which she liked worse: slave-driving Varma or down-on-his-knees-begging Varma. The latter had its temptations, but with a grim shake of the head, Mrs Sidhu knew it was not in her nature to take advantage. 'Mr Varma, I am not suing anyone over a tiny bump on the head.'

Varma let out a long breath. 'I knew that about you, Mrs Sidhu,' Varma said firmly, and not a little bit grate-fully. 'You're an honest person,' he added, causing a flush of shame to flood up Mrs Sidhu's neck. 'And I'll send you the paperwork to sign to confirm that in writing. In return, in consideration of the difficult time you've had, and with no admittance of liability, I will grant your request for a day off. Fully paid.'

So it was that Mrs Sidhu walked back into the kitchen still stunned. A day off, paid, from Varma. She bustled in with the good news straight away.

'Respected sister, I have just heard from Varma that he's giving me the day off. We can go to Bekonscot together.'

Daljeet clapped her hands together. 'This is wonderful news. How I have longed to see its small-scale wonder.'

That was what was supposed to happen next. That was how Mrs Sidhu imagined it. She even rehearsed it. Until something else happened instead, something that changed everything. Mrs Sidhu slid the patila of aubergines back onto the ring.

They sizzled, butter bubbling up, the flesh of the vege-table steaming and softening. It was a sight that made Mrs Sidhu stop. She took the aubergines off the ring once more, the sizzling halted immediately. For a moment the earth stopped revolving. Mrs Sidhu stood absolutely still, her hand on the handle of the saucepan, like a freeze-frame on a TV screen. She was back in Dr Calman's kitchen. The pan with jam in was left on the ring, the pan with the apples was off the ring. She was sure of it.

Daljeet raised an iron-grey eyebrow. 'Well, what did Varma say?' she asked.

Mrs Sidhu paused a long time, watching her aubergines. Outside, the breeze dropped and the laundry carousel creaked to a stop. In the kitchen, Daljeet mopped the last of the mango pickle from the thali.

Mrs Sidhu wasn't listening. She was in a perfect state of Aloneness. Still the aubergine chunks sizzled in the pan as it reheated on the flame and still Mrs Sidhu watched the steam rising from them. With it came the smell of spices and a growing realisation in Mrs Sidhu's brain that she had something to do and that she could not shirk it, because a young man's life and future hung in the balance. That young man had a mother, and in the great pact between mothers, aunts, and the greater matriarchal world she had every reason to expect that her son should be given a fair shake. Sometimes that fair shake needed a representative on earth to do its work. Daljeet waited silently for Mrs Sidhu's reply.

Tez entered the kitchen, shuffling his slippers along the floor. He nudged his mum as he walked past. 'Mum, you're doing it again,' he said.

Mrs Sidhu jerked her head back, her eyes finding focus on her surroundings once more and Respected Sister-in-Law Daljeet's expectant face.

'Tez will take you to Bekonscot,' she said. Her eyes could not meet Daljeet's. 'I will meet you there. I have a small task to undertake first.'

Mrs Sidhu had already left the house before Tez looked up from his cereal. 'Take who where?' he said.

10

'So you see, Patrick couldn't possibly have done it.' Mrs Sidhu beamed a happy smile that could have belonged to the gangly girl who spent her youth unearthing treasures in the back garden of a semi-detached in Slough. Treasure that to everyone else looked like flat stones, sticks and small pieces of broken glass.

Since her moment of Aloneness this morning Mrs Sidhu had found new inspiration. The results of this inspiration were being showered on DCI Burton, who was not altogether sure he was ready for it.

Burton had a morning routine, which since his divorce had somewhat altered. Breakfast at home at the kitchen counter, with only a half-drunk bottle of Glenfiddich for company, had become predictably depressing. So, before he succumbed to alcoholism, and with much cajoling from Mrs Sidhu, he made up his mind to leave the house as soon as he was dressed. Out there, in the pre-work morning hour, he had discovered a world of cafes. Not the sort of cafes Mrs Sidhu encouraged him to go to, the sort that charged five pounds for a cup of hot milk foam and a tooth-breaking biscuit. Burton's preferred venue came with a smear of grease and a frying smell. His latest find was a garden centre just outside Stoke Poges which had a cafe that opened early. Here he could load up on traditional breakfast fare and drink black coffee with two sugars until he was ready to look the day square in the eye. Unfortunately, the weak point of this plan was that eventually Mrs Sidhu would find him. So, when he drew up at the picnic table outside the cafe only to find he was looking into Mrs Sidhu's dark brown eyes, he knew time was up for the garden centre cafe. He was mentally running down a list of alternative breakfast venues while Mrs Sidhu had been talking, and he had not eaten nearly enough of his bacon and eggs, nor had enough coffee to be able to focus on what she was saying. He swigged another mouthful of the brown liquid down with a mouthful of toast and did not bother finishing it before speaking. 'Do you want to explain that again?'

Mrs Sidhu sighed and wiped toast crumbs from her jacket. DCI Burton was a good man, an intelligent man, a slightly disgusting man, but that was something Mrs Sidhu would do her best not to mention.

'You know, yesterday I thought I was becoming desensitised to the horrors of the world.' Burton popped another chunk of sausage into his mouth. 'Then you showed up.'

She tucked her chin in like a boxer taking up a guard and pushed on. Burton chewed and nodded his understanding as Mrs Sidhu spoke.

'This woman, Dr Calman, she was a therapist, yes? And she was on all the village committees and helping with raffles and village fetes and litter collections at the weekend.

A typical do-gooder, couldn't help herself. She was always helping people with their problems, whether they liked it or not. You see?'

Burton nodded wholeheartedly, making it clear that he knew the type all too well. Mrs Sidhu seemed unaware that he was eyeing her with a wry smirk.

'So even though she's retired, she takes a job at the Benham House Retreat, and she gets her patient Patrick a job too. If you met him, you would know that no one in the world needs more help than him. So, what does she do next?'

'Get her oar into his life and make his breakfast times a living hell?'

Mrs Sidhu held Burton's gaze with an icy look until his childish grin faded away.

'What she did was take him in as a lodger.'

Mrs Sidhu could see she was starting to lose Burton's attention. His breakfast was quickly evaporating and it would soon be time for him to be going to work at Newton police station. To confirm this, Burton put on his official police voice. 'I am aware of all this, Mrs Sidhu. Patrick Kirby was Wendy Calman's lodger for the last six months. So what?'

Mrs Sidhu quickened her pace. 'So why did she take the apples off the stove?' While Burton struggled to swallow a particularly dry piece of toast without the aid of coffee, Mrs Sidhu took the opportunity to deliver her coup de grâce. 'Apples stew very quickly, so they must be taken off the heat when you go to answer the door. But if Patrick was living there, he would have his own key. If Patrick was already home, she would have sent him to answer the door. So Wendy Calman answered a knock at the door before Patrick came home.'

107

Burton managed to get the toast down with a strangled gulp. It left his voice dry and hoarse. 'It's something,' he was forced to agree. 'But it's not exactly conclusive. Maybe she did answer the door, but Patrick was in his room, or in the loo, or just too lazy to get up, or he forgot his key.'

Mrs Sidhu made her opinion clear with a snort. These did not seem likely ideas to her. 'An obsessive compulsive forgets the key to his safe place?'

'Do we know that it was his safe place?'

'That woman was a mother to him, or as good as he ever had, I'm sure of it.'

The chief inspector would need more convincing. He waved away imaginary flies, clearing his thoughts before getting up and putting his jacket on. 'Well, it's an interesting thought, and we'll put it to Patrick Kirby when we catch up with him. He did assault you, after all. Or did you forget?' Burton tapped his temple.

The lump on Mrs Sidhu's head throbbed a little and she almost told it to stop agreeing with him. Whatever DCI Burton said, she was convinced that Patrick was no killer, which meant that someone else was.

'So who came to the door if not Patrick? And what happened to Patrick that night? If someone else killed Wendy, Patrick must have arrived after the event, finding Wendy dead.'

Burton grunted. 'And his perfectly innocent response was to steal a box full of cash, disappear for the night and try and pass everything off as normal the next day.'

The wind was out of Mrs Sidhu's sails. She stuttered, 'Yup, yup, yup, that is a reasonable point.' She recovered quickly. 'This is a difficult and complex case. All the more reason we should work together on this.'

'We, and I mean the police, need to find him, Mrs Sidhu, because he's a dangerous, disturbed man.' Burton's eyes shot up to the bruise on Mrs Sidhu's head. 'Who could easily have killed you as well as Dr Calman. Please leave this alone.' He polished his plate with some fried bread. 'Very nice breakfast they do here. It's a shame.'

'What's a shame?'

'That I can never come here again now that you know about it.' Burton rose and put his jacket on.

'I agree with you in one respect, Chief Inspector; whoever did this was not normal. Not what you and I think of as normal. I mean, what is normal, anyway?' Mrs Sidhu said.

'A question we should all ask ourselves, Mrs Sidhu.' Burton wandered away towards the bird feeders. Now what did he mean by that?

Karma, if you believe in it, is a powerful thing. Mrs Sidhu sat in the garden centre cafe for some time after Burton left, swilling cold tea around in the cup. She shrugged. She had failed to get him onside. He was as dead set against Patrick as before, maybe even more so. If DCI Burton wouldn't cooperate it made life much harder for her. She should have let it go right there and then. A normal person would give up, and Mrs Sidhu worried about that for a while. The thing is, Mrs Sidhu reasoned, she had a pigeon to put behind her.

Two weeks ago, she had been driving to a job, a birthday. The back of the car was stacked with boxes of Indian sweetmeats, French pastries, and Vietnamese summer rolls. On the road she had encountered the pigeon and, well, ker-splat.

She shuddered, finished her cold tea, shuddered again and headed for the exit. It wasn't entirely her fault. The blame was shared equally between herself, the van driver behind her who was driving a foot from her back bumper and – and this was in no way victim shaming – the pigeon itself.

She pressed her lips together. Let's face it, with a car bearing down on it, any animal with a sense of self-preservation was supposed to move. This one decided it was staying put, and in a split-second decision, in full expectation that the stupid bird would take wing, Mrs Sidhu kept on driving. She relived the moment, as she had again and again. The braking and the swerve, too late, the blaring horn from the van behind, the stomach-turning thump, the sad spray of white feathers, the heavy feeling in her gut as she kept driving on, shaking her head. Moments later the van overtook and the driver gave her the finger. Half an hour later she was singing Happy Birthday in Punjabi to an accountant from Stoke Poges. Nice house, she remembered, very nice family. Educated people, like herself.

She pushed past a queue of people waiting at a till, mimed an apology that she had not purchased anything and made for the car park.

Since that day, the pigeon, dead as it was, remained with her, and she could not shake off the feeling that there was a price to pay. She had to balance her karma, she told herself. And to do that she would have to lie to her friends, her employer and her family. Karma is a powerful thing. Who was Mrs Sidhu to fight it?

Outside, it was bright, her bottle-green car was nestled between a Range Rover and a Jaguar, both of which had parked sardine-tin close to hers. She sucked her stomach in and squirmed her way to her car door. She edged in through the narrow gap as she opened it – careful not to scratch the Range Rover. She didn't need more bad karma.

On the passenger seat was the paperwork Sienna had given her yesterday. She turned the pages. It was simple enough. Morning tea, lunch, and afternoon tea at the retreat, with a rider for two days' work making and serving cream teas for the village fete. The morning and afternoon teas she could use tray bakes. Lunch, in this weather, was salad, soup or sandwiches. She could hook Tez into helping at the village fete. This could be a lucrative contract without complications, and it would get her into Benham House. The opportunity to atone for the pigeon was right here. The more Mrs Sidhu thought about it, the more she was convinced that a major miscarriage of justice was playing out before her.

Yet, she knew it wasn't as easy as that. With an air of depression she put the contract to one side and asked herself: what could she do about it? Her hands were tied, she was on her last chance with Varma, and she was starting to fear she was losing her knack at winning over DCI Burton. There was something odd about him; she was sure there was something he wasn't telling her. Without Burton in her corner her options were limited. However, she had one golden ticket – a day off. If she was going to put Burton on the right track, she needed evidence that pointed to someone else.

She started the engine. Right now she should be heading to Bekonscot to spend the day with her sister-in-law.

She tapped the steering wheel, drumming out a rhythm. She needed an ally, someone on the inside at Benham House, someone who would help her prove Patrick was innocent. She checked the time. Nine o'clock. She did herself a deal. She would sacrifice part of her day off for the life of the pigeon. She texted Tez: Delayed. Minutes later, her bottle-green car was hurtling towards Benham village once more. Inside was a woman with a clear conscience. The pigeon would be atoned for. What could be more normal than that?

Tez stared at Daljeet. Daljeet stared back at him. The bus rocked, and Tez wished he hadn't taken a seat opposite his aunt. He was never going to win a stare-out with an authentic Indian aunty. After a while his skin felt like it was crawling with beetles. He cracked first, what else? 'So, how's everyone in India?'

Daljeet pulled a face. Everyone was crap in India, everyone was having a crappy time. Tez endured another hour in which she described everyone's problems, sometimes relying on photographic evidence on her phone to back it up.

Tez was thankful when the bus pulled in. They got off. He craned his neck around. 'Mum must be here somewhere,' he said, with a note of desperation in his voice. That was when he got the text. One word and his whole world collapsed. Delayed.

'Never mind,' droned Daljeet, voice as flat and hard as metal. 'We can have a cup of tea and catch up some more. You haven't told me anything about yourself yet. What about your job, and you must have your eye on a girl or two?'

Tez's eyes widened. He hurriedly tapped out a reply: Mum! Come quickly. She's asking questions.

112

11

Dr Calman's former therapy group were on the lawn. Jonny Snakeskin sprawled on his back, Kate Hammond fidgeted on a stool and Edith Pollock smiled beatifically from her wheelchair, with her carer Elliot behind her. It looked like Stephen Eardley had taken over where Dr Calman had left off. He was wrapping up the session just as Mrs Sidhu approached them with a tray of lemonade.

'This is excellent progress, all of you.' Eardley thought for a moment, tapping his lips with his forefinger. 'You will all be thinking about the events of yesterday. It is of course shocking what happened to poor Dr Calman. But first and foremost she was a therapist who, more than anything, would want you all to get better. So we must carry on our good work here, for her sake and your sakes.'

The clients got up and started drifting off in various directions, taking glasses from the tray. Mrs Sidhu waited patiently as Sienna waved down Dr Eardley. 'Here are the notes from the session.' She handed him the red exercise book she carried under her arm; he riffled quickly through the pages, not paying much attention. Then he eyed her with a strange expression on his face. 'These are very good, Sienna, excellent work.' Sienna smiled thinly. He reached out and put his hand on her arm. She flinched – just a millimetre, but Mrs Sidhu saw it before he carried on. 'You're doing really well. Remember, take time out in your day to love yourself.' Eardley gently closed Sienna's notebook and walked away to chat with Kate Hammond.

This was the moment. Mrs Sidhu sidled up to Sienna. This morning she was wearing a lemon-yellow summer dress with white sandals. 'Sienna, can I have a talk with you? It's about Patrick.' She looked different today. Not just the dress, but the subtle nuances of character around her face, and her posture. She was as bright as her dress, smiling and perky. Meanwhile, Eardley was throwing curious glances in their direction. Mrs Sidhu lowered her voice. 'You've heard that Patrick is the police's chief suspect, I imagine.'

Sienna dropped her head to one side. The black button eyes ate up the light and gave no information back. 'Patrick.' She wrinkled her brow in concentration, as if she had forgotten the name. She idly picked a leaf from a tree. Her sharp-toothed mink smile glinted as she eyed it, as curiously as a cat eyeing an injured bird. 'Yes, of course, Patrick.' Then began stripping it with her fingernail.

'It's just I had the impression that you had some feelings for him.' Mrs Sidhu put up her hands, spreading her fingers wide. 'Don't worry, I'm on your side. I think he needs help.' Sienna kept working the flesh of the leaf, but her jaw clenched tight, her shoulders hitched up like a mannequin. 'Maybe I can help Patrick. With a little help from you.'

Sienna twirled the spine of the leaf; she was left with a skeleton. She stared at it, fascinated by the inner workings laid bare. She thought for some time, dropping into a deep state, until something inside her shifted, like a missile finding a new target.

'If I help you,' she said, 'you have to promise not to talk to anyone about me and Patrick. Not Dr Eardley, and not the police.'

Mrs Sidhu nodded, then had another thought. 'Oh, I have all that paperwork you gave me yesterday in my car. I realised I haven't formally accepted the job yet.' Mrs Sidhu narrowed her eyes. 'Haven't actually signed on the dotted line.'

Sienna flicked the leaf skeleton away and cast a meaningful look towards Eardley. 'Come with me, we can't talk here. Let me show you something,' said Sienna.

Mrs Sidhu gasped. It was a garden within the garden. You would never know it was there. A narrow opening between two bushes led back into a secluded enclave. Here there were wildflowers in abundance and the sweet smell of scented plants. It was a secret garden, a lovers' garden.

Sienna stretched her arms wide, spinning slowly, marvelling. 'He made this for me,' she said. 'Can you believe it? Just for me. Me and him. We used it to meet in secret.'

'He must think a lot of you.'

Sienna breathed in a scented rose. 'The police think Patrick murdered Dr Calman.' She turned away. When she spoke, her voice was low and husky. 'How can the man that made this kill someone like that? Explain that to me.'

'I agree, I think he's innocent,' Mrs Sidhu said brightly.

Sienna turned on her heel to face Mrs Sidhu. Tears were running down her cheeks. Her eyes were lit with a new hope. She gripped Mrs Sidhu's forearm with both her hands. They were white like marble. 'You do, don't you? You really do. I thought it was just me.'

My, those long fingers of Sienna's were really digging in. 'It's absolutely obvious to me that Patrick could not have done it,' Mrs Sidhu said. The relief on Sienna's face was visible; she relaxed her grip and Mrs Sidhu extracted her arm. There was no doubting Sienna's passion.

Mrs Sidhu went on and explained her 'apple sauce' theory, with Sienna nodding agreement. In return, Sienna spoke of her growing love for Patrick. His silence and eccentricity were a hole that Sienna's exuberance could never fill – barely touched the sides, in fact. They were opposites that attracted. Over months, secret glances turned to something more physical. She smiled with secret knowledge. 'He loves nature.' Sienna described their passionate encounters in the secret garden and other outdoor places, while Mrs Sidhu listened in silent wonder at their acrobatic sexual encounters and how Sienna longed once more to cleave to his muscular body.

In the end, Mrs Sidhu interrupted the flow of words, holding up her hand. 'It's obvious we both agree that something has to be done to help Patrick, for our own separate reasons, which need no further elaboration. Do you have any idea where he could be?'

Sienna hesitated before answering. 'No. I'm at the end of my tether with worry.' She pulled at her hair.

'Meanwhile the real killer is clear and free. Only the police have the resources to find out who, but they are using all of them to find Patrick.' Mrs Sidhu nodded with birdlike alacrity. 'Unfortunately, DCI Burton won't listen to me. He might listen to Dr Eardley.'

Sienna's hands flew up in front of her. 'Oh no. You mustn't mention any of this to Dr Eardley.'

'Whyever not? He might be able to help. You could tell them about you and Patrick. If he understood that Patrick was in a stable relationship it might affect his judgement. That might just be enough to persuade DCI Burton to look for the real killer.'

Sienna considered this for a while. 'The problem is, staff members aren't allowed to date patients . . . clients.' Sienna corrected herself. 'I could lose my position here.'

Mrs Sidhu remembered Eardley's touch on Sienna's arm and came to her own conclusions. 'Let me guess: Dr Eardley disapproves of you and Patrick?'

Sienna nodded. Anger grew and burned in Mrs Sidhu's chest. How could he? How could a man like that use his position of authority that way? 'Has he ever . . .?' She let the question hang.

Sienna was shocked. 'Oh no, not Dr Eardley, he's not like that. He's more like a father.'

Mrs Sidhu snorted. That was how they all started, she thought. She would deal with Eardley when the time was right, when Patrick was safe and free. For the time being, Mrs Sidhu reassured Sienna that she wouldn't mention to Eardley what they were doing. She saw Sienna's jaw relax and she pushed on. 'Then we have one other choice. To find out who came to Dr Calman's door the night she died. That person either killed her or could have vital information about who did.'

Sienna thought for a while. 'Could be someone from the village fete? That's why Wendy was making scones.

Maybe the Witch knows something.' Mrs Sidhu raised an eyebrow. 'You remember the woman in the wheelchair – Edith.'

Mrs Sidhu stifled a groan. An elderly woman in a wheelchair was not going to wash with Burton as a throat-slashing psychopath. 'Why would she go to Wendy's house, let alone kill her?'

'She wouldn't. But they had a bring-and-buy earlier that day in the village hall. Wendy and Edith helped out. She might have gone round to talk about it. She might have seen something.'

'Bring-and-buy. Is that why Wendy had a cash box? The one that Patrick took? Why would Patrick take that?'

Sienna didn't know. She hazarded some guesses. He knew he'd be a suspect and needed money to go on the run. But no, why wait an entire night and morning to make his escape? Perhaps it had to do with Patrick's obsession with numbers. This was more likely, that the trauma of finding Wendy dead reset Patrick's own trauma, and that the cash box meant something to him.

'He described it as sacred,' Mrs Sidhu mused. 'Perhaps you're right, Edith knows something.'

The only problem was that Edith was not due at the retreat again today. 'But why would I go and see her at home? What excuse could I give?' Mrs Sidhu asked.

This was when Sienna came up with a wonderful new idea. 'I'm inducting you into the village fete committee.'

Mrs Sidhu revelled in the new title. 'A member of the village fete committee. Good. How many of us are there?'

'Well, it was just me and Wendy. Now it's just you and me. Dead woman's boots.'

Mrs Sidhu repeated this grimly. 'Dead woman's boots.'

She looked up at Sienna, eyeing her levelly. 'And you have no idea where Patrick might be hiding?'

Sienna looked away. 'Thank you so much, Mrs Sidhu.' Sienna looked up at the trees and her little teeth glinted with joy. 'I can't wait until we're together again.'

Mrs Sidhu sent another text to Tez. Go in without me. See you soon. She switched her phone off before he could reply. It would be nice for him to have one-on-one time with his aunty.

She handed her signed paperwork to the receptionist, who had to remind her to sign the confidentiality clause. 'Silly of me. I always miss something.' She scrawled her signature on the line.

Warn them, for I am returned, Death, destroyer of worlds.

Patrick's eyes opened suddenly. He was in total darkness.

No, not total. His eyes adjusted. Light edged its way in around the boards nailed over the entrance. His back hurt. The sleeping bag and yoga mat did little to soften the broken cement floor. As he rubbed his numb limbs into wakefulness, the last forty-eight hours came back to him in painful, jagged shards.

A sweat broke out on his massive forehead. He was in a lot of trouble and the police were looking for him. Then there was that strange little woman with the soft brown eyes and the hard mouth. He had hit her. He should not have hit her. Maybe she was dead too. Two people dead, and all his fault. And they weren't going to be the last either. He moaned softly. His eyes fully adjusted to the dim light; he lit the candle by his makeshift bed.

He ran his fingers over his handiwork from the previous night, feeling the bumps and blisters of the wall under the spray paint. He traced out the line making up the design, which was far more detailed and ornamented than the original. Inside each curl was another, and inside that a face or an animal or a plant. The pattern swirled like the numbers that were always there in Patrick's head. His breathing eased. He stood and stretched with graceful movements. The eye and the numbers, they were his new work. The lies were not his life before, they were his life since then. Years he had spent convincing himself that the power of numbers was not real. Wasted years!

Cause and effect, one thing led to another. For many years his work had been simple, he would cycle around Reading town centre playing very loud music and screaming abuse at strangers. Those were the years before he met Dr Calman. She found him. She found him a place and a new job, the gardening work, and she gave him a place to live. She had changed his course in life, and because of her he had been given this task, this task to help people.

Because of her he had come to know the Master and the Master's great works. He did not call him the Master when talking to Dr Calman, because she could never see the symmetry of His work. Because of that, because she did not understand, she was dead. And because of that Patrick had the numbers in his possession and the works of the Master and the mission that Dr Calman had given him to help the others.

People were going to die, but who would be first? Fate could decide. Not Fate, like some kind of goddess, no, fate that was built into the underlying fabric of the universe. Fate that was a result of chaos theory, of quantum physics, and space-time. The Fate that was the goddess of numbers would come to his aid.

It must be done properly. He had folded them up and though there were only three, the choice must be decided by the universe, the gods of chaos. Three numbers, three people, one would die. The numbers were 622, 623 and 624. He swirled his hand around the glass bowl and pulled out the first of the pink tickets. And the winner is . . .

He unfolded the number, and then looked at the name in the book. The first one had been chosen. There was no turning back now.

For a moment he was discouraged. This would be hard. The police were looking for him. What should he do when he felt down? He pulled his shoulders back. Keep a positive attitude. He should do his affirmation. There was a broken mirror in the corner, and Patrick went to it. He plastered on a strange, stiff smile and read from the writing on the mirror. 'You can do anything you set your mind to.' He felt better, he *could* do anything he set his mind to. He washed from the rainwater bucket, dressed and put the winning raffle ticket in his pocket.

For some reason, while he sluiced cold water down himself, he thought about the weirdo girl at work. Her name, he had found out, was Sienna Sampson. He had also found out it was not her name at all. He mused on this for a while. He had thought about asking her out. She was pretty, that was for sure, but obviously she was nuts. I mean, who went around pretending they were someone else? Patrick took a last look in the cracked mirror. He hitched up his smile again and it spangled and fractured in the crazed glass. At least he was feeling more like himself today. More like himself than he had felt in a long time.

12

Mrs Sidhu pottered along the street and paused by the window of the estate agency, sucking her breath at the prices. Her Slough house wouldn't buy her a rabbit hutch here. Still, it was nice to be out in the country. Air and sunshine were free, until the local council decided otherwise. It was high summer, no breeze shifted the leaves on the trees, which drooped in the heat. The sun splashed pretty patterns on a pretty street without a straight line in it. Not like the rigidly regimented grid of Slough's backstreets. The houses here were detached; they stood alone with rustic gravelled driveways dividing them.

Number 12 had a low, black iron gate. On it was a plaque that read BEWARE OF THE CAT. Mrs Sidhu grinned. She wondered if it was referring to the animal that perched on the warm brick wall, or the occupant of the house. The gate squealed on rusty hinges. Mrs Sidhu stroked the cat, which was very amenable to a bit of attention. It stretched itself out on the wall.

'I'd watch Emrys, he can go either way.' The voice was bright but trembled with age. It came from behind the beaded curtains obscuring the door. Emrys licked Mrs Sidhu's fingers. 'He likes you.' Edith pushed a hand through the jangling strips and drew it aside, as if Mrs Sidhu had passed a test. 'You'd best come in.'

You can price it up any way you wanted to, but a floral print armchair was a floral print armchair. Edith Pollock's floral print armchair looked expensive to Mrs Sidhu. The cushions were thick, the fabric luxuriant and it had snazzy extras, like the footrest that flipped out when Edith leaned back, scooping up her short legs. She giggled. 'Most fun I've had all day,' she said. 'Now what can I help you with?' She must have been in her eighties. Her hair was a cloud, white, indistinct and soft.

'I work up at the retreat,' Mrs Sidhu said. Edith stared back at her with a glassy-eyed look, watching with a strange detachment. There was something distant in that look, a hostility? No, a wariness, a long deep figuring out. For a moment, in Mrs Sidhu's perception, there was someone else behind those eyes than the rosy-cheeked old woman whose legs barely reached the end of the footrest on her recliner. Who was it?

Somewhere an old-fashioned clock was ticking. The silence grew long, long enough for Mrs Sidhu to proffer more explanation. 'I don't mean as a therapist, I work there as a chef, I'm helping with the village fete,' Mrs Sidhu added for clarity, watching Edith back.

The rest of Edith's cottage was in tune with the armchair, expensive and tasteless, which was more to Mrs Sidhu's liking than she would like to admit, reminding her as it did of her own parents' taste influenced heavily by the groovy seventies and a modicum of Punjabi practicality. Rainbow rugs, Paisley whorls in the wallpaper, it was cosy, and crowded with china things and old wax candles. Mrs Sidhu could see the fridge peeking through the door to the kitchen, covered in photographs pinned with magnets. There were crystals and mineral rocks out on the table, glittering in the light. There was a sense that there was too much furniture rather than too little. At its centre sat Edith, small, pink-cheeked, like a gnome.

Something broke in Edith's concentration or distraction or whatever it was. A smile returned to her lips, a thin one, colder. 'They call me the Witch up there.'

Mrs Sidhu crossed her palms, drew in her chin and, leaning back, said, 'They call me a witch where I live too. It comes with seeing things that other people don't. It can frighten people. Is that what you and Dr Calman used to talk about?'

Edith drew her eyebrows together and frowned. The clock ticked on, hidden from view, marking out the seconds that elapsed, making each one long, drawn out. Mrs Sidhu had a sense of eternity, as if she and the gnome of a woman could sit like this for a very long time, and that perhaps that was what Wendy had done. The sound was hypnotic and Mrs Sidhu watched Edith's eyelids drooping. She felt her own do the same. Mrs Sidhu shook her head, waking herself up. She clapped her hands together and Edith's eyelids shot open.

'Talking therapy, she called it. I called it a nice chat. My mind's going, you see.' The sharpness in Edith's eyes made that hard to believe. 'Dementia.' Edith's eyelids flickered and, the sharpness dulled again. The strange look

124

appearing in her eye once more. 'We talked about my son. He's gone now. Moved away.' Then once more a flame fanned, burning with mischievous energy. 'My memory's not what it used to be. Did you say you were a chef?'

Mrs Sidhu nodded. Edith smiled sagely. What she understood by it was a mystery to Mrs Sidhu. 'Everybody loved Wendy. She liked to help people,' she said, and her words were abrupt, as if she had come to a decision about Mrs Sidhu, like when the cat had licked her hand instead of scratching it.

'Can you think why Patrick would want to do something terrible like that to her?'

Edith continued as if Mrs Sidhu had not spoken. 'Everything's connected, you see. The whole world is. Not like the fools think, not like the scientists or the politicians. It's connected by our spirits and by the things that happen to us. Do you see?'

Mrs Sidhu didn't. 'Of course. I also understand that you might have gone to see her on the night she . . .' Mrs Sidhu didn't want to say the word.

'Oh no, no, dear, I didn't go over there.' Edith waved towards her wheelchair. 'I don't get about so well, and I was tired out after the day we had.'

Mrs Sidhu compressed her lips. She was wasting her time. Edith was not the one who knocked on Dr Calman's door. Tez and Daljeet would be knee-deep in model village and Mrs Sidhu was not earning any brownie points with Daljeet by not being there. Mrs Sidhu was reaching for her bag when Edith continued. 'She came over here.'

Mrs Sidhu stopped. 'She did? On Sunday, the night she died?' Her reticence with using the word seemed to have gone.

125

'She came to ask about the lost property from the bring-and-buy. But I could tell something else was on her mind. Her aura was all wrong you see. It was all red and angry.'

Mrs Sidhu sat very still. 'She was angry on the night she died?' This was a significant development. If Wendy Calman was angry, she might have angered someone else. Perhaps enough to kill her. Mrs Sidhu kept her voice light. 'How interesting. I wonder what she might have been angry about.'

Edith traced a stubby finger along her chin. 'Let me see if I can remember.'

'Hello, is anyone home?' Wendy had said, shoving her head round the front door. With no reply to her enquiry, she shut the door behind her, and headed for the back of the house. The sound of a nasal snore greeted her.

Edith Pollock was asleep in her recliner. Her surgically stockinged legs were propped up on a big pouffe, her white-haired head rested on a big soft cushion. As her chest rose and fell she emitted a gurgle. Wendy shook her gently by the shoulder. Edith Pollock woke mid snore, choked back some unexpected phlegm, almost fell asleep again, then sat up. 'Edith, it's time to wake up.'

Edith's clouded eyes searched the room in a slowly revolving misted gaze before settling on Wendy. 'Is that you, Dr Calman?' she asked. Her voice trembled. Then she reached into her pocket and, pulling out an acorn, she pressed it into Wendy's hand. Edith smiled. 'Keep you safe, Dr Calman.'

Wendy was about to say something, but the pleading look on Edith's face kept the words locked behind her pursed lips. Wendy dropped the acorn into her pocket. 'I acknowledge your positive thoughts, Edith,' she said. 'But if someone was going to mug me, I fear they would have done it on the way over. Though I doubt it for this lot.' Wendy held up a transparent plastic bag and peered at it through her large spectacles. 'This is the lost property from today's bring-and-buy sale.' The bag was full of hats, spectacles, a couple of purses, a wallet and even a set of false teeth. 'The human mind has long been a subject of study to me, Edith. It has an infinite capacity to obscure and forget things, but I cannot understand how anyone can leave behind their false teeth.' She smiled thinly. 'Perhaps we should call it a bring-and-leave sale. I am convinced we have finished up with more items than we started with. What I want to know is what I should do with it?'

'You should take it home. Then, if people have lost something, they can come over and get it.'

Wendy looked horrified. 'I have to store all this rubbish? For how long?'

'Amateur hour, you see.' Edith broke off from her story. 'The last one holding the bag is the one who has to keep it.' She chuckled. 'Can't believe she fell for that one. She'll have that stuff for months. I've still got stuff from my first one.'

Mrs Sidhu struggled to hide her disappointment. 'And that's what she was angry about?'

'Oh no. She was peeved about it, but you learn the hard way at a bring-and-buy. It was her first, you see.' Edith wrinkled up her nose and nodded, allowances had to be made for newbies.

Mrs Sidhu was the first to agree. Greenhorns, the world over, would always have to be shepherded through these rites of passage by older, wiser women such as themselves.

127

Unfortunately, they were no further forward in their tale. 'So what was she actually angry about?' It was hard to keep the impatience out of her voice.

Edith's gaze drifted away. 'I can't exactly remember.'

Mrs Sidhu was on the verge of leaving when Edith raised a finger to the heavens. 'Oh yes. I remember something.' Mrs Sidhu settled into her seat once more as Edith picked up her tale.

Wendy heaved her arm up and swung the cash box onto the coffee table and dropped it next to the lost property. When she sat down, she peered levelly at Edith and explained to her what she had learned on the grapevine that had upset her so much. 'I've come to ask you if it's true.'

Edith nodded that it was true. They talked for some time, drifting from one subject to another as therapy sessions so often did, but always returning once more to the subjects of Wendy's anger and what Edith had done.

'And what about the others? They have a part to play in all of this, Edith. I fear that you have been used and manipulated by forces far larger than both of us. You don't have to do this, Edith. There's still time.'

Edith averted her eyes and shifted in her recliner as if she could no longer find a comfortable position. 'Maybe. But it's the way it is.' Now her cloudy eyes drifted away. She jumped in her seat when she heard the front door slam. She shook her head, clearing it. She had the clear sense that someone had been here a moment ago, but she had quite forgotten who it was. Never mind. She would close her eyes for a little bit.

* * *

Mrs Sidhu clenched her fingers. 'But what made her angry?' Guilt rippled in Mrs Sidhu's chest. The poor woman had a disease, what could you expect? She uttered a prayer and composed herself. 'And who was the other person Wendy was talking about?'

Somewhere the clock ticked on; Edith listened to it as if the answer might lie in its regular ticks and tocks. Sleep threatened to take her once more, and Mrs Sidhu too.

The tiredness that Mrs Sidhu had fought for two days crept up like a phantom in the night. She consoled herself. There were some intriguing fragments, at least. Something made Dr Calman angry. Edith was involved. There were others involved too and, by the sound of it, powerful people. But these were too vague, nothing here would prove decisive where DCI Burton was concerned.

Edith groped for words. 'I'm sorry, I . . . I . . .' Her misted gaze moved to look over Mrs Sidhu's shoulder. She clapped her little hands together. 'Oh look! It's Elliot.'

Mrs Sidhu was so deep in thought that she hadn't heard Elliot enter the room.

A gap-tooth smile beamed at them. 'Oh, 'allo, what have I interrupted? Girls' night, is it?' He crossed the room to Edith's chair. 'You don't want to get started with this one,' he warned Mrs Sidhu, 'she'll start telling your fortune.'

Mrs Sidhu checked the time and gulped. She should be leaving now if she was to get there in time. 'I was just going.'

Elliot fussed around Edith, checking her cushions. She glowed under Elliot's attention. 'Elliot might remember.' She told him about her memories of Sunday night. 'Mrs Sidhu came to ask about the lost property, you remember, Elliot?'

'You were here, Elliot?' Mrs Sidhu asked, settling back down once more with a thump.

'I put Edie to bed every night.' He moved from Edith's head to her feet. 'Come on,' he said. With a sigh, Edith shucked off her slippers. Elliot produced a pair of nail clippers from his pocket. 'It's that time of the month again. Oh my gawd, believe me I want this much less than you.'

'See the way he talks to me?' Edith grinned. Mrs Sidhu saw it. Elliot was good with older women, his camp charm was just the thing they needed, but there was something about him that didn't ring true. The campness was an act, Mrs Sidhu felt sure of it, a handy shorthand, a quick way of gaining female intimacy and trust. Harmless enough, she supposed, but her instincts told her that Elliot was straight. He held one of Edith's plump mottled feet. 'Little piggy first?' Edith giggled.

'So, what might she have been angry about?' Mrs Sidhu asked.

He shrugged. 'No idea. You know how it is in a village with gossip. When someone has a bit of poison in them, they like to pass it on.' Elliot scowled, trying to take aim at the next toenail. 'The problem with Wendy was she was always helping people – you know the type – couldn't stop herself.'

Mrs Sidhu smiled a brittle smile. She leaned forward, clasping her hands together. 'That's what makes it so confusing. I just don't understand why anyone would want her dead?' She wanted to shout: What poison was Dr Calman passing on, and who had bitten her?

Elliot clipped, and a toenail twanged across the room, delighting Edith. 'She stood up to people,' said Elliot, gently cradling Edith's foot. Edith swung her free leg like a little girl on a swing, she hummed a tune and Mrs Sidhu almost recognised it before Elliot carried on. 'Standing up to people can be dangerous. There, big piggy, last one.'

'Was there someone in particular that Dr Calman stood up to recently?' Mrs Sidhu wondered.

Elliot positioned the clippers on Edith's broad yellow big toenail and grunted. As a matter of fact, there was, Elliot confided. 'Tamzin Grey, she's Jonny Snakeskin's agent. Lives in the village. Some kind of planning issue.' He turned his attention to the other foot. She heard him and Edith on her way out. 'Crikey, Edith, this one needs a wash.' Edith cackled.

Mrs Sidhu was long gone before Edith found the little piece of paper tucked into the side of her chair. 'What's this?'

Elliot read the numbers out loud. 'Six two two. It's your raffle ticket, you silly baggage. Remember, for the village fete on Saturday.' Edith drew a blank. 'I'll put it up on the fridge. Might be your lucky day.'

Tez Sidhu towered over a mock Tudor cottage and cursed his mother. He looked at the message on his phone: Am tied up all morning. Keep your aunty entertained. He wished so many things. He wished he had never taught his mum how to text. He wished he had never agreed to this. Most of all he wished he had an answer to the question his aunty Daljeet had just asked him. 'Good question, Aunty. Why did my dad love this place so much?'

Tez knew from bitter experience that his mother had forgotten him. She had got herself wound up into something more important. He could just about understand her doing that to him, that was old news. But abandoning Aunty Daljeet the Dalek, and leaving him to cope with her, that really burned his buns. He came to a decision. If Tez Sidhu was doing the entertaining, he would do it his way. He sighed. 'Come on, Aunty. We've seen enough here.'

13

After leaving Edith's house, Mrs Sidhu had to prepare lunch back at the retreat. She could hardly let twenty poor chief executives starve, now, could she? They were stressed enough as it was. She had the day off from Varma and she was sure Tez was handling things magnificently with his aunt. For the lunch she made a pistou soup, a light but filling dish from the shores of Southern France. She also set about preparing chocolate cake for the village fete. The sponges were cooling from the oven, it was time to mix the frosting.

Multi-tasking was not a skill for Mrs Sidhu, it was a habit. As her fingers sliced green beans and potatoes, and pressed butter into icing sugar and melted oozing white chocolate, her mind went in another direction.

What ingredients in the Dr Calman murder did she have to work with? On the day she died, Dr Calman worked at a bring-and-buy sale. At that sale, Tamzin Grey said something to her that made her angry. Poison, Elliot called it, and it burned like a snakebite. It burned so much she had to tell Edith, and even if Edith could no longer remember the heat of that impression, it was still in her mind, everything but the detail, like an imprint in wax, or a flavour in a dish you couldn't place.

Mrs Sidhu knew about poison; there was plenty of it in the backstreets of Slough. Think how much of it there was in a grand, moneyed place like Benham village. Only one living person knew what Tamzin Grey had said. But to deal with someone like Tamzin Grey, you needed more than a sweet smile and a packet of biscuits. She needed to wheel out the big guns, and it was Sienna who had loaded the barrel.

With the soup bubbling and the cake cooling down, Mrs Sidhu turned to every small business owner's greatest weapon in the fight against crime. She carried her printer and her laminator from the boot of her car and set it up in the corner of the kitchen.

First, she took a tureen of soup to the white-clothed trestle table in the garden. It soon attracted a crowd, and she ladled it into bowls for those exhausted by their morning's self-actualisation. Finding one's centre for Mrs Sidhu was simple: it was in your stomach. Feed your stomach and feed your soul. Dreams could take sail on a summer soup served with a good slice of sourdough.

Back in her kitchen the sponges were cool enough to start frosting, just as the ID card popped off the laminator, hot and fresh. She stroked the shiny surface of the badge, the old passport photo, the official-looking lettering, then got to work on icing the cake.

This was the stuff of Mrs Sidhu's dreams. A gun and a badge. Well, an icing bag and a badge. 'VFC! Drop it, sunshine, or I'll drop you where you stand.' She was practising in the mirror. She tried another zinger. 'VFC! Put the gun on the ground, your hands on your head, or I'll ice you.' She pointed the nozzle of the icing gun at her reflection and squirted. A blob of liquid sugar oozed out and splattered on the floor. OK, the icing gun was not going to help. But the badge – now that had real potential.

It was two o'clock before she was free to saunter down the High Street once more, past the small shops, the cafe and the estate agent's window where dream houses winked from colour photos. How long before Dr Calman's cottage was up in the window? 'Price on application. Sale forced by family illness.' She walked on and took the next left, circling around onto the lane behind.

Tamzin Grey's 'cottage' was a bigger version of the smaller cottages that both Dr Calman and Edith occupied. It had the thatched roof, the pastel-painted plaster, and the finely trimmed yew hedges, but it was on another scale. It was imposing rather than twee.

Mrs Sidhu dusted the flour off her top and knocked on the front door. She tapped timidly at first, but she soon got the impression that if someone were at the back of the house, they would never hear her. She gave up looking for a doorbell and instead pounded on the door with her balled fist. Eventually, Tamzin came to the door.

It was after lunchtime and she was wearing a dressing gown. So, maybe she liked an afternoon nap or a lie-in. She tipped her sunglasses down her nose to take a better look at Mrs Sidhu and, despite the afternoon sun, there was a chill in her look. Not the chill of dislike, but the impersonal chill that comes when you are used to looking through people instead of at them. The chill of someone

135

who had been interrupted. Beads of sweat, no, water at her chest. Interrupted in the shower, perhaps. But, no, the shortness of breath, the tightness of the muscles around the neck. Interrupted while swimming laps. Mrs Sidhu drew herself up, rocking on the balls of her feet and looked straight back at her. To her chest she clutched the clipboard she had borrowed from the retreat. So that when the curtly asked question came, what this was about, Mrs Sidhu was able to answer with a cheery if efficient smile. 'I'm with the VFC.' She flashed her ID and let it drop onto the lanyard. This wasn't a lie, she told the tidal wave of guilt that battered her heart. 'I understand you had some problems with a planning application.'

Tamzin defrosted very quickly. 'Oh, come in, please.' She stepped aside and waved Mrs Sidhu in.

They went to the bottom of her garden. There was a pair of sun loungers on the lawn and a bottle of champagne in a steel cooler, two glasses beside it. Mrs Sidhu noted the two glasses. She took a discreet look around. No one else seemed to be in evidence, though they might be inside. The curtains were drawn in the upstairs window. And if there was a swimming pool it must be buried away somewhere underground.

Even swimming, Tamzin wore bright lipstick. She was attractive, well-preserved, you might say, with a slightly heavy jaw that lent her the look of a fighter. 'Is it so very much to ask?' Tamzin said. A few puffy clouds had appeared in the early afternoon sky. The white seemed only to intensify the blue, and instead of water they rained hard light. Tamzin pointed to the bottom of her garden, a broad swathe of land that tumbled away from her house and ended in a fence. 'Just a small space to work in.'

'I understand that you work in the music business.' Mrs Sidhu had done her research. Despite appearances, this was no Hollywood housewife. Tamzin Grey was a backing singer turned music agent, and when the global agency that she had represented for thirty years had dumped her, she had taken as many clients as would follow her and set up on her own. 'And this garden backs on to the gardens of the houses on the High Street, is that right?'

Tamzin rolled her eyes. 'It'll be completely soundproofed. I explained that to the neighbours.' She pointed to the clipboard. 'And in my planning application.'

'Soundproofing, yes, I see.' Mrs Sidhu nodded, surveying the garden. She took a quick look at her clipboard. This was the hard bit. A decisive and confident tone was needed, and she hoped she struck it. 'And would you have explained that on Sunday? I believe you had a conversation with . . .' another flicker of the eyes to her clipboard '. . . a certain Dr Calman?'

Tamzin's eyes narrowed to slits. 'I may have had a casual conversation with her about planning matters. I mean we are – well, were – neighbours. And she was such a neighbourly person.' There was little warmth in Tamzin's voice.

Mrs Sidhu may have been a stranger to the well-kept lawns of the Berkshire hinterland surrounding Slough like a green sea around a stone-grey island, but communities she understood. In communities there would always be frictions. Frictions were Mrs Sidhu's business, and it had not taken her long to get to the dry itchy subject that was chafing Tamzin Grey. 'I mean, why would anyone complain about a recording studio?'

'I can't imagine,' Mrs Sidhu said. 'Though I can imagine that if there were such an objection you would want to

137

talk about it with the person who complained, I know I would. I hate misunderstandings, I'm the sort of person who wants to talk it out, get to the bottom of things, come to some kind of arrangement.' Tamzin's eyes were distant and cold now. 'The regrettable thing is that people don't always listen. If it were me, I'd just go and knock on her door and have it out. Is that what happened?'

'I did have a chat with her but not at her house. It was at the bring-and-buy sale.'

Tamzin's eyes sparkled as she remembered.

The Benham village bring-and-buy sale fell one full calendar weekend before the Benham village fete and was almost as popular.

When the doyennes of one of Berkshire's wealthiest villages chucked out their unwanted knick-knacks, you could be sure that among them would be quality merchandise. We aren't talking stained cruet sets and half-used scented candles. The brand names included Gucci, de la Renta, Vuitton, Chanel and Patek Philippe. No wonder, then, that it attracted people from all around the surrounding areas: Reading, Slough, even Swindon. Competition for the finest items was fierce, and arguments were not uncommon. However, as late afternoon turned to early evening, it was winding down. A few remaining bargain hunters turfed through piles of clothes, but the fight had gone out of most of them.

Dr Calman tore a pink strip along the perforated lines neatly marked out in the book.

'That'll be a pound,' she said.

There was a dwindling line of people waiting to buy raffle tickets. At this time of day they were people who lived in and around the village, avoiding the melee of the serious bargain hunters. Without glancing up, Wendy scraped the correct change from the cash-box tray and handed over a crisp new raffle ticket. 'The draw is at the village fete on Saturday, be sure to come. I will be baking my best scones,' said Wendy, then frowned. She had heard a snort.

Tamzin Grey pushed a coin across the table. Wendy put it in the cash box. 'Are you still objecting to my garden office?' She was wearing that knowing half-smile she always wore, and today she half-knew something interesting. 'Because you will be very interested in what I've just heard from Kate Hammond. She's one of your little therapy group, isn't she?'

'I don't discuss my clients outside work.'

'This isn't about the state of her mind.' Tamzin leaned in. The news, when whispered, had burned Wendy's ears hot to the tips of her earlobes. 'They're going ahead with The Sanctuary. They've got all the land they need.'

Then Tamzin picked up her raffle ticket and was about to walk away when she came back. Wendy was still stunned from the news. It took a moment to register that Tamzin was holding something out. 'Someone must have dropped this,' she said. It was a wallet. A thick, fat, heavy wallet, old and worn, filled with greasy-looking cash.

Wendy took it from her and had a look inside, scanning the wrinkled and ageing photograph behind the plastic panel, but she wasn't really looking. 'I'll put it in lost property,' she said in a diminished voice. She reached under the table and hauled out a transparent plastic bag, already filled with a jumble of random lost property. She thrust the wallet inside and put the bag away.

* * *

139

Tamzin threw her head back and with her eyes closed, gave a deep-throated laugh. 'Believe me, she complained about my studio, but that was weeks ago. They're all complaining about my little development, but wait until they hear about what's in store for their precious village.'

Mrs Sidhu picked up one of the half-empty glasses. 'This planning application means a lot to you. Am I right in remembering that you and Mr Snakeskin were once married?' The glass was a champagne flute. 'Perhaps moving close to his rehab centre and building him a recording studio will bring him back. But then I suppose if someone blocked that, you'd be very angry.'

Tamzin's face set hard as cement. 'Who are you?' She grabbed Mrs Sidhu's clipboard, glanced at it and gasped, 'This isn't my planning application – this is a recipe for cake. Let me see that badge?' She snatched it from Mrs Sidhu's lanyard and squinted to read the fine print. 'Village fete committee?'

Mrs Sidhu put the champagne flute down next to the other one. 'But I will offer one piece of advice.' Mrs Sidhu tapped the side. 'Encouraging a man's addiction is a dangerous game.'

Tamzin's face fell. For a moment it looked to Mrs Sidhu as if she was pleading for help. The moment passed. 'I'm not that stupid.' Tamzin reached into the ice bucket and drew out the bottle, brandishing the label for Mrs Sidhu to see.

The slam of the front door rang in Mrs Sidhu's ears long after it was closed behind her. She had wormed more than Tamzin's addiction to Jonny Snakeskin out of her. Benham village had something to brace itself for, and it was called 'The Sanctuary'. Most of all, Dr Calman was angry about it. Interesting. Mrs Sidhu reached for her phone.

* * *

140

When Mrs Sidhu was gone, Tamzin shucked off her robe. She was wearing a swimsuit. She poured two more glasses of champagne. Jonny emerged sweating from the sauna. 'It's already thirty-five in the shade out here, why you got to put me in that oven box? Sheesh. What did the old lady want?'

Tamzin smiled. 'She was collecting for the village fete. Collecting information, I think.'

'What's this? You leave something in a cloakroom?' Jonny held up a pink piece of paper. There were three smudged digits printed on it.

'That is a raffle ticket. It's a quaint English custom that you can see in action at the weekend.'

He read the numbers aloud. 'Six, two, three. Your lucky number?'

'Maybe,' she said, putting a hand on his chest. 'Depends on you.'

Jonny pulled away, poured himself a glass of champagne. 'Don't you have any whisky?' He lifted the bottle and glared at the label. 'Zero alcohol? Not much of a party, Tammy.' Jonny pushed her away. 'If it's not a party it's a business meeting. Are you going to help me or not?'

'Haven't I always been the one who helped you?' She swigged the alcohol-free champagne. 'Time for some cold-water therapy. Follow me.'

Jonny looked around. There was no sign of a swimming pool. Tamzin was heading down to the bottom of the garden. He followed obediently.

14

'This is a three-bedroom property right here in the village.' The young man printed out the particulars and passed them across.

Mrs Sidhu barely looked at the printouts. 'I'm looking for something else. Do you have anything more modern?'

Like all estate agents, he had a shiny suit, shiny hair and a shiny voice. 'Not in the village itself. Have you considered neighbouring locations?' Shiny suit or not, Mrs Sidhu forbore to tell out-and-out lies.

'I'd love to move into Benham village.' Who wouldn't want to move to Benham village? It was paradise. She was just leaving out the part about not being able to afford it. 'I like village life.' *The Sanctuary*, the name itself was suggestive and Mrs Sidhu risked a small gamble. She did her best to look frail and concerned. 'But did I read that a woman had been murdered in the village lately?'

He shifted uncomfortably in his shiny suit. There was no one else in the office but he instinctively looked around.

'There was a death. I believe the police are still investigating. It's a very safe village, lowest crime rate in the area.'

'I really do value security, and some people tell me there are changes coming to the place. What I'm looking for is a sanctuary.' She breathed the last word like a magic spell, and it had its effect.

'Well, not all change is bad. I shouldn't reveal this, but there may be something coming up in the near future. Something a little different. Come with me.' He led Mrs Sidhu to the back of the office. 'I can't say anything official, but unofficially I might be able to take pre-pre-reservations as it were. For the right clients.'

'A new development, here in Benham village?'

'I think I can say this is for you.' He looked around once more then pulled a long flat drawer open and flourished a set of plans. 'The Sanctuary. Fifty acres of exclusive properties, all in a gated community.'

Mrs Sidhu gasped. Open sesame. The bottom right corner carried an architect's mark and the name 'Hammond Homes'. 'I understand Mr Hammond lives right here in the village.'

'We've got a mainline station, which is ideal for commuting into London.' He considered her carefully. 'Or handy for heading west to Bristol and the coast, ideal for retirement.'

Mrs Sidhu adjusted her hair. Cheeky *bandar*. She wasn't that close to retirement. 'And does he? Commute I mean?'

'As it happens, I think he does. I've seen him a few times on the 8.05. We also have London offices, so if you ever think about moving closer to the big city, we can help there too.'

143

She thanked him for the information, remembered out loud that she had no money, and left him with a bemused look and a sweet *ludoo* as a gift. Now what was dishonest about that?

It was late afternoon when Mrs Sidhu got home. She was flushed with her victories of the morning.

She unlocked the front door and smiled to herself with quiet satisfaction on three counts. The first was that her phone showed no new messages from Tez. She had neutralised the two major distractions in her life; they were currently entertaining one another. She was also secretly delighted that Tez had risen to the challenge. He was a good boy, deep down.

Meanwhile, with nothing more than a homemade plastic badge, she had stormed the castle of Tamzin Grey, and then sweet-talked an estate agent into revealing a connection between Tony Hammond, one of the richest men in Berkshire, and the death of Dr Calman. Housing estates had been built before; what was so controversial about this one? The answer to that would have to wait until later. She checked her watch: plenty of time.

She unlocked her front door. She would be able to have some 'me time' in her conveniently empty house. Right now, nothing was as inviting as silence and her armchair.

However, when she got to the living room, her heart fell. They were watching TV. Tez was lying on the sofa and her favourite armchair was occupied by Daljeet. She longed for it, could even feel her buttocks pressed into the yielding cushion.

'You're back then, Mum.' Tez had always been an observant boy.

It was one of those TV shows where people hunted the housing market in sunny places. A fussy couple from Staines were getting the hard sell on a flat in the Algarve but were worried that there was no swimming pool and the bedroom was the wrong shape or size or something. Then they were whisked off to look at another flat which they also found wanting. It was all very exhausting. Perhaps when they got back to Staines they would reconsider moving, decide that home was where the heart was. At least when they got there they would have comfortable chairs to sit on. Mrs Sidhu shifted her weight from side to side to still the numbing sensation that was spreading up through her bum into her lower back.

Mrs Sidhu almost left there and then, with a mind to sit in the garden, but Daljeet waved her in. 'We missed you at the model village, sister.'

'Apologies, ' Mrs Sidhu said through a clenched jaw. 'My work called me away once more. I thought you'd still be at Bekonscot.' This last comment was directed at Tez and came with a side order of glaring eyes. He paid no attention whatsoever.

'I have no idea what my dear brother saw in that place. So we came home,' Daljeet said. 'Come, you must be tired, sit down.'

Mrs Sidhu's heart lifted. For a moment she thought Daljeet was going to vacate the chair. After a prolonged awkward silence it became clear that wasn't going to happen. Mrs Sidhu dragged out a dining chair. It was hard and new, which meant the cushions had not had time to adapt to the human body. Rather than sinking in, she balanced.

'What's the point of going out to look at tiny houses when you've got everything you want right here?' Tez waved his hand at the TV. 'You know what gave me the idea?' A profound sense of bad taste combined with laziness would have been Mrs Sidhu's opening guess.

'I got the idea from Aunty Daljeet. I mean, soon we're going to be lazing around in the sun, ordering servants about and complaining about the swimming pool.'

Mrs Sidhu wondered if the designer of the chair had been inspired by medieval torture devices. It took her a small while to shift her attention from her discomfort to what Tez was saying, because for the most part, she tried to ignore what Tez was saying. 'I beg your pardon? Why would we be doing that?'

Daljeet wrinkled her lips in a very strange way until Mrs Sidhu realised she was smiling. 'When you move to India, of course.' She produced her phone, surprisingly shiny and up to date, and pulled up a photograph. It was a house, not yet complete. A big house, flat-roofed, colonial style, with veranda and balcony. The photograph was taken in bright sunshine, so the white walls seemed to gleam. Daljeet tapped the phone screen. 'This is your house. The one my brother has been building.' When a look of confusion crossed Mrs Sidhu's face she said, 'I'm sorry, sister, were you saving it as a surprise for Tez?'

'Yes, that's it,' she said stiffly. Her voice was cold, but hot fury pulsed through her veins. Mrs Sidhu got up from the chair, which at least was a relief. 'If you'll excuse me.'

In the upstairs bathroom, she locked the door, filled the sink with cold water and washed the tears from her face.

Burton chewed the inside of his mouth. Nearly forty-eight hours after the murder of Dr Wendy Calman and still not a sign of Patrick Kirby. His officers had covered the obvious ground – known associates, family, friends, work colleagues – without finding a trace of him.

This time of night, Newton police station was quiet. Burton knew he had to be patient. In the meantime, learn as much as you can about the suspect. He opened the file, which was disappointingly light. Still, look on the bright side: quicker to read. His eyes scanned the pages with a practised eye.

The official records on Patrick Kirby were thin, but Sergeant Dove had done a good job of pulling together what was known about him from statements from his co-workers. Born in Reading, 1997, working-class background, he had artistic talent but no training. He was diagnosed later with learning disabilities, but back then his parents spent more time fighting with each other than nurturing Patrick. He ended up on the streets, tagging on railway arches, and scrawling on the sidewalks. Until one day he had a bit of luck. His pavement drawings attracted the interest of a lecturer at Reading University. He was enrolled but didn't stick at it. No money, he didn't make friends easily and, after he dropped out, his parents gave up on him completely. At this point Patrick Kirby dropped off the edge of the world, spending long periods off the grid, with occasional arrests for disorder in Reading town centre. Patrick became part of the great and growing swathe of homeless. Until he had a second piece of luck. Dr Calman found him. She helped him, and diagnosed him with an autistic learning disability.

Burton put the file down. He mused over some of Patrick's artwork. It was tangled, detailed and somehow symmetric and spiritual. He had told Dr Calman he heard voices. These voices told him what to draw.

Dr Calman got him a job at the retreat. There, he kept himself to himself. In the days he worked as a gardener and handyman, in the evenings he alternated with one of the orderlies as nightwatchman. On his nights off he came home to dinner cooked by Dr Calman. She was his landlady, his therapist, the person who had helped him get off the street, into a job and into therapy. He owed her everything. Except, last Sunday night, he came home and killed her with a garden tool. 'How bad a chef could she be?' Burton muttered to himself.

He turned the drawing round in his hand, following its lines. It looked like something that had grown rather than something that had been made. It branched again and again and again, turning into descending spirals that had no end.

Patrick Kirby was a confused man with learning problems and a history of violence. So how had he evaded the police for almost two days? This sort of suspect rarely had the resources or the will to stay hidden for long. They weren't organised enough.

Burton put the drawing down. He rubbed his eyes; when he opened them, Sergeant Dove was entering the room.

'Sir, we got into Dr Calman's laptop.' He held the computer in one hand, lid open. 'Looks like she was writing a book, sir, a sort of therapy book. It's just the last chapter, sir, you might want to see what it's about.' Dove put the laptop down.

Burton's face remained impassive as he read the words making up the chapter title. He rubbed the back of his neck where the skin was prickling. 'I've got a very bad feeling about this.'

* * *

Mrs Sidhu banged the dashboard clock then decided to check her phone instead. It was five minutes past nine in the evening and Mrs Sidhu's Nissan Micra was parked at Benham Parkway railway station. The London train was due at ten minutes past.

What was she even doing here this time of night? She could be propped in front of the TV. She could be catching up on family and friends. She could be with Respected Sister-in-Law Daljeet. Mrs Sidhu pushed away the uncomfortable answer to the question. That she was avoiding Daljeet.

No, she didn't know about the house in India! She didn't know that her husband had built it and never said a word about it. Never discussed it, never talked to her. He must have been funnelling money into his little project for years and not a single sentence had slipped from his lying lips to her. Instead he had left her with nothing but debts. Meanwhile, he confided in his sister thousands of miles away. This is how she had to find out, from Daljeet the bloody Dalek.

The twilight was warm. A breeze picked at her chiffon choonie and cooled the hot blood in her veins. So here she was, sitting in her car outside a village railway station avoiding the questions she should be asking and asking questions she should be keeping well out of. That was her, that was her life, a series of upside downs and inside outs. Why stop now? In Punjabi the word for 'upside down' was *ulti* and the same word was used for being sick. It's how she felt, sick, like someone had turned her inside out. A couple of long deep breaths had her simmering somewhere just below boiling. She checked the clock.

Mrs Sidhu had time. She reached for the back seat and flapped her hand around until she felt warm plastic.

She hauled the thermos flask onto her lap and unscrewed the lid. She poured the brown liquid. It was pathili wali tea, sweet and hot. She sipped it and felt her stomach settle and some strength return to her tired bones. She shouldn't add the sugar. She was pre-prediabetic, the doctor said. 'Whatever that means,' she had said when Tez had asked her. She knew full well what it meant, but the body, when unwilling, needed encouragement. Chefs seasoned food with more salt than was entirely good for you, and sugar was the same. A necessary evil, but under its influence her thoughts were coming together.

This was far bigger than a complaint about a garden studio. Wendy Calman objected to the development. That was what made her angry. Tony Hammond knocked on her door that night because she was standing in his way. And he was not the sort of man you get in the way of.

The railway lines hummed. She hopped out of the car and, locking it carefully, she went on to the platform. There was no guard or barrier at the tiny station. There was an automated machine, and Mrs Sidhu diligently paid for a day return ticket, first class, which would take her one stop up the line to Benham village station. The machine had barely spat out the orange and green slip of card before the train whined into the station.

A detailed search of the Great Western Railway website had revealed that this was one of the few express services out of London that made stops at a few well-chosen village stations. Well-chosen meaning well-heeled. She hoped this was the right one, because the next one that made the same stops ran at ten fourteen. She would hate to wait and repeat the journey.

The hustle alarm did its job, and panicked Mrs Sidhu

onto the train. The carriage was hot, with the acrid smell that seems to work its way into train upholstery over time. The rancid tang of delays, overcrowding and clogged toilets.

Being a systematic woman, Mrs Sidhu climbed in through the last set of doors. The doors closed and the train eased forward. The first-class carriage was sparsely populated, most of the commuters would have been on the previous train. Only the real office warriors were on this one. She swayed forward, swinging from one seat to the next like commuter Spiderwoman. Dark-suited men and women, hunched over telephones and laptops, or empty eyes staring at the ceiling, listening to God knows what meditation podcast with jaw-clenched intensity. How many, she wondered, were destined for burnout and then places like the Benham House Retreat? Only to start the process again. She found him in the very front of the carriage.

Tony Hammond had walled himself in behind a copy of the *Financial Times*. The whites of his bulging eyes were washed pink with commuter fatigue. He would be home soon, to Kate. Kate with her issues. He longed to know what Kate's 'issues' were, but Kate would never answer him when he quizzed her. He even asked Eardley, who claimed he didn't know, that it was all bound up in confidentiality. Possession was nine-tenths of the law, and possession was what Kate was to Tony. Which was why he had taken matters into his own hands. It was exhausting though, and he was burning out. He yawned. How much longer could he keep this up?

His jowls wobbled with the movement of the train. The rocking motion and the analysis of the property market were having an effect. His eyelids were just drooping when he was jerked awake by another passenger landing heavily

151

on the seat opposite. He focussed his eyes on the printed numbers once more, forcing himself awake before a small brown finger appeared at the peak of his pink paper palisade and pulled it down.

'Excuse me, but do you mind if I take this seat?' Mrs Sidhu said.

Tony Hammond cast his eyes around the carriage. There seemed to be plenty of seats. He shrugged, muttered something and raised his newspaper once more. Once more the newsprint started to blur, once more his eyelids fluttered and his chin lolled onto his chest. He was just drifting into unconsciousness when a small, brown finger crinkled his newspaper down for the second time.

'I'm so sorry, were you falling asleep?'

Tony's head snapped up and his pink-tinged eyes opened. 'Oh my goodness, you were. I was apologising for waking you the first time, but now I can see you're falling asleep again and now I have to apologise all over again.'

Tony grunted that it was no trouble at all and Mrs Sidhu insisted it was. This went on for a while, and by the time it finished – and Tony never really knew how – they were introducing themselves to one another.

'I work at the Benham House Retreat. Am I right in thinking your wife is having treatment there?'

Tony growled, throwing sour glances around the carriage to see who might be listening. His boiled-egg eyes threatened to jump out of his face at any moment.

Mrs Sidhu put her hand to her mouth. 'I'm so sorry,' she said, dropping her voice. She tapped the front page of his newspaper. 'You need no introduction. Tony Hammond. Our third home was a Hammond home, we loved it, you know.' She remembered the smell of concrete dust and fresh paint. 'A brand-new house, it was a dream come true. My sadly departed husband loved the garage, spent half his life out there.' He had indeed, and stuffed it full of old televisions, washing machines and hoovers that he was convinced would one day be valuable again.

Tony puffed up. 'Damn right, we build good quality homes that people can afford. Many, many people have started out in a Hammond home. We work alongside communities to build stronger.' That was straight out of the brochure; the bit that wasn't in the brochure was that the communities often had other ideas.

The train was slowing as it came into a bend. The next station was Benham Village. Mrs Sidhu did not have much time.

'Of course you do. It must be so hard to with all the planning and the objections. I mean like The Sanctuary project. What a bold vision. That must be so hard to get permission for. And now there's that murder in the village. Nightmare.'

Mrs Sidhu watched carefully. Tony shifted in his seat, resting his arms across his chest. 'We hold consultations, make sure everyone gets a say, it's for the planning people to decide in the end.'

The train howled as it braked, momentum dragging Mrs Sidhu forward like gravity. She swallowed and made her move. 'It's like when my husband built his car port. People were up in arms. We fell out with the neighbours over it. Did that happen? I mean, it gets so personal, doesn't it, when it's in your own village?'

Tony froze, just for a moment. His tongue flicked across his lips. 'Who did you say you were again? You work at the retreat? What are you, a therapist?' He stood, thrusting his arms and legs into black lightweight nylon waterproofs. 'How do you know about The Sanctuary?' The door alarms were already sounding. They were on the platform and she was talking to his broad receding back. 'I'm with the VFC. We regulate, we look into things, we are everywhere, Mr Hammond.' She flashed her homemade ID card with the initials VFC in bold and hoped he wouldn't notice the words 'village fete committee' in eight-point font underneath. She moved on very quickly. 'Did it get personal with Dr Calman? It must have been tempting to talk to her directly about her concerns. Perhaps to knock on her door. Her house is on your way home.'

Now, Tony Hammond was facing her, bloodshot eyes looking straight into hers. 'Wendy Calman was not the holdout tenant. The holdout tenant is Edith Pollock. Or rather she was. She has agreed to sell.'

Tony pointed up towards the hill. Mrs Sidhu could make out a dimly lit circle of boulders picked out by the moonlight. 'That is what this is all about. I'm going to do what no one has done for five thousand years. I'm going to bring that place to life again.'

Mrs Sidhu's eyebrows rose. 'The stone circle? That's where The Sanctuary is going to be built?'

'It will be a living part of a new way of living. Enhancing and enhanced by all that surrounds it. History will be part of people's lives again. Respectfully, of course. The houses will be situated away from it, and the monument will be well protected. In fact, I'm putting millions into its restoration. So forgive me if I'm a little impatient with individuals who don't get the big picture.'

'That was what Wendy was angry about, that Edith was selling? Why would that make her angry?'

Hammond sneered. 'If you're really interested in local planning matters, maybe have a chat with your employer up at the retreat.'

He fiddled in his pocket, pulling out a pair of bike lights. As he did, a tiny pink piece of paper fell to the floor. Mrs Sidhu retrieved it for him. 'You dropped your cloakroom ticket.' She read the number: Six two four.

'Raffle ticket. Village fete on Saturday.' Hammond stuffed it into his pocket. 'My wife is very keen.'

'Stephen Eardley. What's he got to do with The Sanctuary?'

The bike unfolded like a ballet in steel. Hammond had the experience that most people had when they got talking to Mrs Sidhu. 'I fear I've said too much already.'

Tony Hammond made an oddly comic sight, cycling his way down the lane. He was such a large man on such a small bicycle. Soon all that could be seen of him was a winking red light receding into the darkness.

15

The time had come for Patrick to perform a shocking act. He had put it off all day. He was going to take a life.

First he had to decide the best way to go about it. Again, fate played its part. There were old bottles and tools among the half-burned junk in his hideout. The gods of chaos provided, and behind them was the hand of the Master.

He left his hideout as soon as darkness fell. The sun had set, but the earth was still warm. More than anything Patrick missed his garden. The one he had made, tucked away in the retreat, that was just for himself. So many flowers would be in bloom now.

He paused a moment before entering this new garden. It wasn't his garden, it was too tidy, too regular, but it was full of living things. That was something, wasn't it?

It was time for Patrick to act. He shivered. A momentary spasm of doubt crossed his face. He clutched at his dread-locks. What if he had it wrong? There was so little to go on. This was all so confusing, and for another few moments he twisted a finger through his dangling locks. Then a sense of decision seemed to fill him. He breathed into his huge chest. He stooped to pull a white plastic bottle from his rucksack. He unscrewed the lid, pressing down hard and twisting to free the childproof mechanism, and walked purposefully onto the path that ran across the lawn to the front door.

His hesitation, however, must have alerted the woman inside the house. Benham village was the sort of place where people noticed strangers hanging around on the streets. The door creaked open and a head was thrust through it. 'Can I help you?'

Patrick, only halfway up the path, almost dropped the bottle. She didn't sound like she wanted to help him. She sounded like she wanted him to go away. He steadied himself, remembered to smile and reached into his pocket and produced a rumpled raffle ticket. 'Is this your number?'

The woman's brow creased. She tried to read it, but it was a long way away. Yet something about Patrick, perhaps his twitching face, perhaps the long, dirty hair, the filthy hoodie shading his face, the smile that wasn't a smile, the sheer size of him, stopped her from leaving the shelter of her own porch. 'If you don't clear off, I'll call the police.'

'Don't do that!' He could not afford the police. Not now, it was too soon. He stuttered for words, finally finding some. 'It's the raffle. Did you buy a raffle ticket number six two four at the bring-and-buy?'

The woman crossed her arms. Her eyes narrowed. She glanced at the bottle in Patrick's hand. 'What did I win? Some bleach?'

Patrick had momentarily forgotten he was carrying an open bottle of bleach, had almost forgotten his plan, which did not include conversation. 'Is it your number?' he repeated.

The smile was gone. He took two strides forward now, onto the lawn. As he moved, he changed his grip on the bottle.

The woman flinched. 'No, it's not.'

The slam of the door echoed around the street; Patrick felt it like a hammer blow. His heart, he realised, was beating fast. It was the wrong person. He had the wrong house. With shaking hands, he screwed the lid back onto the bleach. He had almost helped the wrong person. For a few precious moments longer, Patrick stood on the lawn taking deep breaths. She would be calling the police, he thought. He was running out of time. Patrick took another look back at the house. He had better do it, just in case.

The next time Tamzin looked out of her window, the giant homeless man was gone. Then she saw her lawn. Her hand shot to her mouth, covering her gasp. She scrambled to find her mobile phone.

'Police? Someone's murdered my lawn!'

'I'm surprised you're still here. Don't you need to get home?'

'I brought you a glass of milk,' she said. Dr Eardley was struggling out of his walking boots when Mrs Sidhu found him. It was late and he was surprised to see her. Mrs Sidhu explained that she wanted to talk to him, professionally. 'You did say your door was open for a chat any time.' Dr Eardley bade her into his office with his usual distant smile.

He finally wrenched his boots free. 'Excellent. I am so glad you took up the offer.' He turned on the desk lamp.

Mrs Sidhu deposited the steaming mug of milk on the desk. 'It's got almonds in it. Good for the brain. I brought myself one too.'

Dr Eardley sipped the milk but said nothing for a while.

Mrs Sidhu sat down opposite him, taking a gulp of her milk before letting out a satisfied breath. She broke the silence first. 'Tastes so good. Good for shock too.'

Dr Eardley leaned back, observing her, fingers steepled on his stomach. 'Yes, how is your head?'

Mrs Sidhu rubbed her temple, having quite forgotten about her bruise. 'It's fine.'

Eardley eyed the ceiling. 'My belief is that as human beings we all tell lies. Good lies, bad lies, lies to make others feel better. But the most damaging lies are the ones we tell ourselves. That we can't be loved, that we can't succeed, that we are beyond redemption, that we're fine really and that nothing is wrong when it is. What lie are you telling yourself, Mrs Sidhu?'

'You're right. My trouble is not so much physical as of the mind. It was about Dr Calman's death. I have been having troubling thoughts that it may not have had anything to do with Patrick's condition.' She left that hanging.

A shadow passed across Dr Eardley's face. He pursed his lips and, leaning forward in his chair, forced a friendly smile. 'Please, I like to help people where I can. What exactly are these thoughts?'

Mrs Sidhu took another sip of her milk and wiped the back of her hand across her mouth. 'Don't let it go cold now.'

Eardley obediently drank some milk, but his eyes were soon back on Mrs Sidhu. 'You were saying?' Mrs Sidhu raised an eyebrow in question. 'About these suspicious thoughts, Dr Calman, Patrick . . .'

'Oh yes, my disturbing thoughts. I suppose they're ideas really.' Mrs Sidhu broke off. 'Let me start again. I notice things. I always have, ever since I was a small girl. Sometimes that's a good thing and sometimes that is something that makes other people . . . well, let's just say it makes them uncomfortable. And what I've noticed this time is that there is so much going on here in Benham, what with summer fetes and planning enquiries and of course The Sanctuary project. Do you know it? It's a major new building development.'

Dr Eardley lost his interest in the ceiling. He shifted uncomfortably in his chair. 'I may have heard something. I think they're holding a consultation.' Those little round spectacles were on Mrs Sidhu now.

Mrs Sidhu smiled brightly. 'Consultation, exactly. So my tiny little nagging worry was that were someone objecting very strongly to the plans, and that person found out something suspicious, that they might be better off dead. To certain other people, anyway.'

'Well, you'd have to talk to Tony Hammond about that.'

'Oh, I have.' Mrs Sidhu smiled at Eardley, who was alert now, leaning forward in his chair. 'You know there are quite a few links between the village and the retreat. Take Mr Hammond's wife, Kate. She was a client of Dr Calman's. I see you've taken over her group.'

Eardley gave a good-natured grimace. 'Obviously I can't discuss her case – client confidentiality.'

'Oh, I quite understand. Then there's Mr Snakeskin, the rock star, also one of Dr Calman's clients. He has an ex-wife in the village, Tamzin Grey. Do you know her?'

Dr Eardley was losing interest. 'Yes, she moved here to support Jonny.' He took his glasses off and polished them. 'Really, it is getting late. These "connections" seem perfectly normal to me. Lots of people have thoughts and suspicions

160

and anxieties about all sorts of things. The pressure of constant news and social media makes us very susceptible to paranoias. Maybe we should continue this in the morning, or we could schedule a mindfulness session and a healthy digital diet. We all need to take time out now and then.'

The trail was going cold. Mrs Sidhu recollected that overheard phone call. What had Eardley said when she first had her ear pressed to his office door? '*It had to be done. This is simply not the time to start dredging up all that nonsense. She had no right to treat her, she's my client now, Anthony. Which is why I'm terminating her.*' The implication was clear. He was sacking Dr Calman because she was interfering.

Eardley was rising from his chair. Mrs Sidhu cleared her throat and spoke quickly. 'Then there's Edith Pollock. She used to be Dr Calman's client but a few weeks ago you took over. Why was that?'

Dr Eardley sat down again, slowly. He put his little round glasses on again. 'Yes well, Edith isn't strictly in need of rehab. She is suffering dementia; it was felt that my touch might help her more. Wendy was completely onside.'

'Until she found out about the land deal. Not Tony Hammond's, but your land deal. Now you're buying the land from her. Isn't that what's called manipulating a client? Or do you think it's all right to do that? Is that the lie you're telling yourself, Dr Eardley?'

Dr Eardley was hunched forward, toying with the glass on the table, making milk rings on the wood. He tried to wipe them away but only succeeded in smearing it around. He stopped abruptly. Suddenly he chuckled. 'You are certainly a very observant person. But what you don't understand is that it was Edith's idea to move over to me. She had already made up her mind to sell the land. She wanted to put it all to rest, that's what she said. And I need the land to expand the retreat. Then I had a better idea. Why not make mental wellness the centre of how people live. That's what The Sanctuary will be: an entire housing estate designed with the human spirit at its core. And in the very centre a heritage centre dedicated to the stone circle, a symbol of holistic wisdom.' Eardley's eyes had lit up with wonder while he spoke, and now he did his best to recover a sense of detachment. 'Tony Hammond loves the idea. For years he's wanted to do something more than build little boxes for people to survive in. So The Sanctuary was born. Edith was worried Wendy would talk her out of it. Wendy kept asking her about the deaths, you see, wouldn't leave her alone.'

Mrs Sidhu raised an eyebrow. 'The deaths? What deaths?'

'The Pollock suicides. Most people have forgotten them. In 1997 Justin and Sandra Pollock joined the E cult. "E" for enlightenment. They took poison, and the cult leader burned their bodies and their house. Wendy Calman was obsessed with it; it was supposed to be the crowning glory of her book. She gave me a copy, wanted me to talk to my publishers.' He pulled a thick manuscript from his drawer. 'Wendy was an academic, a great therapist, and an appallingly dull writer.' He thumped it down on the table. Mrs Sidhu pulled it towards her using both hands. 'Edith became uncomfortable about it a couple of months back. I didn't talk Edith into anything, you can ask her yourself. I'm sure the police have.'

Mrs Sidhu was at the door when Eardley spoke again. 'You should know that Edith carries a lot of guilt about those deaths. She feels that she is responsible because she is a Druid herself, and she introduced her son to that world. To the world of William Mackie.'

'People used to laugh, you know.' Edith laid down her knitting. She looked out of the window at the sliver of moon in the sky. 'But I say it keeps you grounded. You think about the seasons, and a lot of it is about nature. It'll be Midsummer soon.' Edith winked scandalously. 'We had a lot of fun in the summer.' Mrs Sidhu believed her.

To Mrs Sidhu's relief, Edith seemed quite lucid tonight. Elliot didn't seem to be around, and Edith welcomed her in. She accepted Mrs Sidhu's offer to make them tea. As before, the house smelled of an old woman: liniment, potatoes, laundry and an indefinable hospital smell, a mixture of an ageing body, medications and cat food. The heating was on, even with the sweltering temperatures, and the room was warm. Edith's chin was dropping. Mrs Sidhu spoke quickly before she fell asleep. 'Tell me about William Mackie,' she said.

Edith's grey head jerked up from her chest. Her fleshy face was pink and soft. Her crab-apple cheeks bulged. 'He was a handsome man, tall – real presence, you know. When he talked it was like the Sermon on the Mount or one of them gurus. People followed him around like sheep with a shepherd.'

'Did you follow him?'

Edith nodded. Mrs Sidhu swallowed back her excitement. The next question was a hard one and it was difficult to predict how Edith would react. Mrs Sidhu had no choice but to ask it. 'Did you introduce your son to him?'

That brought on a long silence. Edith looked out of the

window while she flexed her thickly stockinged foot. She drew her cardigan tighter around her as if the room was freezing rather than the balmy twenty-five degrees she always kept the thermostat at, winter or summer. Eventually she spoke, her voice barely a whisper.

'The dead are always calling.' There was a quiet intensity in her voice, and the room was filled with an electric charge. Edith looked at Mrs Sidhu closely, staring into her head, as if she could see all the workings and clocksprings inside her mind. 'You know it. They call on you too.'

The hairs on Mrs Sidhu's arms stood on end. She remembered her dreams, the free-falling ghosts in her tumble dryer. She shivered and tried not to return Edith's gaze. 'Tell me about the ones that call on you.' She poured more tea and sipped the dryness out of her mouth.

'I tell myself it's not my fault. The thing is, there's a curse up there. My son bought all that land and he wanted to make himself rich off it. He paid the price.'

'You're telling me your son died because of a curse? Surely William Mackie had something to do with it.'

'Oh yes, well, he was the tool. But if you want to know why they went along with it, it's because those stones protect themselves. Ten men, they've stood there for who knows how long. The ten men stand. People can try and change it, but there it is, go up against the ten men and you'll fall too.'

'And now Patrick is the instrument, the tool.'

'Can't say. But them who go against the Ten don't last long.'

Edith's face underwent another reset, her gaze unfocusing, looking away, then returning to Mrs Sidhu with no recognition. She could not afford to lose her now.

'Edith, you were talking about your son,' she said firmly, 'don't forget Justin.'

'I haven't seen my son in over twenty-five years.' Edith's head jerked forward. 'On the good days I know he's gone. Or maybe I mean the bad days, depending on how you see it.' Mrs Sidhu nodded. She did not want to push too hard. It would be easy to open up a chasm of grief. Fortunately, Edith was in confessional mood tonight. Perhaps she was missing Dr Calman's therapy. 'He was a good boy. How much he loved that girl, Sandra. He married her in the end.

'And then William Mackie came.' She spat the name like it was a hair on her tongue. 'He picked them out because they were so open, so trusting, especially my Justin. My fault, I always brought him up to believe in things that other people laughed at. I thought it would make him independent-minded, and it did. He was smart but he didn't bother with university. He said it was for sheep. He went straight to work, and in a few years he was making money on property. But it's what made him open to Mackie. He didn't know the limits and I couldn't teach him them, because I barely knew them myself. You learn though, the hard way. The way of death.' She said this as if Mrs Sidhu would know what she meant. 'He set his eyes on Justin and Sandra the moment he arrived. He reeled them in. They weren't the only ones. He wasn't talking about nature, he was talking about spaceships and the life beyond. When words came out of Mackie's mouth, people believed.' Edith drew in a sharp breath and wiped a tear from her eye. 'Now I've made a decision about it. I'm selling the old house. The living can use the money, and the dead can rest.'

'But where will you live?'

'Oh no, dear, I'll live here. I'm selling *their* house, the one they built out in the woods. The one that burned. I'm selling to that Hammond fellow, and Dr Eardley, of course. He'll get better use out of it than me.'

'Even though they'll be swallowing up the standing stones? You don't mind? Aren't they important to you?'

'They were once. But they've brought me nothing but misery. I'll walk the Scapegoat path one more time before I'm done. Same as Justin and Sandra did that night.'

The cloud passed; the moon crept out with strengthening light. 'It's still there!' Mrs Sidhu gasped. 'The house is still there.'

16

All Kate ever wanted was to get better. She desperately wanted to get better. She always felt she was letting Tony down. Tony her rock, her saviour.

The Hammonds' house was altogether more modern than the little cottages in the centre of the village. On the outskirts, there was land enough for something much larger and imposing. It was modern architecture, glass and steel, the kind that some members of royalty tut and write angry letters about.

As she woke this time she lay in a perfect square of silver. The moon was deathly white and the light pressed through her eyelids onto her retina until she could sleep no more. She checked the time. It was late. Tony was still not home. She longed for him to be home so he could put his arms around her and make her feel safe and the ghost would go away. She shook off the covers. It was hot; that was why she left the curtain open. Now if she was to get any sleep she would have to get out of bed, traverse the room and close it. Better to do it quickly while the sleep was still in her eyes. Her feet found the floor and she was across the room in a few strides. Her hands were ready to draw the curtains together when she stopped.

He was there. He was there again. He was standing out there in the shadows, between a tapestry rose and a small bay tree. He was looking up at her. Normally she would be so frightened she would run straight back to bed, pull the covers over her head, and phone Tony. But not tonight. She remembered Dr Eardley's words from earlier that day: 'Your recovery starts with the admission that he's not real.'

She liked Dr Eardley. He was kind and he had charisma. When he spoke, you listened. She knew she was being silly, but Dr Eardley had made her feel like she was the only one in the group class. He made her feel that she could take control of her life. That was what his books were about, weren't they? And they had helped millions of people across the world. Kate believed in Dr Eardley.

She pulled a thin silk gown on, tying it at the waist with a narrow cord. She put her chin forward and moved purposefully out of the bedroom. The house was filled with acres of luxurious carpet, and her feet made no sound as she took the stairs two at a time. She passed the huge framed photograph of her and Tony on their wedding day. She passed the hall table. There was the newspaper open at the article about the terrible murder of Dr Calman, poor woman. Kate's eyes opened with worry as she pressed her hand onto her chest. Should she really be doing this? Maybe she should wait for Tony. But when would Tony get home? And anyway, he was getting fed up with her delusions; she felt his impatience. She looked again at the newspaper. She realised the article was not about the murder. It was a follow-up piece. Tony must have been reading it. She wondered why. It was about the Pollock suicides. They had printed an old photograph of the young couple celebrating. They looked so happy sitting on a sofa holding glasses of wine. Kate's eyes rose to her wedding photo again. How carefree she and Tony looked. She wanted to be that woman again. She put her shoes on. Tonight, Kate Hammond was going to get better.

The path left the road at the point where the first trees grew, and that was where Mrs Sidhu made the fork to the right. She soon left the village behind, and the trees grew thicker and the ground softer. She was following directions given her by Edith. There used to be a road here, planted with saplings, but after the fire it had been abandoned. The whole site had been forgotten about until now.

Twenty-six years ago, William Mackie had left this village on Midsummer Night, after 'helping' Justin and Sandra Pollock to die. He had poisoned them and then set fire to their house. Most people had forgotten about it. Dr Calman had done her best to understand why it had happened, and she was writing a book about it. Mrs Sidhu had an idea of what was going on.

Twenty-six years, and strong saplings had grown into mature trees. It was hard to see where the driveway had been, but Mrs Sidhu found her way through the undergrowth. After twenty minutes' walking she found gravel under her feet. She followed the crunching sound.

As she walked, ideas were spinning in her head. What if Dr Calman had come across something in her research, something that was both incredibly exciting and incredibly dangerous to her? But, no, she would have told someone.

Mrs Sidhu slapped her forehead. Start again. The under-growth here was thicker and she had to leave the gravel and push her way through until she found a foot-trodden path. Made by whom, she wondered. Teenagers, she told herself, remembering her own wanderings as a youth – wanderings that were frowned on, and curtailed by night curfews by her over-anxious parents. But she already knew it wasn't teenagers. Wanderings could be dangerous.

She put that thought out of her head and walked on. She screwed up her cheeks and thought more deeply, as her mood of being alone in a secret place overtook her. Secret places, yes, Sienna had shown her a secret place. You show me yours and I'll show you mine. Secret places were for secret things. But what of William Mackie?

Wendy Calman had found out something that got her killed, something that she knew but did not know she knew. That was it. That was why she told no one. She opened the door to a stranger. It did not have to be a stranger, of course, it could be a face she knew. A face she had looked at for years and was only just coming to realise was right in front of her. William Mackie. William Mackie was here, somewhere in the village, and there was a danger that Dr Calman would expose him.

Her thoughts returned to the present when she heard a noise. She stopped. The noise stopped too. For a moment her breathing stopped. She had made a terrible mistake coming out here alone, perhaps making the same mistake Dr Calman had made. After a minute of standing perfectly still she saw what it was and breathed again. A squirrel, its grey tail curled up along the length of its back, locked to a tree. With the well-tuned instincts of an animal, it was aware that it was being watched by an apex predator and had frozen perfectly still. Mrs Sidhu moved on quietly and shivered. Where had those instincts gone in humans? Did Wendy Calman feel it the moment before she was struck down? Mrs Sidhu kept walking.

The last sunlight was long gone now, replaced by moonlight, and the temperature was dropping. A low mist was suspiring from the springy soil, playing mysterious shadows from tree trunks and branches.

The heavy woodland opened into a wide space, which she guessed had been the turning place for cars, because beyond stood a boarded-up double garage and above it the shattered, blackened frame of what had once been a house. More than that, a home.

She felt along the boards until she found a loose one. There was time to turn back, get DCI Burton to come back with her. The board moved, creaked and fell out, followed by its neighbour. There was a dark space just wide enough for her to squeeze through.

Mrs Sidhu took a last look at the forest around her, then ducked inside the old garage.

She saw a candle and, taking her trusty cooks' matches from her pocket, she lit it. The yellow light spilled out onto the floor, where her feet kicked into something soft. She shook them free of a dirty sleeping bag, which landed in a heap at the foot of the rear wall. She went to retrieve it. That was when she saw the picture.

Mrs Sidhu gasped. It was a shriek in peeling paint, a fang-toothed cry of howling insanity, a mind-burrowing insectoid, flaming, multicoloured scream of pain. For a moment Mrs Sidhu felt something strange inside her, an unacknowledged something that she would come back to later. For now, there was too much to take in. With a trembling finger she reached out to touch the brickwork, almost fearing that the apparition would reach out and bite her, or worse, take her soul. That's what this was, someone's soul. Patrick had etched out his soul on bare stone in spray paint. Holding the candle up to the wall she could clearly see a pattern that ran through the demonic drawings. From the centre a single huge eye looked out at her.

She heard a scraping sound, almost inaudible. Goosebumps raised on her neck and the backs of her arms. With the unfailing instincts of a squirrel, Mrs Sidhu knew she was not alone. She blew out the candle and stood very still.

Timidly, she opened the door to Tony's study. The light was on, but there was no sign of Tony.

Kate looked out of the patio doors. Outside all was dark. She pulled back her shoulders, she was quite determined. Again she looked around, hunting in the shadows between the plants and flower bed. For a moment she thought, *This is it. I've done it. I am facing him down, and he's gone, like all ghosts*. Then her eyes found him. He was still there, standing perfectly still, watching her.

She always hated the way you could see into the house from almost all angles. Tony's idea, it had been. He said the foliage around the house would provide privacy. It did, in that the house could not be seen from the road or neighbouring properties; but anyone inside the grounds could see right through the house. There was no escaping his gaze.

Tonight he was different. Usually he was all in black, but tonight he was in white. Was that because she had changed? Had he turned somehow from black to white because Kate was making progress? Her breathing was coming in short gasps and she forced herself to do some of Dr Eardley's breathing exercises. For a moment she even wondered if she should go and get the podcast episode about breathing. Then the ghost did something new.

Kate gulped. The ghost man, the apparition, was moving. He had never done that before. He was moving right towards her. She took a step backward, almost tripping over a chair. She recovered herself.

Tap, tap, tap.

It was him. He was tapping at the glass. He had never done that before. He was becoming more real, and Kate's head spun in dizzying reels. She was getting worse. She could just see Tony's face – his sympathetic confusion and, worse, his pity. That was why he stayed out late. That was why he worked when he could be at home. She buried her face in her hands and sobbed. She wanted to run away. She wanted to be someone else. She wanted to be normal like all her friends at the spa, at the expensive shops she went to. Her tears soaked the silk of her gown, which was pulled up over her palms.

There was only one way, Dr Eardley's way. She had to do it.

Her jaw clenched and with shaking jerks of her neck she raised her eyes. *When I look he won't be there. He will be gone and I will be normal.*

Tap, tap, tap.

This was a test. This was what Dr Eardley had prepared her for. This was a test of faith, and Kate had faith in Dr Eardley's teachings.

He had never worn white before. He had never knocked at the door before. Maybe it wasn't Him. Maybe it was someone else. Maybe it was Tony, he had forgotten his keys and now he was locked outside, waiting to come in. To give her a hug and kiss on the head and complain about all the silly legislation that was getting in his way on the building project. She laughed with relief, and the air escaping from her lungs released the tension in her shoulders. She felt like a balloon that had been pumped up too much. She tightened her gown and wiped her wet fingers on the sides of her legs. She was so stupid. Creeping round her own house, terrified of her own husband. She heard the patio door slide open, only seeming to realise after that it was her own hand that had opened it. A tiny spark of triumph glinted in her eyes. She had done it. 'Tony?' she said bravely, but she could not keep the tremor of recently vanquished fear out of her voice. There was no reply.

Kate edged out of the study into the darkness of the garden. He was there, standing absolutely still in the dark. Ice filled her lungs, the clock spring of fear in her chest that had slowly unwound, tightened itself to shrieking point. She could see his face now. She had never seen his face before, because ghosts don't have faces.

'You're not real,' she said, but the tremor in her voice belied her uncertainty.

The man raised the rusty smiling blade and Kate knew she was going to die.

17

Mrs Sidhu puffed the candle out and held her breath. There it was: the sound of shoes on the gritty concrete floor. It was faint, but the sound was unmistakable. Mrs Sidhu's shoes had made the same sound when she had dropped in from the dirt floor of the forest onto the cracked paving of the garage. That either meant that someone had just come in behind her, or that someone had been standing silently watching her. And now they had decided to make their move.

Fright, well that was done with. Flight? Mrs Sidhu was standing two feet from a solid wall built into the bank of the hill. There was nowhere to run to that way, and the only way out was behind her, in the darkness occupied by grinding footsteps. Footsteps that were getting closer.

Mrs Sidhu turned, slowly, lifting her feet and placing them so as not to make a sound. If she had one advantage, it might be that whoever was approaching did not know she was here. On the other hand, she might have been followed here. Or, if her own theory was right, Patrick was living here, somewhere in that darkness, and he had just come home. To find Goldilocks in his house. She rubbed the bump on her head and hoped he was in a friendlier mood than last time.

Suddenly everything happened at once, and an instant before Mrs Sidhu had prepared herself. Mrs Sidhu choked back a cry. A beam of intense white light cut through the dark, crazed around the garage, until it shone hard in Mrs Sidhu's eyes. Her pupils tightened fast, she threw her hands up to protect herself, to deflect the blow that must be hurtling towards her from behind the blizzard of light.

And then, nothing. Mrs Sidhu waited and nothing happened. She was starting to wonder if somehow she had triggered an automatic system, like a security light. That no one was standing there. That thought was scotched by the familiar dry cough and stolid voice. 'So, you found it then,' said DCI Burton. 'Where's Patrick Kirby?'

'You utter, utter git,' said Mrs Sidhu.

Burton poured coffee from his flask. 'A tip from a professional cop. If you're going blundering around woodland and abandoned buildings at night, take a torch and a flask with you.' Burton took a swig from his own plastic mug and indicated that Mrs Sidhu should do the same from hers.

Broken from her trance, doing her best to disguise the shake in her hands, Mrs Sidhu took a sip and waited for the tremor to go out of her voice. She swallowed and grimaced. 'A tip from a professional chef. Brew the coffee fresh and clean the grounds filter once in a while.'

'This is nice, two old pals catching up. I always thought we should hang out in psychotic lairs more. Beats the garden centre.' They clinked plastic cups. 'And they don't

176

come more psychotic than this.' Burton drew the torch beam across the walls. There were more drawings than the few Mrs Sidhu had seen by the light of the candle. The same symbol repeated again and again.

'The Eye of Ra, an ancient Egyptian symbol,' Burton said.

'I saw it in Patrick's drawings in his shed. It seems likely that Patrick is bunking down here,' Mrs Sidhu said.

'I agree, and given the Eye of Ra symbol, and that this is the location of the Pollock suicides, I'd say there's a connection. What exactly, I don't know yet. Unless there are two maniacs on the loose with a fixation on the same ancient symbol.'

Mrs Sidhu opened her mouth hopefully at this point. Burton was quick to jump in. 'Which is vanishingly unlikely.' Mrs Sidhu was forced to agree with a shrug of the arms. She looked crestfallen. Then she raised her finger, remembering something. 'There's something that happened at the village bring-and-buy.'

Burton grinned. 'Don't tell me. One of the biddies who does the Victoria sponges got riled up in a taste test and carved Wendy Calman's throat open with a cake slice?' He snapped on a pair of latex gloves. 'That would make an interesting new round in *Bake Off*.'

Mrs Sidhu grimaced. 'Not exactly, but Wendy Calman knew something. She knew that Stephen Eardley was putting pressure on Edith Pollock to sell this land to Tony Hammond. She was one of Wendy's clients. That's motive for murder.'

Burton was searching, peering in drawers. He looked up sharply: this was news to him. 'OK, go on.'

Mrs Sidhu hesitated. The idea that William Mackie had returned was firmly in her mind, but she was reluctant to put it on the table. She finally had Burton engaged again. A wild idea like that could drive him away. She could bring it up now, but it might sound like a desperate gambit to swing suspicion back away from Patrick. 'Ah, but what if it was Mackie himself who's come back,' she would say. She could already see the dismissive smile on Burton's face. He would shake his head, he would rub his neck, he would say something kind, words to the effect that Mrs Sidhu should drink less coffee, and Mrs Sidhu would feel foolish and that would be that. This was not the time for wild theories. She had enough work to do to convince him that someone other than Patrick could have killed Wendy.

'What else did Wendy know about? She had a pen out when she died, but there was nothing to write on. Maybe she was writing on something that the killer took.'

'Like this?' Burton pulled out a thick ream of printed A4 paper. He tilted the cover sheet into the light. '"Dysfunctions of the Mind by Dr Wendy Calman" – catchy title, might be your next aeroplane read.'

Mrs Sidhu peered at it. The pages had handwritten notes in the margins. She remembered Dr Calman's uncapped pen. 'Let me see.'

Burton tugged it away from her grasp before she could lay hands on it. 'This is evidence, and it'll tie Patrick Kirby to the crime scene. Well, it will when forensics find his prints and DNA all over it. And no, I don't have another pair of gloves. You can read it when it hits the shelves.' Burton flipped through it to the last page.

'Doesn't look like she's finished though, ends in mid-sentence.'

'Luckily, I know the ending. Patrick Kirby stole her book.' He flipped the pages back to the beginning of the final chapter. 'My guess is, to feed his obsession with this.' He tapped his finger on the page. 'The question is, where is that obsession going to take him next?' Burton asked.

'William Mackie and the E cult,' Mrs Sidhu read out loud. Seeing William Mackie's name there in print made her heart jump. Her resolve to keep her theory to herself waned into doubt. If she said nothing now, Burton would push forward even faster on his flawed path. She pressed her hand into a small fist. 'What if it's not Patrick's obsession? What if William Mackie has returned and he's the one who killed Wendy?'

Mrs Sidhu sagged as she saw Burton's smile, his hand reaching to rub the back of his neck. Before he could speak, the garage was suddenly filled with the sound of jarring steel scraping on steel. Mrs Sidhu jumped, her heart thrashing in her chest. Burton calmly pulled his phone from his jacket pocket. 'Sorry, new dial tone. Jonny Snakeskin. I was a fan boy back in the day.' He answered, while Mrs Sidhu silently cursed modern technology and terrible music. What was wrong with a nice love song?

'Yes, I am in the area,' said Burton, then a pause before he wearily exhaled. 'Noise complaint? Yes, I suppose I could go and have a look. I am only a chief inspector.' Whatever underling was on the line clearly began backtracking, because Burton smiled wryly and flapped his hand. 'No, I'm joking, don't wake up a constable. Like I say, I'm in the area, and I'm awake.'

He switched the phone off. 'Duty calls. I can give you a lift back to your car. Unless you want to walk back.' Mrs Sidhu was at Burton's car before he was.

* * *

Arif woke up. He wasn't sure what he was hearing at first. There was something travelling on the night air. Slowly it resolved itself. It was music. That bloody rock star again. Arif swung his legs off the hard mattress he preferred and thrust his head and shoulders out of the window. Down below in the courtyard and across the lawn, nothing moved.

He sniffed. He could smell smoke. Maybe Snakeskin was smoking. He was weak, a slave to addictions. Arif had been told not to judge but he couldn't help it. None of these people – rich, comfortable – had been through the things he had been through, that his father had been through. They would never know deprivation or real pain. His father had made a life for them, provided for them, and finally given Arif a start in life.

Arif remembered a time when he had leaned back in the firm, unyielding chair while his father poked around his molars and spoke to him. 'My son, our lives have been hard but now they will be easy. For the first time we have more than enough.' Arif asked where the money had come from. His father's eyes narrowed and he pressed a finger to his lips. 'The money comes from silence.'

For his father, silence was not hard. There were so many things they did not talk about, things they had left behind in the war. His teeth were fine, and his father cracked a match, and lit another of his black cigarettes. For a moment the flame lit up the sadness in his eyes. 'There is no sense in questioning who lives and who dies.'

But this smell now was not cigarettes. Arif remembered the cigarettes his father smoked. Russian cigarettes, black tubes, long and straight as a rifle, and as surely as a rifle they would eventually kill his father. Not before he had taken ownership of the small dental practice on the High Street and put his son through a nursing school. A higher education, he had said, was not possible – Arif's grades had not been good enough – but this country needed nurses and it would be a job. When father died, Arif sold the dental practice; he had a nest egg tucked away, enough soon to buy a house of his own, perhaps in the new place they were building. Oh yes, he listened, he heard, he watched Dr Feelgood and Mr Hammond.

The music, he decided, was not coming from the retreat. Arif thought about going back to bed. He stopped, halfway onto the hard mattress. The retreat's inmates were his responsibility when he took his turn on the night shift. Arif took his responsibilities seriously. The music was loud, and if one of the retreat's pampered little clients complained about noise, it would be Arif who would be blamed. Madness, these people had no idea what true madness was. Perhaps one day he would sit down with the good doctor and tell him what thoughts ran through his mind.

The music was not the kind the snake man played. Not the discordant, frankly horrifying jumble of noise that idiot produced. My God it was worse than the noise of war. This was more the sort of music his father would have liked. Lilting, a man's voice, and anyway it was too far away to be from the retreat. It was one of the neighbouring properties.

Arif put his tunic on and grabbed a torch. He paused at his door, then went back and hunted in his sock drawer. There it was, he pulled it out and felt its weight. He drew the steel from the leather pouch and inspected the blade in the light from the window. None of these people knew what real madness was. Arif went out into the night.

As soon as he was outside he knew it was a big one. He started running, breaking into a sprint. 'Fire!' he shouted. 'There's a fire.' He fumbled for his phone, dropping it onto the grass before snatching it up again, juggling it into the air and catching it on the third try. By the time he got to the Hammond house, the flames were screaming up into the sky.

Mrs Sidhu watched, numb from toes to fingers. Burton was shouting, from a distant place, like words heard through a shell.

'Get out of there!' Burton hammered on the glass doors. Inside, flames were already licking up, spreading from the carpet, up the curtains. The occupants of the house sat dumbly on the sofa, looking for all the world like they were watching TV. Like Tez and his aunty Daljeet earlier that day. *Escape to the Country*. Mrs Sidhu would have laughed, if this weren't really happening. They had had minutes to get out. She knew they were going nowhere.

Burton tried the door. Locked. He stumbled around in the flower bed and came out carrying a rock.

'I don't think you can save them. Look,' Mrs Sidhu said, dreamily. She pointed and Burton strained his eyes. Each of them, Tony and Kate Hammond, seemed to have an extra mouth gaping open in ragged smiles, only these mouths were halfway down their necks. But her finger wasn't pointing into the house, it was pointing at the lawn, where the moon and the fire picked out a pale design etched into the grass.

There was no time now, the glass on the downstairs windows exploded. Burton had to drag Mrs Sidhu away, her legs would not move for themselves.

A flock of birds took flight and whirled around the house, cawing. They were speaking to her. Screeching that she was a long way from levelling her pigeon-based karma debt, and that the man she was trying to help may well have killed two more people.

PART III

Hot water is the most common cooking ingredient in the world. Finding yourself in it is the least comfortable experience.

Life With a Knife, Mrs Sidhu's memoirs

MIDSUMMER DAY, 1997

Tonight they would walk the Scapegoat path. The path that crossed the causeway. The notch in the landscape where the sun would set just once a year.

It wasn't called Scapegoat path; the Druids would never have called it that. They were all into it, all joined up with nature and life and death and the circle of life that was wrapped up in the circle of stones. He was wearing white, they were all wearing white and in his right hand was the sickle, bright and shiny and new. He had ordered it made from a blacksmith, and it was said to be the same type of blade used by the ancient Druids to harvest mistletoe. He may have got that from a history book, or an Asterix book, it didn't matter, because there was truth in all books and sometimes real knowledge was buried away in fictional works. The collective subconscious worked that way, even Carl Jung thought the same, and Carl Jung was a famous psychotherapist, a founder of the science of psychiatry. I don't believe in Jung or Druids, he told himself, not a word of it. He was just executing a plan.

A cloud roiled away from the moon in the sky, and the whole scene was lit up like a stage set. You couldn't ask for a better night for a wedding, he thought, and chuckled to himself. She looked absolutely perfect: dressed in a single piece of cotton – a white sheath – and when she turned her eyes on the man, it was like she and he were made for each other. And they would be, they would be joined together, they were all waiting for them up there in the middle of the circle. Tonight was the night.

The path followed the spiral energies of the earth lines that lay beneath. Oh yes, someone had come and measured them. A bearded man with prongs that penetrated the soil had spent months, back in the sixties, making charts, proving once and for all that ley lines lay down there. But who cared? It was all nonsense, a means to an end, and the end was in sight.

For now, he put one foot in front of the other as he had from the beginning. You don't build anything overnight, you build it in steps. Like the E cult. E for enlightenment. That doesn't happen overnight. He looked around at the pitiful specimens he had collected so far. The toothless, the homeless, the hopeless. It didn't matter, they were also a means to an end. The couple were the main event, and they were far from hopeless.

A little bit of pride stirred in him. Good plans don't happen overnight; they have to be brought to life. Like the house out in the woods, which was built in steps, in careful stages so that it would last. But he knew it wouldn't last, because that was where it was all going to end. That would establish the legend for real.

The couple were within the circle now, crossing the boundary from this world to the next. He was standing before them, long hair, beard, classic messiah complex stuff. He had his face turned up to the sky and the comet was just visible. A smudge in amongst the clear twinkling stars. Their steps fell into synchronism, funny how that happened sometimes. She really was very beautiful. And he had seen the changes in her recently since they joined the group. The growing confidence, how these days she would speak up instead of falling silent. That she would have ideas, new passions. She had always been so shy, but now she she was someone else, someone new, reborn they all said, and, he reflected grimly, he was the one who had made it all possible.

He wanted her more than anything, but she was not his. There was still time to stop, to turn back.

'Are you sure you want this?' He asked them both but his eyes were on her only. And her eyes were on her husband-to-be. They smiled and nodded coyly with shy smiles, and his heart broke in two like dry clay.

'Then put out your hands.' There was no turning back.

They stood before him now, the sickle came up. Sacrifices would have to be made, they always had to be made. Before we move forward, the umbilical must be cut, blood is always spilt. They winced, sharp hot pain for an instant. They looked down at their hands, blood flowed in a line across his palm and hers too. She smiled and looked to the comet in the sky.

Tonight, they walked the Scapegoat path, tonight there would be sacrifices. Tonight, fire would cleanse everything.

18

'We've got a copycat killer,' Burton said.

Firemen were dousing the last of the embers on the ground floor. A blue tape kept the onlookers away. He would not be able to enter the house until it was declared safe. Safe, he grimaced. There were two bodies inside, he knew that much. He just hoped there was enough forensic evidence left after all the hosing down to be any use, but he had few doubts who the bodies belonged to: Kate and Tony Hammond.

His throat was still sharp from shouting, 'Get out! Get out of there!' The flames had been too intense for Burton to get to them. It was the second time the fire brigade had come to Benham village in a week. They knew the way, he observed grimly. The soaked timbers were still smoking, Burton hovering over the broken shell like a spectre.

'I saw Tony Hammond last night. He was on his way home,' Mrs Sidhu said. She was wrapped in a foil blanket, for shock more than cold. 'On his bicycle.'

'He might have been the target. Patrick's wrapped up in all the mystical Druid stuff. Maybe he knew about this

190

new building development. Patrick kills them both. Then he sets them up like dolls and torches the place.'

'What makes you think that?'

'There's clearly a place the fire started and there's clearly a load of accelerant. My guess is they were dead before the fire started. This is a copy of the Pollock suicides. If you need any more proof, then this is it.' Burton crouched on the lawn in front of the Hammond house. He pointed at the symbol etched into the front lawn. 'The Eye of Ra.'

Mrs Sidhu circled around outside the blue tape, like a jailer around a cell. 'There's an alternative explanation. William Mackie has unfinished business in this village.' She stroked her chin with one hand and thrust out the other like a blade. 'Like I said before, he's come back, and Wendy Calman found out, so he killed her.' Mrs Sidhu ignored Burton's dubious look and pushed on. 'OK, tell me this. Why aren't the Pollock suicides big news?' Mrs Sidhu asked.

'Because the E cult never got going. William Mackie's first success was his last. He fled the country. He died in a fire in the Columbian jungle eighteen years ago. He tried to set up his cult again, only this time he ballsed it up and ended up killing himself. If you play with fire . . .' He left it hanging.

'Deaths can be faked, Chief Inspector, especially one that's in a far-off place like a South American jungle.'

Burton shook his head. 'No, the local police sent Thames Valley Police their forensics evidence. It was confirmed as William Mackie.' He raised a finger as Mrs Sidhu opened her mouth to speak. 'And even if somehow he fooled forensics, and did fake his own death, why on earth come back? He's out of the country and in the clear.'

Mrs Sidhu's shoulders slumped. 'I don't know.'

Burton regretted his sarcasm immediately. 'Take it from a cop. Two deaths isn't a good result. But you got something right. You found Patrick's hideout and, in a sense, William Mackie has come back. He's come back in the brain of Patrick Kirby. Kirby's our man.' Burton's voice went hoarse. 'Kirby is copying Mackie's idea, only he's in more of a hurry. He's not waiting for them to do themselves in, he's giving them a little helping hand. And I'm going to get him before he does this again.'

Mrs Sidhu turned her key in the door and hoped and prayed that she did not wake anyone. The house was like an oven. Respected Sister-in-Law Daljeet was not one for ventilation. Mrs Sidhu tiptoed to the kitchen, where she opened the window and let some night air in. The red lights on her clock display told her it was two in the morning. She smelled of smoke. She undressed in the dark, brushing mud, ash and leaves from her hair. Taking a shower risked waking Daljeet and a lot of awkward questions.

She thought about what had happened in the burned-out house. For one moment, when madness was about to overtake her, she knew how she had reacted, and she had not expected it of herself. When the madness of Patrick's creation had reached out to her, she had not flinched. On the contrary she had reached out to it, wound herself around it, until of course she had realised what she was doing and recoiled; recoiled from it and from herself. The boy had talent, and talent of that kind lives on the margins of sanity. What lay over that edge? What did those who looked into the abyss see? Could

192

they ever come back from it? Mrs Sidhu hoped, for Patrick's sake, that they could.

Mrs Sidhu yawned and fell asleep, face down into the pillow.

There are many kinds of tea. There is the first tea of the day. There is the working cuppa. There is the half-forgotten cup, which when reached for in a moment of concentration meets the lips with wretched coldness. There's fine-leaf tea served in a pot on the lawn with lemon. But for thinking, there is only one kind of tea: Pathili Wali Chai.

Mrs Sidhu rubbed her eyes. Sleep had not refreshed her. Her bedroom had been like a steam oven, the air so thick you could carve it with a knife. Her dreams were also hot, unsettling and repetitive. The flames of the house on fire were fixed into her retinas. After barely two hours of sleep she gave up, padded down to the kitchen in gown and slippers, dawn glimmering behind the roofs of the houses opposite. She ran fresh water into a saucepan and snapped the gas on the stove. Her movements were addled this morning. The gas hissed out, filling her nose with its dull smell while her thick fingers took three goes to light the match. When the blue flames finally sprang to life it was with a small explosion which burned yellow in her eyes. She fumbled the pan onto the stove and settled in to wait.

At the centre of that retinal burn there was a shadow, a clearly seen silhouette of a man and a woman sitting, holding hands, leaning oddly to one side as the flames tore up the curtains and the walls. A man and a wife, burning like kindling. Mr and Mrs, be nice to one another. Were they nice to one another?

She compressed her lips and tapped them with her fore-finger and put the images out of her mind. Clear thinking, not emotion was needed here. Dr Calman was aware of the property deal between Edith, Dr Feelgood and Tony Hammond. It certainly gave motive for Eardley to kill Wendy. Whatever Eardley said, if there was even a hint that he had manipulated a patient into selling him land, he would be finished. He could easily have knocked on Dr Calman's door and killed her. And last night Mrs Sidhu had left Eardley in his office, but there was time enough for him to slay Kate and Tony and set the house on fire. But why would Eardley kill Tony and Kate Hammond? Tony Hammond was helping him and Kate was a valued client at the retreat.

The gas ring hissed and steam was gently rising from the water in the saucepan. She tore open a PG Tips teabag and the black leaves quickly formed a crust on the warming water. She added cloves, crushed cardamon pods with the flat of her knife until the seeds spilled onto the counter and perfumed the air. She took a deep breath and opened up her lungs.

Then there was the symbol etched out on the lawn in front of the Hammond house. The Eye of Ra, which both she and the chief inspector had seen in Patrick's lair. She had tried to ignore it, but the fact was, the more she tried to convince DCI Burton that Patrick was innocent, the more evidence appeared to point the finger right at him, and Mrs Sidhu was the one leading him right to it.

Pathili Wali Chai was an invention of her parents' generation. Arriving in a country where tea was served in a bag, boiling water poured on and then cold milk added seemed alien to them. They longed for the steaming, sweet, aromatic, churned, frothing drink of their homelands.

Nowadays, you could walk into a coffee shop and have yourself a chai latte, a vanilla chai, a chai of a thousand kinds, but back then choice was limited. Pathili Wali Chai was the answer. The secret to it was that it took time. The secret was the secret of all great culinary inventions: process.

There was one fixed point in Mrs Sidhu's mind. Patrick did not kill Dr Calman. Apple sauce recipes might not hold up in a court of law, but they were ironclad in the kitchen. She had to admit it looked like he had killed the Hammonds, but appearances could be deceptive. If that were true, there was no connection between the two deaths. Except that all of them were connected by the method of killing. More than that, the Hammonds' death was connected to the Pollock suicides by the staging of the bodies and the fire. There was a connection to the E cult. So all the deaths *were* connected, that was definite – and if Patrick didn't kill Dr Calman it meant he didn't kill the Hammonds either.

Mrs Sidhu grunted, threw her hands into the air and stamped her sandals. Where did that leave her? All these were dead ends. Bloody heck, three people were dead and she was getting nowhere. Her back hurt and her head was sore and her mouth tasted of burning house. She added milk to the brew on the stove, and the chai turned the colour of monsoon clouds at dusk.

So, she clenched her eyes shut. Without sleep she had to will herself to concentrate on separating them out. If Dr Calman was killed because of something she knew, it had to be something she knew about the E cult. There were too many connections for that to be a coincidence. So the Hammonds were also killed because of something they knew about the E cult. She opened her eyes.

The surface of the tea puckered and bubbled, foam rising to the surface like a milky brown tidal wave. Mrs Sidhu killed the gas ring before it reached the lip of the pan, and poured it, steaming hot, into a cup.

One last push. So if there was a connection between Dr Calman's death and the Hammond murders, it had to be Kate Hammond – not Tony Hammond, as Burton thought. The Pathili Wali Chai only made it halfway to her mouth. Kate was a client in Dr Calman's therapy group. Only five people knew what went on in that group. Two were dead and one was senile. That left one client and one other.

She put the cup back down. Hours later Tez found her cup of Pathili Wali Chai cold and untouched.

19

'Hey there.'

Sienna was crossing the garden with her notebook tucked under her arm when the voice rasped close to her ear. Jonny laid a tattooed hand on hers. She flinched. 'Don't be scared. I just wanted to say hi.'

'Uh, hi,' said Sienna. She tried to continue along the path but Jonny, with a movement of his sinuous hips, eased in front of her. She looked down at his hand, the tattoo gazed back up at her, it was of a single staring eye. He pulled his hand back quickly.

'Sienna, right? I'm Jonny.' He allowed his slow smile to do its work, like it probably had on a thousand impressionable girls. 'But you know that. I saw you in the session with Dr Calman on Friday. I guess I was still a little high when I came in here and I can't even remember what I said. I noticed you taking notes. Maybe I could take a look in your little book there.'

Sienna clamped the red notebook tight between her arm and her side. 'I can't do that. It's confidential.'

'It's my own words, what's the problem?'

Sienna was unmoved. 'You'd need to talk to Dr Eardley about that.'

Jonny's slow smile eased back down. 'Yeah, I guess I will,' he said stiffly, adding, 'I'm a nice guy, you know. I notice you have a great look, stylish. Let me know if I can help you in any way to achieve your dreams.' With that he turned and sidled away.

Sienna realised she had been holding her breath. She eased her chest, in the way Dr Eardley had taught her, concentrating on each breath as her chest rose and fell. When she was ready, she drew herself up straight and walked on.

She hadn't got very far when an arm reached round from behind a bush and yanked her in. She yelped half a cry before a hand covered her mouth.

'I have a new theory,' Mrs Sidhu whispered urgently. 'I wonder if we could have another chat. In private.'

'Mmm mmm mmm.'

'What?'

'Mmmm mmm mmm.'

Mrs Sidhu realised she still had Sienna's mouth covered. She released it and Sienna's wrist at the same time.

'It's only me – Mrs Sidhu.'

Sienna rubbed her wrist. 'I can see that now. Did you have to grab me like that?' She glowered.

'I'm sorry. I haven't had much sleep. If I could take a look at your notebooks from last week?'

Sienna hugged the notebook to her chest. 'Not you too.' Mrs Sidhu shot her an enquiring look. 'Jonny Snakeskin just asked me the same thing.'

'Did he? Now that is interesting.'

'Anyway, neither of you can look in the notes; they're confidential.'

'Can you tell me what Kate was suffering from?'

Sienna's eyes opened wide. She put one long hand on her chest. 'I can't tell you that. I said when you started here that all those details were confidential.'

'Of course, I was completely forgetting. Forgive me, please.' Sienna let out a breath and nodded, relieved. Mrs Sidhu continued earnestly. 'Ask anyone in Slough, Mrs Sidhu is not a poker or a pryer. Mrs Sidhu is very discreet, it's part of the Sidhu Fine Catering Services promise, discretion is guaranteed. I wouldn't even have asked if it wasn't important in helping Patrick. But put the question from your mind. Mrs Sidhu has offended your professional code, and that is the last thing I wanted to do.'

The pause hung for a little while. 'You think it could help Patrick?' Sienna said.

Mrs Sidhu raised an eyebrow. 'It might.'

Across the garden, Eardley stopped talking and looked in their direction. 'Is everything all right, Sienna?'

'Yes, everything is fine. Just talking about . . . the lunch menu.'

Eardley nodded and went back to his conversation.

Sienna grabbed Mrs Sidhu by the arm and whispered, 'What are you doing? Stephen can't know about us. I told you.'

Mrs Sidhu apologised and walked alongside Sienna. 'Come on, VFC meeting.' There was mischief in her eyes and it was infectious.

Sienna grinned. 'VFC.' She put her hand on Mrs Sidhu's like they were taking an oath.

* * *

199

'You swear not to tell anyone?' Sienna said. Mrs Sidhu nodded.

They went again to the secret garden; they had made it their place, a fitting headquarters from which Sienna could save Patrick. 'OK, Kate was seeing men.'

Mrs Sidhu's nose wrinkled. 'You mean she was some kind of nymphomaniac?'

Sienna laughed, squealing and covering her mouth at how her words must have sounded. 'No! I mean she literally imagined she was being followed around by men. Or just one man, it was hard to tell because she never saw his face.'

They sat on the grass. Sienna twirled a pink wildflower in her fingers. Mrs Sidhu kicked her sandals off and buried her toes in moist grass. 'Oh, that feels good.' She peeled back the cellophane from freshly cut sandwiches, offering the silver platter to Sienna.

Sienna's hand hovered. 'Should we? Aren't these for them?' She jerked a thumb back towards the tightly wound business leaders.

'I have a feeling my skills will stretch to making another round of sandwiches. Is it not possible that Kate did have a stalker after all?' Mrs Sidhu asked.

Sienna plunged in and started to eat while talking rapidly. 'Maybe. I mean someone killed her. Do you think it was him? The ghost was real? There's no connection with Wendy?' When Mrs Sidhu shrugged, Sienna shook her head. 'But no, you see, that was what Kate thought at first, so she went to the police and they looked into it. She never got any suspicious messages, or phone calls, and she never got a picture of him or anything, she never had any witnesses. The police said they couldn't put a restraining

200

order on a ghost. It was in her head. I know, I sat in on the sessions with Dr Calman.'

'What did Dr Eardley say?'

'He didn't know. Well, he knows now, because when Wendy died, he took over and got her notes. Kate wanted it confidential so it was strictly between her and her therapist. Mr Hammond never knew either. She never wanted him to see her as sick or unwell.'

'It's not actually rehab, though, is it? Should she not have gone to a specialist?'

'Wendy was qualified. It's what Kate wanted. We were close to home for her. When she knew Mr Hammond was going to be away for work, she would spend the night in the retreat.'

'And while she was staying here, did she ever see this man?'

Sienna pulled at a loose strand of hair for a moment. 'I don't honestly know. Anyway, how could she? He wasn't real. It was in her head, wasn't it?' She looked at Mrs Sidhu with worry growing on her face.

'Of course it was,' Mrs Sidhu reassured her. 'You don't have to worry, Patrick will be back with you safe soon. You'll be back in this garden together. I promise.'

Sienna struggled with something. Her face went blank, her voice was flat. 'Patrick,' she said, her brow wrinkled. 'Yes, of course, Patrick?' Sienna shook her head clear and got up abruptly. She looked around her as if in an unfamiliar place. 'I have to go now. Dr Eardley will be waiting for me.' Sienna leapt up and scuttled out through the break in the hedges.

Mrs Sidhu followed. 'Wait, can you tell me which room Kate stayed in?' Sienna told her and left Mrs Sidhu deep in her own thoughts. 'Odd girl.'

20

It was daylight and Burton still crouched by the symbol on the lawn. He put a gloved finger to the soil and sniffed. The choking tang of ammonia reached his nostril and he pulled back. 'Bleach,' he said to no one in particular.

'One way to weed the lawn, guv. Another hot one, sir.' Dove was standing behind him, legs astride, sweating freely and looking at the skies. With a look Burton enquired why he was holding a file. 'Forensics results are back on Wendy Calman.'

Burton raised an eyebrow. 'Good. That was quick.'

'Must be my charm. They were very keen to get me on my way. Anyway, the interesting thing is the wound on her neck. It had traces of iron and rust, but it also had traces of gold in there. Gold leaf, they think.'

Burton stood and dusted off his knees. 'Gold? From jewellery?' But Dr Calman had not been wearing any jewellery. What else did you put gold leaf on that you could cut someone's throat with? There was no time for Burton to ponder that.

'Sir?' A flustered uniformed constable was calling out, walking towards him with quick strides. 'Sir, there's been another report, sir.' When Burton enquired what of, the harassed constable collected her thoughts before replying. 'Of this symbol on someone's lawn. Happened yesterday. This is the address.'

Burton took the piece of paper. 'If it happened yesterday, why am I only finding out about it now?'

The constable stuttered before answering, 'No one took it very seriously, sir. We were all looking for Patrick Kirby. But now it's turned up here . . .' The constable did not complete her sentence, partly because there was nothing more to say, but mainly because Burton was already halfway to his car. 'Dove?'

'Yes, guv?' Dove adjusted his shirt, which was sticking to him in a number of places, and then pulled at his crotch, which was sticking to him in even worse places. Burton changed his mind. 'Dove, stay here.' He eyed the constable. She looked hygienic. 'Constable, come with me.'

Dove looked disappointed; the constable looked even more flustered. Burton started his engine.

Anyone watching Mrs Sidhu now would have been curious, to say the least. She crept between trees and around herbaceous borders while snatching glances up at the house. 'Oh, I am sorry,' she said, almost tripping over a small group of meditators in bright lycra sitting cross-legged in the grass. She turned to the nearest one, an earnest-looking finance officer for a major global accounting company. 'Excuse me, but from down there, can you see into that window?' The finance officer shook her head and concentrated instead on convincing herself that her life was like

203

a gushing waterfall and that somehow breathing regularly would make up for the next twenty years, wondering what her children looked like and if her husband still loved her when she barely had time to look at him. That's what Mrs Sidhu imagined she was doing, but then Mrs Sidhu had a very active imagination. An imagination that was currently whirling with the idea that Kate Hammond had a real honest-to-goodness stalker. What she was looking for was some evidence that would prove that it was possible to watch Kate, and even better, some evidence that someone had.

Mrs Sidhu moved on to the next spot. 'Oh dammit,' she said to herself as another promising location yielded no view of Kate's window and another group of disturbed de-stressers, an art therapy class this time. 'Very nice lines,' Mrs Sidhu said, 'but if you're drawing that woman over there, it's a good likeness, and you've certainly caught the shape of her, very sexy.' The director of a supply chain disruptor's cheeks flushed red, as did those of the woman (the marketing director of a start-up) whose anatomy was in question. Mrs Sidhu moved on, leaving him to cast his eyes to the ground, and her to zip up her fleece top and glance shyly at him. Romance had blossomed on less fruitful trees, Mrs Sidhu knew that.

She stumbled on with her mission, but a half hour later she slumped herself onto a beanbag and sighed. There seemed to be nowhere that allowed someone to spy on Kate's room. Nowhere, she thought, that was on solid ground. A new idea sprang to her fertile mind.

She edged her way into one of the planted areas, and slowly one edge of the window came into view. She moved another foot to the right. She could see more of the window.

She raised a foot to take one more step, the step that would surely yield a full-frontal view right into the room, when she stopped herself. Luckily, she looked down first. There, next to her sandalled feet, was exactly what she was looking for. In the loose earth were two deep depressions: large, heavy footprints. Footprints made by boots, with a zig-zag tread and a distinctive cut in the third tread on the right boot. She tapped her pursed lips with her finger. Now, she had seen a pair of boots somewhere.

'Just look at what he did to my lawn.'

It was the same symbol, drawn out in pale brown grass against a sea of green. Burton leaned in and smelled the same aroma of bleach.

'When are the police going to do something to protect ordinary people?' Tamzin Grey assessed Burton coolly.

Burton cast his eyes around the ordinary two-hundred-acre plot of land, the ordinary seven-bedroom house. He was about to make his speech, the one about doing everything they could to protect the community, but her manner made it clear she was in a hurry to get away.

'That's what I'm here to do. Find out everything I can.' He smiled back. Burton was standing on the lawn, with the constable taking notes. 'So he was standing here?'

Tamzin shook her head. 'He was much further down the garden when I saw him.'

Burton reversed his steps and bade Tamzin stay where she was. She tutted until he was in the right place. 'That's it. And he said something.'

'What did he say?'

Tamzin shrugged. 'He was mumbling about all sorts of things. Numbers, something about what my number was.

A raffle ticket, that was it. I thought originally he'd come from the village fete committee. That I'd won a prize.'

'And then he poured bleach on your lawn?'

'No, no, no.' She tapped her foot, her large jaw hardened. 'Look, is this going to take much longer? I mean, the damage is done now, I'll just have to get it re-turfed. I'm sorry to have troubled you. If we're done?'

In long, unhurried strides, Burton made it to the front door in time to stop the door closing. 'There is a bit more, ma'am, if you don't mind.'

Tamzin checked her watch again. 'Then you'd better come into the back garden. I'm afraid I'm getting hot.'

Burton looked to the unrelenting sun in the sky. 'I'm hot too.'

'Not like me you're not.' She disappeared inside. Wearing a puzzled look, Burton and the constable followed her.

21

There were the boots, in the corner, sole down on a boot rack.

'I brought you a mid-morning snack.' Mrs Sidhu entered the office with a tray.

Eardley, bent over some reading, looked inclined to refuse. The smell of coffee and her freshly baked pastry rose up and changed his mind. He stopped reading. Mrs Sidhu arranged cup, plate and fork and tried to work out how she would get across the room to look at the boots.

'You will have heard about the fire at the Hammond house.' She was looking into Dr Eardley's little round spectacles. Funny, on the back of his book jackets he wore sleek oblong ones, the type Mrs Sidhu thought of as 'media' glasses. She wondered idly when he had changed to the little round ones and if it was just another piece of theatre, a look designed to give an impression.

Eardley nodded gravely. 'Terribly sad. Some kind of accident?' he asked. 'You seem to know DCI Burton, has he said anything?'

She placed a clean white napkin across his lap. 'I am but a humble chef, he tells me as little as he can.' That at least was no lie. 'I'm sure the police will get to the bottom of it.' She cast her eyes around the room, until they fell on the bookcase, which gave her an idea. 'My concerns are more for my own state of mind. You know, I've always taken inspiration from your books.' She jerked her head towards the bookcase. 'May I?'

'Help yourself, borrow any book you want.'

Good, that would get her halfway to the boot rack.

'This smells divine.' Eardley bit into the pain au chocolate and sipped the coffee, her own French blend that she had sourced to go especially well with her pastry. Eardley's eyes misted over; a childish grin played across his face. 'We used to holiday in France when I was a boy.'

Mrs Sidhu had started to deviate her path towards the boots, but deviated it back towards the bookshelves when Eardley looked over at her. 'I'm taking some solace in words too. I'm reading Wendy's book manuscript, her theories on William Mackie are quite something.'

Mrs Sidhu stared at the shelves blankly. She had to get Eardley thinking. 'What if he's back?' Eardley's eyebrows rose over the glasses in surprise. 'What if William Mackie has returned to Benham village?'

'Now that is an interesting idea.' He swivelled his chair towards the window and settled his eyes on the distant horizon, just as she knew he would. 'But it tells me more about you than about the case. You really are a very fascinating woman, Mrs Sidhu. This imagination of yours is quite something. I may use you as a case history yet. Why would William Mackie return here – not forgetting the fact that he's dead?' He tapped Dr Calman's manuscript.

Mrs Sidhu was finally at the object of her search. Now she was up close, she could see that the boots were caked in mud. She quietly picked them up and turned them over. No good, the soles were stuck up with thick clay.

'Unless you believe in ghosts, Mrs Sidhu. Not sure I'd put that past you.' Mrs Sidhu jumped. The voice seemed to come from inside her head. She turned slowly. Eardley was so close he must have whispered in her ear. She could smell coffee on his breath. He took a savage chunk out of the pastry, shedding big flakes of choux over the rich, red carpet. He was smiling. 'What's so interesting about the boots?'

Mrs Sidhu steadied herself, making her voice natural. 'I just noticed how dirty they were. They could use a good clean.' A shower of dry mud fell to the carpet. 'Kate Hammond believed in ghosts, didn't she? That's what she called the man who was stalking her.'

The smile diminished on Eardley's face. He swallowed his delicious mouthful as if it was a brick. He turned a hard gaze on her. 'How did you know that? Only the people at the sessions would know that.'

Once again she cursed herself, for speaking before thinking. She mustn't get Sienna into trouble. 'I must have overheard when I was serving lemonade. I try not to listen in.' She looked into the round spectacles. 'I can barely understand the technical stuff. I mean, you psychiatrists have a different language, don't you?'

Eardley relaxed, went back to his desk and allowed himself a sip of coffee. 'It is a very involved profession, but I am not actually a psychiatrist myself,' he said stiffly.

He was becoming suspicious; she needed to put him at his ease. The round glasses gave her an idea. 'You wouldn't know it, to hear you talk on the subject. You know, when I came here, I loved your popular books, but I can see there's a real depth behind them.' That did the trick. Eardley relaxed, and Mrs Sidhu poured it on. 'I mean, all those people have academic qualifications, but you've lived in the real world.' Funny, the human mind, you can spend all day teasing people's secrets out of their skulls and understanding how their brains worked, but there wasn't a person on earth who was immune to a bit of flattery. 'For instance, I notice you dedicated your first book to Emily. Is that your wife? Was she the one who inspired you?'

Eardley spoke in a thin voice. 'Something like that, yes.' His face fell and his eyes searched the room for something that he could not find. Mrs Sidhu worried that she had poked at a sore point, like a dentist finding a cavity. His pain seemed very real, no pretence or theatre there. Regretting the pain she had caused, Mrs Sidhu changed the subject.

'I suppose with Mr Hammond dead, the deal for the land and The Sanctuary won't go ahead.'

'Not at all. Edith has already signed, and Hammond Homes is already being run by its vice president. A big company like that can't afford to stop, even in death.'

So if the killer's plan had been to stop the development, it hadn't worked. More strength to her theory that Kate was the target, not Tony.

A knock at the door was followed by Arif's head craning around. 'Dr Eardley, your session is due to start in the garden.'

Eardley grunted. 'Uh, I was forgetting, I am taking over Dr Calman's group, or at least what's left of it. Poor Kate.

I'd better go.' He walked to the door. Finally, a chance for Mrs Sidhu to knock the mud off the soles of the boots and get a clear look at the tread. Except that Eardley stopped in the doorway for a moment. 'And yes, those boots could use a clean. Arif, could you?'

Mrs Sidhu watched on in mute frustration as Arif roughly took the boots from Mrs Sidhu and followed his master out of the door. She ground her teeth. Another dead end, what was she going to tell Sienna? She was no closer to helping Patrick, and no closer to understanding why three people were dead.

This was when Mrs Sidhu's eyes fell on the manuscript. Her heart beat a little quicker. This was her chance, her chance to read Dr Calman's book. There was one problem.

Arif was hovering in the doorway, watching Mrs Sidhu while trying to keep an eye on his master. He had a black plastic name badge pinned to his tunic at his breast. Begovic was an unusual name, she thought, and in her mind there were echoes of war and chaos. 'Arif, I'm going to need you to pitch in on Patrick's duties,' Eardley called out, already well down the corridor. 'Come on, I haven't got all day.'

With great reluctance, Arif was forced to abandon his vigil over Mrs Sidhu. When he was gone, Mrs Sidhu reached for the manuscript. Something made her pause.

It was wrong to steal, Mrs Sidhu knew that, in fact she had instilled this into her son and her own nephews and nieces from the very first moment they sat on her knee. Borrowing, on the other hand, was the dancing partner of sharing, and sharing was the essence of being a good citizen. Was it not Dr Eardley himself who had said to borrow any book she wanted?

Moments later, Mrs Sidhu was leaning heavily to one side as she made her way to her bottle-green Nissan Micra. She hauled the bag two-handed onto the back seat. She needed to get some serious reading done.

Tamzin Grey was heading rapidly down her back garden. Burton was alarmed to see that she was shedding clothes as quickly as she could. 'Can you possibly imagine what it's like having the menopause, Chief Inspector.' Burton had to admit he could not. 'No surprise there. Men don't have any idea.' She was down to a bra and panties. 'It's like hot ants crawling all over your skin. Do you think you can imagine that?'

Burton flushed red. 'I think I can.' Burton was doing his best to walk in the same direction as her while looking in another direction completely. 'Perhaps we should come back at a better time? Or maybe we could do this at the station?'

Tamzin ran a hand over her skin as if brushing away hot ants. 'Drives you mad. Come on, let's just get this over and done with.' And there went the bra.

Burton's cheeks reddened. 'Getting back to the man who came calling. It was yesterday, you said.'

'That's right. I didn't notice at first that he was carrying a bottle of bleach. I told him to sod off, and when I looked out again he'd done his bit of handiwork. I mean, all these people are constantly on about going green, but is it green or eco to go round killing perfectly good patches of grass?'

Burton admitted it wasn't. They were heading towards some trees, and as yet Burton had not spotted a swimming pool. Tamzin ducked under a tree branch and disappeared.

Burton glared at the constable. 'Go in there and take her statement.' She shook her head. 'All right, come with me and witness that this isn't an inappropriate . . . whatever.'

From among the trees, Tamzin called out. 'For crying out loud, Chief Inspector, get over it. I haven't got a lot of time today and I need cold water.'

He took a deep breath and entered, with a constable by his side. They were in time to see her jump into the water, disappear, then breach, wet and slick like a dolphin. She let out a long breath. 'Such a relief.' She began an athletic breaststroke, her arms and legs spanning and disappearing into the deep green water. 'River swimming. It's great for the menopause. Female or male, of course.'

Burton didn't hear her. He looked around, his jaw hanging open. They were in a deep green glade of trees split by a wide and meandering river. He knew this area. The only river was the Thames and its course did not bring it through the middle of private land. 'You mean you've got a stretch of river going through the back of your garden.'

'One thing you need to know about me. I don't like sharing,' she said through clenched white teeth. 'So I had a section of the Thames siphoned off so it goes across my land. The rivers authority were very good about it. It rejoins a bit further up.'

Burton's eyes followed the path of the water away and down, and he wondered how much it cost to put all this in and make it look like it had been here for hundreds of years.

There was a blue two-seat kayak on the bank. 'You like your outdoor sports.'

'Feel free to borrow the kayak. Or, if you're hot, why not jump in. If you're shy, I'm sure I've got some men's trunks back there somewhere. People do leave them lying around.' She winked.

Burton cleared his throat, smiled faintly and declined. 'Just as I feared. You get to an age where as a woman you become invisible.' She picked a leaf of weed off her cheek then floated on her back. Tamzin Grey may have broken the fifty barrier, but she was far from invisible and she knew it.

Burton looked away. 'Can you describe the man, the one who decorated your lawn?' She took her time filling in a description that Burton already knew would fit Patrick Kirby to a tee. A white guy with blond dreadlocks, large frame, torn jeans.

She swam to the far bank where a basket sat incongruously stacked with clean, white towels. She wrapped herself in one and began drying her hair with another. 'So why would Thames Valley Police send a chief inspector down to Benham over a bit of garden graffiti?'

Burton realised that he was going to have to break two pieces of bad news to her. 'Do you know the Hammonds? Tony and Kate. You may not have heard that unfortunately they died last night. There was a fire at their home.'

Tamzin towelled her scalp vigorously. 'I had no idea. Poor Kate and Tony.' She wrapped the towel round her and sat down. 'Is that a coincidence? Two fires in one week, after Dr Calman as well?'

'In Dr Calman's case it was an oven fire – we think that part of it was accidental. In the Hammonds' case the fire was set deliberately.'

'What a horrible way to die.'

'That's not how they died. They were murdered first, in the same manner as Wendy Calman. Throats cut.'

Tamzin rubbed her own throat. 'That's terrible. But I don't understand, what has that got to do with me?'

Burton frowned, there was no easy way to say this, so he'd better just get on with it. 'There was a symbol bleached onto the lawn in front of the Hammond house. It was identical to the one in front of yours. The Eye of Ra. It's Egyptian.' He let this sink in.

'So, you think that this nutter is after me too?' She shook her head. 'I don't believe it. What would he want with me?'

'That's what I don't know yet. He was the gardener at the Benham House Retreat. Do you know it? One of those new age places.' Burton stifled an internal grimace. Saying 'new age' almost certainly showed his old age. There must be a more up-to-date expression.

'Of course. It's a mental wellness retreat.' Burton wrote that down for future reference. 'I have a client up there, in rehab.'

'Client? Are you a therapist too?'

Tamzin's laugh was deep-voiced and throaty. 'Need a therapist, more like. No, I'm in the music business. Ex-wife, ex-agent, ex everything to Jonny Snakeskin. Jonny's driven completely by his urges. Rock-star stuff like drink, drugs, sex, public urination – it's a rich tapestry. There's two things he can't shake off. His addiction to powerful substances, and his old girlfriends. I'm the latter, in case it wasn't obvious. He left me for the younger model, then a runway model, and a string of them. But when he's low he comes back, and I'm a fool, so I moved to this village so I can be round the corner from his favourite home away from home.'

Burton rubbed the back of his neck. 'Let me guess: Wendy Calman was his therapist.' When she nodded,

215

Burton pushed a little further. 'And Jonny Snakeskin is no stranger to your house.'

'Of course not. He stays over all the time when he's had enough of the asylum. He was here the night poor old Wendy Calman got hers.'

Burton's eyebrows were tingling. 'You getting all this, Constable?' She nodded, scribbling rapidly.

'And last night?'

'He stayed over again.'

'So you're an agent with benefits?' he said.

Tamzin laughed again; it was a laugh that Burton liked, just like his ex-wife's laugh. 'The last thing I need in my bed is an overgrown man-child.' Just like his ex-wife. 'I'm here to get Jonny clean and get his career back on track. He hasn't had a download that's gone over ten thousand hits since "Into the Night". If you can remember that one?'

DCI Burton nodded distantly; he did remember it. Another sign of old age, but he had something else on his mind. The prickling sensation spread up from his neck onto his scalp. He was pretty sure he knew what connection Patrick was making. He needed to talk to Stephen Eardley urgently.

'Stay inside, lock your door, and if you remember anything else, call me straight away.' He dropped a card on the blue kayak. 'The constable here will stay with you while you pack some things, you can't stay here tonight.'

'Where's your aunty Daljeet?' By arriving late last night and leaving early this morning she had avoided her respected sister-in-law. Since the 'India House Incident' (as she was calling it) she didn't know if she could trust herself to keep her emotions in check. Her husband had told his

216

sister but not her. She glared at the photo of her husband. Her jaw tightened. Well, that was just fine. It was clear who her husband had loved more. No wonder she could barely remember his face.

They were in Mrs Sidhu's kitchen where Tez was mooching through the fridge, throwing out cabbages, carrots and cucumbers until finally he reached the real treasure, a chocolate yoghurt. 'She went out, with Varma. Now, do you mind? I want some time with my yoghurt.'

'Varma?' Oh great, not satisfied with stealing her husband's memory, she was going to take Varma too. By the day after tomorrow she'd have shares in Mrs Sidhu's business. 'What's she doing with Varma?'

Tez didn't know.

'This is what she does. She's the dalek, she sucks the joy out of everything.'

'We had fun at Bekonscot. You should have come.' Tez licked the spoon. He gave her a sly look. 'So, when were you going to tell me about the big move to India?'

There were pots, pans and frying pans everywhere. Mrs Sidhu moved from one to the next, each one needing urgent attention. 'We are not moving to India.' She grabbed for a panhandle and burned her fingers.

'I know that.' Tez peeled the lid from his yoghurt. 'Why would I want to move to India? I've got loads going on here.' Mrs Sidhu decided not to tell Tez that eating yoghurt in your pants wasn't a career move. He continued: 'Makes a lot of sense for you, though – put your feet up, retire.'

Mrs Sidhu doused her fingers under the cold tap while prodding at some burning onions with her free hand. 'Does it look like I can retire?' She added a dash of water to one pot, and a dash of cumin to another. 'Tez, I didn't want to tell you this, but your father never told me about the house in India. He kept it secret. He and your aunty plotted it all behind my back.' There, it was out, the betrayal.

But instead of anger, Tez was nodding sagely. 'Makes sense. If they'd told you, you wouldn't let them do it. You never do any fun stuff.'

'Don't you see, this is what she does. Daljeet the Dalek destroys everything.'

Tez tapped the side of the yoghurt pot. 'Maybe you're the dalek.' He drifted away to the living room, leaving Mrs Sidhu speechless.

How could this be happening? First Daljeet turned her husband away from her, now she was doing the same with her son. Well, you know what? There was one thing she was going to stop feeling guilty about right this minute.

If Daljeet and Varma were now in communication, she was going to find out that Varma gave her the day off and she'd been lied to. This had weighed heavily on Mrs Sidhu's conscience, but no longer. That was not going to play on Mrs Sidhu's mind at all, because one lie begets another. That was in all the major religious texts and in a couple of TED Talks too, and if it wasn't, it should be.

Mrs Sidhu came to the fuming end of her blazing train of thought and finished prepping her smouldering food. She had other things on her mind, the lumpy weight in her bag told her. She needed time and space and a place to read Dr Calman's masterwork.

She heard the key in the front door rattle and saw two silhouettes through the rippled glass of the front door. Both of them! Mrs Sidhu would have to deal with Daljeet and Varma later. She grabbed her bag to her chest and marched upstairs to the only place she was guaranteed any privacy. She raced to claim her place of refuge, barely making it before the front door creaked open.

22

They were in a semicircle. Eardley was at the centre. Jonny Snakeskin lay on the grass looking up at the sky through dark glasses. Edith was staring into space, Elliot holding the grips of her wheelchair. There was an empty cushion for Kate. Sienna took her own seat, beside them, her notebook on her lap, pen poised. She kept her head down, but they would be watching her. Most of all she felt his gaze on her; since this morning, she was aware that Jonny was watching her. Perhaps he had always been watching her. Perhaps when she had looked at him, he always quickly looked away, pretending to be interested in something else. That was it, and that new reality began cementing itself into Sienna's mind. When she took her cushion, next to Edith's wheelchair, her face was flushed and she kept her eyes on the ground while she wrestled her notebook open and twisted the lid off her pen.

'OK, so you're our therapist now. I want to set some new ground rules. Is she going to keep taking notes?' Jonny drawled. 'I hate it.'

Dr Eardley looked somewhere into the distance, while making it somehow clear he was addressing Jonny. 'Now why does that make you angry?'

'Because it's stupid to let her do that. If I'm supposed to stop drinking, then she can sure as hell stop writing.' He smouldered for a while, and during that while Sienna scrawled on her notepad.

Edith, interrupted, tapped her walking stick. 'Could we get started, m'dears?'

Dr Eardley smiled. 'Someone's in a hurry today.'

'I'm losing my mind, Doctor, I'm fully aware of that and it is the curse I live with, but while I have a couple of marbles still rolling around to appreciate all you're doing for me, maybe you can actually do something for me.'

Dr Eardley considered all this with a lightly amused smile while he cast his gaze kindly on some nearby bushes. He paced around the little circle. 'We are going to have to address the elephant in the room first.'

'We're in a freaking garden, man, not a room,' Jonny said.

'Two of our number, Dr Calman and Kate Hammond, are not here. They are dead, alongside Tony Hammond. How do we feel about that?' There was a pause. Sienna stopped writing. 'Is no one going to say anything?' Eardley looked dismayed. 'Then I'll say it. The Hammonds deserved everything they got.'

Edith put her hands to her mouth. 'Shame on you,' she said. Sienna too was shocked. Jonny Snakeskin applauded, enjoying the chaos. 'This is more like it.'

Eardley raised a hand to quell the noise. 'It's a learning moment. We will all die, one day.' The group settled down. 'Their deaths are a learning opportunity. You own your futures, that is what you have to open your eyes to.

Kate and Tony failed to own theirs, and they perished sadly in a fire. An accident, but what do I say in my fifteenth book, *Your Life: You Made It, You Own It . . .* ?' he waited for the droning chorus to come back at him.

'There are no accidents,' they intoned.

He smiled. 'That seems extreme, I know, but if we can accept that is what happened, then we can use that. Because if we're responsible for our own deaths, then we are responsible for our own lives. Once you feel that, in reality, in your hearts, you will be back in the driving seat, no longer passengers. When we die, it will be at our own hands. In our own gift. That is transcendence, that is mastery, that is the secret to living for ever. Their deaths are the greatest gift.'

'That could be very timely advice, but I'm not sure how much control they had over their deaths. The Hammonds' deaths weren't accidental, and they weren't suicide. They were murdered, all of them.' DCI Burton was there, standing as tall and unmoving as a statue.

Eardley blinked. 'I see, Chief Inspector. That is unexpected. Do you want to talk in private?'

'Actually, I think this involves all of you.'

Jonny and Edith looked at each other. Eardley remained smiling and impassive. 'We've lost enough time this morning, Chief Inspector, so you'd better just join in.' He waved Burton towards Kate's vacant cushion.

Burton scowled. 'Maybe we could all go inside.' We could sit on chairs, with a nice solid wooden desk between us, he wanted to add. Instead his enquiry came out as more of a plea and he hated the weakness in his voice. Eardley firmly gestured him to the cushion, and Burton took it.

*   *   *

222

The sound of water has a profound effect on the human mind. As a species we come from water, only in relatively recent times dragging ourselves onto land and evolving legs, but the sound of it is still in our ears. Mrs Sidhu felt the calming power of water rushing, gurgling, swirling and pouring, and finally coughing to a halt, followed by the discreet whine of the cistern filling. She lowered the lid, sat heavily and rested her head on her fists. Now this was a place to think.

Mrs Sidhu was a fast reader. Her head was a sponge for any kind of knowledge, and as a child she devoured books, reading them from cover to cover so fast that her mother would take her to the library twice a week. Within an hour, she had consumed most of Dr Calman's manuscript, speed-reading the heavy parts and pausing over the salacious details.

Dr Eardley was wrong, Wendy Calman wasn't such a terrible storyteller, not when she was on to something. It was a book both serious and exciting. It was just missing a conclusion. At its centre was William Mackie, the high priest of the cult that had all but vanished when he did.

The spare upstairs bathroom was the ideal place to get away from things. When Mrs Sidhu had detected quiet lulls in the house below, she had rounded up useful items, even gone to the library. A stack of books on symbolism teetered on a foldout table next to her laptop and a pad of Post-it notes. The Wi-Fi signal was strong up here, thank goodness. She had also gathered up her glasses, a foldout garden chair, some cushions, another table to put the manuscript on, a pencil and paper to make notes and even a kettle, which she was running off an extension lead that ran through the gap under the door. She was calling it her 'Toilet Office' and she was really getting things done.

She sipped on a cup of hot Darjeeling and kept reading, underlining passages that caught her attention:

William Mackie blended ancient myth, folklore, and Druidic rites and mixed it with space-age and science fiction themes. I have spoken to people who have met him and described him as handsome, charming and likeable. Others call him a predator. One thing is known. He arrived in Benham village in the spring of 1995. By summer 1996 he had gained a small following among a group of homeless people. By the following summer he was responsible for the deaths of two wealthy, respectable locals. Justin and Sandra Pollock poisoned themselves in their home. Afterwards, Mackie set the house on fire in order to send them on their way through a portal into another universe, where they would rub shoulders with Egyptian gods and little green men and live happily ever after.

Someone ran the taps downstairs, and the pipes in the bathroom gurgled. Mrs Sidhu scooshed herself further into her throne and plucked a chocolate macaroon from a plate beside the knitted toilet-roll holder. She read on.

Mackie was convinced that the Hale–Bopp comet was a doomsday harbinger, and that the portal to the new world, a world he called 'Balamshazar', was through the stone circle at Benham village known locally as the Ten Men. This would open only once, on Midsummer Day at midnight. The ancient Druids had built the circle knowing all this, and had spoken to Mackie via an alien presence he called 'Xerbor', a four foot 'grey' who visited him often.

Mrs Sidhu stopped reading and frowned. If the portal was the stone circle, why did the Pollocks die at home? Surely the whole thing should have happened at the Ten Men? The inconsistencies were frustrating. Mrs Sidhu took a break to reflect on what a hodgepodge of made-up nonsense Mackie had concocted, and what demons had chased his sanity down the plughole of life.

She took a look around. She was hiding in a bathroom so she could read half-baked nonsense, just so she could avoid her sister-in-law and the embarrassment she felt because her husband did not share more of his life with her. Maybe we all need to think twice before pointing the finger. Mackie created a make-believe world because the real world was uncomfortable and hard and, more often than not, something he wasn't ready for. It was a retreat to a childish safe space. Only it had been anything but safe for the Pollocks, for Edith's son and his wife.

It was Xerbor who prophesied that the world would end and gave Mackie the title 'destroyer of worlds'.

Warn them, for I am returned, Death, destroyer of worlds. Now Mrs Sidhu recollected why the phrase was so familiar to her. It was like what Oppenheimer, the nuclear scientist, had said when he built the first atom bomb: 'I am become Death, destroyer of worlds.' This was itself a quote from Hindu mythology. Mackie had blended world culture and myth and borrowed from other cults to create a new belief system, and not a word of it rang true. He could barely decide if he was a reincarnated Druid, pharaoh or alien being. It was hollow, made-up even, certainly badly thought through.

So, the central question was: how had he driven the Pollocks – a happy, newly married couple with money

225

and prospects – to their strange deaths? They were intelligent people. How had they come to believe in such obviously fabricated gibberish? She read on:

'The Eye of Ra was central to William Mackie's belief system, a potent symbol that he used to confer authority on himself.' She was reading out loud to herself. 'This was the one consistent piece of symbology that he used.'

Mrs Sidhu turned from the manuscript to a library book, riffling through pages until she found the entry she had marked out. There, her finger traced the words. 'The Eye of Ra and the Eye of Horus were both symbols of protection.'

She peeled off a new Post-it note, took the pencil she'd had clenched in her teeth while she turned the pages of the book, and sketched the Eye of Ra, then took another Post-it for the Eye of Horus. She stuck them up on the shower screen. Together they made up two eyes of a face, Ra was the right eye and Horus was the left. She thought back to Patrick's pictures; the ones in the shed, the one spray-painted on the wall of the garage at the burned-out Pollock home. She shuddered again at the memory of fear. Both those pictures were the Eye of Horus. But – and here was the interesting thing – the one bleached into the lawn at the Hammond house was the Eye of Ra, she was sure of it.

Patrick Kirby was distinctly drawing the Eye of Horus. Someone else was drawing the Eye of Ra.

She quelled the excitement in her chest. She put her pencil down. 'The Eye of Ra confers protection on royal persons. The Eye of Horus on ordinary people.' Patrick Kirby was protecting ordinary people. William Mackie was protecting himself. More proof that Patrick was warning people, not killing them.

There was a knock at the door, then another. 'Sister, are you feeling all right?'

Mrs Sidhu snorted. Like anyone cared if she was all right. 'I'm fine, thank you.'

'It's just you've been in there a long time.' Daljeet's dalek voice was muffled through the door, which was mercifully thick. 'Will you be out soon?' Mrs Sidhu hoped she couldn't hear the rustling of paper or the munching of biscuits. 'I'm fine, respected sister. I am just . . . having a bath. Please use the other bathroom.'

'Oh. I see, of course. Please, when you've finished, come downstairs. Mr Varma and I would like to speak with you.'

Mrs Sidhu bet she would. What other little surprises did she have in store for her? What other little humiliations? She grunted and turned her thoughts back to the case.

Then there was the matter of the missing last page of the manuscript.

She turned to the final page. There was little to distinguish it. It was a list of acknowledgements, that was all. Of course, on her own copy, Dr Calman might have made some kind of note, but what that note was she could only guess at. She was about to put it away when a name caught Mrs Sidhu's eye, an unusual name that had stuck in her mind: Arif Begovic. Why would the orderly at the clinic get an acknowledgement in Dr Calman's book? She looked again. These weren't a list of dedications, these were sources. Arif Begovic was a source on William Mackie.

Burton had asked her why William Mackie would return now. Because it was a useful distraction, that was why. Patrick was being used by someone who was trying to cover up something else.

227

As Daljeet's footsteps retreated, Mrs Sidhu opened the bathroom window. Outside was a flat roof. Mrs Sidhu flitted across it and scaled down the garden trellis into her own back garden and out through the rear gate. She felt like a little girl again.

The piece of wood was shattered in two. Arif lifted the axe to strike again when a voice stayed his hand.

'Begovic is a name from the Balkans, isn't it?' Mrs Sidhu asked.

'You ask a lot of questions.'

'And you have no accent at all, so you grew up here. Your father was a refugee.'

Arif placed another log on the block.

'Bosnian. We came over in 1993, my father and me. I was two, I don't really remember it. My mother didn't make it. It was just me and Dad. I don't remember any of it. Dad had plenty of memories for both of us.'

He lifted the axe again. 'Best not come too close,' said Arif, grinning. The blade came down with a crunch. Mrs Sidhu covered her eyes. They were showered with tiny pieces of wood. Tiny flecks of it landed on her hair and in his goatee. A wedge of wood fell from the block.

'More work for you with Patrick gone.' She dusted herself down.

'Whoo!' Arif exclaimed and raised the axe once more. 'Dr Eardley says work in the garden is good for the spirit.' He was wearing protective glasses and thick gloves, but his bare forearms glistened with sweat and wood chippings.

'Hungry work, I expect.' Mrs Sidhu put a paper bag down on a log. 'I saw you out here and I thought you could use some sustenance. My best samosas.' She had

228

made them fresh. The smell of hot, softened potato, spices and pastry filled the air. Arif eyed Mrs Sidhu with suspicion and the samosas with wet lips and interest. He embedded the axe in the block, making Mrs Sidhu jump, and left it there like some gravity-defying sculpture. He unwrapped the food and sat down on the grass. 'I brought tea and coffee, both.' Mrs Sidhu jiggled two thermos flasks like a mother entertaining a crying child.

'Coffee, thanks,' Arif said. She poured and watched him chew, his eyes fixed on the distance, washing it all down with fast gulps of the coffee.

'I'm surprised to see you out here. I thought you would be with the clients. You are one of the nurses, aren't you?'

He shook his head. 'I do what they tell me to.'

'You're like me. You don't belong here, do you? I mean here, but not there.' They were sitting in the woodland that was part of the Benham House estate, but they could still see the big yellow homestead.

He chewed some more, shrugged, glugged and swallowed. 'Maybe I belong in there more than you think.'

Mrs Sidhu joined him on the ground. 'Tell me.' And Arif shrugged and told her. He told her what it was like to be brought up in a tiny English village by a father driven half mad by grief and war. How he taught him not to love but to survive. 'It wasn't all bad. He was a strong father and he made a life for us here. In Bosnia he was a dentist, and with some help from people here he became the local dentist. He passed away last year. I thought he was finally at peace, but at the end he gave me his hunting knife. He told me to keep it under my bed because at any minute, at any time, the people of the village might turn against me.'

'And do you keep it under your bed?'

There was silence for a while. Arif munched on another samosa, while Mrs Sidhu searched for any words of comfort, until Arif broke the tension. 'As you can imagine, I didn't make a lot of friends at school.' He chuckled uneasily. 'And look, you couldn't imagine a safer place to live.'

'Until a few days ago,' said Mrs Sidhu. 'You work on the night shift, is that right? You reported the fire at the Hammond house.'

He nodded again, now eyeing her a little suspiciously. 'The music, it woke me up. Frank Sinatra, "Fly Me to the Moon". My father was a big fan.' Arif drew the knife from the sheath on his belt. 'I keep it with me to remind me of him.' He stroked the blade and put it away again hastily. 'I think you and I both belong in there because we don't think like them. That's the irony. We're crazy and they make us work here to look after the crazy people,' he said.

'Crazy might be a bit strong. It's a retreat, not an asylum.'

'Believe me, there's craziness here,' said Arif.

Mrs Sidhu spoke. 'You know when I was young, all I wanted to do was to run around in fields and woods all day with dirty knees and muddy hair. But immigrants are over-protective parents. They wanted me to be indoors, where they could see I was safe. Which was also ironic, because where they had come from, in India, all they did when they were my age was run around in fields, chasing cows and running up and down dungheaps. They told stories about it. So, I got out whenever I could, whenever I got the chance to escape.'

Arif nodded. Something in his eyes told her he was remembering.

'I used to love to hide and to watch people. Oh, the things I saw!' Mrs Sidhu clapped a hand to her mouth and laughed. When it was quiet again, she said, 'Do you like to get out and watch people, Arif? Is that why Dr Calman came to talk to you about her book?'

Arif didn't answer the question directly. 'I saw Him, when I was young.' The him was spoken with a capital 'H'. 'The one they're talking about again. William Mackie. He came to my father's dental practice down in the village the night he did that couple.'

'They knew each other?'

'Mr Pollock came with him. He sat in my dad's chair and he did his teeth.'

Mrs Sidhu rubbed the bridge of her nose. 'Why did they come together?'

'Mr Pollock helped my father, helped him become a dentist here in the village. Helped him buy the practice. Maybe he was helping Mackie too. I never understood, but one night I went up to the circle and saw them. They were all in a ring and in the middle was Mrs Pollock with no clothes on. I mean Sandra, not Edith. It surprised me, because she was very shy. She came to dentists a lot, she had cavities, but she could hardly look anyone in the eye. Mr Pollock always kept her close to him, like he was protecting her.'

'But she didn't come that night?'

Arif finished the coffee and leapt up. He grasped the handle of his axe, and Mrs Sidhu felt for just a moment a spark of concern.

'In my case, it was war. That's why my father was scared for me. I grew up around here so I never saw what he saw, but I could hear my father screaming at night.

231

He was a dentist. In the camp they ripped every tooth from his head. So nights were a good time to be out.'

'And now? Do you still like a night walk?'

Arif finished his lunch. He pulled the head of the axe out of the block and raised it. He looked back up at the house, where Stephen Eardley was standing in the middle of a group of seated clients, each one with a look of bliss on their faces. Beside him, Sienna took notes. 'Now, I keep my mouth shut. In case someone steals my teeth too.' The axe head came down like a guillotine and carved its way through another wedge of wood.

'Did you clean up those boots Dr Eardley gave you?' Mrs Sidhu asked. Arif looked away, there were the boots, clean and polished. She turned them over. The soles were as clean as the rest of the boots. They had a zig-zag tread and a distinctive cut in the third tread on the right boot. 'Why don't I take them back to Dr Eardley?' she said.

Arif said nothing, and launched his axe at the next log.

23

DCI Burton's most natural position to conduct police business was not sitting on a cushion with his hands folded in spiritual bliss. He had experienced very little spiritual bliss in his life and he was not sure this was the time to start.

'Let's begin.' Eardley pressed his palms together. The others followed suit. Sienna put her pen down, even Jonny Snakeskin swivelled into seated position and adopted an easy, cross-legged position.

Yeah, he would be a yoga buff, thought Burton. 'Two people are dead, one of your therapists and one of your clients. You and your retreat seem to be the connection.' Burton creaked his long legs into place, curling his arms round them. He looked like a praying mantis.

'I didn't mean you, Chief Inspector. I meant the group,' Eardley replied. 'First let's empty our minds. Close your eyes and focus on your breathing, in and out.' Burton did, inhaled and exhaled in unison with the others. 'Now, carry on.' Silence. 'I mean you, Chief Inspector, what were you saying?'

'Oh, right.' Burton cleared his throat. 'Patrick Kirby is after a group of people. Specifically this therapy group of people.'

Silence. Burton continued breathing. Sunlight glowed red through his eyelids. Leaves stirred nearby. His shoulders relaxed, even his legs unstiffened and folded out naturally. 'You know what, this is good.' He really was feeling more rooted in the here and now. Eventually, when he was ready, he opened his eyes. Five pairs of eyes were staring right back at him.

'You're saying he's trying to kill all of us?' Eardley said, eyebrows raised, looking with concern at Sienna, who looked away sharply. Jonny sat up, and Elliot tapped Edith on the shoulder, seeming to jerk her out of her daydream.

Burton rubbed the back of his neck. 'That is the line of enquiry we are pursuing, sir. Patrick Kirby has formed some kind of animus against this group. He killed Dr Calman, and then Kate Hammond – and given that he killed her husband too, we have to assume spouses and partners are also at risk. He is leaving a symbol – the Eye of Ra – at the places he intends to kill next. We found one at Kate's house and this morning we found one at Tamzin Grey's house.' Burton looked at Jonny. 'You and Ms Grey were married, weren't you?'

'Yeah.'

'And Patrick knows that?' Jonny mumbled that it wasn't a secret. Burton continued: 'Patrick was intending to kill you there last night. For some reason he changed his mind and turned his attention to the Hammonds instead.'

Jonny snorted. Edith and Elliot rolled their eyes. Eardley spoke up: 'No, I think we should listen to the chief inspector. If there's any danger to any of you, we have to make sure you're all protected.' He was still looking at Sienna, who was staring at the ground. 'I want to keep you safe.'

Jonny was horrified. 'What are you saying? We can't go out?' Jonny said.

'I'm putting officers here at the retreat and I'd like you all to stay here for the time being.' Burton had to raise his voice over the groans. 'I've let Tamzin Grey know as well. She might be under threat too. I will ask her to move up here for the time being. It's much easier to keep watch over everyone if you're together. We are going to catch up with Patrick Kirby very soon, so I promise it won't be long.' He turned to Eardley. 'Do you have enough rooms for everyone?'

Eardley nodded. 'Of course.'

As Burton was getting himself slowly into standing position, Mrs Sidhu appeared, striding across the lawn with Dr Eardley's boots in her hands. 'Chief Inspector!' she called out cheerfully. Burton closed his eyes, blinking long and hard, hoping that when he opened them Mrs Sidhu would be gone. She wasn't.

'Chief Inspector, I have something to show you.'

Mrs Sidhu held the boots out. Before Burton could take them, Dr Eardley reached out a hand for them. 'These look excellent.' He was gone before Mrs Sidhu thought of anything to say. She stared open-mouthed, with Burton looking at her mildly confused. 'Yes?' he prompted.

Mrs Sidhu glowered. 'Come with me,' she hissed, 'I know who did it.'

'I think Patrick is protecting the therapy group. The proof is in Dr Calman's book manuscript.'

'Mrs Sidhu, I really am very busy.' DCI Burton was being towed across the south lawn of the Benham House

Retreat like an oil tanker by a tugboat. The smaller vessel in question was, of course, Mrs Sidhu.

'The Eye of Ra and the Eye of Horus. In each instance that Patrick is known to have drawn the symbol it was the Horus, the left eye. Which eye was it at Tamzin Grey's house?' My goodness, Mrs Sidhu thought, even for a big man he was surprisingly difficult to pull and even more difficult to change direction. But change his direction she must if she was going to help Patrick and Sienna.

Burton checked himself. 'Hang on, how come you suddenly know so much about Dr Calman's manuscript?'

'Errr, I may have managed to get a sneak look at a copy.' Mrs Sidhu squirmed under Burton's gaze. 'OK, I borrowed Dr Eardley's copy. Which eye, Chief Inspector?'

Burton grumbled but checked his phone for the photo of Tamzin Grey's lawn. 'Left eye.'

'That's what I mean. Whereas the one outside the Hammonds' was the right eye. The Eye of Ra. William Mackie called himself "destroyer of worlds". Patrick is warning these people that he has returned.'

Burton looked exasperated. 'Do I have to explain yet again that Mackie is dead? We know he's dead. It's all in Patrick's head. You have no idea the kind of pressure I'm under here. My superintendent is already all over me. Three murders and I'm no closer to finding Patrick Kirby. Where are you taking me, anyway?' They were heading away from the house and, more importantly to Burton, away from his car. 'I've already questioned everyone at the retreat.' He finally managed to pull his arm free.

'Someone else wants it to look like this is all to do with William Mackie. That's the person Patrick is protecting them from.'

'And who is that?' Burton asked.

Mrs Sidhu thrust her chin out. 'What about Dr Feelgood?'

Burton searched the skies before uttering a single syllable. 'What?'

'I knew you wouldn't believe me. I have proof positive.' They had apparently arrived at their destination because Mrs Sidhu stopped. Burton looked around; all he could see was a flower bed. Mrs Sidhu continued. 'Kate Hammond had a stalker. The police dismissed it as part of her mental condition, am I right?'

Burton shoved his hands into his pockets. 'Clearly, Patrick had been following her for a while.' He could not meet Mrs Sidhu's eye.

She pointed up at the house. 'This is the only place you can get a view of Kate's room anywhere in the garden. So if Patrick was the one who was stalking her, explain these footprints.' She aimed her finger at the ground. 'There.'

'All I can see is dry mud,' Burton said.

Mrs Sidhu rubbed her eyes. 'There were footprints right here.' In the distance, Arif was raking at another flower bed. 'They had a tread with a scar across the sole.' She appealed to Burton. 'Go and get those boots off Dr Eardley – you'll see that boot sole is as unique as a fingerprint.'

Burton's chin dimpled. 'And what would I compare them to?' he asked.

Mrs Sidhu clenched her fists. 'I don't know.'

Burton rubbed the back of his neck. 'Mrs Sidhu, you know I am always very grateful for your help, but we're dealing with a serial killer here and I know exactly who Patrick Kirby is targeting. He has a specific group he's after.'

'You think the murderer has a kill list?' Mrs Sidhu looked far too excited for Burton's liking. 'That's exactly the sort of phrase that is hugely unhelpful.' He tried to ignore the gleeful smile on her face. 'Dr Calman's group are all in danger, so I'm asking them all to stay here tonight. We can protect them here. So, thanks, but for now I've got this under control.'

Burton seemed poised to end the conversation right there, until Mrs Sidhu spoke. 'You want to tempt him here and finish it tonight! You're setting a trap!'

Burton hushed her with a finger to his lips. 'This is all under control.' He paused a moment and glanced at the bruise on her head. 'Maybe you should take the day off.'

'Don't you start! You're going to find out that Patrick isn't the killer, Chief Inspector. What if it is Eardley, or one of them? You're locking them all in here together. What you're doing is putting everyone at risk by chasing the wrong man.' Mrs Sidhu stormed back towards the house, leaving Burton standing in a flower bed. He stood for a while, grinding his teeth, wondering if he could retrieve that moment of bliss he'd experienced earlier. Maybe he should give one of Eardley's podcasts a go.

24

'What are we going to do now?' asked Tamzin.

Jonny stood bare-chested at the window, his skin a network of tattoos. They were in his room at the retreat, which was pretty much identical to all the other rooms, a mixture of hospital efficiency and old-world luxury. 'We stay on plan.' Down below, Sienna was writing in her red book. Snakeskin's heavily made-up eyes followed her. 'Is everything in place?'

'Yes, but there are police everywhere.'

Jonny sneered. 'That cop thinks he can get the gardener guy to come here. I can see it in his eyes. So we go to yours.'

'They're going to be watching my place too,' said Tamzin.

He ignored her. 'We're going to need a girl.'

Tamzin joined him at the window. She followed Jonny's gaze. 'Her? You've got to be kidding.'

'She's perfect. Reminds me of a young you.' Down on the south lawn, Sienna Sampson sat, her red notebook in hand, taking notes while Dr Eardley waited for the group to join him.

'I need fresh blood. You want to help or not?' Jonny held Tamzin's gaze until finally she averted her eyes. 'Good. She's perfect, and tonight is going to be a very special night. Tonight is my comeback.' He laughed. 'Only how are we going to get out of here?'

'Leave that to me,' said Tamzin. 'You don't mind a bit of exercise, do you, Jonny?'

Jonny soured. 'Let's get back to Dr Feelgood, recess is over.'

'Listen to your inner voice. What is your inner voice telling you?'

Mrs Sidhu took a guess. Jonny Snakeskin's inner voice was telling him it was time for a drink. Edith Pollock's inner voice was either looking forward to seeing her son, or remembering once more he was dead. And Sienna . . . well, who knew what roads crossed in Sienna's mind. 'Listen to your inner voice.' What had Kate Hammond's voice told her just before she died?

Eardley clapped his hands, like a stage hypnotist bringing his volunteers back to the conscious world. Mrs Sidhu, too, jerked, nearly scattering the cups and saucers in her tray. 'That concludes this session. Well done, everyone, you're all making excellent progress,' he applauded, encouraging the others to do the same. 'We have to give ourselves congratulations for every hour, every day of progress. Keep listening to yourselves, you're your own best doctor.' They were on the south lawn. Mrs Sidhu gathered up the remnants of tea, coffee and tray bakes. The class stretched, looking refreshed, and

240

began dispersing. Mrs Sidhu watched as Sienna gathered her notes up under her arm. As Dr Eardley passed, she hailed him. Interrupted and confused for a moment, it took him a while to realise what Sienna was offering him. 'The notes,' she said, 'you need the notes from the session.' Dr Eardley looked at the red notebook as if it was the last thing he wanted, but with a sigh he relented. 'Yes, of course, you've worked very hard on these. Well done,' he paused before saying her name, 'Sienna.' He walked away.

Tamzin Grey saw her chance. She had been waiting for the class to file out, like an expectant mother at the gates of a school. She wasn't waiting for Jonny, though. They shared a look. Jonny wandered off into the bushes. It sounded to Mrs Sidhu like he was taking a leak. Tamzin gritted her teeth. The man was determinedly a rebel. Tamzin, though, was undeterred and took the opportunity to sidle up to Sienna.

'Hello, why don't you and I have a little chat? I've been meaning to talk to you for quite a while. Jonny and I are loving your vibe.' She led Sienna away.

Interesting, thought Mrs Sidhu. What would those two have to talk about?

Mrs Sidhu made a point of skirting round in their direction and straining her ears. She could make out very little except that Tamzin was complimenting Sienna on her looks and her style. Sienna glowed shyly. She did manage to hear one thing. 'You can be part of something bigger. Part of a new family.' Mrs Sidhu's ears were tingling now. What could Tamzin mean by that? She was pressing her hand to Sienna's arm.

Until, suddenly aware that Mrs Sidhu was watching,

Tamzin quickly took her hand away. She whispered in Sienna's ear and walked off.

'What was all that about?' Mrs Sidhu asked when Tamzin was gone. Sienna shrugged innocently, but her little black eyes were following Tamzin, who had grouped up with Jonny and was talking to him, leaning close in. Jonny looked round, shining that crooked, craggy smile on Sienna, who – Mrs Sidhu could not help but notice – was smiling back shyly.

'But what about Patrick?' Mrs Sidhu said.

For a moment Sienna seemed to be searching her memory to place the name, until finally her eyes glowed with triumph and certainty. 'That's not important any more.'

Mrs Sidhu did her best to hide her shock. 'Why don't we regroup in the secret garden?' She nudged Sienna. 'You know, VFC,' Mrs Sidhu whispered.

When at last Sienna responded, there was a shining light in her eyes. 'I'm so sorry, Mrs Sidhu, I have to go now. Lots to do. Another time.' Her little mink teeth were fixed in a blissful smile. Something about it was repellent, frightening.

Slightly at a loss, Mrs Sidhu agreed faintly and headed back to her car.

242

25

Circles, there were circles everywhere.

Mrs Sidhu was back in her toilet office. She had managed to move more equipment in. There was a side-by-side hotplate so she could continue working on her aubergine bhaji orders. Each was a circle and on top two circles made by saucepans. Like the saucepans on Dr Calman's stove. Music hammered out from her laptop.

> Into the night, into the night, my darling, won't you take me
> into the night.
> The Eye of Ra is watching us we can do no wrong
> Even if it don't feel right, this circle is our home
> The ancients have spoken and we have nowhere to fall
> Come on give your spirit up and we will join them all.
> Into the night, into the night, my darling won't you take me
> into the night.

Mrs Sidhu finished copying the lyrics onto an old enve-lope and turned the volume down so that she could think straight. Jonny Snakeskin's 1998 song 'Into the Night' was, like so many of his numbers, a guitar-thrashing anthem to the darker side. What was very clear was that it contained references to William Mackie's ideas about the afterlife and ideology. She underlined the lyric 'this circle is our home'. It was another circle, another connection. She stuck it up on the tiles over the sink.

These were not the only reference to circles in the room. Starting with the Eyes of Ra and Horus as her inspiration, Mrs Sidhu had begun tracing out patterns and symbols. The eye turned up throughout history. From the 'eye of providence' – that floating eye framed in a triangle which turns up in Renaissance art and the United States dollar bill – to the third eye, a symbol of wisdom and transcendence in Eastern religion, the eye is a sign of enlightenment. Hence it had a prominence in Mackie's Enlightenment cult. She had filled the shower screen with quotes, occult references, and drawings. They now spilled out onto the walls, the mirror, even the cistern.

Her thoughts were interrupted by a gentle tap at the door. 'Mum, you all right in there? What's that music?'

Mrs Sidhu hurriedly closed the music player app and closed her laptop. 'What music? There's no music? It must have been the toilet flushing.' She flushed the toilet.

It all went round and round in Mrs Sidhu's head. Patrick didn't have the personality to kill. Patrick was obsessed with Mackie. Patrick killed Wendy and the Hammonds, confirmed by evidence that he was present at both crime scenes. But Patrick didn't have the personality to kill. Circular patterns, circular reasoning, it was like a snake swallowing its own tail. Another circle, the Ouroboros.

Then there were mandalas, fiery circular emblems used in meditation all over the world. The mandala was a symbol of perfection, and its simplest purest form was the circle with a dot at the centre. It was on the cover of Snakeskin's album. Head cocked to one side, she carefully traced it out, humming in childlike satisfaction. 'This circle is our home,' she sang.

In 1997, the summer that the Pollocks died, Jonny Snakeskin had played Reading Rock Festival, just a stone's throw from Benham village. Another coincidence?

Mrs Sidhu was cooking up a new idea. What if Mackie wasn't the leader of a cult? What if he was a shill, a front for those who really ran the cult? He had conveniently died abroad, which protected the identity of who was in charge. Jonny Snakeskin was and is part of the E cult. It's all so obvious now. And if this is a conspiracy, it could go all the way to the top. All the way to Burton's bosses. But she had to get some real evidence to contact Burton. Mrs Sidhu needed real evidence, and she had a chance to get to it. Sienna's notebooks.

Tez knocked at the door again, more insistent this time. Mrs Sidhu pulled on rubber gloves, unbolted the door and opened it a crack. Tez pushed on it straight away, eyes narrow, but it held firm against Mrs Sidhu's foot.

'What are you doing in there?' Daljeet was close behind him, flapping the air with her hand. 'Hai, hai, it smells terrible.' Then she stopped to sniff the air. 'Actually, it doesn't smell bad at all. Sister, is your lower bowel all right? I have a number of medications which I am certain will clear things out.'

Mrs Sidhu waggled her gloved fingers. 'I'm just having a deep clean in here, that's all.'

Tez narrowed his eyes. 'With the door locked?'

Mrs Sidhu shrugged. 'I used the loo first, and I must have forgot to unlock it.' She watched Tez, who looked dubious. Daljeet was rustling through a washbag, probably looking forward to unleashing her medications on her. Heaven only knows what kind of stuff she might have brought over from India. You didn't mess with Indian gut medication. She winked at Mrs Sidhu in a confidential way. 'We will talk later, sister, when we have time alone. My brother explained to me that the workings of your inner plumbing was often an area of disagreement between you.'

Mrs Sidhu closed the door and bolted it again. She growled. Was there anything that man had not shared with his sister? It didn't matter, she had more important things to do. She listened. It sounded like Tez and Daljeet had gone. She reached for her phone.

Burton answered the phone despite his misgivings.

'DCI Burton?' The voice at the other end was hoarse. 'This is an anonymous tip-off.'

She heard DCI Burton sigh deeply at the other end. 'Mrs Sidhu, I know it's you, your name shows up when you call.'

Mrs Sidhu spoke in her normal voice. 'Yes, I forgot that. OK then, let's just say it's a tip-off.'

'Where are you talking from? It sounds very echoey.'

'I'm in the bathroom, as it happens.'

'Lovely.'

'Though I'm not doing what you'd expect in the bathroom.'

'That hasn't made anything better. Or clearer. What can I do for you?'

'You said yourself, how has a confused, delusional

individual like Patrick stayed hidden? The answer is simple. He has had help.'

A slow look of incomprehension was creeping up on Leslie Burton, and it was no stranger to his face when it came to dealing with Mrs Sidhu. It was already making itself at home and putting the kettle on by the time he spoke again. 'Why don't you take it slowly, for me. You know how I struggle to keep up.'

Mrs Sidhu was not a fan of sarcasm; it was the lowest form of humour. 'Someone's sheltering him,' she snapped. 'What happened to William Mackie's cult after he left?'

Burton shrugged. 'Nothing. Without the leader it collapsed, melted away. After his failure here, Mackie went to South America and started again, but ended up killing himself.'

'What failure? I mean he convinced two perfectly happy, moneyed people to go along with his ideology. That was a success, in his terms at least. Do you know, that after years of research Wendy Calman was only ever able to identify a handful of cult members, homeless people. No one else – no one who would talk about it, anyway. Surely, after all this time, someone would break the silence. So my question is, if you were recruiting for a cult, where would you start?'

He rubbed the back of his neck. The look of incomprehension that had made a temporary home on his face signed a long-term lease and started shopping for curtains. He said nothing, because he knew Mrs Sidhu and he knew she had asked a rhetorical question, and he knew that she was about to land her killer blow and he didn't want to deliver her what comics called a feed line. So as the silence continued, the pressure built up until, as do all people who start a stare-out with an Indian aunty, he broke first. 'Why would I be recruiting for a cult?'

'William Mackie was a cult leader, albeit small-time. Perhaps others were involved too. I'll ask again. Where would you recruit? Somewhere there are vulnerable people, people who are already distanced from reality, perhaps people looking for answers in their high-pressure lives. Look around you, what do you see?'

The sun was setting on Benham House, dandelion seeds and pollen drifted around in the last sunbeams picking out smiling people sitting cross-legged in circles, some painting, some talking, some eyes closed in blissful meditation. Fairy lights came on, twinkling like stars.

Burton stood dumbfounded. His mouth hung open; his lower jaw sagged like a beagle's. Incomprehension had just got evicted; now total disbelief was opening a squat. 'You've got to be kidding me. Here? The Benham House Retreat?'

'The Pollock deaths were murder, not suicide. Why kill your best two recruits? Because something happened. Dr Calman says in her book that William Mackie was a predator. What if he was hot for Sandra? Maybe he sexually assaulted her and the Pollocks threatened to expose the whole thing. They all had to die, Chief Inspector, to save the cult itself. The E cult is still going and it's going on all around you.'

'Are you sure about this?' he whispered, through clenched teeth. 'Because you'd have to be pretty damn sure before I made an arrest, Mrs Sidhu.'

Mrs Sidhu hesitated. How sure could she be? All she really had were her instincts. Yet, she had seen what was happening to Sienna, and she had to stop it before it went too far. 'You'll find out tonight, because Tamzin Grey and Jonny Snakeskin are initiating a new member. Sienna Sampson has been brainwashed.'

248

'But how? The place is crawling with police.'

'I don't know. All I know is that this whole thing is based on the symbol of the circle, the most perfect shape in geometry.'

She did not sound entirely grounded to Burton, but that was not always a surprise with Mrs Sidhu. 'Look, tell you what I'll do. Why don't I go and check in on Tamzin Grey, Sienna Sampson and Jonny Snakeskin? There's bound to be a logical explanation for all of this.' He ended the call quickly.

In her bathroom, Mrs Sidhu traced out another mandala and added it to the others. She rubbed at the sore spot on her head and went back to the photograph of Justin and Sandra Pollock, which she had stuck up on the cistern. They were smiling, happy and with a look of such perfect, shining certainty in their eyes. She had just seen that look again. It was there in Sienna's eyes. What went on behind those button black eyes and that little toothed smile? What went on in those group sessions? What was going on between Sienna, Tamzin and Snakeskin? Burton wanted evidence, and she knew where to get it.

'Hello. Who am I talking to now?' Eardley asked.

'You're talking to Sienna.' The voice on the phone was low and calm. 'What is it?'

Eardley gave a good-natured smile. 'Sienna. I only wanted to ask you about something that I found in your room.'

'You've been in my room. Why?' She sounded angry.

Eardley ignored the question. He had a rectangle of plastic in his hand, roughly the size of a credit card. He turned it over in his hand. 'Where did you get this card?

It says VFC,' he read and squinted to read the fine print. 'Village fete committee. Sienna, I've never seen you make anything like this.'

There was a pause. 'My handler provided it for me. It's a cover, obviously. I can't say much. I'm working undercover now.'

Eardley's eyes crinkled. 'Undercover? Really, how very interesting. Tell me all about it.' He peered over his glasses, talking genially, as if speaking to a child.

'It's a secret organisation, and we are tracking a cult.'

'A cult?' The geniality disappeared from Eardley's manner. He sat up straight. 'Now, listen, Sienna, perhaps you should come to see me.'

Sienna laughed. 'I'm in the middle of an operation. I can't stop now.'

'Please, is Emily there? Can I talk to Emily?'

Sienna's voice trembled. 'Emily isn't . . . Emily isn't coming back. You know that, Doctor.' The call ended abruptly.

Eardley placed the phone back in his pocket and put his head in his hands. This was a new and unwelcome development.

26

Burton knocked at Tamzin Grey's door. 'Hello, Ms Grey? Tamzin?' He waited. The door remained closed and there were no sounds from within. Something was stirring in Burton's stomach, a feeling he didn't like. He dialled and spoke sharply into his phone.

'Dove. I want you to check on Jonny Snakeskin. Is he in his room?'

'Ah, no, sir. They wanted to collect some things from Ms Grey's house. I drove them here personally, sir. The girl too.'

'What girl?'

'Sampson, sir. Works at the retreat. They said she was needed.'

Burton controlled his breathing. 'Where are they now?' The word came out oddly, his mouth was dry.

'In the house. I'm waiting in the car for them.'

'Go and get them.'

After a few moments the answer came back. Dove was breathless. 'They're not answering the door, sir.'

The floor fell out of Burton's stomach, like an elevator plummeting.

'They can't go anywhere, sir. I'm right here.'

Burton remembered; he knew how they had got out. 'They're using the river.' Burton threw his phone across the corridor.

The kayak barely made a sound as Tamzin pulled it up onto the bank. Jonny wheezed and helped by collapsing on the ground. 'Come on, Jonny, you say you want this. Put some back into it.'

'Where's the girl?' he whined.

'I've sent her up there.' She watched Jonny slipping around in muddy water and took pity. 'You'd better get up there too. They'll be waiting.'

The moon was out.

It was night and Sienna approached the stone circle. She was alone, with no sign of Tamzin, nor of Jonny yet. She shivered. Since the sun went down, the temperature was dropping, and while it was not cold, Sienna was only wearing the plain shift, a sheath of cotton, that Tamzin had given her. She was walking along the avenue, the ancient path that led from the village to the Benham circle. In medieval times it was renamed the Scapegoat path, as rumours of witches and human sacrifices abounded at that time. The idea of human sacrifice at the stone circle had been put to bed in the age of reason, but the image persisted in popular culture of Druids making blood rituals among the stones.

She was almost at the stones now, standing throwing dark shadows, and still no one around. She started to wonder if she was the victim of a practical joke. Where were they all? Then she saw him standing in the centre of the circle.

He was tall and lean and almost naked, his body covered in lines and twisted drawings. Ice filled her chest. 'Hello?' she said; she had to force her voice out of her lungs as if she had jumped into cold water. He beckoned her forward with a long finger. He was Death, she was sure of it, Death himself.

Light! Sienna put her hands up to cover her eyes, and still the light blinded her. Slowly her eyes adjusted, and still the writhing, dancing figure in the stone circle urged her on. She trembled and tried not to cry. She felt a hand on her arm, and she was led forward towards him along the Scapegoat path, like a bride towards a gruesome groom. She shouldn't have come here.

27

Mrs Sidhu's car squealed to a halt outside the Benham House Retreat. She waited for Cher to stop wishing she could turn back time before snapping off the radio. The engine clicked and clacked as it lost heat to the cool night air. She pulled out Wendy's manuscript. She could return that at the same time, but her focus was on those little red notebooks. The time for niceties like privacy and client confidentially had long gone, in Mrs Sidhu's mind.

She approached through the outer office. She put her ear to the door. It was quiet inside. The touch of the cold wood to her earlobe reminded her that this was the exact position she was in when she first met Sienna. Sienna must have been coming in to help Dr Eardley with his ten o'clock client. Something about that seemed wrong, but Mrs Sidhu couldn't put her finger on what. She listened harder. There were no signs from inside.

'Can I help you?'

A cold sensation seeped up into her legs. The voice was as clear as a bell and came from beside her. Dr Eardley was standing close enough for her to feel his breath on her neck. He was wearing his amused smile. 'Why don't we both go into my office?'

Mrs Sidhu had little choice; Eardley was blocking her way out. She opened the door and led them both into the room. 'Please, take a seat.' Eardley dumped himself behind his desk and watched Mrs Sidhu take her place on the chair in front. She could make a run for it. She eyed Eardley. There seemed little threat in his demeanour. 'You really are a very interesting woman,' he said. 'So what brings your ear to my door tonight?'

Mrs Sidhu took a deep breath. It was time to risk all. 'I know what's going on.' She thumped the manuscript down on the desk.

He drew it to him with two hands. Then he polished his little glasses and put them on. 'I've been looking for this.' He leaned back in his chair, interlacing his fingers over his belly. 'Interesting reading?'

'Very interesting. But first I'd like to see the soles of your boots.' When he had the gall to raise an eyebrow, Mrs Sidhu put her knuckles on the desk and leaned in. 'The ones you used for your little night walks.' Eardley nodded to the boot rack. Mrs Sidhu grabbed the boots and turned them face up and showed him the tread. There it was: a zig-zag with a distinctive cut in the third tread on the right boot. 'These imprints were left in the rose bed outside Kate Hammond's window. Explain that!'

'Were they?' Eardley paused, thought for a moment before speaking. 'Those aren't my boots,' he added with an odd kind of embarrassment. 'Those are Tony Hammond's boots. We took some night walks together, when we were scheming about acquiring all that land for The Sanctuary. Look, mine are on the rack below, much smaller.'

Mrs Sidhu seemed to wake from her trance. Her eyebrows rose in surprise. 'These are Mr Hammond's boots?' She slowly put the boots down.

'Don't know what to do with them. I suppose I'll have to wait until there's another bring-and-buy – they'd never fit me. Tony was a big chap.'

'Why would Tony Hammond watch his own wife?'

Eardley rose from his chair and took a long look out of the window. The reason for his embarrassment soon became clear. 'Kate Hammond wasn't the only Hammond who suffered from delusions. Tony suffered from a kind of morbid jealousy. He was convinced that his wife was having an affair. I allowed him to observe her while she was here. I thought that proof that she was devoted to him would clear her in his mind. Unfortunately, it had a secondary effect that I was not aware of.'

'Kate Hammond thought she was seeing a ghost. She was seeing her own husband.'

'I'm afraid that due to client confidentiality, Dr Calman did not reveal to me what Kate's condition was. Meanwhile, Tony swore me to secrecy that he was following his wife around, and in return he promised to help me acquire the land I need to expand.'

'That's what Mr Hammond was doing. He was taking an early train home while pretending he was staying in London, in the hope of surprising Kate and her lover.'

'There was no lover. When Wendy died and I read Kate Hammond's case notes, I realised what a mess we were all in. So as soon as I had my first session with Kate I tried to repair the situation.'

'You told her to confront her ghost.'

'I genuinely thought it would be better if it was out in the open, that they could resolve their problems with minimum impact on the retreat.'

Mrs Sidhu gasped. 'Instead, she opened the door to her killer.'

The three of them were gathered outside the upstairs bathroom. Varma tried knocking again. 'She's not answering. How long has she been in there?'

'All afternoon.' Daljeet's forehead puckered. 'You think she's done something?'

Tez's eyes widened. 'She said she was a bit depressed about the house. How Dad told you and not her about it.'

Varma banged the door again. 'Mrs Sidhu, please! If you don't answer, I will be forced to break down the door.' They all waited. The only sound was the rattling of the pipes. He looked down and saw the electricity cable coiling under the door.

'Right.' Varma took as many steps back as the landing would allow and dropped his shoulder. 'We're coming, Mrs Sidhu!' he cried.

Confidence can give you wings, but it can also deceive you about how things really stand. And that is the moment that the air under those wings sags, swirls and plunges you into a nosedive. And to get out of a nosedive, you have to beat your wings even harder. There was no backing out now.

Mrs Sidhu took a deep breath. 'I've been talking to your assistant.'

257

'You have?' Wrinkles of good-natured bemusement gathered around Eardley's eyes. 'I wouldn't put much faith in what she says.'

'Is that what you and Jonny do? Build them up, then gaslight them?'

'Sienna isn't my assistant.' Suddenly Eardley's voice was ice-cold. 'There is no Sienna Sampson.'

Mrs Sidhu spluttered. Maybe she had overestimated Dr Eardley. She had expected any number of ploys, but simply dismissing the existence of Sienna out of hand was laughable. The woman who Mrs Sidhu saw at ten o'clock every morning coming into the retreat very clearly existed. Ten o'clock, regular as a pendulum, every day, and that nagging worry was starting to drag at Mrs Sidhu's chest. The cold feeling was seeping back into her legs. She felt like a chess player who was only now realising that she had made the wrong move three turns back and was scrambling around wondering if she could retrieve the situation.

'Sienna Sampson, as she calls herself, is one of my clients. My regular ten o'clock.'

The smile that had frozen itself on Mrs Sidhu's face was melting like ice cream on a hot day. 'But, but, but the sessions, the notes, it's all in her notes. That's what I came here to see.'

Dr Eardley opened his drawer, took out one of Sienna's red notebooks and slid it across the desk to Mrs Sidhu. 'Please, take a look.'

She opened it, hardly daring to look at the meaningless scrawlings inside. There were pages and pages of squiggles and doodles. 'I don't suppose this is some kind of shorthand?' Another thought came to her. 'The secret garden, Patrick made it for her. There's a hidden garden just for them.'

'That garden is for individual sessions. It's been here years; we don't use it much for group work, because there's an ants' nest in there. Sienna has barely said two words to Patrick Kirby.'

The air under Mrs Sidhu's wings died, she was in a dead stall. 'Nothing was true, not a single thing that Sienna has said to me.'

Eardley shook his head slowly. 'Her real name is Emily. Emily Eardley.'

'Emily? You mean the inscription in your book?' She recollected the dedication. 'To Emily, who taught me to follow my dreams and to believe in the impossible.'

'She's my adopted daughter and I love her dearly. But she has a disorder.' Eardley's eyes took on a distant look. 'The damage was done long before I adopted her. Emily's trauma was caused by her abusive birth parents. They were deeply religious and strict. If Emily misbehaved, they would lock her in a cupboard for hours, sometimes days. To deal with the wounds, she invented Sienna, a woman who was in control of her life, had a fantastic career, and was free to do all the things Emily could not.

'She was diagnosed with paranoid schizophrenia, but we made no progress. Until she met Wendy Calman. It was Dr Calman who diagnosed her with dissociative identity disorder. It was her idea to indulge Sienna and have her take notes as a way of engaging with the underlying trauma.

'Unfortunately, Dr Calman's death seems to have locked her into the Sienna persona. I can't seem to get my daughter back. She's even developed new branches of the character. She thinks she's a spy.'

Mrs Sidhu cleared her throat and spoke in a small voice: 'Oh dear. The E cult. It's still here. They've got your daughter.'

'Cult?' That word again. Eardley narrowed his eyes. 'Hang on, you're not responsible for this, are you?' He dumped the plastic VFC card on the desk. His lips were white. 'What exactly have you done?'

'Circles.' Mrs Sidhu blinked for a long moment. A circle with a dot at the centre. This circle is our home. 'The stone circle. They're taking her to the stone circle.'

28

There were other figures around her now, wearing white clothes and masks. Pushing her along until she stood before him. There was a deafening noise, a screaming, screeching, singing. It was a chorus. 'Into the night, into the night, darling, won't you take me into the night.'

She was standing in front of him, his crooked smile, his ravaged face, every muscle on his body oiled and drawn tight, and as he parted his lips she saw red fangs. He put the palm of his hand to her head, she stood, her chest heaving in sobs of air. Sienna was falling apart, she knew it, all the people living inside her were fighting to get to the surface, clutching for the meniscus between unconscious and conscious like fingers breaking the surface of water, until with a shriek one broke free.

A high-pitched keening sound came from all around. The gathered group turned their faces upward and Sienna did the same. For a moment it looked to her like the stars were shining extra brightly tonight. Yet the constellations looked strange and unfamiliar. Then, slowly, they began to move. It was true, the stars were moving. Sienna's knees weakened, her legs buckled. Before she fell, she was steadied by the man on her right. Above her the tiny white lights circled, and the whining rose to a buzzing, the buzzing of a million bees.

The scream was long and loud and it took almost thirty seconds for Sienna to realise that it wasn't coming out of her mouth. It couldn't. Her mouth was full of pulsing flesh and pounding blood.

Jonny Snakeskin's face was contorted into a grimace, his mouth was open and he was howling. 'Get her off my arm!'

Someone shouted, 'Cut!' and the music slowed to a halt. The three witches on the rocks stopped singing backing vocals, and two runners sprang forward and tried their best to get Sienna's teeth out of Jonny Snakeskin's arm. In the distance police sirens approached.

The bathroom door hung open; the broken bolt was on the floor. Varma, Tez and Daljeet entered and stopped almost immediately. All three gasped at the same time.

Post-it notes with illegible scrawlings covered the walls and shower screen. A kettle and a hotplate were plugged into the extension cable. A makeshift desk straddled the toilet seat.

'What madness is this?' Varma whispered. Varma sniffed a saucepan. 'Oh my God. She's been cooking my aubergine bhajis in here. This is a toilet kitchen.'

Daljeet was at the open window. 'She went out this way. And her car is gone.'

29

Patrick waited patiently. He had traced out his message on the small lawn outside the cottage. He looked at the raffle ticket and checked again the number on the list where the name was written in Wendy Calman's neatly printed hand alongside the three raffle ticket numbers. 'Elliot Chase.'

He watched Elliot leaving the house with a bag. He would be taking Edith her clothes for the night. He knew they were all holed up at the retreat. It was announced on the news. But it was Elliot he wanted to help the most. Because Elliot was the one, the one Wendy was most concerned about. So much so she had scrawled his name on the last page of her manuscript.

Patrick followed silently. He had to get to him before he reached the gates of Benham House.

Elliot jammed his buds into his ears and turned up the music. The holdall dangled on his right arm. It was heavy and dragged at his shoulder. It didn't matter. No one knew when they'd catch up with Patrick, so he'd packed a few days of clothes and supplies for Edith. He smiled to think of her, sweet old thing, and he was glad he had found her. End-of-life care was what it meant. He would see her through to the end, that was a certainty. After that, well, he'd think about that when it happened.

The gates of the retreat were coming into view. There was Arif. He waved and Arif unlocked them. Elliot wondered where the coppers were. When he'd left there had been two of them either side, like those stone lions people put outside their doors to ward off evil spirits.

Arif saw him a moment after he saw Elliot. He shouted but the idiot had his earbuds in. There were moments, barely seconds to act. He ran towards Elliot, just as Patrick ran towards him from behind. He fumbled in his back pocket for the syringe, flipped it round but his fingers were tense, cold and unyielding. The syringe dropped to the ground. Arif's brain whirled, while the whole world slowed. Patrick was nearly on Elliot and he knew he had to save him. Then his hand found the sheath on his belt. It was there; his father's gift was in the palm of his hand before he could think.

Elliot saw the gates open, but something was wrong. Arif was yelling something, hands cupped either side of his mouth. Now, he was running towards him, pulling something out of his belt. Something shining, made of steel. Elliot pulled the earbuds out and threw his hands up with a scream as Arif's knife flashed up. He choked and fell to his knees, the cry for mercy stuck in his throat. Blood, there was blood everywhere. Then a moment, a blissful, tearful moment later, he was still alive. Arif's face was frozen in shock staring at the space behind Elliot.

Elliot turned awkwardly, still on his knees. Patrick lay face up, looking at the stars. An expanding pool of blood made a moon-like circle around his prone form. He reached a hand towards Elliot. 'I am returned, destroyer of . . .' The light drew back from his eyes and they glazed over.

Arif found his voice. 'Bloody hell. I've killed him.'

Elliot's lip quivered. 'You saved my life.' He stood up, his white uniform soaked in blood.

PART IV

Good cooking is like solving a murder. You've got all the ingredients, but they won't make a dish until they're combined in the right way.

Life With a Knife, Mrs Sidhu's memoirs

MIDSUMMER DAY, 1997

Time was short, but he couldn't suppress a chuckle. He had two dead bodies. Have to get them to the church on time, wouldn't want to be late. He was certainly getting no help from either of the bodies. Arms flapping, legs flopping – it was worse than helping a drunk. There wasn't much time to enjoy himself, but it was important to take time to celebrate your wins, to acknowledge how far you had come.

The ceremony at the stone circle had gone well. This final act, the fire, would really establish his name and the E cult in the minds of people.

He hauled the second body into the front passenger seat of the car, with help from Begovic, who was compliant enough, though it was easy to read the disgust and hatred in his eyes.

He could kill him too. It would be easy to establish him as another E cult member, but the boy had seen them, and another body so young – now, that would be hard to explain. Plus he had nothing against these two. It was the other two who had betrayed him. He was no cold-blooded killer. If anything, he acted out of passion and love. It was just his way to turn that heat, that passion into cool, calculated planning.

It was dark outside, and the sweat was cooling on his forehead. Sweat made of nerves and of hard work. And if he was tired now, wait until later. The night was far from over.

The boot of the Land Rover was already well stocked with petrol in jerrycans. When the house went up in flames, with the two of them inside, only then could he relax just a little. Safely inside, he chuckled again. He would sleep on the flight.

Sandra, she had been the difficult one. Not because she had put up a fight, quite the contrary. When he gave her the choice, she had drunk the glass of fizzy pop laced with phenobarbital in one gulp. The difficulty was how quickly she had come to her decision. This one, he hefted a dangling arm into the car and closed the door, this one had been a pleasure. Time to digest these emotions later, he sniggered once again.

Begovic cleared his throat; he had to stop chuckling lest he appear mad. The refugee dentist was rheumy-eyed. 'It's getting late,' he said. 'Our business here is complete.'

'What will you tell your son?'

'Arif is a good boy. He will say nothing, he is young, his head is full of ghosts. As is mine.'

He walked around to the driver's side. 'Then the price of your silence is due. The documents will be with you tomorrow. I have already instructed my lawyers.'

As he drove away, Begovic waved as if they had just enjoyed a meal and a nice bottle of wine and now sadly the evening was coming to a close. In the rear-view mirror he could still see him dwindling smaller into the night. Next to him was the boy, holding a knife. The boy loved his knife. Maybe he too would make a fine killer one day.

30

There they were, lumpy, fleshy, featureless faces rolling round and round in the laundry. They were as bland as bedsheets, empty, eyeless sockets made from panty leg holes and mouths from socks.

As she woke, Mrs Sidhu recalled what Edith said. 'The dead are always calling. They call to you too.'

Mrs Sidhu shivered. There was someone in her bedroom. She lay in bed. She felt hollowed out like an eggshell, like an aubergine skin, like a baked potato that you've scooped the flesh from prior to crisping and baking and now longing for its mushy innards to be replaced and to feel whole again.

The figure stood over her. She couldn't move. Maybe this was her own funeral and this was Death.

With extreme reluctance she recollected the previous night's work. It was a scene of chaos. If only she had stuck to eggs and aubergines and baked potatoes. There was Jonny Snakeskin screaming, first in pain and then in rage. There was Tamzin's slow smile as he turned to her for comfort, there was DCI Burton marshalling his troops trying desperately to regain order. At the centre of it all, two people, a father and a daughter.

Stephen Eardley cradled Sienna's head in his arms. She was a shattered vase; he was trying to hold the pieces together. They were at the centre of the stone circle, which was at the centre of a storm whose winds were made of dashing police officers, confused film-makers, onlookers from the village and members of the press. It was a storm of *ka ka*, and it had hit Mrs Sidhu full in the face.

She almost wished this was her own funeral. Above her now were the whorls of Artex her departed husband had made in the ceiling to give the bedroom 'a bit of class'; opposite her was the woodchip wallpaper he had put up to hide the cracks in the plaster. Death, meanwhile, wasn't making any moves, looking more like a nervous teen, shifting from foot to foot. So, she was most clearly alive, only momentarily trapped in that state known as catatonia, where one's muscles don't respond. In sleep, the body disconnects from the brain, sometimes leaving a person paralysed when they wake.

Catatonia passed and with relief Mrs Sidhu moved. Next to her, miraculously, was a cup of tea. She touched it. It was hot. Slowly her eyes came into focus and the figure leaned over. It wasn't Death. It was Tez.

'Mum?' He spoke gently. 'I made you a cup of tea.'

With a small smile and great anticipation she tasted it, swishing it round her mouth, bubbled air through it, and after much supping and lip-smacking concluded that it was terrible. Tez waited for her response. 'Thank you, Tez. It's lovely.' He smiled.

Life is what you make it, and in this case she had better make her own tea. She took a deep breath, swung her legs round, her feet finding her slippers, her arms finding the sleeves of her gown. 'I'd better make breakfast for you and your aunty.'

Tez didn't move, and the look in his eyes drew a sharp pang in Mrs Sidhu's heart, a reminder of the looks from everyone the night before. 'She moved into a hotel,' said Tez.

Mrs Sidhu was already at the bathroom door before she heard him. She stroked the wood around the door bolt. Splinters pricked her fingers.

'Uncle Varma broke it down. We were worried about you when you didn't reply. Then when you weren't in here, he called the police.'

The door was a quarter open; she pushed through it and saw what they must have seen as they would have seen it. A kettle, a hot plate, Post-its and notecards and envelopes with scribbled writings, fluttering in the breeze of an open window. She gathered up some of her Post-it notes that must have been blown off the shower screen: 'lost property' 'village raffle'. Her chin dropped to her chest. 'What must they all think of me?'

Tez spoke innocently. 'It's OK. I told them it was normal. Normal for you, anyway.'

Mrs Sidhu thanked Tez absent-mindedly. The stairs groaned sadly as they bore her down them with her unsatisfactory tea.

'Oh. Aunty Daljeet says she's flying home tomorrow. She gave me the flight details. Maybe we should see her off,' he called out.

Downstairs the gas flames jumped on and water swashed into the pathila. It steamed and wobbled on the ring as Mrs Sidhu tore open a teabag, crumbled in the contents

274

and thought most deeply while she waited for it to boil. It took her a while to see she had a message on her phone.
There will be a meeting in my office at 10 a.m. Eardley

OK, she was wrong about the cult.

The tyres of her bottle-green Nissan Micra were eating up country road as quickly as Mrs Sidhu's highly acute mind was coming to conclusions. She had to be honest with herself, she had been led astray. Sienna, whose real name was Emily, had been telling Mrs Sidhu exactly what she wanted to hear. She had adapted her own story into it, and between them they had dreamed up an occult nightmare sitting at the centre of the village.

Mrs Sidhu's style of driving was what she described as cavalier and debonair, and what everyone else described as dangerously unhinged. In her own mind, once she got outside Slough and hit the Berkshire countryside, she was in an open-topped Bugatti and the green fields of the Home Counties melded as one with images of the French Riviera which she had clipped from magazines. In the mind of anyone that encountered her she gave the impression of a wayward green missile with a guidance system prone to making last-minute decisions on the subject of which lane she was in and how fast she was going to take a corner. So the man crossing the road as she entered Benham village had to make several changes of direction, before realising in horror that his best option was to jump into the ditch. Pigeons – well, pigeons, as we know, are forewarned.

If Mrs Sidhu was convinced that she was wrong about the cult, then she was equally convinced that she was right about Patrick. Just because Sienna's romance with him

275

was a work of fiction did not mean he was less deserving of Mrs Sidhu's help. Apple sauce does not lie. He was trying to help people, not murder them. He was trying to protect them with charms and symbols, and there was another reason that connected the deaths of Dr Calman and Kate and Tony Hammond. That reason would become clear when they found Patrick, as she felt sure they would soon. How long could he stay hidden?

The tyres kicked up handfuls of gravel as she stalled the car to a halt at the Benham House Retreat.

That was what she had to convince DCI Burton of, that there was a connection to Patrick, yes, but that connection was not his murderous intent, or his psychosis. She cast her eyes around the front of the retreat. There was Burton moping around in his car. He needed a little bit of Mrs Sidhu motivation.

With a slam of her car door that left the shell juddering and knocked a wing mirror askew, Mrs Sidhu strode across the car park.

Burton had been sitting in the Benham House forecourt for a long time. He checked his watch. Five minutes to ten. He had no desire to be early for this particular meeting. The leather upholstery of the car seat creaked for a moment as he slid his hand under his backside and came back out with his wallet. He plopped it open. It was old, leather, and some of the stitching was going at the seams. He didn't really need it, it had become home to a wad of receipts he didn't know what else to do with, but it was home to one other thing. He ran his nail over the scuffed plastic window and stroked the face in the picture behind it. It was taken right here, in the gentle sunshine of better times, not the neon, reality-hardened sun of today. She was holding a huge teddy bear, her brown eyes shining, and he was next to her. Her hero.

'Doesn't do to dwell on the past.' Mrs Sidhu propped her arms on the open car window. 'Let me see.'

Burton slapped the wallet closed. 'None of your business.' He climbed out of the car, unfolding himself, long legs first and heavy body next. He started a funereal trudge towards the house.

3 1

'Hey, come on, please, we need to talk.' Mrs Sidhu increased her stride to catch up with the long-legged policeman. 'I realise what happened last night was a debacle, of course, but in the midst of it all something occurred to me.' Their feet grated in unison on the gravel path, an uneasy rattle of dragging heels. Mrs Sidhu continued briskly: 'What if things happened as I said?'

Burton walked with his back bowed, his wrists together behind his back. His face was unreadable, a mask. His lidded eyes stayed firmly on the path ahead of him, as if each footstep needed to be watched. The tread of a wary soldier in a minefield.

'What if Patrick found the body, but, and this is the important thing, what if Wendy was still alive when he did?' This point seemed important to Mrs Sidhu, and at this point she got quite excited, emphasising her point with jabs of her finger on Burton's upper arm. 'Perhaps she told him something.'

'She had her throat slashed open. Pathologist confirmed that she couldn't have said a word.'

The pen, she had a pen, and a new thought thrilled through her synapses. 'Maybe she wrote it down. On the last page of her manuscript. The missing last page. When you catch up with Patrick, he'll have that last page and on it will be the name of the killer. Bet you anything.'

'We've caught up with Patrick.'

'Oh, and what did he say?'

'Not much. He's dead.' Burton's voice was dangerously flat calm. 'He was killed last night while we were all running around like idiots up at the stone circle.' He didn't add that they were there at Mrs Sidhu's insistence; he didn't need to.

Mrs Sidhu's stride faltered. This was unexpected news. 'You don't understand, I thought Sienna . . . Emily,' she corrected herself, 'was being groomed by a cult.' She fell behind Burton, who was ploughing forward like a cross-Channel ferry. She doubled her stride to catch up once more. 'Well then, that proves it, doesn't it? He knew something. Just like Wendy, he died because he was trying to help. Like Kate he could see something better around the corner of his life, if he could just reach out and grab it.'

'He died because he was about to kill the next man in line, the next person who was at Dr Calman's therapy sessions. He came at Elliot Chase with a claw hammer.' Burton balled his fist and smashed it into the palm of his hand. 'The one person who was present at all the therapy sessions who we hadn't put a watch on.'

Mrs Sidhu was taken aback. 'A hammer? That's odd, isn't it? All the others had their throats cut.'

'Maybe he was bored, maybe it was symbolic, who knows. We never will, because he's dead.'

'I don't understand. So how did Patrick die?'

Burton explained to her that Elliot was lucky that Arif had seen what was about to happen and had fought Patrick off. In the struggle, he had used his knife and stabbed Patrick. 'We've got Arif in custody, but it looks like self-defence.'

Mrs Sidhu's brow furrowed. 'Arif?' She shook her head.

'Apparently he carried a hunting knife around. Given the circumstances, I suspect he'll get off with a warning. He saved a man's life.'

'But what about the case against Patrick?'

'It leaves a great big mess. Our main and only suspect is dead, and we can't close the case without affirmative proof that it was him. We still don't know where he's been since we found his little lair at the Pollock house. We still don't have the murder weapon – something rusty with gold on it. Yeah, go figure. The only plus side is that at least now the killing will stop.'

'I have an idea about the murder weapon. Are you familiar with Druidic practice? No? Well, I've been doing some reading, and it was common to cut mistletoe with a golden sickle. So an iron implement, maybe with gold spray paint on it.'

'So, the sort of thing a gardener might own. Especially one who does his own graffiti?'

Mrs Sidhu gulped. 'You're still certain it was Patrick.'

Burton muttered something under his breath along the lines of how much more did she want.

'I'm only going by your standards of proof. You say you don't have enough evidence. Maybe there's a reason for that.'

Burton had always been a man who was slow to anger, but anger it was that was turning his face pink. 'You really don't know, do you? You really don't know how far you've gone this time?'

Mrs Sidhu appealed to Burton. 'I only ever wanted to help.'

'Helping others comes at a cost. Policemen learn that early. We keep our heads down and our tails tucked in. That is wisdom.'

'Is it?'

'It is. It's a cost you don't know before you start. The bill always comes at the end. You're about to learn that.'

Mrs Sidhu blinked. 'I don't understand you. What am I about to learn?'

They had reached the door of the Benham House Retreat. Mrs Sidhu stood back and waited for Burton's reply. When none came, she finally took in Burton's even-more-stolid-than-normal air. 'I must say, Chief Inspector, you don't seem your usual self this morning.' Or maybe too much his usual self.

Burton swallowed. For a while it looked like he wanted to say something. Quite a lot, actually. A number of conflicting emotions spasmed across his features, none of them gaining any long-term purchase.

'Are you having some kind of fit?' Mrs Sidhu asked. 'Should I call an ambulance?'

Burton gained control of his features. 'Mrs Sidhu, I think it's better if you let us handle the situation from here on in.'

'We've had that discussion before, Chief Inspector. I don't know what makes you think anything has changed.'

'Very well. I want you to know I did everything I could.'

Burton opened the door and walked away, flapping his arms like a giant penguin.

'Are you saying I should try and prove it?' There was no reply. Mrs Sidhu looked for the space inside where she should have been upset. There was nothing there. Mystified, Mrs Sidhu entered the house.

32

When Mrs Sidhu entered Benham House, everything was quiet. She heard murmurs from Dr Eardley's office. Her burning ears yearned to join with the cool wood of the door. After the events of the previous night, it was better not to.

When Mrs Sidhu read Eardley's text message, she had naturally assumed that he was asking her to help with the catering. So now she entered discreetly with tea, coffee, pastries and homemade cookies.

They stopped talking when she opened the door. She muttered an apology for being late and began pouring drinks for the assembled group. Around the room were familiar and unfamiliar faces. At first she thought she must've walked in on a therapy session. There was Jonny Snakeskin, Edith was there too, with Elliot behind her, scratches on his hands and face. Some people Mrs Sidhu didn't recognise, who had an official look about them, she guessed were from the board of trustees. And of course Eardley. His spectacled eyes never left Mrs Sidhu; he watched her with white-faced detachment.

That impression was dispelled when she saw Tamzin Grey and a mousy-looking woman holding a briefcase (Mrs Sidhu guessed a lawyer). All in all, Mrs Sidhu noted cheerfully that there was an atmosphere of barely contained hostility. Someone was in for it, that was for sure.

DCI Burton was seated too. He sat sternly at the centre, contemplating the carvings on the ceiling. The investigation must have moved into a new phase if he was questioning a wider group of witnesses. It was odd, though, that he had neglected his notebook. Another curious thing was that there was an empty seat beside him. Who were they all waiting for? Mrs Sidhu fell back on her usual gambit. To move around the room delivering drinks and food while gleaning what information she could.

They resumed their conversation. Jonny Snakeskin was speaking.

'We were filming, all right? That's what we were doing at the stone circle.'

'We did it on the quiet, guerrilla viral style,' Tamzin said acidly. 'We all know how hard it is to get permission to do anything in this village.'

'It was a rock video, I understand,' Burton said.

Jonny rubbed his stomach, and in a low rumble said, 'No, a life insurance ad. It was Tamzin's idea. I got full artistic control.' He grimaced. 'That's where I am now, OK? I am happy to have full artistic control over a life insurance ad.'

Tamzin squeezed his hand. 'This is the beginning of the comeback.' Jonny looked unsure.

'Look, back in the nineties, I did this song, I wore these vampire teeth and I bit into a virgin's neck.'

'I remember it – "Into the Night". Classic.' Burton grinned, and then stopped.

'Yeah, well, in the ad, it's lucky because the virgin has a mutual policy that pays out to her dependants even in the event of a life changing injury. Like becoming a zombie bride. Is that so hard to understand? I figured the girl looked like a virgin. She's not supposed to bite back.' Jonny rolled up his sleeve and displayed his forearm to everyone. A set of white mink teeth had made a row of sharp red indents.

Jonny sat back and rolled his eyes to the ceiling and Tamzin took over: 'The cost of abandoning a night's filming is quite considerable.' Pages were passed from lawyer to Tamzin and on to Eardley.

He examined the numbers; his eyes widened momentarily, then he blew out of his lips before speaking. 'In summary, we are talking about delusional behaviour. About deceit, about a mind that is clearly suffering from a disorder. She seems to be completely buried in an alternative reality.'

Poor Emily, thought Mrs Sidhu, but what could you expect? The girl had a mental health condition, and because of that she called herself Sienna Sampson. However, Mrs Sidhu was surprised that Eardley, who had finally revealed that he was Emily's adoptive father, was being quite so clinical in judging his own daughter. That was the professional in him, she presumed.

'You can stop that now, Mrs Sidhu, the incessant pouring of tea, the slices of cake, the admittedly delicious snacks.' There was a murmur of approval about the delicious snacks. 'All the perfect front to hide what is clearly a very troubled mind.'

'Me?' Mrs Sidhu gulped. All sound ceased in the room.

Burton beckoned Mrs Sidhu to the middle and the empty chair. It was for her. All this was for her. She took in the sea of angry faces, her knees trembled. She sat down before the ground dropped out beneath her. With eyes wide, she cast looks about the people gathered. Gathered, it now dawned on her, to watch her downfall.

'This woman came here as a chef, and yet her behaviour has caused disruption, nay, chaos. An already disturbed patient was nurtured – groomed, some might say – in her fantasy.' Sienna sat hollow-eyed in a corner of the room. Mrs Sidhu was shaking her head. Eardley continued unabated: 'Consequently, a talented musician suffered serious injury' – Jonny Snakeskin waved his arm again for everyone to see – 'and has suffered a relapse in his quest for rehabilitation.' Jonny Snakeskin waved a bottle of whisky which he had miraculously obtained. Tamzin snatched it from him before he could take a swig. 'The good name of this retreat has been dragged into disrepute . . .' Dr Eardley paused, his voice softening. 'And more than that, my own daughter has been psychologically damaged, possibly beyond repair. All because of her.' Eardley's finger quivered as it pointed at Mrs Sidhu.

Mrs Sidhu's head was shaking from side to side, as if she was trying to loosen a pea that had got stuck in her ear. It was as if the dark spaces between her and her assembled accusers was a sea, a writhing, swelling mere that she had been cast into. 'No, no, don't listen to him,' she said. Everyone's eyes were fixed on her, receding behind the waves of panic that threatened to drown Mrs Sidhu. No one was throwing her a lifeline. 'I've done nothing that any ordinary citizen wouldn't have done.'

Eardley ignored her interruption. 'I have been in contact with her employer, a Mr Varma, who it seems was surprised to hear that Mrs Sidhu was working at the retreat. He was under the impression that she was taking time out due to a head injury sustained while working for him. Until last night, when he called on her at home. Suspecting she was depressed, he broke into her bathroom and found this.' Eardley circulated a picture. It raised eyebrows as it was passed from hand to hand until it found its way to Mrs Sidhu. She winced. 'She has constructed what he could only describe as a toilet kitchen.' There was an audible gasp around the room at this.

Mrs Sidhu raised a wobbling hand. 'With the greatest of respect, er, your honour, that is a toilet *office*.' An even louder gasp of disapproval followed. 'Please, let me explain, you'll see it's quite simple. I needed a place to think and work, and my sister-in-law – who is bonkers, by the way, and dead set on stealing everything and everyone in my life away from me – was taking up the kitchen. So I set up a toilet office. The cooking' – and this was an important point – 'was purely secondary.'

'A toilet office,' Eardley repeated gravely. 'And from the cookery equipment in this photo, are we to understand that you prepared food you've served here in this toilet office?'

In a small voice Mrs Sidhu said, 'Some of it, yes.' There followed the sound of cookies, pastries and rolls dropping on plates. Several faces turned green.

'Chief Inspector Burton.' At Eardley's call, Burton hauled himself to his feet. With the eyes of the assembled group upon him, he swallowed hard. 'Chief Inspector, do you know this woman well?' Burton thought for a moment, but there was no denying it. He nodded curtly, once. 'Has she inserted herself into police business on more than one occasion?' Burton thought about speaking, thought better of it, and nodded once more. 'Are there no penalties in place for interfering in a police investigation?'

Mrs Sidhu stared at Burton with wide, unblinking eyes. This was the moment when he would surely step up. 'Tell them, Chief Inspector. All I've ever done is help. Help you, help the police. Tried to help the people of Benham village.'

'Yes, please tell us, Chief Inspector,' Eardley said.

The world waited. Burton seemed to have lost even the ability to stand properly. He moved his hands uncertainly, trying one in his trouser pocket, then the other, like a man looking for the correct change that he was certain that he had, but realising slowly that it was in his other pair of trousers. Eventually, Burton cleared his throat. 'This woman . . .' he started, then changed his mind and started again. 'What you need to understand about Mrs Sidhu is that there is not a bad bone in her body.'

Mrs Sidhu nodded brightly. This was more like it. Now the likes of Eardley and Tamzin Grey and Jonny Snakeskin were going to get it from the horse's mouth. 'She's an extraordinary woman, whose first and only instinct is to help people who are in trouble.'

Mrs Sidhu let go of the breath that had bottled up in her lungs. The relief that spread through her tired muscles was so all-encompassing, so deep, that it took her a moment to catch up with the words that Burton was speaking.

'But I think we can all see that she has a problem. A severe problem.'

Mrs Sidhu waved her hand, as if she was signalling for a bus to stop. 'She's nosy to the point of obsession, she's irritating, and she never listens to anyone.'

'No, no, no, hang on please . . .' she twittered. The bus was not stopping.

288

Burton continued: 'Not only that, her imagination is so wild that she allowed a person with as fragile a grip of reality as Emily Eardley' – Burton nodded an apology to Stephen Eardley, who grimly accepted – 'to convince her of the existence of a cult here in Benham village.' They all chuckled.

'Hang on a minute. Something very fishy is going on here.'

Burton cut her off. 'But we have an opportunity to help her.' The room fell silent. 'So rather than recrimination, or severe legal action . . .' Not only was the bus not stopping, but it was swerving deliberately into a huge puddle, sluicing a huge wall of muddy, brown water directly onto Mrs Sidhu. 'I am going to suggest an alternative course of action.'

All she had to do was admit she wasn't Batman.

'It feels like we've had this date with destiny from the moment you walked into my office,' Eardley said. 'Do you remember when I mistook you for a client? It looks like it wasn't my mistake after all.'

Mrs Sidhu lay on the couch, looking up at the coffered wooden ceiling and saying nothing. If she didn't talk, he couldn't get anything out of her. If she didn't listen, he couldn't convince her of anything.

'Now you . . .' here Eardley paused and let out a barely audible chuckle, '. . . you, an ordinary woman from Slough, have become invested in the idea that you alone can solve this crime. Why is that, I wonder?'

Things had moved rapidly after Burton's submission to the board of the Benham House Retreat. Mrs Sidhu, her face burning with embarrassment, had been presented with a piece of paper which would put her under the care of Dr Eardley, who would assess her mental and spiritual condition and recommend further help if needed. Burton had been dubious about Eardley's qualifications to do this, but Eardley was holding all the cards, it was his confidentiality agreement that Mrs Sidhu had broken, and it seemed a small concession under the circumstances. Mrs Sidhu, after all, was a fan of his techniques.

With hangwoman Tamzin Grey standing over his shoulder, itching to start legal proceedings against her, Mrs Sidhu had little choice. She was defeated, her arms lost all strength, hung like spaghetti from her shoulders. Then the final humiliation. Tez, Varma and (Mrs Sidhu shuddered at the memory) Respected Sister-in-Law Daljeet were led in. Each carried a look of pity and concern like a burden on their faces. Mrs Sidhu was left in no doubt that she had let her family and her colleagues down. Tez was wearing a suit, which, through welling eyes, Mrs Sidhu appreciated. She had always wanted to see him in a suit. He put a hand on her shoulder and with the other offered her a pen. She took it and signed. Next to her mark, a tear splashed, smudging the ink with a crown of regret.

Mrs Sidhu had cleared her throat. Her hands were clamped together, palm to palm, the fingers of each hand folding over the back of the other, making an entreaty. 'If you would only ask DCI Burton, he will confirm that I have helped him with a number of cases.' She could feel her palms beginning to sweat. Realising that she was making a poor impression, she released her hands and by effort of will sat back in her chair. She could not resist grasping her knee for support.

In his office, Eardley cleared his throat, bringing Mrs Sidhu back from her recollection. 'People are usually standing in the way of their own happiness, pushing on the door that says "pull". Give way to it, stop resisting, and life becomes so much easier and more rewarding,' said Eardley.

He sat silhouetted in the window. His face was in shadow, but Mrs Sidhu could feel his eyes on her. When he broke the silence, his voice had a smile in it. 'It's because you're unhappy. Your life is raising a son, running a business. It was once being a wife. And for you, it doesn't seem like enough. But you have to come to terms with life as it is. There's no shame in being a chef. There's no shame in not being Batman.' His voice was unreadable, lacking in all sentiment. He came and sat beside her. 'Don't you want to get better? To be well?'

Mrs Sidhu tried not to listen. Her legs felt numb and her thoughts lumbered uneasily through a fog of – what was it she felt? – numbness mixed with humiliation with exhaustion. 'I have solved cases. I have helped people.' She wanted to sound defiant but heard the weakness and complaint in her own voice.

'How you resist. Come, Mrs Sidhu, give yourself over. You are an animal in pain, yet you won't trust me. I can end the pain.'

How had it come to this? The anchor around her heart was pulling Mrs Sidhu down. Mrs Sidhu asked herself if she was mad. She felt normal, just as she always had. Yet even when she felt normal was it not true that she had, all her life, felt adrift? Never had she fitted in, always she had chosen the other way, the way of turning her back on the standard, boring way of doing things. This, then, was her punishment. Society did not endure those who went against the grain. They, like her, were sooner or later pulled down into the murky depths, spiralling down a plughole. That anchor was dragging at her still.

Eardley sat back stiffly. 'You're here on DCI Burton's recommendation. But you could see a psychiatrist, I mean a clinical one. They might prescribe drugs, medications, stays in institutions. You're familiar with the well-known Section 8 of the Mental Health Act?'

Coldness gripped her heart. Mrs Sidhu raised her hand quickly, banishing the idea. 'No!' Her voice was taut with strain. 'No, please, I'd rather not.'

His voice soothed again. 'I'm sure that won't be necessary,' Dr Eardley mused, 'as long as you are cooperative.'

She heaved and lay on her side, curling into the foetal position, with arms wrapping over her head. There it was, he had broken her, she felt it. She was a sinking ship, her back shattered by the torpedo of wellness and reason. She was a little girl again, holding a broken vase, her face stinging from her mother's anger, and tears leaping to her eyes. 'Denial,' she heard Eardley say as if from a great distance, 'to acceptance, and with acceptance comes healing.' She knew it was true and she longed for it. She had longed for this couch and Dr Feelgood's calm eyes from the very start. She longed for her mother's forgiveness. And in place of her mother she saw her sister-in-law Daljeet, whom she had wounded and ignored. Why resist? Why not dissolve into Eardley's grey gaze?

She glubbed up a sob. 'I have been wrong, wrong all along, wrong all my life. I'm not Batman, or Batgirl or Bat anything. I'm just batty,' Mrs Sidhu said.

'There, not so hard at all,' Eardley soothed. 'Good, a sign of acceptance is a chance to leave your old world behind and to start your new one,' Eardley went on. 'Tell me everything.'

And she did. She told him about her groundless suspicions, about her pointless investigations, about her arguments with Daljeet, about her lying to Varma, about the Post-it notes she still carried in her pocket that read 'lost property' and 'village raffle', about her vainglorious dreams of solving the case before the police did, and her mistaken faith that Patrick was somehow not responsible and that she could reunite him in a romance which never existed with Sienna Sampson, a girl who existed even less. She wrung every last bit of penitence from herself, burying her head further into her arms, sobbing, wailing and apologising to Eardley, to her mother, to Daljeet and to the world she had wronged. At the end she was just the last piece of wood floating on the water after the ship had sunk.

33

On Saturday, Mrs Sidhu was wrung out like a wet rag. She exuded wellness. Every pore of her body had been flushed through in every possible way. She had meditated, cogitated, and de-constipated. Dr Feelgood made good on his guarantee. She felt good. The whole world looked like a different place.

Benham House certainly did. The lawns that were usually populated by meditators and art classes and tai chi-ers were turned over to gaudy stalls. There were all the things common to the Great British village fete. There was a tombola, second-hand books, toys, a coconut shy, jumble, stalls selling hot food, stalls selling cold food, and of course a raffle.

'Carm and git yer raffle tickets.' Unfortunately, in a mistaken attempt to add authenticity, some braying million-aire was selling raffle tickets in an ironic costermonger voice.

She glanced round at the winding line of people buying tickets. A raffle, something about that struck Mrs Sidhu, a dim memory. She shook her head; ah, now there was one of her triggers, these vague feelings that something was out of place. Mrs Sidhu smiled, she was going to stay on course, stay on the golden road.

This was what being well felt like. It felt like sitting in golden sunlight, in a pagoda on top of a mountain, under a golden umbrella. It was like being born again – crying, laughing, bloody – into the world anew. The darkness and disease we all feel we have accumulated, the bad karma, was flushed away. All her life Mrs Sidhu had been unwell. This had been explained to her. The absence of that unwellness was all she needed to free her into wellness. It made perfect sense.

In the Benham House kitchen, she wiped the jam off her hands and went to the oven. Mrs Sidhu was in the moment, fulfilling her purpose. After all, she had come to Benham to make scones. At this, a snapshot memory clicked into Mrs Sidhu's mind: Dr Calman's kitchen, the smoke pouring out of the oven, burned jam stuck to one pan, and half-softened apples sitting in another. The apples that told her as loud and clear as the blue sky outside that Patrick Kirby hadn't killed Wendy Calman. With determination, Mrs Sidhu pushed that image to one side. She had promised Dr Eardley, Burton, Varma and her whole family she would not go back there. She was on a golden road to recovery. She had to stop this train of thought.

She had a golden road to stay on and a train of thought to get off. She had everything she had wished for, didn't she? She, along with Jonny Snakeskin and new members of the group, had intoned: 'We are standing in the way of our own happiness. We are opening the doors and stepping onto the golden road.' The grass under their bare feet felt real and lush and the earth – when had Mrs Sidhu stopped smelling the earth, simple mud? – smelled sweeter than dark chocolate ganache.

As for sleep, she had never slept so soundly. The bad dreams had gone. That ache where her back met her hips had gone. The numbness in her feet, the heat under her skin that threatened to burst open her veins had gone. Mrs Sidhu had simply left the concerns of the world behind her.

'He's good, isn't he?' Jonny Snakeskin had rattled in her ear after the first group session, breath smelling of rancid sativa. She could only look at him, unable to speak. Dr Feelgood lived up to his name.

It was all so clear. She had everything she had wanted on the very first day she arrived at the retreat.

She wanted to stop cooking aubergine bhajis. She no longer had to deal with her drudgery of those endless dishes, at least temporarily.

She wanted to spill her heart to Dr Feelgood. She had spilled her heart to Dr Feelgood, and Dr Feelgood had made her heart whole again.

She had come here to help at a village fete cooking scones. Here she was at a village fete, cooking and serving scones.

Mrs Sidhu's three wishes had come true. Now she was walking a golden mile, a shimmering road through winding acres of swaying grass. It was a road that had a beginning, and like all roads an end, and like all the best magic roads, you resisted being tempted off the path.

Trains of thought are hard to stop. Wendy Calman had found that out. You apply the brakes but there is weight behind the movement.

'As you can see, our latest client is doing wonderfully,' Dr Eardley said as she came out of the house.

She had believed in Patrick. Foolishly seeing something of him in herself. She let out a dry chuckle. Well, they were similar in at least one way: everyone thought they were mad. And what of Patrick? If he had truly butchered three people and had been about to butcher a fourth, why? Yes, they were connected by the therapy group, but that alone was surely not enough to attract Patrick's murderous attention. No matter, it wasn't her problem.

She was in the sunshine, offering people scones and jam. Not as a caterer, but as a patient – or client, as Dr Eardley insisted – an example of the fine work the Benham House Retreat did in the field of mental wellness. She had collected glowing smiles, supportive glances and loving hugs. Mrs Sidhu kept smiling through it all – until she heard the voice. That was when she felt the doubt.

'Carm on, stip right up, wunnerful prizes to be won.' The voice of the ironic ticket seller chattered across her like warning shots.

Mrs Sidhu again tried to bring that train of thought to an end.

No. Mrs Sidhu was supposed to be 'getting better', to be putting aside thoughts of . . . she could barely bring herself to think of it, the crushing embarrassment of it all . . . of being some kind of detective. Now she thought it, she was hit by how ridiculous it was, how ridiculous she was. Even now she had the delusion that there was a pattern to the murders that she could almost see. Something at the edges of her vision, which when she turned to look at it with the full force of her concentration moved like the floating threads that clouded her vision more and more these days. It was just another facet of her unwellness.

'Carm on, last few tickets.' The queue had dwindled to a handful, and following the whirls and currents and movements of the crowd that she had somehow become lost in, Mrs Sidhu found herself joining the line.

Trains, even those made of thought, are hard to stop. Dr Wendy Calman had learned that on the last day of her life.

'Come on, come on, don't want to miss it, do we?' Elliot beamed his gappy, tombstone smile down on Edith. He stroked her greying hair. 'Not every week there's a village fete. And you do love them.'

Edith tipped her head back and smiled gently, wagging her finger. 'Not as much as you do.' Her eyes were clear today, her face was firm, not slack. It was a good day. The firmness came to the fore when she shook her head. 'But I'm tired. You go. You need some time off, looking after me all day, every day.'

'Oh come on. We can go together. I'll buy you a new raffle ticket.'

'Raffle ticket?' Edith was getting that clouded look again.

'You remember, don't you? When I bought you that ticket at the bring-and-buy?'

Edith smiled weakly. 'Of course I remember.' It was clear she didn't remember a thing. 'But I'm tired out today. You go.'

Elliot came round to face her, dipping at the knees and taking her hands in his. 'You sure? It's been a tough week but it's over now. He's dead. We should be grateful we're all safe and that we've got a village fete to go to. There was talk about cancelling it.'

'I am grateful.' She stroked his face. 'I'm grateful for every minute I've had.'

Elliot eyed her for a few moments. Edith watched him back, her chin set forward. This gnome of a woman could be stubborn when she wanted. 'Well, I know you, dearie: once you've made your mind up, you've made your mind up.' Elliot fetched his baseball cap. 'Anything you want?'

Edith thought. 'Get me a scone. Maybe one that Wendy made. That'll cheer her up.'

'Wendy Calman? Dr Calman's . . .' Elliot abandoned it. Let her be happy. 'She'll be made up. You'll probably be her only sale.'

Elliot closed the front door gently behind him. As he left, the mist in Edith's eyes cleared. She had made her mind up, all right. She read her note again, then sealed the envelope. On the front she printed the words *I'm sorry*.

All roads have an end. This one was a level crossing.

The queue was short now. Mrs Sidhu was at the back, third in line. The woman at the front bought her ticket and as she passed Mrs Sidhu she dropped it. Mrs Sidhu picked it up straight away. 'Hello, excuse me, you dropped your ticket.' Mrs Sidhu looked at the number. 'Seven seven four.' The woman took the ticket with thanks. Mrs Sidhu did the maths. 'If everyone buys one ticket each that'll make me seven seven seven. Lucky me.' The woman smiled politely and moved on, mildly disturbed by Mrs Sidhu's intensity, her staring eyes and her total stillness.

The train of thought Mrs Sidhu had started earlier

thundered across her golden road and ripped the tarmac right off the ground.

She heard the sound of money dropped in a box. Another happy soul walked away with a pink ticket. The queue shuffled forward a few inches. And another. And another. It was like a machine.

Clink, clank, tear.

Tamzin had been in the raffle queue. Elliot said he'd bought a ticket for Edith. That was two of the three targets on Patrick's list. Tony Hammond had a raffle ticket too. If Kate was in the queue as well, that meant there was another connection between the deaths, not just the therapy group.

Clink, clank tear.

'Well?'

It took Mrs Sidhu a while to realise she was at the front of the queue. She paid. 'Could I take your name and contact details?'

'Why would you want those?' Mrs Sidhu asked.

Mrs Sidhu watched in fascination as the braying millionaire wrote her details down neatly on a sheet of paper. She took her number. Seven, seven, seven as she had calculated. A lucky number. A number decided by fate. Their deaths had been decided by numbers and fate.

Mrs Sidhu had the answer in her lap, like a stunned bird. She stood very still. An idea is as easily frightened as a bird; it can take flight and be gone in an instant. She examined what she had from all angles. Until, finally, she knew she was right.

She had to talk to DCI Burton.

34

The time from the moment Mrs Sidhu had her epiphany to losing her shiny wellness-based glow was three minutes.

The first minute was indecisive. She actually felt happy for the first time in a long time. She had shrugged off the cares of the world and was living her own existence. Looking around her, she was on a sun-drenched lawn, surrounded by accepting and supportive faces. She was in the sun.

In the second minute, the shadow of a cloud fell. She was a mother and an aunty and her duty was to other people. In this case, to dead people. There is an inbuilt engine to an Indian aunty and it revolves around the axis that this world is not here to be enjoyed. This lesson was passed down to Mrs Sidhu by her mother. This life was to be tolerated, suffered, mastered even, but enjoyment and guilt-free frivolity was not a list topper.

The third moment was a goodbye, a goodbye to the soft golden road, a goodbye to the sun, and a hello to the stony path of real life. That path began with a simmering bitter-ness. To have experienced the blissful way was to have

301

made the sharp rocks on the path of pain only sharper. One man, and one man only, was responsible for that. Mrs Sidhu growled. 'I'm back, and I'm as mad as hell.'

'They won't even let me near the knife drawer,' Mrs Sidhu was hissing in Burton's ear. As each word was stabbed out, Burton flinched. 'I had to make everything using a spoon. Have you tried cutting sandwiches with a spoon?' Mrs Sidhu thrust a plate of badly cut sandwiches at Burton, which he dodged only narrowly.

They were at the coconut shy, where Burton had been happily hurling cricket balls at tropical fruit. Families frolicked on the lawn, others played at the coconut shy, the hoopla, others enjoyed tea, cakes and sunshine. Mrs Sidhu glowered. It was the perfect day for a village fete.

'These look good.' Burton pecked a sandwich from the plate, then hopped back out of Mrs Sidhu's reach. It was a singularly nimble act, more suited to a sparrow or robin redbreast than a seventeen-stone policeman with knee complaints. Burton managed it, nonetheless. He felt the heat of Mrs Sidhu's gaze. 'You'd rather be sectioned, then?'

'I've had to lie on a couch drivelling nonsense to Dr Feelgood for days on end.' It was true, Eardley had made her his top priority and barely took his eyes off her. Even now he was throwing concerned but loving glances at her.

'That sounds nice, you love a good natter.'

'It is not nice!' Mrs Sidhu growled. 'Actually, all right, it was nice and yes I do like a nice natter.' Her voice became low and dangerous. 'He made me feel like I've never felt before, like I'm whole again.'

'Well, there you go.'

Mrs Sidhu pointed the spoon at Burton. 'That's what

makes me so angry. Because of you, I had to experience something nice. I had to believe for a few glorious days that I'm the centre of my own universe and that nothing else really matters but my subjective existence. That making myself happy is a perfectly good goal in life.'

'That's what's bothering you? That you had a nice time?' Burton scoffed.

'It's a lie. I'm not allowed to be happy while people are dead and the criminal is getting away, and nor are you.' She snatched the cricket ball and swung it at a coconut. It smashed, pouring its milky innards onto the ground. 'Do you know how hard it is to give up nice things when you've had them?'

The stallholder handed Mrs Sidhu a teddy bear. 'Good shot, you win a prize.'

Mrs Sidhu grabbed the teddy bear and strangled it while she talked. 'You stabbed me in the heart. You could have told them about our other cases. Now look at you, waltzing around enjoying my best spoon-made sandwiches. And not only that, everyone, everywhere, believes what they've suspected for years: that I'm not right in the head. It's your fault!'

'I couldn't tell them we'd worked together. If that got out, I'm finished. I did what I could. I am sorry, truly.' Burton gently took the teddy bear from Mrs Sidhu before she tore its head off. He stared at it sadly. 'I know how you feel, mate,' he whispered.

Mrs Sidhu grumped for a while, but eventually, with an ill-natured grunt, accepted Burton's apology. 'I really shouldn't be helping you any further, given your betrayal, but as it happens, I've been thinking and I've come to some conclusions about the case.'

Eardley glanced over in their direction. Burton smiled blandly and waved to him, then when Eardley went back to his conversation, he grabbed her and pulled her to one side. 'Are you mad?' Mrs Sidhu looked hurt. Burton winced. 'Sorry, figure of speech. You know the conditions. You have to abandon any idea of solving crimes. If Eardley or Tamzin Grey find out, it's litigation time all round, and you get sent to the real big house. Nurse Ratched and all the gang waiting for you.'

Eardley looked again in their direction, eyes narrowed. Mrs Sidhu chewed her lip. Finally, she got her freshly bought raffle ticket out. She spoke in a bright, clear voice, which immediately raised Burton's curiosity. 'You're right. I'm just here to serve cream teas and to enjoy the fete. Have you bought a raffle ticket yet?'

'Um, no,' he said, alerted by the sudden change in subject.

'They've had to start the raffle sales from scratch, because the old cash box is part of police evidence.' They watched the ticket seller. 'You see what they do? They sell the ticket, and then they write down the name and details of the person who bought the ticket. That way, if you win a prize and you're not here to claim it, they can contact you later.'

Eardley looked reassured and stopped shooting her glances.

'The people in the queue will have numbers that run in sequence. I wonder what might connect those people, or perhaps the people who bought the original tickets from Dr Calman. I've got one number.' She leaned in and whispered in his ear.

Moments later, Burton scurried away with his phone attached to his ear. 'Dove? I want you to go the evidence lock-up and get the Benham case stuff. It's the raffle list I'm interested in. Who had tickets around the number 624?'

Edith hauled herself to her feet. Pain grabbed her wasted thigh muscles into balls of hot lava. She grimaced and got the crutches under her arms and tottered across the room to the drawers. Some thoughts had been troubling Edith in her more lucid moments. One was that she missed her son dearly. The second was that she was going to say something one day when she was less lucid. The last was that the chef woman was not the sort to stop. There was only one way to get out. Edith opened the drawer and found them lying on top.

The car keys jangled as she slid them into her pocket. Now Edith's eyes turned to the window and the great, grey asbestos garage. It was time to put an end to this.

She groped around in her pockets. There it was. She pulled it out so she could look at the little pink slip. She was going to collect her prize.

As she unlocked the door, she found the length of rubber hose on the shelf where she'd left it long ago. This was going to be a struggle. 'So many people are dead because of me,' said Edith. There was a meow from near her feet. 'You'd better come too.' She scooped up Emrys in her hand and went out the back door. 'There won't be anyone to look after you.'

35

In the Benham House kitchen, Mrs Sidhu lifted a tray of freshly baked scones from the oven. The air was filled with the smell of warm pastry, sultanas and sugar. She breathed it in. It was the smell of summer. She put them down and started transferring them to a tray.

Burton entered, closing the door behind him. 'OK. They all bought raffle tickets at the bring-and-buy last week. Kate Hammond was six two four, Tamzin Grey was six two three and Elliot Chase was six two two.' He went for a scone.

Mrs Sidhu slapped his hand away. 'So Elliot bought his ticket, and behind him was Tamzin Grey and then behind her Kate Hammond.'

'So they've got raffle tickets – half the village has probably got raffle tickets. It doesn't necessarily mean anything.'

'That's one victim and two intended victims, all in a row. It's too much of a coincidence,' she said.

She took the tray and headed out the door, with Burton on her heels.

'So Patrick Kirby was killing them by raffle ticket number. We knew he was disturbed. That's good to know. Well done.'

'He wasn't disturbed. Not in the way that made him a killer. He was acting from a sense of logic, his own kind of logic. There's a reason he approached the people with raffle ticket numbers. It means that something happened in that queue that got Wendy Calman and Kate Hammond killed and put a target on Tamzin Grey and Elliot Chase.'

'What was that?'

'I wish I knew. What about the lost property bag?'

'It was never recovered at Dr Calman's house.'

'But Edith saw Dr Calman take it home.'

Out in the garden, they were drawing raffle numbers and calling them out. Prize winners ran to the front to claim their wins. Mrs Sidhu continued past, walking with a purpose.

'Where are we going?'

Mrs Sidhu ignored the question. 'Just because Edith Pollock has dementia, no one thought it was worth following up.'

Burton raised his arms in protest. 'We have been devoting most of our time to tracking down Patrick Kirby.'

'As was intended by the killer. But there's one person left who did see the lost property bag. Not at the bring-and-buy, because she couldn't go. But at her house when Wendy waved the bag around, the transparent bag. One person might remember what was inside it.'

'Edith Pollock?' Burton said.

Mrs Sidhu had arrived at where Eardley was standing. She handed him the tray of scones. He looked at her with surprise. 'Are these for me?'

'If you could hand them out. We have a murder to solve.'

Eardley was confused. Tamzin Grey threw Burton an outraged plea for support. Burton could only shrug apologetically. 'We do unfortunately have to do exactly that.'

Mrs Sidhu clutched Eardley's shirt in her fist. 'I'm Batman, and I'm back,' she growled deep, like Christian Bale.

'Mrs Sidhu,' Burton warned.

Everyone was looking at her in shock. She released her hold on Eardley and smoothed his shirt. 'And I'm not mad.' With that she turned on her heel and marched off.

'Jury is out on that one,' said Burton, adding weakly, 'I'll get back to you.' Hurried strides took him out of the Benham House garden.

It was Arif who found Elliot.

Elliot was returning home from the village fete with a bag full of goodies. Scones, of course; she loved a nice scone. The summer air was sweet, and the day was long. Someone was playing music from their house, an old-time song, but it was too muffled to pick out the tune. Now the days would get shorter, which was always a depressing thought, but at least when it got colder they could snuggle up in front of the fire. The old bird had time in her yet.

The High Street was quietening down now. Days like this, cars were parked up and down the road, double yellows and everything. The village fete had always been popular. Someone was idling their engine. You could smell it, the exhaust. He coughed. The music got louder.

He passed the estate agents. There were signs up about The Sanctuary, coming soon, plots available. He chuckled, maybe one day he'd be able to afford one. He was in a good mood, and he played a childhood game he had played before on this street, kicking a pebble and keeping it on the pavement.

There was that engine idling, getting closer. Funny, no cars around. The pebble zigged and zagged along the pavement, as he stretched his legs in crazy directions trying to keep it in play. He abandoned the game when he got to Edith's driveway, knocking the stone into the flower bed and celebrating, arms wide, wheeling around at the imaginary crowd. 'He scores!'

The engine sound was strong now, and somehow distant. There was a smell too. He wrinkled his nose. A flat, smoky rank diesel odour. He saw the smoke and couldn't quite believe it. A fire? Here, now, again? Then he heard the music – Frank Sinatra's honeyed voice begging to be taken to the moon and stars. He ran towards the garage door. It wasn't fire.

The door groaned as it swung up and over, and exhaled smoke into the outside air like a purring dragon. Inside was what Elliot knew was a 1994 registration Jaguar XJS, mint condition, two careful owners. It hadn't been driven for years but Edith made sure it was in perfect working order, MOT up to date, road tax paid, because it belonged to her one and only son, Justin Pollock. The exhaust fumes cleared. Elliot caught a sob in his throat. The hose stretched from the exhaust pipe round to the driver's side window. Edith lay there, seat in recline, for all the world as if she was asleep on her favourite chair, listening to her favourite song. Her mottled hands were closed around Emrys' soft form. Elliot let go, his chest collapsed, and heaved, the weight drained into his legs and he broke down. That's how Arif found him, walking back to the retreat. He put his arms around his shoulders, helped him stand up, and called the police.

36

'She was killed because of what she saw,' Mrs Sidhu said.

Burton pursed his lips. 'Not possible. She's locked herself in here from the inside, she had the only key to the garage in her pocket. Plus, there's no signs of a struggle, and she's left a suicide note.'

He held up Edith's note. Mrs Sidhu read it.

I'm sorry.

It's my fault so many people are dead. I let William Mackie into this village and into this family. When he left I became the leader of the E cult. Patrick got interested in Mackie and the E cult, and got Kate and Tony to join too. They had an unhappy marriage and Patrick wanted to help them the way William helped my boy and his wife. Help them reach peace and get to the stars.

Then when Wendy found out about us, I got Patrick to kill her. After we sent Kate and Tony to the stars, I wanted to share the greatest gift with Elliot. He's looked after me so well these last six months. I wanted to help him too, but it wasn't to be. I'm sorry, Elliot, I'm going to a better world and I was hoping to see you there too. Anyway, it's over now. The E cult dies with me. I'm losing my brains, but while I've got a little left, I'm taking the chance to check out and join the spaceship in the sky and see my son again.

Edith Pollock

'And Patrick killed them all. So much for your raffle ticket theory. But you were right about the most important thing, there was a cult here in Benham village.' He patted her on the shoulder. 'You're right. You're not mad after all.'

Mrs Sidhu forced a weak laugh. 'So it seems.' But Mrs Sidhu was mad, she had to be. What sort of person is proved right and then doesn't believe the proof of it in black and white. 'But I got it wrong, it wasn't Eardley and Snakeskin and Tamzin.'

'Thought you'd be happy. Play your cards right, you won't have to see Eardley any more. No one can say you're delusional when you're the only person who spotted a cult operating right under their noses. I'll back you up.'

'For once,' Mrs Sidhu said. 'Do you believe it? I mean, if she owns up to any more murders, she'll be the one who killed President Kennedy.'

Burton opened the plastic bag he was carrying. Inside could be seen blue nylon and a zipper. 'Sleeping bag. We found it and a bunch of Patrick Kirby's things on the back seat of the car. She's been hiding him here all along, then sending him out at nights to do his grim stuff.

'And if that isn't enough, here's the clincher. We found the last page of Dr Calman's manuscript.' Another evidence bag was produced, this one with a crumpled sheet of paper. 'It's got the raffle ticket numbers on and the letter E. E for E cult. Dr Calman wrote out the raffle numbers of the members of the E cult. Edith sent Patrick to kill Dr Calman because she found out who was in the cult. As we already know, the Hammonds were members and victims of the cult itself.' Burton pointed at the garage wall. The capital letter E was emblazoned on the wall. 'Patrick Kirby's handiwork. That's everything, it's all wrapped up.'

Mrs Sidhu's phone pinged. 'Oh my God, I have to get going.'

It was like the name itself was cursed. All the Pollocks were dead now, all by their own hands. Maybe William Mackie was more powerful than anyone had imagined. From beyond the grave he had somehow arranged the deaths of four people. Mrs Sidhu was not a superstitious woman, but this thought caused a shiver to pass down her spine. It was her name that would be cursed if she didn't make it in time.

She slowed down as she turned out of the retreat. Her brakes squealed before she mistimed the clutch. The engine whined and spluttered and complained its way into an erratic acceleration. 'Oh, don't let me down now.' Mrs Sidhu pounded the steering wheel. The car slowly picked up speed.

The winding lanes around Benham soon gave way to the M4. Windows wide open, the car flat out at sixty miles an hour, Mrs Sidhu let her hair bounce in the wind. This was the closest she ever came to aircon.

There would be two FOR SALE signs up in the High Street now, not to mention the plot of land vacated by

313

the Hammond house. There was suddenly a lot of high-end property available in Benham village. Would they be hard to sell? An interesting proposition. Two perfect cottages in the most desirable village in Berkshire, both with mysteriously dead previous occupants. An unstoppable object versus an immovable wall. That was a problem for the estate agents. She had her own paradox.

Edith Pollock was probably the last living person who could identify William Mackie. And yet it was certain that she committed suicide. Just as her son and daughter-in-law did. Again, a shiver passed through Mrs Sidhu's bones. Something here didn't feel right, but for now Mrs Sidhu had other concerns.

The little car was swallowed up by the tunnel into Heathrow Airport. She fiddled with the lights; they blinked a couple of times before shining yellow onto the tarmac ahead of her and the arrow that pointed towards Terminal 2 short-stay parking. This was going to be awkward.

'I was just wrapping up the evidence for the Benham village case . . .' Dove paused, looking uncertain.

Burton decided to prompt him. 'Yes, Dove?'

'We finally got a message back from Bogota police on the Mackie remains. They had some kind of computer virus and lost a load of records in 2005.'

Burton looked worried. 'So?'

'They eventually recovered them, but they have no record on file for the request made by your predecessor, nor sending us confirmation from the dental records we supplied.'

'OK, well they lost the records. We have a copy on file here, signed off by . . .' Burton tapped at his computer,

'. . . a Detective Inspector Guillermo Miguel Clave. We just need him to confirm what he saw.'

'That's the thing, sir. They don't have a record of a Detective Inspector Guillermo Miguel Clave ever working for them.'

Burton blinked. He pulled his keyboard towards him and searched on a Spanish translation tool and mumbled as he typed. 'Guillermo Miguel Clave.' He hit return.

'William Michael Key. William Mick Key. William bloody Mackie sent his own death certificate!'

37

Heathrow Airport has always had the air of a temporary structure. At any given time, half of it is being built while the other half is being knocked down. It is a hodgepodge; the original three terminals have been added to over decades, connected by temporary structures that seem to have become permanent while the building of brand-new structures seems to carry on regardless. Nothing finished.

Terminal 1 no longer even exists. In the unending paradox that is Heathrow Airport, the oldest terminal is the newest. The Terminal 2 rebuild was finished in 2014. What had been an enduring reminder of the golden era of travel was replaced with something brisk and modern – which is another way of saying busy, distracting and overcrowded. The walls and floors are steeped in the dead-flower scent of cheap disinfectant and goodbyes. This should have been just another one of those goodbyes.

Mrs Sidhu gave Daljeet the orange plastic bag. 'It's your favourite.'

Daljeet peered inside. It contained a crinkly foil package and the smell of warm parathas. She grimaced. She pointed to the sign. 'Sister, I cannot take these through security.' Mrs Sidhu took back the crinkling orange bag. It was the thought that counted, wasn't it?

'You know, I proved I'm not mad.' Mrs Sidhu stared at Daljeet stiffly until she realised she looked quite mad.

'Oh,' said Daljeet, 'I never thought you were.'

'Why did you come to England, respected sister?'

'I came to see you and Tez, and I got what I wanted. At least I got to see Tez, we had a wonderful day out and we got to chat. I'm just sad you couldn't join us. But your life is your own and I don't like to pry.'

That's my line, thought Mrs Sidhu. Maybe we're all like this. We're all daleks, engaged in a universal war of thoughtless destruction. 'I'm sorry. I should have spent more time with you.'

At the check-in desk there was a long line. Daljeet insisted that Mrs Sidhu could leave, but she stayed, eyeing the suitcase. Two men ahead of them in the queue smiled and joked with each other, one telling the other he was sorry the stay had been so short. Should she feel relieved that Daljeet was leaving? Guilt lay a heavy hand on her shoulders. So when they got to the front, it was Mrs Sidhu who swung the bag onto the belt with a grunt. An electric whirr as it was tagged and gobbled up through a hole in the wall. It really was time to say goodbye, but in modern air travel there is always another queue. The world these days was made of queues; traffic queues, shopping queues . . . raffle queues.

The queue for the departure gates moved in fits and starts. The two men ahead of them were already at the barrier. One smiled, the other had a tear in his eye. They embraced

317

warmly. When had men got better at expressing their emotions than women? She could give Daljeet a hug, but a curt handshake would have been more appropriate. In the end they groped their way through a one-armed embrace, side-on, avoiding eye contact.

'Well, I suppose this is goodbye.'

'This has been very nice.'

They both spoke at once. Cancelling each other out, they fell into silence, broken only by Daljeet's throat-clearing. 'Sister,' she started and then fell quiet again. Mrs Sidhu changed hands with the orange bag. She had cooked too much food; why did she always cook too much food? 'Sister,' Daljeet said again, 'I have two confessions to make. First is that I always wished I could be more like you.'

Mrs Sidhu's eyes widened. 'You do?'

'Yes. You always did exactly what you wanted, you always have and you never cared a moment what other people thought. Like marrying my brother; you married him when everyone said no. My second confession is that I was the one who told respected brother not to marry you. I've regretted it ever since, not least because it put a distance between me and him.' Daljeet breathed a relieved sigh. 'There, I've finally said it.'

The queue was moving again now.

Mrs Sidhu looked at her shoes. 'I have a confession too. I knew about your advice to him, and it was me who drove a wedge between you.'

Daljeet considered this. 'Then, sister, we have both sinned against each other. Our crimes are equal. I'm sad it took so long for us to be honest with each other.'

'I think he might have married me only because everyone said no.'

'Nonsense. He married you because he wanted to, and you showed him that he did not need to live his life in misery if he would only do as you do. A lesson all of us should have learned.'

Daljeet pressed her boarding pass to the reader. It bleeped and the gate swished open.

'And now you're involved with all these police investigations. It sounds like so much . . . fun.' It was a foreign word in Daljeet's mouth, part of a language that she had once tried to learn and given up on too soon. 'You have a talent. If you have the means to help people, you should do it. Always.' The queue surged forward, but something about Daljeet's severe demeanour held it back. She wagged a finger. 'Don't let them put you in a box. Not before your time, anyway.'

Mrs Sidhu looked at her again and saw it. The hollowed-out eyes, the weakness in the muscles, the skeletal frame. The dead are always calling, sure, but no one expected them to come over from India and stay for a week.

'Why did you come?' Mrs Sidhu blurted quickly. 'It's not just the land and the house, is it?'

Daljeet shook her head. 'I'm getting old. International flights aren't for me any more. Who knows when we will see each other again.'

Mrs Sidhu reached for something to support her. She found Daljeet's hand. How could she not have seen it before? 'How long?' Mrs Sidhu asked.

Daljeet shrugged, drew the corners of her mouth down. 'This is not important. So far it hasn't spread. There's time and there's hope.'

'Hope?'

'So much depends on the treatment.' She beat her hands on her chest. 'It's expensive.'

For a moment, Mrs Sidhu enjoyed a mental picture of what she could do with the money from the house. She could buy a brand-new van, with an integrated cold space, air conditioning, a clock that worked. She gave herself a moment to imagine it. Then she pushed it off a cliff.

'You're right. I do have a chance to help people. I want you to have the house.' She silenced Daljeet before she started to talk. 'Your brother didn't build it for me; he built it so he could be close to you. I want it to be for you. Use it or sell it. Perhaps the money will help, or perhaps you'll feel closer to him.'

Daljeet pressed her bony chest against Mrs Sidhu and put her thinning arms around her, and then she was gone, the sliding gate closed behind her and she was part of a milling line of bright-shirted holidaymakers filing forward for the luggage scanner.

She came to see me one last time, and I squandered that time. There was an echo here, of something, but it was unclear. Mrs Sidhu tucked it away.

Perhaps the sadness of parting with Daljeet was too much; she had to think of something else. As she turned away, a new thought came to her. Edith Pollock could identify William Mackie. The people in the queue all saw something that got them killed. What if they could identify him too? But none of them had ever met him, so how? What did they see in the queue for raffle tickets? Then she realised that she was wrong about Edith. There was one more person who could identify William Mackie.

Mrs Sidhu's chest tingled. She had more people to help. More dead people. She went into one of those trances, those moments of Aloneness where the world stood still.

Trolleys stopped wheeling, baggage carousels stopped moving, aeroplanes froze in their flightpaths.

She turned her mind back to the raffle queue she had stood in, when the other woman dropped her ticket, and Mrs Sidhu had picked it up for her. Something had happened in the queue for raffle tickets at the bring-and-buy. Everyone who was targeted saw it. Mrs Sidhu knew what it was. Human nature was what it was, and it was human nature to help people. There's a price to helping people, DCI Burton had told her; Mrs Sidhu knew all about that. What had Daljeet said? 'Who knows if we'll see each other again.' Finally, Mrs Sidhu had all the answers.

The car started on the third attempt; Mrs Sidhu swerved out of her parking spot. A few moments later, the Heathrow tunnel spat her green Nissan Micra onto the M4 westbound like a well-chewed olive stone. Only one thought pressed itself into her mind. 'She came to see me one last time.'

There was one other problem. Not only was Tamzin Grey still alive, but no one had tried to kill her. She was in the queue, she had a raffle number right between Elliot and Kate, but there had been no attempt on her life. Could it be she hadn't seen what the others and Dr Calman saw? Was she looking the other way? Odd. Dr Calman would have been facing them, and they would have been facing her. What could they all have seen? Nothing, there would have been nothing but air between the front of the queue and Dr Calman.

Mrs Sidhu's green Nissan Micra gave up on Benham High Street; the engine temperature needle was so far off the scale it nearly snapped off. She ran the last of the way to the retreat.

'You're the last one left in the group.' Mrs Sidhu met Jonny and Tamzin at the gates. 'Last man standing.'

'Yeah, it's pretty weird,' Jonny said. 'I guess I'm lucky I didn't buy a raffle ticket. That dude was seriously twisted.' Jonny was carrying a suitcase. His guitar was strapped across his back.

'Are you leaving the retreat?'

'Yeah. You know, I had my day. It's where I am, I'm just going to roll with it.'

Tamzin nudged him. 'Don't worry, Jonny. We're going to get a place on a reality show. They love a recovery story.' She smiled.

'I don't wanna do it.'

Tamzin's face dropped. 'We've got to revive your career. It's why you came here.'

'No, we don't. We need to let it lie, with the dead. I can do without the pressure to get into the top ten again. I came here to get my head together and I know what I want. I'm quitting while I've got a shred of dignity and integrity left.' Jonny swung his luggage onto the back seat of his taxi. 'Just take me to the station.' The taxi drove away.

'I guess you were right.' Tamzin watched the car departing. 'There goes my ten per cent of nothing. Ungrateful little git. I should never have tried to help him.'

Tamzin allowed Mrs Sidhu to take her by the arm. 'You know, maybe he's right. It's time to retire. I understand there's a vacancy for village helper.'

Tamzin snorted at this. 'I'm not exactly the helpful type.'

'That's what I thought. Please, can I ask you something,

Tamzin. Do you find it odd that you bought a raffle ticket but no one tried to kill you?'

Tamzin frowned. 'You're forgetting Patrick came to my house, he scrawled that eye thing over my lawn.' She meant the Horus, Patrick Kirby's symbol of protection.

'He had a bottle of bleach with him, but was he carrying a weapon?'

Tamzin thought. 'I don't think so.' Then she added with more certainty, 'No, he was just carrying the bottle.'

Mrs Sidhu nodded as if this was significant. 'One last question. On the day of the bring-and-buy, you bought a raffle ticket. And you also handed something in to lost property – a wallet, I think.'

'That's right.'

'Now I want you to think very carefully. Did you look inside?'

Why would he come back, why would William Mackie come back now? She had asked Burton that, and she had asked herself again and again. Now, she had the answer, but she needed one more piece of confirmation.

'You saw William Mackie once. Would you recognise him again?'

Arif was clearing away paint brushes and paint pots, the aftermath of a wellness session. 'It was twenty-five years ago, and it was dark. But, yes, I think so. He had a very distinctive face.'

'Have you seen him?' Mrs Sidhu nodded, helping Arif clear away the remnants of an art therapy class. 'I mean lately.'

Arif looked at Mrs Sidhu quizzically. 'Of course not, he's dead.'

'Please, think carefully. Is there anyone here at the retreat or in the village, who might resemble him.'

Arif stroked his goatee. 'No. No one.'

'What your father said, about stealing a man's teeth . . .'

'Keep your mouth shut or they'll steal your teeth too?'

'What did he mean?'

'Someone gave him money. Enough money to buy his practice. He never said who, but it had something to do with William Mackie's visit. I always assumed it was him. Though he never looked like he had enough money for dental work, let alone property.'

'Thank you. That makes things much clearer. And what about the man who was with Mackie that night?'

'I told you, I never saw his face.'

'Good. If anything happens to me, make sure that everyone knows that. It could save your life.'

Arif's eyes widened. 'What's going to happen to you?'

'Nothing, I hope. Where's Elliot?'

'He's gone. Said he was selling Edith's house and he's going travelling.' When Mrs Sidhu looked confused, he added, 'She left him everything.'

Of course she did. 'Where is he now?'

There was a small urn on the table.

'She left me everything.' Elliot was red-eyed. 'Including these remains. God knows what I'll do with them.'

Mrs Sidhu eyed the small pot. 'Emrys,' Justin said. 'Edith'll have a woodland burial, it's what she always wanted. When the coroner releases the body.'

'Of course. Makes sense to leave it all to you. She had no one else left.'

'I didn't ask her to,' he insisted. 'People think that's why we do the job. It's not true. I've looked after a lot of old people. Some you like more than others.'

'She was special to you.'

Elliot looked a little embarrassed. 'I suppose she was. I mean, she was bonkers with her crystals and her herbs and her Druid stuff and that stone circle. I had no idea she had that lunatic Patrick in the garage, can't believe she sent him to kill me.'

'I don't think she did. It was all part of a bigger plan.'

'Crikey, you sound like her now.' He went into the kitchen, calling out from behind the open fridge door. 'Can I get you a drink?' Mrs Sidhu said she was fine. He returned with a bottle of cola and a glass.

'What will you do with the house?'

'This one? I'll sell it. The one in the woods, I don't know. It's always the sort of place I've dreamed of living in. But I can't really do that, can I, not right now?' He swivelled to face her, tombstone teeth smiling. 'When did you realise it was me?'

38

'It never made any sense for William Mackie to return. But it did make sense for a son to come back to visit his mother for the very last time. To look after her in the final days, while she still had enough mind to remember him. Fuss her, cut her nails, buy her raffle tickets. How did you do it? How did you convince William and Sandra to take their own lives? It was poison, wasn't it?'

He poured a glass of cola, the brown liquid frothing up to the neck of the glass before subsiding. The foam looked thicker than usual.

'Phenobarbital. They told me they had been having an affair. They wanted a marriage, can you believe it? So I gave them one, a made-up one with all sorts of rubbish, up at the stone circle. I even told them they could have the woodland house. I built that house for us, for Sandra really.'

Out there in the woods, to keep Sandra to himself. A young woman who was finally finding her confidence and moving out of the shadow of her husband. 'They were in love.'

'William Mackie was desperate to be loved. Not just by Sandra, but by everyone. It was easy to convince him that I didn't mind about him and Sandra, because he wanted to believe it. All he ever wanted was my blessing. Pathetic.'

'So why did they kill themselves?'

'You know the ending of *Romeo and Juliet*?'

'They each think the other is dead and commit suicide.'

'I gave it a helping hand. I told Sandra that William was dead and asked her if she wanted to carry on living, with me.'

'And she drank the poison.'

'Without a second thought.' The tombstone smile faded from Justin Pollock's face. He toyed with the glass, turning it this way and that. 'And William, poor Bill, I did so enjoy seeing his face when he found her dead. He thought he could join her on some bloody spaceship, so he took it too. It's sort of beautiful really. That man really did have the faith of his convictions.'

Outside it was getting dark, and neither of them had thought to put a light on.

'And Kate and Tony Hammond?'

'I offered Kate Hammond the same choice, but she wanted to live. And when Tony found her, he didn't. He virtually offered his neck up. Love conquers all.' Justin laughed. 'You know, he wasn't right in the head. He was obsessed with her. He watched the whole thing, thought I was her secret lover, until he saw me kill her.'

'You still carry Sandra's photograph with you, don't you, in your wallet.'

'Clever, clever.' Justin wagged his finger. 'That's what's so bonkers. We could have avoided all of this fuss.' Fuss.

327

Three dead in as many days. A mild irritation drew up in his eyes. 'This place hasn't changed in twenty-five years. New faces, same old same old nosey people. They had to look inside, didn't they?' He chuckled. 'Do you want to see it? Of course, I took the lost property when I paid Wendy Calman a visit.' He leaned up on one buttock and pulled it out of his back pocket. It was ordinary, brown leather, worn. He flipped it open and ran his finger over the shiny plastic window. Behind it, a faded photograph, two people with dated hairstyles, arms wrapped around each other. 'That's us before she met him. He put ideas into her head. She started wearing new clothes, wanting to go out, she started daubing bloody watercolours, and writing poetry. I wasn't enough for her any more. That's why I had to do it.'

Mrs Sidhu changed the subject. 'How on earth did you manage to keep a fake career as a carer from the police? I know DCI Burton. He must have done background checks after Dr Calman's murder.'

'It's not a fake career. In South America you can buy a new identity quite cheaply, and I have been playing the long game. Once I decided it was time for William Mackie to die, I had to find something to do. I missed Mum. Elderly care seemed a good choice. All my work credentials are real. For almost twenty years I've worked in private care homes all over the world.'

Justin put the glass down with a thump. The liquid fizzed.

Burton's mind was reeling. Since learning that William Mackie's death was fake, he had put Dove and everyone else in the office on digging up what they had on him and on the E cult deaths, going over every last piece of

328

paperwork. He tackled Dr Calman's manuscript himself. When he got to the end, he remembered the final page was in a separate evidence bag. He found it in the lock-up. Under the single swinging light bulb, he read again the pen-written scrawl on the page. Something caught his eye. He read it again; it was still the same ink-pen scrawl.

When he was a young detective sergeant, his first boss Detective Inspector Reems had told him that sometimes the conscious mind missed what the subconscious mind already knew. It sounded like something Eardley would say. He went through the exercise of unfocusing his eyes and not looking at the writing, allowing his mind to do what it would, like trying to look at one of those 3D pictures of dolphins that had been so popular in the nineties. The ones his ex-wife could always see instantly and he could not. He tried not to think about where she was now and, in doing so, two thoughts came to him.

The current theory was that Dr Calman had written these things moments before Patrick came in and killed her. He took them to cover up the cult that he was involved in. Later, Edith Pollock also killed herself for the same reason. And yet, nothing about this cult rang true for Burton. Where was the internet presence? In an age where cults can grow like bacteria on the petri dish of the internet, there was very little E cult out there on social media or the dark net. Burton had been searching for days. Ironically, since the recent murders, there was a lot more, which was a headache he did not want to start.

The other thought that came to him, as he tried to emulate the long-ago retired Detective Inspector Reems and his long-ago remarried ex-wife, was that he was getting a headache. He wasn't seeing anything on the page, certainly not a three-dimensional dolphin. He pulled up the version on Dr Calman's laptop instead. Without the ink scrawl and the blood splatter, it was suddenly very clear what he was missing. It was the name Arif Begovic.

39

'Do you know what I learned?' Justin pushed the glass of fizzing cola towards Mrs Sidhu. 'There is a moment in grief, before our animal instincts kick in, where we all want to die. We want to give in, give ourselves up to it, to give up the struggle and join the dead. It's quite interesting.' He said it as if discussing a new scientific advance in the newspapers.

'And when you offer them a choice.' The blade landed on the table with a dull, steely thud. She looked at the thing, a wicked rusty smile in iron, semi-circular with a worn wooden handle. 'People so often take the painless way out. It's a golden sickle; I had it made for the Druid marriage ceremony. Most of the gold has gone now, but it's still sharp. You see, I'm not really ready to leave here. I want to bury my mum, put flowers on her grave and live in my old house. But you know who I am, and while you're alive I can't very well do that.'

They sat for a while. Mrs Sidhu watched the fizzing glass. Bubbles appeared at the bottom and rose to the top

331

where they popped out of existence. Then new ones would appear at the bottom and rise again, like tiny quivering souls on an endless cycle. A wash cycle, in which featureless faces spun and groaned. The wheel of life, the wheel of death, the dead are always calling. This would be a painless end, Justin said, so easy to finish and give up on it all. It was not herself she was thinking about, though.

Mrs Sidhu knew full well that life was a gift, and gifts are things you accept with grace, even if it's an unwanted mustard yellow jumper knitted by your cousin Bindhu, or the world's worst scones. You make the best of it.

'I'm not ready to leave either. I decided I wanted to live a long time ago,' Mrs Sidhu said.

Justin picked up the sickle. 'The hard way then.'

Burton was standing with Arif, who he had only recently released from custody for the death of Patrick Kirby.

'I told you, I had no choice. He was coming for Elliot.'

'I'm not here about that. What did Dr Calman speak to you about regarding William Mackie?'

Arif recounted to Burton his childhood encounter with the E cult leader.

'Your father did William Mackie's teeth in the middle of the night?'

'He was the only dentist around here. If there was an emergency, he did it. There was another man with him, I didn't see his face. He and my dad helped him into a car.'

'Helped him? Couldn't he manage it alone?'

'My dad said it was the anaesthetic. He couldn't walk.'

'Dental work!' The sun was dipping, but for Burton it was a new dawn. One in which he realised his team had missed something very important and that Dr Calman had held back something she should have told the police a long time ago, instead of waiting for it to come out in paperback or coming back from the grave to kill her. Burton rubbed the back of his neck. 'William Mackie was dead. Pollock switched places with him. He's still alive.' Burton grew angry at Arif's sullen silence. 'You bloody knew!'

'Look, William Mackie isn't here. I'd recognise him. If he was here, I'd have said.'

Burton glowered.

'Anyway, your chef friend from Slough already asked me all these questions.'

'She did what?' Burton's shoulders slumped. 'When was this?'

'This afternoon. She went looking for Elliot. You know, bloke whose life I saved. The one with the big teeth.'

The blade glinted in the half-light. Suddenly, antifreeze was running through Mrs Sidhu's veins. She forced her voice to be calm. 'I'm not suffering from grief. You, on the other hand have just lost your mother. She took her own life because of you.'

Justin froze. Mrs Sidhu watched him like a bird eyeing a worm. 'It's true, isn't it?'

'She killed herself because she knew she would stop recognising me. And to set me free, so I could get away. It was the last act of a loving mother.'

'She did it because of what you are: a killer with no remorse. Another woman who would rather die than live with you.' Mrs Sidhu added an edge to her voice, sharper than the sickle in Justin's hand. 'You hid Patrick in the garage, you sent him out to give you an alibi, and then you went out and killed three innocent people. Is it any surprise that the two women who loved you most on this earth took their own lives rather than spend the rest of their lives with you? Where does that leave you?'

In the distance she could hear the police sirens. 'That's my golden sickle on the way. There's two ways out for you. The easy way and the other way.' She pushed the glass back across the table. In the dark, bubbles popped. Justin's face was unreadable. He sat still, hunched over the drink.

Mrs Sidhu found the strength to push back from the table and stand up. 'There is a moment in grief, before our animal instincts kick in, where we all want to die. We want to give in, give ourselves up to it, to give up the struggle and join the dead.' Mrs Sidhu walked to the door, her heart beating blood into her head and her ears, expecting any minute to be struck down and seeing red spray shoot from her own neck. Somehow she made it out of the room. She did not look back, accelerating her steps to the front door. She almost fell the final few steps, regaining her balance on the last one. Outside, blue lights were already twinkling through the trees. She slammed the door behind her and breathed in big swallows of air.

'Are you all right?' Burton was running, spider legs eating up the ground between him and Mrs Sidhu. 'What happened to Justin Pollock?'

Mrs Sidhu sat heavily on the garden wall where a few days ago she had stroked a curious cat. 'To be honest, I don't know.' He's inside the house, half dead and half alive, she told herself. Until we open the door, he's both.

40

How much can birds change your life?

Burton stared at the cage with infinite sadness. He ran a thumb over it and twanged the wire with his nail. It sang. He sighed. Did he really want a bird feeder? Would the provision of fat and protein to migrating avians somehow fill the hole in his life?

'I can see the way your mind is moving. Attracting birds, attracting women.' Mrs Sidhu twanged the wire too. 'Plays a nice tune.'

Burton grimaced. 'How did you find me?' He put the bird feeder down.

'Classic double-bluff. I knew you'd come back here. It's got the highest cholesterol breakfast in Berkshire.'

'You can't teach that.'

'I've had my problems with birds too. Mine was a flattened pigeon, bad karma.'

'And how did you get on with that?'

'Work in progress.' Mrs Sidhu picked up the bird feeder.

'Maybe I should get one of these too, it might appease the bird gods.'

'So? What is this? Come to tell me "I told you so"?'

'Nonsense. Not at all.' Could she really resist rubbing it in? 'I mean, yes, I did tell you Patrick was innocent, Chief Inspector. People lie, circumstances lie, but apple sauce does not lie.'

'You'll be glad to hear that Justin Pollock aka Elliot Chase chose the way of life. Life imprisonment.'

'So, don't you want to know what all this was about before you submit your report?'

'Ridiculous.' Burton picked up another bird feeder. 'I know what this was all about. Justin Pollock killed his wife and Mackie because they were having an affair. He paid off the local dentist, a refugee desperate for money, to X-ray the dead man's teeth and switch dental records with him, so he could disappear. Afterwards, he ramped up the myth of the E cult, which he pretty much created out of thin air to explain their apparent suicides.'

'That's the gist of it. So how come he then went on to kill three more people in the village?'

Burton put the bird feeder down and picked up another one which was guaranteed only to attract small birds. 'Obvious. The two women knew who he was, so he had to kill them. Tony Hammond came home, so he killed him too.'

Mrs Sidhu narrowed her eyes. 'And how did they know who he was?'

Burton fiddled with a third bird feeder. 'You have to buy special balls of compacted fat for this one.' He picked up a bag of fat balls.

Mrs Sidhu uncrossed her arms. 'You're avoiding the question.' She held out her hand. 'Give me your wallet.'

Burton knew what was coming. He reluctantly handed over the pork-chop-sized lump of leather, worn at the edges and gently curved by the pressure of being sat on over many years. It was full of cash and old receipts, with a clasp that strained to keep it all together. Mrs Sidhu weighed it carefully in the palm of her hand. She waited, perusing the customers until the right one was passing. Then she threw it across the aisle towards the pet treats section.

'Hey!' Burton protested. 'What'd you do that for?'

Mrs Sidhu silenced him with a finger to his lips. 'It's a boomerang, I promise you.'

The woman who picked it up was middle-aged, kindly, attractive. She had a little dog on a lead. 'Excuse me, I think this is yours.' She held it open for Burton at the picture page. 'Is that your wife? She's beautiful.'

Burton nodded, thanked the woman, and patted the dog. He held the wallet open, his thumb tracing his wife's face. 'Thanks for the demonstration. I get it, he killed the people who looked inside his wallet and saw his picture with a dead woman. But who's going to recognise either of them twenty-five years on?'

'Wendy Calman, naturally, because she spent half a lifetime looking at pictures of the Pollocks. She even had this one in her file.'

'OK, Wendy Calman. That's her marked for the grave,' Burton said drily.

'And then things really got out of control. With a tragedy in the village, it was only natural that the press would revisit the past.'

'The Pollock suicides.' Burton was getting it now.

'In fact, the *Slough Observer* printed that very picture. The other victims were new to the village, but it was only a matter of time before they connected the photo in the paper to the one they saw when they helpfully looked in Elliot's wallet. That is also why Tamzin Grey was spared. She didn't look because she had no instinct to help.'

'Or she wasn't nosy.' Burton raised an eyebrow. 'I wonder what got under his skin about nosy, if helpful, people.'

'That's not the point I'm making.'

Burton sighed, because he knew the point she was making. She made it anyway. 'We all love the people we've lost, Chief Inspector, but sometimes, for our own health, we need to let go.'

Burton waited a long while, looking deep into the picture in his wallet. Slowly, he pulled the credit cards out of their sleeves, then the cash from its pocket. He dumped the wallet into a dustbin on the way out. 'Never needed all those receipts, anyway.'

When they left the garden centre, Burton and Mrs Sidhu each carried a brand-new bird feeder and a bag of fat balls guaranteed to attract only the most discerning of garden birds. No one can bring a pigeon or a person back to life. The best you can do is sustain what life is around you.

Varma was a clever man; he had built an empire of cash-and-carrys, and he had done it by managing costs, attention to detail and extreme efficiencies. These, as far as Mrs Sidhu was concerned, were all different ways of saying he was cheap. Cheapness exuded from his every pore, from his bad shoes, up through his shiny suit to the cheaply buttoned-down collar of his cheap rayon shirt and his clip-on tie. He was a man of busy movements, marshalling activity around his flagship cash-and-carry store like a cut-price general on a discount battlefield. On a cold day, there was enough electricity generated in his polyester weave clothing to power the grid for Slough. On a hot day like this, he was a fire hazard.

Mrs Sidhu had reached a decision. She had to follow her dream, and her dream had never been cooking endless aubergine bhajis. There were several problems with this decision. First of all, with no fixed income and a failing car, how was she going to make a living? The answer to that question would have to wait, because there was a more pressing question, which was how was she going to break it to Mr Varma?

When not in one of his stores, Mr Varma, as has already been noted, conducted the bulk of his business from the lounge bar of the Heathrow Holiday Inn. This was where Mrs Sidhu found him. It was lunchtime and he was finishing a frugal plate of salad and working. She waved for his attention.

He shut his laptop straight away. 'Mrs Sidhu, so nice to see you. Please join me. Can I offer you a drink? A tap water, perhaps. It's a hot day. Ravi! Tap water! Jaldi!' Ravi, an elderly waiter, reacted as fast as his wobbling legs would carry him. Varma grasped his hands together. 'I've been meaning to call you. How are you?'

'Not mad, if that's the question.'

Varma laughed a little too loud. 'Did you hear that, Ravi? She hasn't lost any spark of her humour.' Ravi doddered, smiled, and deposited an empty glass on the table. Varma swallowed. 'We're training him.'

Now it started to dawn on Mrs Sidhu, who was a sharp-witted woman, that from Varma's nervousness and body language, she had the upper hand here. She could not be

339

sure why, but she decided not to charge in with her piece of bad news. This turned out to be an astute move.

Varma swallowed again, his throat suddenly dry. 'I'm afraid I have an awkward subject to broach.' He wrung his hands together. Tension and ozone seemed to fill the air.

Mrs Sidhu worried his suit would catch fire before he found the strength to speak. Instantly she cautioned herself for thinking such things. Despite his tight-fistedness, Varma was the man who had saved her, lent her money when she was penniless. 'Please, Mr Varma, I just want to help in any way I can.' As long as it didn't get her killed.

'This is very hard, Mrs Sidhu, but I'm afraid I have to terminate your aubergine bhaji contract with immediate effect.'

Mrs Sidhu held her breath a moment. Play it cool, Mrs Sidhu, play it cool. The silence hung for a second longer. 'Oh, Mr Varma, that is terrible news.' She put her hand to her heart as if to steady a fluttering beat.

'I know how much this job means to you, Mrs Sidhu. But if people around Slough think that my dishes are being cooked in a toilet kitchen, it could ruin me.'

She was in the clear, and it only got better.

'What I'm going to suggest is that you leave all the Slough-based work for now, and let's see how you get on without me getting in the way. Maybe you can get more work in Berkshire. You seem to get on well with those nobby types.'

There was a triumphant smile in Mrs Sidhu's heart and a look of heartfelt grief on her face. 'Only if I must, Mr Varma.' Another thought occurred to her, and she put the back of her hand to a feverish brow. 'Alas, my car is on its last legs. If I'm to go to jobs in Berkshire, perhaps it could be fixed.'

Varma stroked his chin for a while. 'Let me see what I can do.'

Mrs Sidhu's phone hummed rhythmically while she decided if she was going to wake up or not.

In her dream she was in a tumble dryer. That was as far as she got. A second later, she jolted upright. She had no money and no job, and no choice about if she was going to answer the phone. This was real life, and dreams could just go park themselves in the subconscious for another twenty-four hours.

'Mrs Sidhu's Fine Catering, Slough and environs.' She downed the glass of water on her bedside table and pulled her dressing gown on while she made for the bathroom. Her voice was still thick from sleep, but she tried to lay down a layer of sales gloss on it. 'How may I help you today?' She put her hand over the phone while she barked into the other bedroom. 'Tez! Up, get the kettle on.'

Tez grunted, rolled out of bed. 'Yes, Mum.' Like a sleepwalker, he padded downstairs to the kitchen.

She dropped back into a silky sales voice. 'Yes of course I can come over. Yes, that does sound like a very interesting job.'

She gulped her tea, looking out of the window. The bird feeder was up and doing a roaring trade in sparrows and a robin too. With joy, Mrs Sidhu saw a pigeon was stalking the ground underneath, pecking up loose seeds. In the skies, thunderclouds were gathering. It looked like the weather was finally going to break. The garden could do with a bit of rain. 'Tez, mow that lawn before it rains.'

On the way out of the door, she kissed her fingers and placed them on the lips of her departed husband's photo. For a moment she tried to remember what her waking dream had been, but the memory of it had simply gone, like the steam rising from her half-drunk tea in the kitchen.

ACKNOWLEDGEMENTS

Let me start by thanking my wife, Tess Recordon. She's an artist (a real one, with paint and canvas, not just a hacky writer with a broken laptop). She taught me how hard but worthwhile it is to create something from inside yourself. She's been by my side and in my thoughts throughout my writing life, and without her I wouldn't have made it.

Then there's my family. My parents who raised me, my mum who still worries about me, my brother and sister with whom I share a sense of humour about all things Asian and beyond. They've always been there to turn to for a kind word or a belly laugh. Plus, I can't write a book about a formidable aunty without thanking my formidable aunties. You were at the centre of this endeavour. Thanks for all the love, all the food, all the telling-offs.

Thanks to Harper Collins, and mega thanks to my publisher, Julia Wisdom, commissioning editor, Kathryn Cheshire, and my agent, Adam Gauntlett, for making this book possible. Special thanks to my editor, Angel Belsey, for holding my hand through this first novel. She did it with skill and a smile, a rare combination of gifts. Also Jo Kite (marketing), Fliss Denham (publicity) for making me presentable to the public (almost impossible) and Toby James for his delicious cover design.

Friends, so many friends, where to start? I don't think I'd have been a writer without Richard Pinto and Sharad Sardana (R.I.P.). They got me involved in *Goodness Gracious Me* and in *The Kumars at No.42*. It's where I met Meera Syal, who became an ally in the making of – and the outstanding star of – BBC Radio 4's *Mrs Sidhu Investigates*.

So, so, many, many thanks to Meera. Also comedy legend Gordon Kennedy and directing legend Marilyn Imrie (R.I.P.) and all the cast and crew who made the radio show so special.

As you can see, a number of my friends didn't make it. Maybe I'm a dangerous guy to know! There are three more people who shaped my young life, and departed too soon: Tejinder "Roj" Gill, Andy Calver and Gary Hird. Big gaps, you're in my heart always. It's hard to list all the writers and pals who have kept me sane over the years, (you know who you are) but George Jeffrie, who also passed on, was a special fellow and inspiration. Also, a big thanks to the crime writing community, who have welcomed me in warmly.

Institutions: St Catharine's College, Cambridge. I worked hard to get there, and my education changed my life and created opportunities. Thanks to all my friends for getting me into trouble – and to my tutor, Dr Paul Hartle, and his wife Wendy for getting me out of it.

Finally, YOU. Yes, you! If you're reading this, you're reading this book. I wrote it to connect some of my thoughts to you. Don't you think reading is like telepathy? Someone spews ideas and images into words, and when you read them back at speed the words stop being words and become pictures and ideas again. Like those old fashioned flick-books, and early cinema. It's a miracle. It was hard to write this; I had to find a whole new way of expressing myself without sound or actors. So, thanks to you for taking the time to read this book. I hope you've found something here that will keep you smiling, thinking, wondering for a beautiful hour or two. That it took you out of yourself, that it laid out a world to enjoy through characters that you wanted to get to know. That would make me happy.